A World Full of Strangers, Fairytales, The Days of Winter, Portraits and now, Cynthia Freeman's triumphant saga . . . *Come Pour the Wine.*

Her Jewish grandfather married for love and lost his family.

Her Christian father reclaimed his past and was buried as a Jew.

Janet Stevens, the woman who had everything, was torn between two worlds and a divided heart . . . until she met a man who took her back to her roots—and forward to the ends of the earth.

"Readers savor and enjoy the tragic flaws in beautiful people. . . . They will get just what they want . . ."

—*Publishers Weekly*

Come Pour The Wine

A Novel by
Cynthia Freeman

BANTAM BOOKS
NEW YORK · TORONTO · LONDON · SYDNEY · AUCKLAND

*To those special few whom I
love. I need not mention their names
since they know who they are.*

COME POUR THE WINE

*A Bantam Book / published by arrangement with
Arbor House*

PRINTING HISTORY

Arbor House edition published November 1980

*An Alternate Selection of Literary Guild Book Club March 1981
A Selection of Doubleday Book Club Summer 1981
Bantam edition / October 1981*

ISBN 0-553-26090-1

Published simultaneously in the United States and Canada

Bantam Books are published by Bantam Books, a division of Bantam
Doubleday Dell Publishing Group, Inc. Its trademark, consisting of the
words "Bantam Books" and the portrayal of a rooster, is Registered in
U.S. Patent and Trademark Office and in other countries. Marca Regis-
trada. Bantam Books, 666 Fifth Avenue, New York, New York 10103.

PRINTED IN THE UNITED STATES OF AMERICA

KRI   20   19   18   17   16   15

Acknowledgments

To my dear husband whose shoulder was always
there when I needed it.

My deepest gratitude and profound thanks to my
publisher, Don Fine, for all his efforts.

And to Jessie Crawford, who started out as my
senior editor and ended by becoming my dear
friend. For her devotion, which went beyond the
call of duty, she has my warmest gratitude.

Chapter One

JAPAN ORIENT LINES
S.S. Eastern Pearl

April 19, 1981

Dear Kit,

It hardly seems possible that two years have passed since we said good-by, but what a time this has been.

You and I have shared a great part of our lives together . . . perhaps the most important events. Now we also share the joy of two grandchildren, and I thank God that your son Mark and my Nicole were destined to give us that happiness. I received the pictures of our youngest grandchild, Eden. Need I say how full my heart is?

I sit here devouring the magical sight before me. Today the blue Pacific is calm and serene. Her mood matches mine. Oh, dear Kit, if only I were able to articulate the gift of love that is mine, the joys and the wonders I have seen. Since we have been away I've had time for deep introspection and have definitely decided that this is the best time of my life.

Last month I turned forty-seven and I have more vitality than I did at twenty-seven and surely a greater appreciation of what life is all about. Why do we fear growing older? I, for one, am certain that if offered the chance to go back to the uncertainties and frustrations of my twenties I would refuse. Love at *this* age is so much better, more gentle, more tender, the thrill—yes, and I don't apologize for the word— even greater. The tempestuous urgency may be gone, but the need for love is just as great. And the fulfillment is greater, since nothing needs to be proven any longer. The time for testing is over, and now the years I hope we'll be blessed with can be savored.

I've seen the Taj Mahal, the ancient bazaars of Tunis, the pyramids of Egypt, the shrines of Jerusalem, the beaches of Tahiti—but best of all, I have discovered a new world within myself that I might never have known had I refused to pour

1

the wine of life. The world seems to move on and on, round and round. And if we learned the importance of moving with it, at the end we would surely be able to say we had truly lived, that the excursion had been worth every moment.

My life is so full that if I sound terribly romantic, you are quite right. Yesterday we left Honolulu. It was paradise. We danced, as they say, 'til dawn, made love in the fragrant night, swam in the surf. The sensation of gliding between the giant waves is incredible. Who said second honeymoons aren't better? I never thought anything like this could or would ever happen to me.

I'm not quite sure when we will be home. Neither of us seem quite ready for that, but eventually home we must go, and when we do, these memories will be stored away in a very safe place where few are permitted—in my heart. Until the next port of call, dearest Kit, as always I remain with abounding love,

Janet

Janet put down the letter case and lay back in her deck chair to gaze out into the glorious mixture of sun and sea in the distance. Closing her eyes, she gave way to total relaxation. Why were people so frightened of growing older, more mature, she wondered? Between youth and middle age there should be no cul-de-sacs, no blind alleys. Getting on with life should merely be a continuing process, but somehow people were not prepared. What a pity. It should have been taught from the cradle that youth was a temporary condition from which one recovered. No, if Janet were offered the chance to relive the frustrations and uncertainties of being young again she would reject it. Indeed, she would.

Her memory wandered back through time, back to 1953. She could remember so vividly that eager, excited, naive nineteen-year-old Janet Stevens, late of Wichita, Kansas, standing at the airport saying a tearful good-by to her mother and father, family and friends. How pathetic and unsure she had looked as she boarded the plane, holding a bouquet of red roses held together by the wide red satin bow and streamers in one hand and a large box of candy in the other.

As she waved good-by from the top of the stairs it didn't enter her mind how much this one special day would change her life, that it would never be the same.

All she knew or thought about was that at long last she had captured what she had dreamed of for so long. She was on her way to New York to pursue the career she had been preparing for since she could remember. Janet Stevens was going to be a famous high-fashion model. . . .

The first night she registered at a hotel on 59th Street near Fifth Avenue. It was quiet and most respectable, and her mother had selected it very carefully through the travel agent back home. But what Janet really wanted was the flavor of Greenwich Village, where she could live the Bohemian life she had heard so much about. It would not meet with her parents' approval, she was sure, but once she was settled she was sure her mother and father would understand.

She woke early the next morning and eagerly set out to explore the city. New York was overwhelming and intoxicating. She walked along the streets like Alice in Wonderland, peering up at the tall buildings that seemed to embrace the sky. There was an energy and excitement that permeated the air. As she left the uptown area, however, and gradually worked her way down to Greenwich Village, her spirits began to fall. For all her fantasies about the quaint cobblestoned streets of the Village, the reality turned out to be squalid and depressing, unlike anything she had ever seen or imagined. The bearded and sandaled Bohemians she had envisioned were unkempt, ravaged-looking people who huddled together in coffee houses, reciting incomprehensible beat poems to a tuneless guitar accompaniment. Men wearing wigs, rouge and mascara loitered in the streets and doorways. Women with gray fedoras and pin-striped suits swaggered about, and prostitutes, pushers and would-be poets wandered the Village in a marijuana high. The street-corner musicians playing exotic instruments only added to the grotesque carnival atmosphere, and Janet began to feel panicked. This was a nightmare that she couldn't escape fast enough.

Frightened and shattered, she cried behind a locked door in her hotel room. Maybe she should never have left home . . . But to go back now would be too great a defeat. Her parents had asked her to wait a year or so but

3

she had persuaded them that the time was now. It wasn't just that she was eager to get started but also that a young age was **basic** in establishing herself as a model with a future. After all, it was a business in which one's career lasted only as long as one's looks.

The next morning she looked through the classified section of *The New York Times* . . . "Lovely, sunny furnished apartment on West 53rd Street." It sounded promising, but her heart sank when she arrived at the building that afternoon and the super showed her the apartment. It was dark and looked out to a faded brick wall. The sofa and matching velour chairs were a bilious green and the carpet, once rosy red, was now orange and threadbare. The kitchenette was barely large enough to accommodate a midget, but worst of all, in a way, was the grease that clung to the walls. The porcelain washbasin was worn down to the gray metal. The only redeeming feature was the rent: $65 a month without utilities.

She returned to the living room, where the super waited impatiently.

"Where is the bedroom?" Janet asked uneasily.

"You're standing in it."

"But . . . I thought the ad read three rooms."

"It is—a kitchen, a living room and bathroom. What do you want, the Waldorf Towers?"

No, at this moment she wanted her wood-framed home in Wichita, with the crisp organdy curtains at her bedroom windows and the fragrant sheets that Effie ironed so meticulously and the rose garden and the porch and . . . Lord, why had she ever imagined she was ready for New York?

"Look, girlie, do you want it or not? I ain't got all day."

On the verge of tears, she said, "I've just come to New York, can I ask you a question—?"

"So ask."

"Is this pretty much like most furnished apartments?"

"Unless you want to move up to Riverside Drive or Central Park West. But this is what you get for sixty-five dollars a month."

Well, there was no debate. Of course, she *could* write

4

home for a larger allowance . . . She had devised a budget that seemed enormous back in Wichita, but honor was honor—not to mention pride—and this would have to do until she was able to sustain herself on a slightly grander scale.

Sighing, she said, "I'll take it."

"Any cats, dogs?"

"No."

"That will be two months' rent in advance."

"But I thought it was rented by the month."

"It is, but I got to get a cleaning fee."

"I'll clean it."

"*You* can do anything you want, but I still got to get a cleaning fee."

When Janet moved in, there was little indication that the cleaning fee had been put to use. She bought a mop, a scrub brush, cleaning detergent, Bon Ami and window solution, then scrubbed until her knuckles wore through the rubber gloves. Her hands were raw. If only Effie could see her now. . . .

The first night she lay awake on the uncomfortable couch, listening to the dripping faucets and the pounding steam pipes. The tenant above her practiced on the piano until midnight, and she could smell the odor of cabbage and other unidentifiable delicacies when the painter across the hall clattered about his kitchen to prepare his one A.M. dinners.

She cried herself to sleep. . . .

The next morning she sat in Schrafft's, having a cup of hot chocolate. She felt alien and disconnected. Should she go home and admit she'd been overwhelmed by the reality of her childhood dreams or should she stop feeling sorry for herself and go to Powers to take the modeling course? The decision had to be made today since she was scheduled for an interview. You'll get used to it, Janet. It's just a whole new world you've entered and you're not giving it a chance. *Forget* Kansas and the hollyhocks.

Janet sitting on her deck chair of the *S.S. Eastern Pearl* of the Japan Orient Lines, in the middle of the Pacific, could laugh benignly at the Janet of yesterday. Hard to believe how those two Janets had merged into one. How

5

strange. When this older Janet looked back she saw in her mind's eye that timid young woman of nineteen picking up her portfolio and leaving Schrafft's with a million trepidations. . . .

She sat in the office of Miss Phillips, the director of Powers, waiting nervously while her stills were being scrutinized.

"Would you mind standing, Miss Stevens?"

She stood quickly and obediently.

Miss Phillips gave her a long look from head to toe. "Would you turn sideways, please . . . Lean a little forward to the left . . . Now, would you turn around . . . Very good."

She was asked to be seated again and her heart pounded when Miss Phillips took a folder and dictated to her secretary all the information pertaining to the agency's requirements.

Resumé—Janet Stevens

Height	— 5′, 7″
Weight	— 100 lbs.
Shoulders	— 22″
Bust	— 33B
Waist	— 23
Hips	— 33
Eyes	— Almond-shaped
Color	— Deep violet to blue
Hair	— Thick, shoulder length
Color	— Amber to brown
Lips	— Sensuous
Face	— Heart-shaped
Cheekbones	— High and extraordinarily sculptured
Contours	— Reflect light and shadow uniquely
Skin	— Clear, transparent, bordering on alabaster tones
Classification:	Wholesome, sense of style and fashion, has enormous potential

Summation

Shy, but energetic and will evolve with sufficient aggressiveness

Goals	— High-fashion model

When the secretary had finished, the director of Powers stood and extended her hand to Janet. "We're very happy to have you with us, Miss Stevens. I have high hopes for you."

Janet almost fainted. And if this wasn't enough to lift her spirits after her uncertain welcome to New York, after eight weeks of instructions at Powers, she was ready to sign with an agency. She was on cloud nine when she was accepted by Conover, one of the most important modeling agencies in the world.

But being a model wasn't quite the glamorous, exciting profession that people thought it was, she soon discovered. The pace was so grueling she had neither the time nor the inclination to add on a social life. By the end of the day she was often so exhausted she skipped dinner, showered and collapsed into bed by seven. Each day began at six in the morning, when she rose and dressed in the uniform of all models. She would zip up the back of her black shift, adjust the small straw hat, step into the high-heeled patent pumps and leave her room with the ever-present portfolio under her arm and a heavy tote bag. She was aware that her glamorous appearance brought whistles from construction workers or looks from young aspirants who wished that they too could some day be a part of what they imagined was her exciting world . . . If only they knew, thought Janet, that her life consisted of running from one assignment to the next or waiting nervously by the phone and hoping to be called for an assignment. No indeed, modeling wasn't quite what she had dreamed it would be. It meant going to an interview and often waiting with a half dozen other girls for hours, only to be told that somebody else had been selected. She was beginning to become disenchanted with hailing cabs in snowstorms, or getting on a stuffy, crowded bus in the sweltering heat. All the models she knew were striving for the greatest possible exposure and recognition, but Janet was discovering that hers was a temperament that didn't seem to require such great acclaim. Perhaps it was that lack of eagerness that made it appear she was overly selective, a quality her peers resented. They labeled her a snob, and because she was shy and lacked the New York savvy of the people she met she was able to make few to no friends.

Still, though her social life might be all but nonexistent,

she *was* doing well professionally. Within a very short time she had become a face that was recognized in the industry and top photographers were beginning to ask for her. Imagine, Janet Stevens . . .

She found herself being helped into Christian Dior, Oleg Cassini and Chanel creations and being whisked away to pose in front of the cameras with a fan gently blowing her hair and billowing her gown seductively against her body.

In spite of the things she disliked about modeling, these moments of make-believe lifted her. And, to be honest, it was difficult not to succumb to near intoxication when she saw herself for the first time on the covers of *Vogue* and *Harper's Bazaar*. Her heart skipped a beat, her pulse quickened as she stood in her capris and cotton shirt at the newsstand looking at the face . . . her face . . . on the covers of the magazines. Yet for all her pleasure there was also a residue of embarrassment that went back to her Kansas upbringing . . . vanity . . . beauty was inherited, God-given, not manufactured. Beauty shone from the heart . . . Those sage tidbits made her happy that no one recognized her as they picked up the magazine from the newsstand and paid for it without a glance in her direction.

Embarrassed or not, that day she walked through the streets of Manhattan five feet off the ground. But the sensation did not sustain her for long, there seemed to be so much missing in her life . . .

Although her days were filled, the nights were long and lonely. At times she wondered what she was proving and why she went on. Yet she was unable to convince herself that the thing to do was go home. That indecision kept her on an emotional seesaw, that and her loneliness. A part of her wanted this life and another part longed for Kansas, love and family, reassurance and stability.

Sundays were the worst. She dreaded the prospect of week's end. . . .

Janet woke and lay listlessly. She sighed. Sunday . . . What was there to get out of bed for? Her gaze wandered around the room. The sight of it depressed her. Sunday in Kansas . . .

Quickly she got up and went to the bathroom. As the tub filled she brushed her teeth. What are you going to do today, Janet? she asked the reflection in the mirror. She sighed and answered the echo in the silent room, I don't know . . . I really don't know. Immersing herself in the soothing water, she took a bar of scented soap in her hands and watched as the lather became iridescent tiny bubbles. She blew on them and watched as they floated in midair. Somewhat like you, isn't it? It's pretty, but soon it will burst and disintegrate and—

Oh come on, Janet, stop feeling sorry for yourself, this is what you dreamed of. You couldn't wait, remember?

Yes, but I had no idea what I was giving up. I didn't realize I'd be so lonely, I only thought about the excitement and glamor . . . well, it isn't exciting or glamorous and I'm not the most adventuresome person in the world . . .

True, but on the other hand you have to sacrifice something to achieve what you gained.

What have I gained?

A position most girls would give their eyeteeth for . . . remember the feeling of seeing your face stare back at you on the cover of—

I remember and I'm still lonely, so I guess it didn't really mean that much . . .

Okay, Janet, that's enough, you're going to get around more. You're going down to Orchard Street today. It's something you've been promising yourself ever since you saw Aggie walk into the make-up room with that green silk suit she made.

I don't know if I really feel like it . . .

Stop acting like a ninny. Of course you feel like it. What you need is something to occupy your time instead of mooning around. Do something constructive. Remember what they say in Kansas, idle hands make idle thoughts. Maybe they don't know about that expression in Manhattan, but it's a philosophy a lot of people could profit by. Including you.

That's absolutely right. Besides, my French grandmother didn't teach me to sew those fine stitches by hand for nothing . . .

Now you're getting a little gumption . . .

She reached for the towel and rubbed herself so vigorously her skin tingled. A new spirit rose in her, a feeling of purpose that seeing her image on the cover of *Vogue* hadn't equaled. Quickly she opened the dresser drawer, took out a pair of brief panties and a lace bra. Should she wear the black sheath? No. She wore that all week. She reached for a pair of yellow capris and drew them on over her long legs, then tucked the tails of a striped cotton shirt into the waistband. She buckled her sandals, tied her hair back with a red bandanna, picked up her purse and ran from the room down the stairs to the street, then breathlessly boarded the subway train.

After what seemed an eternity Janet found herself on Hester Street. So this was the Lower East Side, that famous, fabled part of New York. She hadn't ventured further east than Third Avenue and 59th where she had stopped at Bloomingdale's. The first time she wandered among the endless aisles in that gigantic department store she was staggered. The largest store in Wichita could have fit easily into one corner. But if Bloomingdale's with its multitude of shoppers had surprised her, the panorama that lay before her now was even more startling. Ragged children played in the streets, bearded old men in skullcaps seemed to be discussing something of enormous moment. They were seemingly unaware of what went on around them. Garbage cans overflowed. Women screamed at a vendor because his carrots weren't large and plump and they argued over the price of a pound of potatoes. Young mothers and some not so young sat on the door stoops exchanging gossip as they breast-fed their children. Strangely dressed men gesticulated as rapidly as they spoke, in a tongue that fascinated Janet. There was an asceticism about their bearded faces and their black, broad-brimmed beaver hats. The black frock suits they wore were shabby with age but their demeanor seemed lofty, even spiritual. Somehow she felt very humble. Her eyes wandered to the roofs of the dirty tenements. Clotheslines stretched from one end to the next. The winds of Manhattan were brisk, making the sheets billow out like sails on a sea. Children ran down the alleys, disrupting a small group of men who were playing a game of dice. Little ones in their bare feet ran into the gushing

10

water of an open hydrant, slipping and sliding and laughing.

Janet started to weave through the milling crowds, totally caught up in the carnival-like atmosphere of this strange new world. It didn't seem possible this could be a part of a borough called Manhattan with its sophistication and culture. It was a far cry indeed from Bergdorf Goodman on Fifth Avenue or from Carnegie Hall. For all its squalidness and poverty, it far from repulsed her . . . quite the contrary. Its abject simplicity and liveliness were somehow beautiful. Strange, she thought, Greenwich Village had been a frightening place but here she forgot her loneliness, and her mind conjured up a long-forgotten story of her father's grandfather . . . He'd been a Jew as these people were and the sudden realization that she was a part of this scene filled her with feelings she could not quite articulate. She moved on excitedly . . . This was not the slick, impersonal world of Fifth Avenue, Madison or Park. There was a togetherness she felt these people had with one another that was unique. . . . *These* people? Really my people too. She had a strange feeling . . . of wanting to embrace them . . .

Inside of Nussbaum's Kosher Delicatessen she stood on the white tiled floor and observed the assortment of salamis hanging on a hook. The smell of stuffed cabbage mingled with garlic and onion rose from the steam-table and wafted through the air. There were slabs of smoked salmon, pastrami and fat juicy corned beef ready to be sliced, then put on large slices of Russian rye bread accompanied with crisp kosher dills and slices of pickled green tomatoes.

Janet was startled when the proprietor, Mrs. Nussbaum, called out from behind the counter, "Next." For a moment Janet stared at the ample woman whose cherubic face was framed by curly black hair. "*Nu,* girlie," Mrs. Nussbaum said as she wiped her hands on her apron. "So, what's for you?"

"Ohh," Janet replied, "I think I'll have . . . ah . . . a pastrami on rye." Having said that, she felt, somehow, enormously proud.

Janet watched the pudgy nimble fingers place the meat

11

on two thick slices of rye, and cut the bulging sandwich in half.

"So what do you want, cole slaw or potato salad?"

"Ah . . . yes."

"What do you mean *yes?* You can't have both unless you pay for it. So, cole slaw or potato salad?"

"Oh . . . I'll take the cole slaw."

"*Mazel tov*. And what do you want to drink, cream soda or seltzer?"

"Cream soda."

"*Mazel tov*, enjoy."

Janet smiled and answered, "Thank you. How much is that?"

"You pay at the end of the counter."

"Oh. Well, thank you."

"You're welcome. Come again."

"I will."

"Next," Janet heard as she paid the toothless old man who sat on a high stool punching the keys of the nickel-plated cash register, which was older than he.

Janet was all ears as she sat at the round table, listening to a language she had never heard before that somehow didn't seem at all foreign. To the contrary, it sounded lovely, melodic. She was struck with the feeling that she was a part of these people—maybe only a small part, but in her veins ran the same heritage as in theirs. She had a surging desire to know more about her heritage—the roots from which a part of her had come. She was fascinated, she wanted so badly to know more about these people . . . about herself . . .

As she munched on the sandwich, Janet observed the camaraderie among the customers, and a feeling of closeness she had never felt before came over her. She was so absorbed in the sights and sounds about her that she was startled by the voice of the young busboy when he asked if she was through. Looking up from the half-eaten sandwich into his bespectacled young face, she realized it was an invitation to leave. She looked at her watch. Without realizing it, she had been sitting here for forty minutes. Flustered, she apologized for having overstayed, then got up and left.

As she wandered down Hester Street she saw a little

boy sitting on the curb and crying. He seemed so pathetic, and sitting alongside him on the cement she asked, "Why are you crying?"

The child looked wide-eyed at the stranger. "Because I lost my ball."

Taking out a handkerchief, Janet wiped the small nose and dried the blue eyes. "Where did you lose it?"

"In the street. A guy picked it up and wouldn't give it back."

"Oh. How old are you?"

"Five."

"Five? I thought you were at least six."

"No, my sister's six."

"What's your name?"

"Jeremy Cohen."

"That's a nice name. How would you like an ice cream cone, Jeremy?"

He shrugged his shoulders. "Okay," he answered, although he would have been happier to have been offered a new ball.

Janet bought him an ice cream cone and once again they sat on the curb, Jeremy having forgotten his loss for the moment and contentedly licking his cone.

She observed his tattered clothes and the hole in his left tennis shoe where his large toe stuck out and thought how the children she'd known in Kansas were different, and yet not so different, from Jeremy Cohen. It was a question of being privileged at birth, and now she felt both guilty and grateful that she'd had the luck to be among the privileged part of humanity . . . "Well, it was a pleasure meeting you, Jeremy. I hope we meet again." Jeremy's response was a nod of the head. As Janet got up, she looked at the little boy once again, took out a dollar bill and handed it to him. "I want you to buy a ball, Jeremy."

He blinked. A ball didn't cost a dollar, he thought, but *goyim* didn't know any better. . . .

Janet walked further down Hester Street until she came to Orchard. Masses of people occupied the sidewalks but there were few children. The surrounding buildings were much the same as on Hester Street, crumbling tenements with laundry flapping in the wind, and here and there were street vendors who sold shoes, handbags and belts. She walked slowly, peering into windows that looked as though they hadn't been washed in years. Pausing at the entrance of a store, she heard the sounds of laughter as the women in a back room stuffed pillow casings with soft white eiderdown for the ladies and gents of Park Avenue to lay their heads on. She stepped aside as several of the women, with white feathers clinging in their hair, walked out to the street and stood in front of the store to smoke a cigarette. One took out a package of Luckies and shared it with her co-workers. Janet went inside to look at the magnificent satin comforters. When the owner asked if there was anything she could help her with, Janet smiled and said she was just looking.

"So go look, *mein* dear. Enjoy."

"Thank you, I will." She browsed for a while longer, then left.

Next door the sign read, Kowalski's Fine Fabrics. As she walked into the dimly lit store, a voice from the back, Fayge Kowalski's, greeted her. "So what can I do for you, *dahlink?*"

Janet answered, "I'm looking for some silk, can you show me something?"

"Yardage I don't sell. If you look, you'll find."

Janet rummaged through the bins of fabric until she found a three-yard remnant of lovely orchid taffeta. At one corner was a large grease stain. Would there be enough material when she cut the stain off, she wondered as she held it up. Yes, she felt she could work it out. "How much is this?"

Fayge chewed and swallowed her mouthful of hard-boiled egg before saying, "Make me an offer."

Janet didn't have any idea what it was worth. "How much do you want for it?"

"Make me an offer," Fayge repeated as she salted the egg and took another bite.

Janet stood there, bewildered. "I don't know how much to offer you."

"So how much is it worth to you?"

"I really don't know."

"Make a wild guess, I'll take it or I won't."

"All right . . . ten dollars."

"Twelve."

Janet was beginning to catch on. "Ten-fifty."

"That's a very fine piece of silk—100 percent. Ten-fifty I wouldn't take."

"Eleven?"

"Eleven-fifty and it's yours."

"I'll take it."

As Mrs. Kowalski stuffed the taffeta into a brown grocery bag she looked Janet over and thought . . . such a pretty little *shiksa*. It really wouldn't have hurt if she'd given her a better price. She looked like such a sweet little *nebbish*.

When Janet handed Mrs. Kowalski a twenty dollar bill she glanced first at the money and then at Janet. "This is the smallest you got?"

Janet went through her wallet again. "I only have a ten and a five."

"Give me the ten. You owe me the dollar and a half."

"I'll change it and come right back."

"No one would change it for you. You'll owe me."

Janet smiled. "It's very sweet of you to trust me."

"What's sweet? If you trust, nobody cheats you."

It was early evening when Janet let herself into her room and leaned back against the door. Somehow the room didn't seem as depressing as it had that morning. What she had seen and experienced had washed away the emptiness she felt. And the thing that impressed her most was the fact that Mrs. Kowalski had trusted her. It was rather like Kansas. She undressed, showered and contentedly got into bed. Sleep came blessedly easy tonight. So many of her misgivings seemed to have gone. She fell asleep with thoughts of next Sunday in that special world of Fayge Kowalski.

The week that followed was no different than others had been, but she knew when Sunday came there would be no question of how she would spend it. The experience had sustained her for a week. . . .

This Sunday morning Janet awoke eager for the day that lay ahead. On the way to the subway she stopped at the bakery and bought a strawberry torte to give to Fayge in exchange for her trust. As she wove through the crowds of Hester and Orchard streets, retracing her steps of last week, once again the curious scene gave her a feeling of belonging. She *did* belong here. This place made her feel that way.

When she walked into Fayge's store she found her eating a chopped liver sandwich at a table in the back. Janet smiled. "I'm so happy to see you, Mrs. Kowalski."

Fayge continued munching and looked up at her vaguely, wondering who she was. Then she remembered, the little *shiksa* who had been here last week, the one from the orchid taffeta. Wiping the crumbs away from her mouth, she answered, "Likewise, I'm sure. You came for more material?"

"No, I want to pay you your money and thank you for trusting me," Janet said as she handed Fayge the cake box.

If Fayge was surprised that the *shiksa* had remembered to give back the money and that she herself had forgotten the money was even due her, she was astonished by the cake box the girl had presented her with. Who remembered Fayge? To get back the money and to get a present on top of it . . . "This you didn't have to do."

"You didn't have to trust me and you did."

Looking deep into Janet's almond-shaped eyes, Fayge felt ashamed that she had charged her eleven-fifty for the piece of material when, in fact, it wasn't worth five dollars . . . *Nu,* God, so I was a little greedy. "Listen," she said, "I got a pretty piece of brocade upstairs where I live. On you it would look beautiful. Come, I'll show it to you." Taking a ring of keys in her hand, Fayge got up, her bulk protruding beneath the loose cotton dress, and on her turned-over heels made it to the front of the store to turn the sign to CLOSED and lock the door behind them. A step or two beyond the entrance to the store she slowly proceeded up a narrow stairway, holding onto the banister. When they reached the top Fayge paused, her breathing labored, and put her hand against her full bosom and felt the thumping of her heart. *Oy vay,* those stairs would kill her . . .

Janet followed down the dark hall, unable to avoid noticing the warped wooden floors and the chipped painted doors which led to the four bedrooms. When they reached the living room, Janet was shocked at the condition of it. In the corners there was material stuffed into paper bags and cartons that looked as though they were ready for the trash bin. A threadworn sofa with protruding springs sat against one wall. In the center was a large round table and surrounding it were six unmatched chairs. Fayge pulled out a box, sending the bags on top tumbling to the ground, then reached inside and plucked out a creased but magnificent brocade in startling colors of gold and peacock blue. Handing it to Janet, Fayge said, "Here's a present. On you it would be beautiful . . . it's you."

Janet couldn't accept it. "Thank you, Mrs. Kowalski, but really, I couldn't—"

"What do you mean you couldn't? Then I couldn't take the cake."

"Well, that's different, it was my way of telling you how much I appreciated your trusting me—"

"A cake you didn't have to bring me for your appreciation. Why shouldn't I trust you? You're a nice girl," she said, placing the fabric in Janet's hands.

Janet had tears in her eyes when she looked at it. "I don't know what to say."

"What's to say? You'll make a nice dress. Now, maybe you'd like a cup of tea?"

"Thank you, I'd like that."

"Fine, so you'll sit." Fayge quickly took off the food-stained newspaper on the dining room table and replaced it with a clean issue of the Yiddish *Forward*. After all, she was entertaining a beautiful young guest.

As they sat drinking the tea and eating the homemade sponge cake Fayge asked, "In New York I know you weren't born. Where do you come from?"

"Kansas."

Fayge squinted. "Kansas?" It was as far away as Pinsk.

Janet nodded. "Yes, that was my home until I came to New York."

"Your family still live there?"

"Yes."

"You live alone?"

Janet toyed with the crumbs and merely nodded.

From the sad look on Janet's face, Fayge knew she was very lonely. *Shiksa* or not, lonely could happen to anybody. "How come a nice girl like you comes to New York?"

"I wanted to be a model."

Fayge shrugged. "A model was the best thing you could be?"

For a moment Janet wondered the same thing. "Well, you know how it is when you're young and have crazy dreams."

Fayge sighed. When had she been young? She was forty-five already and the foolish dreams she'd had were long gone. "You miss your momma and your poppa?"

"Very much."

"You got brothers and sisters?"

"No, I'm an only child."

An only child wasn't so *only*. One of Fayge's dreams had been to have many children, but God had had a different plan. But at least she had Mendel. Only two weeks ago she had brought him back from the sanitarium in Denver where he had been recovering from tuberculosis. Thank God . . . thank God for giving her back Mendel. "You're not eating your strudel. Eat. Tell me, what does your poppa do?"

"He's a doctor."

That, Fayge liked. After God, doctors were the most important. "Well, finish the tea. Sunday is the best day for business and I gotta go downstairs to open the store."

Janet got up and thanked Fayge for her generosity. When she picked up the piece of material, without thought she turned and put her arms around Fayge's bulk and kissed her on the cheek.

Fayge held her close. Sweet little girl, she seemed so lost. "You'll come Friday night for dinner? You'll have a good *Shabbes* meal. *Oy vay,* you don't even know what *Shabbes* is. It means sabbath. It's like your day of rest. You be here at five."

In the subway, Fayge's words haunted Janet. *You don't even know what Shabbes is . . .* Unfortunately, that was very true. She should have known, should have been taught that part of her legacy. Had her great-grandfather's decision been different, she might have belonged to these people. Janet recalled having heard bits and pieces of his life. Now she longed to know how she had evolved into a Christian . . . part of her roots came out of the land of Canaan. Now there was a burning curiosity that would refuse to be stilled. . . .

Janet knocked on Fayge's door precisely at five on Friday evening and when Fayge released the door with a lever at the top of the stairs Janet walked into the stairwell, carrying a basket of fruit.

Fayge called down happily, "I thought maybe you could have forgot."

"I couldn't wait for tonight," Janet responded, smiling.

"Good, good. Come now, *dahlink*."

Janet went upstairs and embraced Fayge and then found herself being led down the hall to the front room. It was so different from the first time she'd been here. The table was set with a snow-white cloth, and there were two candlesticks placed at the head of the table, a bottle of wine and a tray of homemade *challah,* braided and baked to a shiny, delicate brown so artfully that it was hard to believe that it was merely a loaf of bread. There were pieces of gefilte fish adorned with slices of carrot and a sprig of parsley, and small ruby red glasses completed the setting. But even more impressive was Fayge. Her curly black hair had been shampooed and fell in small ringlets around her really lovely full face, and her eyes, the color of soft ripe olives, sparkled. The rosy plump cheeks needed no rouge and her lips were natural red. Gone was the ill-fitting dirty cotton dress. Tonight she wore a beautiful black silk, with a cameo pinned in the center of the white lace collar. Small diamond earrings shone in the dimly lit room. As Janet handed her the basket of fresh fruit, she said, "You look so beautiful, Mrs. Kowalski."

Almost shyly, Fayge answered, "Well, on *Shabbes* you wear your best. It's a very special night to sit with God. Every woman should look like a queen." Looking at the basket Janet had just handed her, she said, "This is very nice, but so many presents you don't have to bring. It's enough you brought yourself. Now sit down, *dahlink*."

19

As Fayge went back to the kitchen to baste the chicken, Janet seated herself on the sofa, trying to avoid the sharp springs that stuck through the worn fabric. She had just settled herself comfortably when she looked up and saw a man with the most extraordinary flaming red hair and beard she'd ever seen. His blue eyes, though, seemed sad. He was emaciated and bent. In that fleeting moment Janet knew this was Fayge's husband and that he was very ill. Janet smiled tentatively and was about to introduce herself, but just then Fayge bustled back into the front room.

"*Nu*, Mendele, you had a good rest?"

He nodded. "I had a good rest."

"Sit, Mendele, sit," Fayge said, helping him into the wooden chair. Like a loving mother she said, "Mendele, let me introduce you to—" She broke off, suddenly realizing she had invited the girl to dinner but had never thought to ask her name. Flushing in embarrassment, she said, "You should excuse me, but I don't know your name."

Janet had been called "dahlink" so many times, she hadn't even noticed. Nor was she offended now. "It's Janet Stevens," she said simply.

"Very nice name. And this is my Mendele," Fayge said. "Mendele, this is the nice little—" She was about to say *shiksa* but she caught herself just in time. "This is the nice sweet girl I told you about who gave us the cake. And now she brought a basket of fruit."

Mendel said, "Very happy to meet you."

Janet smiled. "It's a pleasure to be here."

Before another word could be spoken an old lady hobbled into the room with the aid of a cane. The resemblance to Fayge was unmistakable. The old lady was Fayge's mother, Rivke. Her shoulders were bent, her face was etched with deep furrows. Her hands were arthritic and her legs swollen. Fayge hurried over to help her, saying, "You couldn't have waited, momma? I was just going to get you."

"When I need you, I'll call you. In the meantime, on my two legs I can still stand."

Fayge and her mother spoke in Yiddish, but Janet

could tell the old woman resented being fussed over. Still, as though Fayge hadn't heard, she helped her to a straight-backed wooden chair.

"Janet, this is my mother."

Janet was surprised when the old lady responded in broken English. "You brought the cake? It was very good."

Before Janet could answer, the doorbell rang and Fayge went quickly down the hall. Janet could hear profuse greetings from the doorway and when Fayge reappeared it was with her two uncles, Itzik and Yussel. This was Fayge's entire family; the rest had perished in the Holocaust.

After the introductions were made, Fayge asked everyone to be seated and she began the ritual of *Shabbes* which had been performed for centuries. Putting a white lace shawl over her head, she struck a match and lit her candles. They gleamed like jewels in the evening shadows. Fayge put her hands over her eyes and swayed back and forth, silently reciting the prayer. Janet felt herself responding. It was somehow more personal than being in a cathedral. When the prayers were concluded Fayge took off the lace mantle, folded it carefully, then cut the *challah*, handing each member a piece to be eaten after the *motzi*, the prayer led by Uncle Itzik, who, being the oldest, was given the honor. Holding the bread in his hand, he blessed it and in Hebrew recited the benediction. "Blessed art Thou, Oh Lord our God, King of the Universe, who brings forth bread from the earth."

The others bit into the bread, and Janet followed their lead. The wine was blessed by the younger brother, Yussel, and then Fayge poured it into the small glasses. The red horseradish was passed and the meal began.

As Fayge was removing the fish plates Janet said, "Please let me help you, Mrs. Kowalski."

"You call me Fayge. And if you feel like, it would be my pleasure."

Janet helped Fayge clear the table and then set out the next course—bowls of yellow chicken soup, each containing three succulent matzoh balls. When she and Fayge were seated again, the conversation began, all of it in Yiddish. Itzik inquired how his sister Rivke's rheumatism was. She answered him with a shrug. "How should it be?"

The question having been answered with a question, Yussel asked Fayge, who was swallowing her last matzoh ball, "Where did you find the little *shiksa?*"

"She came to the store last Sunday."

"So every *shiksa* who comes into the store you invite home? What, you're so rich you can afford to invite everybody home for dinner?"

"Never mind. She's a very lonesome little girl. *Goyim* get lonesome too. And try to speak English so she shouldn't feel left out." Fayge glanced at Janet, taking in the untouched bowl of soup in front of her. "You don't like it?"

Janet had been so caught up in all that was going on that she hadn't even tried the soup, but she said, "It's very good."

"How would you know? You didn't even taste it."

"I'm sorry . . ." She took a large mouthful, then another, and found that she enjoyed it very much indeed.

The rest of the meal passed with little conversation, everyone turning their attention to the steaming platter of chicken, the bowl of *tsimmes* and the compote of stewed fruit that Janet helped Fayge to serve. After the dessert of tea, sponge cake and Janet's fresh fruit was eaten, Fayge passed a bottle of seltzer water and they all helped themselves.

Now the questioning began, and Yussel's frank curiosity about Janet's background soon had her opening up and feeling at ease. She told him why she had come to New York and they laughed together about her experience in Greenwich Village. She talked about modeling, then about Kansas and her family, and when she mentioned that her father was a doctor Yussel was as impressed as Fayge had been. She told them about the French ancestry on her mother's side and ended by saying, "And my great-grandfather came from Russia. He was Jewish." A hush could be heard.

Narrowing his eyes in disbelief, Yussel asked, "Your *zayde,* I mean your great-grandfather, was a Jew?"

"Yes," she answered.

Immediately Yussel said, "In that case I have a lovely boy for you."

His earnestness almost made Janet laugh. Smiling she answered, "I'd be delighted to meet him."

"*Nu,* so next time you come I'll introduce you." ...

Chapter Two

The companionship and pleasure of that evening rushed into Janet's mind at almost every idle moment during the following weeks. Now her Sundays were complete. She spent the day with Fayge and Mendel and Fridays were a standing invitation. Somehow the young man Yussel had promised never materialized, but Janet was so pleased to be in their company that she never even noticed.

The only disruption to this pattern came when Janet decided to go home for a week.

When she told Fayge of her plans, the older woman had brushed aside her apology for missing their usual weekend gathering. "Go and enjoy, Janet. Nothing in the world is more important than a mother and father."

True, Janet thought. She had missed them more than she'd ever thought she would. And they might hold a key that would help her understand more of who she was, make her feel more at home with herself in the frighteningly impersonal world she'd entered the day she set foot in New York.

Janet sat in the library across from her father. "Dad, how much do you know about your grandfather?"

He looked at her in surprise. "About my grandfather? A great deal. Why do you ask?"

"I wrote to you about meeting the Kowalskis. Ever since I've known them I've had a deep curiosity about us. I mean, we're part Jewish but we seem to have ignored it, and that part of me feels . . . well, deprived. I've heard so much about mom's side of the family but we've talked very little over the years about *your* origins . . . I have to know who I am, dad. Tell me all you can."

"That would take quite a while, Janet."

"Well, it's little enough time to find out about . . . my heritage . . . who I am . . ."

James Stevens looked out the window and saw the lovely garden, but his mind went beyond as he began to tell his daughter about things he remembered having been told in his youth . . .

His grandfather, Yankel Stevensky, was born in a remote part of Russia. But remote as it was, the men of his village were scholars, and from the time he could speak he had grown up with the idea that he would become a rabbi like his father before him. But the tentacles of Jewish persecution reached out and destroyed both his dreams and his isolated home. When the fires of the pogrom died, Yankel found his father sick and wounded. "You must leave, Yankel," and so, painful though it was, he left his village, his parents and his roots. Knowing that he would never see them again was the most painful of all. . . .

When he arrived on the shores of America two years later it was with few worldly possessions. His pockets were bare, his clothing worn and the strain of the ordeals he had suffered was evident in his appearance, but he still had his *tefillin,* his *tallis,* Bible and Talmud and he reasoned that he was rather a rich man to have been blessed with the spiritual assets that a man could feed his soul on. Like so many others, he went to the Lower East Side but he discovered it was not the place for him. He couldn't stand the crowds, the bantering, the hollering. If there was a sky, you couldn't see it . . . not a tree, not a flower. At least his little village in Russia had been pretty, everyone polite enough to greet each other. Here he was just a faceless person in the crowd. Who invited Yankel to a *Shabbes?* No one. No, this was not for him. So with his little vending case filled with pins, ribbons and thread, he decided to take the advice of someone who mentioned a place called California where giant redwoods grew. That was for Yankel.

Yankel soon found himself in the backwoods and byways of America, safely away from the noise and uncaring crowds of the city. He slept contentedly in a meadow, a forest and an occasional hayloft, wherever was handy as he moved west. And no matter where he was, whether at the side of a stream or deep in a glade, a morning never graced the sky that Yankel didn't commune with his God. The ritual started by putting the *tallis* around his shoulders and placing the *yarmulkah* on his curly black hair. Then he took out the phylacteries containing the sacred text, slipped the thong of one of the small square boxes around his forehead, wrapped the thin leather strip attached to the other around his left arm and began to recite from Exodus 13:9. "And it shall be for a sign unto thee upon thine hand, and for a memorial between thine eyes, that the Lord's law may be in thy mouth." He ended with a similar commandment in Deuteronomy 6:8.

After he had finished his morning prayers, Yankel lifted his eyes toward heaven and sighed contentedly. "Good morning, God, I slept very well last night. I'll have my breakfast and then we'll move on." Yankel fried the fish he'd caught and as he sat on the ground with his back against a tree, he said, "So, God, where do you think we should go now? Just walk, you say? That's a good idea. We'll walk." Yankel rolled up his bedding, put the tin pans into his knapsack while whistling an old Hebrew song he'd been taught sitting on his mother's knee, and was again on the road west.

After many days and nights trying to defy the elements, Yankel found himself in a place called Wichita, Kansas. The only resemblance between Wichita and Riga was that they both happened to be on the same planet. There the similarity ended, but somehow it looked like a place he might stay for a while on his way west. He didn't know why. It just felt right to him.

Yankel stood in front of the white clapboard boarding-house and looked at the garden with the dahlias and yellow hollyhocks. Wisteria and sweet peas wound around each other as though embracing. The white picket fence reminded him of the one his father had built . . . *nu,* so it wasn't exactly the same. His father had only used wood stakes cut from a tree, but a fence it was. Opening the gate, he walked up the path, up the four wooden stairs and stood before the door admiring the stained glass oval window. He knocked on the door. When it was opened he took a step backward. The young woman before him with soft, taffy-colored hair was not at all what he expected.

26

When he had been told that Pegeen O'Hara had rooms for rent, he had imagined she would be a middle-aged lady. Pegeen was far from that. She was slender, rosy-cheeked and maybe nineteen . . . twenty at the most. In the purest Irish accent she asked, "And what would you be wantin'?" This was a new English accent to Yankel—from the northern part of Protestant Ireland, as he would later learn—and he didn't quite understand. How did he answer when he wasn't even sure what she had asked? But she realized that Yankel was new to these parts from the attire he wore, especially the broad flat beaver hat and dangling earlocks, and looking at his confused face, Pegeen repeated, "Would you be lookin' for a room?"

The word *room* Yankel understood. He nodded, and Pegeen opened the door wider. Yankel found himself standing in the front hall gazing at the golden oak banister which led to the second floor and then looking uncomfortably downward to the hooked rug. He knew he shouldn't be looking at Pegeen. He remembered his father's warning—not only was it wrong for a young man of twenty to gaze upon a girl, but it was forbidden to gaze upon one who wasn't Jewish. His eyes remained steadfastly poised on the carpet. It wasn't until Pegeen said, "Gentlemen remove their hats," that he looked up. His eyes focused to the right side of her face as he took off his hat and immediately replaced it with a black *yarmulkah*. The custom was new to Pegeen but she respected it. She wasn't quite sure what nationality he was or why he was wearing such peculiar clothes, but that was none of her affair.

"Now, would you be wantin' to see a room?" Yankel nodded and followed her up the stairs to a small immaculate bedroom at the far end of the hall. Yankel was pleased. He hadn't slept in a bed for so long he'd almost forgotten what one looked like. And when he took in the lace curtains, the iron bedstead, the kerosene lamp that stood on the golden oak bedside table and finally the comfortable-looking rocker, he thought that, yes, this could be home until he moved further on. For a long moment Pegeen stood watching. He was the most curious man she had ever seen. But her chores downstairs were waiting, and she couldn't stand here any longer waiting

27

for him to decide. Clearing her throat, she asked, "Would this be pleasin' you?"

She knew from the look on his face that he had not understood her. She rephrased it. "The room . . . would you be takin' it?"

That was a little clearer to Yankel. "How much?" he asked in his accented, minimal English.

"Two dollars a week, room and board."

Yankel knit his eyebrows together. "Room . . . und *vat?*"

"Room and food."

That sounded very good to Yankel. He gave Pegeen the two dollars, dollars of which he had very few. But up to now he'd saved the little he had by not paying rent and by traveling across country either on foot, the back of a wagon or an occasional horse.

Dinner that night was not to his liking. Beans and ham hocks, Yankel wouldn't eat. He wasn't crazy about the turnip greens but a man couldn't live on bread alone, so he ate. When he was passed a corn muffin he refused it also, afraid that it might be *trayf,* not kosher. He'd never seen bread like that in his life and he wasn't going to take the chance. When the apple cobbler was served he said to God, "Listen, what could be so bad about a piece of apple strudel? All right, so I'll only eat the fruit."

Pegeen looked across the table at him, then at the other boarders in their shirt sleeves and arm garters. Yankel was aware of her look and of how out of place he must seem sitting among these men and wearing his *yarmulkah,* but he wouldn't remove it—not even if he had to give up this haven.

Yankel rose at dawn the next morning to commune with his God, but as he started his prayers he felt a sudden attack of dizziness. His face began to feel hot and tiny beads of perspiration appeared on his forehead. By the time he finished his prayer and put his *tefillin* away, he didn't feel just right . . . maybe it was the unaccustomed luxury of a soft bed . . . maybe it was God telling him he shouldn't be too cocky to have found such a nice place, that a little humility was in order . . . Whatever it was, he didn't feel too good . . . maybe he'd lie down for a while, just until it passed . . .

When Yankel was jarred out of his sleep he was surprised to see that it was night. He looked around the room, disoriented, then heard the knocking again that had awakened him. Pegeen called through the door, "Mr. Stev . . ." but it was too difficult to pronounce . . . "are you all right?"

"I'm all right, thank you," he answered, his voice weak and scratchy.

"You're sure?"

"Thank you, I'm sure."

Pegeen walked away feeling somewhat uneasy, knowing he had missed both lunch and dinner that day. . . .

After breakfast the next morning she knocked on Yankel's door again. "And how would you be feelin' this morning?"

When there was no answer Pegeen opened the door slowly and found Yankel with his eyes closed. From the sound of his breathing she knew he was very ill. Immediately she got a basin of cold water and a wash cloth, brought it back to Yankel's bed, washed his face, then applied the cool cloth to his forehead. For five days and nights she looked in on Yankel as often as she could. On the sixth day, when Yankel finally opened his eyes the first sight he saw was Pegeen, who sat in the rocker by his bed.

"I've been sick . . . no?" he said quietly.

"You've been sick . . . very."

"You took care of me?"

"It's no more than I would be doin' for anyone."

"I'm sorry to be so much bother."

"Oh, saints be praised. You were no bother."

From that moment on Yankel's affection for Pegeen O'Hara grew rapidly. Despite his father's warning that it would be wrong for him to even look at a non-Jewish girl, he reasoned that she had been good to him, that it was only natural that he should like someone who had been so kind to him. God could hardly blame him for that. . . .

Life became very good for Yankel. He found a job as a dishwasher and when he had some money saved he decided it would be a nice gesture to repay Pegeen for her kindness by hiring a horse and buggy so that they could ride into the country. He waited until after dinner was over one night to tell her. He stood in front of her in the sitting room, watching shyly as she embroidered a sampler. Clearing his throat, he said softly, "Maybe if you wouldn't be busy this Sunday . . . maybe you wouldn't mind if I asked you to take a nice ride."

She finished a stitch and looked up at him. "That would be lovely."

On Sunday they drove out into the country, and Yankel gave way to his curiosity about Pegeen. As they sat in the lazy afternoon he asked her where she had come from. Until she was thirteen her home had been Ireland, she said. Her mother had died when she was four, and when her two brothers were killed in an Irish rebellion her father decided to send her to the safety of his brother's home in America. Tragedy was no stranger to Pegeen, and her seven years in Wichita had not substantially brightened her personal life. She had sat at the bedside of her aging uncle and watched as he breathed his last breath, and when he was peacefully laid to rest Pegeen found herself the owner of O'Hara's boardinghouse.

Yankel sighed when she finished her story. It seemed that the violence in Ireland was little different from the pogroms he'd run away from, and his heart went out to her. When he told her about his escape from Russia, about the family and dreams he had left behind, the expression on her face told him that she understood all too well what he had been through. Now there was a common bond between them—a bond of loss that had brought them together.

After Yankel recited his prayers that night, he sat up for a long time trying to reconcile his feelings for Pegeen with his father's teaching. You heard what she said today, he thought. Like for me, life was not so good. She's a kind and understanding person—and if she's not Jewish, it's not her fault. I would have been happy if she was, but she's not. I think I should marry her. Please, God, don't be angry. You remember the book of Ruth? She wasn't Jewish either. And neither was Moses' wife. I'm not Moses, but what could be so wrong with it, God? . . .

The next Sunday they took another ride into the country and stopped at the same meadow. They talked for a while and then sat in comfortable silence until Yankel said, "I don't know you very long and you don't know me very long, but long has nothing to do with liking someone. It may come as a big surprise to you but . . . if you wouldn't mind, I would like to marry you."

Pegeen stifled a smile. "Why, you've never even called me by my name."

"I know, but not because I don't like you. I can't pronounce it."

She laughed. "That's why I never called you by your name. Every time I try to say it, it sounds like Yankee."

"It sounds like what?"

"Yankee," she said.

"*Nu*, if it sounds like Yankee, call me Yankee. And since I can't pronounce your name I'll call you Pegela."

Six months later they were married. With a small loan from his wife, Yankel opened a restaurant. Nine months later Yankel and Pegeen were blessed with a son. As Yankel looked down at the child he said, "What a *shayn* little boy."

Pegeen asked, "What did you say?"

"I said the little boy was *shayn*."

"Then that's the name . . . Sean."

On the birth certificate was written Sean Stevens, at Pegeen's request.

Despite Yankel's deep affection for Pegeen, he couldn't help regretting that a son who was descended from generations of rabbis should be called Sean. And the changing of Stevensky to Stevens was almost like having to cut his earlocks. But this was America and in America one forgot the old ways. The things that Yankel would not forget or give up, even in this promised land, were his *tallis*, his *tefillin* and his Talmud. The ritual began at dawn as Yankel wound the thin strap around his arm and placed the little square black phylacteries on his forehead and on his arm, while Pegeen was in the adjacent bedroom with baby Sean at her breast. . . .

When Sean was four, on Saturday mornings he could be seen walking into Temple Emanu-el with his father. It was the only temple in Wichita, founded by German Jews in 1851, and because it was Reform and Yankel couldn't use his skullcap and *tallis* during their services he wasn't especially happy to be worshiping there. But it was 1904 now, and Yankel was waiting patiently for the ground to be broken and the cornerstone to be laid for the Orthodox *shul*. It wouldn't be built for three years, but for Yankel the wait was worth it. The disenfranchised of the old world had found Wichita, Kansas. That lovely city had acquired enough Russian and Polish Jews to make the miracle possible. Now he'd be worshiping in a *shul* like a real Jew.

On Sundays Pegeen and little Sean could be seen walking up the wooden stairs under the peaked roof of the Protestant church. Both Yankel and Pegeen held to their beliefs without conflict. The respect for each other's heritage was complete, instinctive. It didn't need to be talked about.

When Passover came, Yankel taught Pegeen to make matzoh balls, and on Easter Sunday she decided to forgo the traditional dinner of ham in deference to her husband's belief. He built a booth in the backyard at Succoth to commemorate the Festival of Tabernacles. Pegeen came home on Ash Wednesday with a dot of ash on her forehead. Pegeen became so accustomed to Yankel's traditions that at Purim she prepared crisp, lacy potato pancakes. At Christmas the presents under their brightly decorated fir tree seemed to reflect the light of the candles that burned in the menorah on the sideboard. Instead of being confusing to Sean, the mingling of the two traditions was exciting and rich. It all seemed natural, normal.

One of the great joys in Yankel's life was Sean's *bar mitzvah* at Ahavach Achim Synagogue, when he saw his son standing before the congregation in his *tallis* and *yarmulkah* reading a portion from the Torah. He sought out Pegeen's face among the women, and when she returned his look with a warm smile it seemed to him that his life had become very full, more so now than ever before.

At Rosh Hashanah and Yom Kippur Sean *davened*, praying at the side of his father. The only time Yankel sat alone was during the memorial service when the highest of holy days came to a close with the setting sun. Yankel walked home in the dwindling shadows. Although he hadn't eaten or sipped a drop of water from sunset to sunset, he was not weak. His spirits had been restored, his life was full.

But it was not to be long-lived. At forty-two Yankel lay on his deathbed. Sean, who had just turned twenty-one, was seated on a chair at his side. Yankel looked deep into his son's eyes and said, "I have tried to live my life as best I could and in my heart I have kept God's commandments. You are my *Kaddish,* my immortality. Through you I will live, my blood will run through the veins of all the generations to come. When God calls me you will cut the lapel of your coat and you will sit without shoes for seven days. Each year you will observe *yahrzeit* and light a memorial candle. You have been taught the Mourner's Kaddish and as my son, whom I love, will recite it. I ask you to do this for me so that I will not leave this place I've loved without it being remembered that once I, too, walked upon God's green earth . . ."

A week later Sean stood at the graveside of his beloved father, silently watching handfuls of dirt thrown over the casket. Pegeen stood next to him among the Russian and Polish congregants with whom Yankel had worshiped. She felt blessed that she had shared her life with this quiet and loving man, and if she wept it was because Yankel was someone for whom time should have stood still. The world had become a better place because he had lived in it. Listening to Sean that evening as he sat in his stocking feet on an orange crate, reciting the traditional prayer for the dead . . . *Yis-gad-dal v'yis-kad-dash sh'meh rab-boh* . . . she prayed that their son would carry just some of his father's goodness into the world . . .

And he did, in his own way. Sean became a doctor and married Laura Benton in the chapel in which Pegeen had worshiped through all the years. Two years later she was overjoyed to hold her grandson, James Stevens, as she had held Sean. If only she could have shared this blessed event with her very own beloved . . . her Yankee, her Yankel. But even as the thought came to her it seemed that he whispered in her ear, "*Mein* dearest Pegela, I thank you, but remember that God in his wisdom always knows best. Live for our child and enjoy the years." She remembered that when she was privileged as a very old lady to celebrate their son's fiftieth birthday. . . .

One evening after having supper with her grandson James, she sat in her bedroom reading Yankel's Talmud.

Such beautiful words . . . such magnificent poetry. Yawning, she climbed into bed, turned off the bedside lamp and closed her eyes. She died in her sleep that night as gently as she had lived her good life. . . .

Only fifteen years later, it was Dr. Sean Stevens' hourglass that had run low. When the days of his years had come full circle, he called his son James to his bedside. Sean lay reviewing his life as once his father had done with his only son . . . "Unlike my father, I've not lived my life as a Jew, but I want to be buried as one. I've kept my word through the years and repeated the *Kaddish*. I didn't teach you as I had been taught, but in the last days of my life I ask that you say those holy words for me . . . 'you are my immortality as I was my father's.' " . . .

When James Stevens had finished his long recital, some of it laced with unspoken reminiscence, they sat silently, father and daughter. He looked at his beloved Janet. "I thank you, darling, for reminding me. Until today I hadn't thought much about this . . . but we are the products, and the inheritors, of those who went before us. When my time comes I too want to be buried with a *tallis,* the way my grandfather and my father were . . . and you, Janet, you are my immortality. Apparently I'm not quite the *gentile* Dr. Stevens I'd always thought I was. Well, I'm glad of it . . ."

Janet went to her father as he stood up. The two looked at each other, and then they reached out, arms enfolding. Father and daughter united as never before. With each other . . . with the beauty of the past . . .

When Janet returned to New York she came with a far deeper sense of herself. Her first thoughts, not surprisingly, were of Fayge, and she could hardly wait until Sunday . . .

She walked eagerly down Orchard Street, which today she found had a different look for her. Something down deep in her reached out to embrace these people even more than before. Almost breathlessly she walked to Fayge's store, only to find that the CLOSED sign was out. Something was wrong . . . quickly she walked beyond the store and knocked on the door to Fayge's flat. It took a while before it was opened. When she entered and looked up, she knew her fears were well-founded. There were no tears but somehow she knew that Fayge's jolly face was a mask for sadness.

She greeted Janet with an embrace and a kiss, affecting her usual manner. "Well, Janetel, you had a nice visit with your momma and poppa?"

"Lovely," Janet answered, watching Fayge trying to put on a brave front. "How are you, Fayge dear?"

Fayge swallowed, paused for a moment, then said, "How am I? Fine. Come, I'll make a nice glass of tea, then we'll talk."

As they sat at Fayge's kitchen table drinking iced tea, Janet studied her friend's face over the rim of her glass. "I was . . . surprised to see that you weren't open today, Fayge."

"*Nu,* so I'm entitled to a Sunday. Tell me, what happened with your family?"

Fayge was obviously reluctant to talk about herself at this moment, and respecting that, Janet began to tell her the story of her great-grandfather, ending with her father's request to be buried in the tradition of his people. And as she talked, Fayge sat there reflecting on the story that in one way or another had affected the lives of all Jews. Poland . . . How painfully vivid were the sounds of hobnail boots running across a cobblestoned courtyard, the sound of a siren, a car coming to a screeching halt, a door being bashed in, the screams, pleading, the cries of children . . . the herding into boxcars . . . numbers on tattooed arms . . . emaciated bodies . . . families separated . . . gas chambers . . . Auschwitz . . . pits in the ground . . . arms and legs, by the hundreds . . . Fayge closed her eyes and put her hands over her face. Did one ever forget? How was it possible to forget? At least Mendele would die in the warm sun of Miami.

"Fayge, what's wrong? Tell me."

She shrugged. "Mendel got sick. The coughing started all over again. The doctors said he should go back to Denver, but I said no, not this time. No more separations. I'm selling the *shmattes* to Mrs. Goldstein. Rags I can buy in Florida."

Janet was stunned. She was losing a part of herself. Fayge had represented a link between her and what she

35

longed for, to know more about . . . It had little to do with Judaism in any religious sense. What she wanted to know were the songs, the humor and storytelling, the taste of the food, the experience of sitting in Fayge's shabby front room with the newspapers on the table and feeling the richness that they had. They were rich, rich from the long years of survival. Fayge and the remains of her family wore the signs of a survival with dignity, even beauty. Although Fayge was a part of the silent generation that refused to discuss the unspeakable horrors that had been visited on them, without knowing, through a word dropped here and there, she had revealed things that she might have liked to have kept hidden.

"When are you moving?" Janet asked quietly.

Fayge shrugged. "A week maybe."

They sat silent, each with her separate thoughts. Then Fayge said, "I want you should know I feel like you're my child."

Janet got up and kneeled in front of Fayge. Putting her face to Fayge's, she allowed the tears to come . . . It wasn't fair, that Fayge should suffer like this . . . or that she, Janet, should lose her . . .

Fayge smoothed Janet's hair away from her face. "You shouldn't cry. God has been good to me. I have Mendele, my mother and my two uncles. With them, how bad off can I be? Wipe your tears. Now come, I have something I want to give you so you would remember where you came from."

As she went down the hall Janet looked around this place that had been her haven and realized how much beauty she had been given. But as Fayge would have said, "Nothing lasts forever." There are moments of joy and misery. Without the bad, how would we appreciate the good, how know the difference . . . ?

Janet looked at Fayge as she sat down alongside her on the worn red velour sofa and handed her a small green velvet box. Janet's hand trembled as she accepted it. For a moment she hesitated, then opened it. Inside lay a gold Star of David. It was impossible to hold back the tears. "Oh, Fayge, thank you . . . you've been so good to me, I've learned so much from you. *How* can I thank you—?"

"You can thank me by wearing this. You can thank me

by remembering your *zayde,* by remembering your Jewishness, by remembering to repeat the story to your children."

"I promise."

"Now, let me put it on."

Janet looked at the star, and felt as though God had put his arms around her and that Yankel Stevensky was looking down from heaven, and smiling . . .

And now the moment she dreaded . . . Lingering at the top of Fayge's stairs she looked for the last time at this beautiful face and heard Mendel's coughing behind the bedroom door, smelled the pungent odor of liniment that wafted under the crack of another door. She kissed Fayge, then walked slowly down the stairs. Fayge called, "And thank you, Janetel, for the candy. They're sweet as the memories I'll always carry of a beautiful girl who I pretended for a while was my child."

At first it was impossible for Janet to realize when Sundays came that she no longer had Fayge to run to. Friday nights were spent in bittersweet memories. But time softened the sense of bereavement and in its place Janet heard the distant laughter of Fayge and the others on *Shabbes.* Forgetting the pain was also more easily managed when Janet was very tired, and so she urged herself to accept more assignments. Her earnings became much more than she either wanted or hoped they would be. But when she thought about it, it had its compensations, not so much for the money itself but for the gifts she was able to send to Fayge and her family. And, at last, it also allowed her to furnish a lovely apartment. Life, at least on the surface, seemed good.

Chapter Three

Along with her sense of achievement, Janet also found a new source of personal happiness. After being in New York a year she finally met her first real friend—except, of course, for Fayge and her family. Janet and Kit Barstow were quite different in temperament and backgrounds, and their attitudes were far from the same; nonetheless, they were completely taken with each other.

Kit had been a freelance model since she was eighteen, and now that she was twenty-four she was taking a long look at her life. How many more years did she have as one of the top fashion models? Four, maybe five? She'd had it all, made the front cover of *Harper's Bazaar* and *Vogue*. Sure, it was exciting . . . who—as Janet too had discovered—wouldn't like seeing their image staring back at them from a magazine rack? Yes, she'd loved it but now her best days were numbered and she knew it. For reasons other than Janet's, the raven-haired, olive-skinned, green-eyed, five-foot-eight Kit Barstow had lost her drive. Who *needed* it? It would be nice to have a sense of, well . . . of belonging, to have a place to use to get out from under the rain. And so, secretly, she began to toy with the idea of marrying Nathan Weiss. . . .

Strange, thought the forty-seven-year-old Janet sitting in her deck chair . . . What would have happened if she hadn't gone to Kit's party that particular Saturday night? She'd had no intention whatsoever of going, but Kit was adamant, wouldn't take no for an answer, and so she finally, reluctantly went. What a difference one small word could make—a *no* or a *yes* might have changed the direction of her whole life. If she'd said no that evening, chances were she also would not be on this magnificent voyage today. Twenty-seven years had passed, and yet she recalled each and every detail of that event as if it were yesterday.

It was the night she met Bill McNeil for the first time . . .

When she walked into Kit's exquisite apartment it seemed as if most of the population of Manhattan was there. She looked around uncomfortably at the unfamiliar faces and searched for Kit, but there was no sign of her. People stood huddled in close groups, talking about whatever it was that people huddled in small groups talked about. Ten minutes later, Janet was still standing alone and feeling so ill at ease that she was tempted to leave, but just then she caught a glimpse of Kit, who waved "hello" from across the room.

Janet accepted a glass of champagne from a server and started across the room to join her friend, but her progress through the dense and shifting crowd was slow.

Suddenly someone backed into her, jostling her arm, and she was dismayed when she realized that the champagne that had been in her hollow-stemmed glass a moment before was now dripping down the front of a Brooks Brothers suit. She began to apologize, but as she looked up into the man's face she broke off mid-sentence, stunned by her overwhelming awareness that he was the most handsome man she had ever seen. All she could do was to stand mute as he took out his handkerchief and began to wipe the front of his jacket. Finally, she said, "I'm so sorry . . . I . . . I really am . . ."

"Forget it," he answered, mopping up the remains. Without looking at her, he went on, "I'm going to give this damned suit away. It's a jinx. Three times I've worn it and three times I've had it cleaned. I don't know what there is about it, people just don't seem to like this suit."

"I . . . I know what you mean. I have a white dress like that . . . I'm really so sorry—"

"It's *okay*. Think nothing of it," and the next thing she knew he was gone.

She was so embarrassed and surprised by the effect he'd had on her that, without stopping to say goodnight to Kit, she promptly left the party.

In the lobby she asked the doorman to call a taxi, then walked out of the building to wait. Her heart thumped. *He* was standing there, also apparently waiting for a taxi.

They looked at each other. He nodded almost imperceptibly, as if he only vaguely remembered it was she who had rained on his evening—or rather his suit—and then looked away. When the taxi arrived and he was about to get in, he hesitated and looked at Janet with some annoyance. "You take this one."

"I wouldn't think of it, but thank you. Mine will be here any time now."

"Oh, come on, we'll share this one."

In a semitrance, she found herself sitting in the back seat, he in the extreme left corner and she in the right.

It was the voice of the driver that brought her back to earth. "Where to?"

By now she was so unstrung she couldn't remember.

The next voice came from the left corner of the back seat. "What's your address?"

"The Hotel Barbizon on—"

"I know, lady," the cabby said.

After what seemed an eon of silence the man next to her said, "My name is Bill McNeil."

"Janet Stevens . . . I want to apologize for spoiling your evening—"

"You didn't spoil my evening, just my suit. The truth is, I wasn't going tonight but Kit can be damned insistent."

"That's strange," she said, more to herself than to him.

"What?"

"I didn't want to go either. Tonight, I mean. And you're right. Kit doesn't take no for an answer."

That was the beginning and end of their conversation. As the cab stopped at the curb in front of the Barbizon Hotel, Bill asked the driver to wait, helped Janet out, escorted her to the door, said goodnight and was back in the cab before she could even say thank you for the ride.

Somehow she made it to her room and found herself leaning against the now closed door and staring into the dark. The heat of the room was not nearly as intense as the burning she felt. It was as though she had been hit by a kind of stroke. Quickly she opened the window and tried to catch her breath. No man had ever affected her the way Bill McNeil had. She probably would have fainted if he had kissed her goodnight or even if he had shaken hands. What in the world had happened to her tonight? And what was wrong with her . . . acting this way? She'd had her share of dating since she'd arrived in New York, but no one had really excited her. In fact, quite the opposite. Sooner or later, and usually sooner, they all got around to the same old line. *You're gorgeous . . . simply gorgeous. Love to see it without the draperies.* Which was usually followed with . . . *my place or yours?* The propositions were so constant and so predictable, and the men so utterly lacking in desire to know anything about her beyond what met the eye, that she had felt almost inhuman. She began to find them repugnant, and she was exhausted by her efforts to fend them off tactfully. Finally she had given up the lovely apartment she had eventually taken and furnished to her taste and had moved to the Barbizon, a hotel for women only. She wasn't a prude and even in Kansas girls knew about sex. But the opportunities that had been offered her could have made her the most underpaid, overworked bed partner in Manhattan, and so far she had never made love with a man. She'd saved the experience for someone very special, and somehow she had the feeling that that someone might be Bill McNeil. Perhaps it was because he hadn't come on strong like all the others. For that matter, she reminded herself, he hadn't even noticed her, much less made a pass or asked her out. But somehow she knew that he would. He *had* to. The more she thought of him, the more her feelings went into turmoil. At the moment, at least, nothing for them except a very cold shower.

After a sleepless night she looked at the bedside clock. It was only six in the morning, and another empty Sunday lay ahead of her. Well, one thing was sure. She couldn't lie here any longer fantasizing about what it would be like going to bed with Bill McNeil. She had run the gamut on that one since two this morning. Quickly she got out of bed, went to the bathroom and took another shower. With the towel wrapped around her hair, she went back to the bedroom and dressed in a pair of plaid wool slacks, a cashmere turtleneck sweater and boots. Replacing the towel with a knit cap, she then buttoned her navy blue

41

jacket, flung a muffler around her neck and grabbed up coin purse and keys as she left the room.

It was an extraordinarily mild and invigorating day for February, not a cloud in the sky nor a threat of rain on the horizon.

Finding a coffee shop a few blocks away, she ordered tea and toast. No butter, thank you . . . had to keep those pelvic bones showing. Munching on the dry toast, she tried reading the Sunday paper but found that she could read no further than, "It has been rumored that before Joseph Stalin's death last year, he . . ." when her mind wandered back to Bill McNeil. She visualized him as he lay in bed, his thick chestnut-brown hair in disarray, the deep brown eyes shut in repose, and his long, nude body sprawled under the sheets. In her fantasy she saw him getting out of bed, stretching away the last vestiges of sleep as he yawned . . . Now he was doing a dozen push-ups . . . now dashing quickly into the shower, letting the spray pelt against his lean and muscular body. Wiping the steam from the mirror, he lathered his face, took up his Schick razor and shaved. No, wait a minute, that's what my father uses. Bill probably uses an electric. Refreshed and still nude, he went to the kitchen, measured the coffee grains into the Silex. Waited until the water turned a rich dark brown, poured a cup and brought it back to the living room, where he opened the front door, stuck out his hand and retrieved *The New York Times*. He scanned the pages as he sipped at his coffee, then threw the paper aside to read later and decided to dress and face the day. Leaving the bed unmade, the coffee cup unwashed, papers strewn on the floor, he dressed in a gray sweat suit and left the apartment. Where would he go? To Central Park? More than possible . . . Why not? Sunday mornings were the only time to get out into the fresh air after a long week in a stuffy office. The more she dwelled on it the more logical the fantasy became.

She got up quickly, leaving much of the toast and tea untouched, paid the check and proceeded toward the park.

Once inside the park she was deluged with a dozen overlapping thoughts—all negative. How in God's name would she find him, *if* this was where he would be going? It was a good-sized park with plenty of trails and was it possible that she could accidentally bump into him? Stupid . . . STUPID . . . This is just a fantasy, she reminded herself, and you can't manipulate reality. But there was an urge that compelled her on. Perhaps some unknown source *had* led her here, and him as well. There *was* such a thing as fate, or destiny. Don't be ridiculous, Janet. Things happen spontaneously. This isn't a movie, where you can change the script and make happy endings.

Abruptly a new thought occurred to her . . . maybe he could be at the skating rink. She walked quickly past the zoo and all but ran to the platform above the rink, where she had a perfect view of the skaters below. She scanned the panorama, carefully observing each face. The skaters pirouetted and twirled in pairs to the sound of a Chopin waltz coming over the loudspeaker. It was a romantic scene that made her sigh all the more deeply as she realized Bill wasn't there. Slowly, she turned and walked away, the lovely music fading behind her.

By eleven that morning she'd given up, feeling like a female Walter Mitty. Slumping down on a park bench, she lectured herself, Well, you didn't really think it would happen . . . In fact, you knew it wouldn't. I'm sorry, Judy Garland, but you're absolutely wrong. Wishing will *not* make it so. She sat looking out to the greenery beyond for a moment longer, then decided to go back to the hotel. Mission impossible not accomplished.

She sat on the edge of the bed, staring out of the window. God, how lonely Sundays were. Particularly this Sunday. Imagine, somewhere in this city was a man who had aroused feelings in her she'd never even been aware she had, brought out a kind of compulsive, irrational behavior . . . If this wasn't love she couldn't find a different or a better word for it. If her parents could see the state she was in and the reasons for it . . . Their words sounded in her ears . . . "Your father and I are not for your leaving college and going off to New York by yourself, but as much as we're against it, we do give our consent . . . Janet, you're very mature for nineteen and we know we can depend on you to do the right thing . . . you're a very level-headed young woman, we're very proud of you, and we know you won't do anything to embarrass us or yourself . . ."

Well, mother darling, you wouldn't be so sure at this moment about that, not when I'm burning up and crazy in love with a man who doesn't even know I exist. If I could, right now at this very minute, I would encourage him to seduce me. So there, mother, that's your adorable little Janet, Girl Scout leader, pom-pom girl of the year, Miss Kansas Corn and runner-up for the Kansas Miss America. And, damn it, he didn't even look at me. And you know something else, dear mother? The most shocking thing of it all is I would never have guessed such passion was even a part of cool, calm and collected Janet Stevens. Cool? Some bad joke . . .

She got up, paced the floor. It was only eleven-thirty now and she couldn't call Kit. Especially not on Sunday morning, after Nathan Weiss had spent the night. He always stayed over on Saturday nights. "Nat always screws best on Saturday night and Sunday morning," Kit had said. What the day had to do with how well one made love remained a mystery to Janet. But then, it seemed she had a lot to learn in that department.

For lack of anything better to do she lay down and glanced through *Harper's Bazaar,* which did little to distract her. She tossed the magazine across the room. *Damn* him. He hadn't even noticed her. Damn, damn, *damn.* She went to the dresser and pulled out her album of stills. Back in bed once again, she braced herself against the backboard and carefully scrutinized the photographs. They were good. Hadn't they been her passport to the best modeling school in New York? But he hadn't noticed. Oh, nuts to it. So he hadn't noticed her . . .

By noon she was climbing the walls and impulsively picked up the phone and called Kit.

A sleepy Kit answered in her morning basso profundo voice. "Hello and what the hell do you want?"

Janet was almost embarrassed enough to hang up, but instead said softly, "Kit, it's me, Janet. I'm sorry I woke you—"

"Me too. But now that you have, what's on your mind?"

"Kit . . . could we possibly have dinner tonight?"

An annoyed silence, then, "That's what you called for? At this time of the morning?"

"Well . . . no, not really. The truth is I . . . have to talk to you."

Nat was awake now and beginning to claim her attention.

"Listen, Janet, I'll call you back about four." The phone went silent.

Oh, God. What was she going to do until four? She hadn't felt so panicked and alone since she had first come to New York. And all because of a man who didn't even know she existed.

Quickly she dressed again and left the room. Instead of waiting for the elevator she ran down five flights of stairs. Once outside the hotel she stood wondering. Maybe she'd go to a movie. Or . . . maybe the Metropolitan Museum. No, not today. The nudes of the old masters, with their inward-looking satisfied gazes, would be no solace for her now.

She walked aimlessly down Fifth Avenue, stopping from time to time in front of a store window, but all she saw reflected in the glass was the face of a woman who was all but invisible to Bill McNeil. Damn him, he hadn't noticed her and it hurt. Somehow he had gotten down deep inside her, unlocking all the hidden doors she'd so carefully guarded, and opening others that she hadn't known existed.

Finally she took the bus uptown to 59th Street, got off and walked toward the hotel . . . home.

It was three-thirty when she let herself in, weary from her sleepless night and the emotional turmoil of the day. She undressed, sat on the edge of the bed watching the clock. The minutes seemed like hours, as though they were standing still. Would Kit remember to call, or would her sexual idyll push the outside world from her mind? Was sex so all-consuming that reason was forgotten? With each passing moment her desperation built to such a pitch that she was more and more tempted to call Kit back. It was a quarter past four. Unable to control herself any longer, she was about to pick up the phone when it rang.

For a moment she froze, her hands shaking as she took the receiver off the hook. "Kit?"

"How'd you guess? Now tell me what you called for this morning."

Haltingly, she said, "I thought we could go to dinner . . . just the two of us . . . Look, Kit, I have to talk to you."

There was a long pause.

"Kit, are you there?"

"Barely . . . I'm really beat."

"I know, I can imagine after giving such a large party last night—"

"After the party ended the party began. One thing about Nat, his stamina improves with time. One volley after another. If he could package it he could make a fortune. So you don't misunderstand, I happen to love it . . ."

"I guess it must be wonderful to be in love—"

"You'd better believe it, kiddo. I love the way he makes me feel, before, during and after. Now about tonight . . . look, I really am sort of beat."

Tears came into Janet's eyes. Much as she loved Kit, she felt a resentment she couldn't deny. There really weren't any friends, not when you needed them. God, she missed her mother and father, maybe she should go home . . . People here were just too tough for her, too glib, too self-centered, didn't really give a damn when it came right down to it. Or maybe she was too much a part of Kansas, where neighbors were always willing to help, no matter what, or when. She'd thought that everyone was like the people she'd grown up with . . . That was partly why she'd been so drawn to Fayge. But now she realized how unprepared she had been for New York after all, for its big bad impersonal world. Or maybe it was just the profession she'd chosen, maybe not everybody here was like the people she'd come in contact with in the fashion industry. She still remembered the shock she'd felt when someone said, "Here, get your ass into this one," as if she were just a hunk of meat ready to be hung in a butcher shop. And the four-letter words that everybody used. *Everything* was a four-letter word. She had heard it often enough since coming to New York. It was just a part of the lexicon. The f—— camera . . . what the f— . . . and

46

so on. Effie would have washed their mouths out with soap. But come to think of it, she was a prude. She remembered being on the edge of tears after a photographer had thrown a white chiffon dress at her and yelled, "Get your ass into this, double-time." That was the day she'd spoken to Kit for the first time . . . "Don't take it to heart, sweetie," Kit had said. "It's nothing personal. That's called communication. It goes with the territory. In one ear and out the other. F— 'em."

Janet had also been shocked by Kit's language; Kit didn't seem the type. But she had since taken it as part of Kit's frankness . . . She sat now, trying to keep back the tears.

"I understand, Kit. Thanks for the party last night . . . I had a great time." She felt like using the Anglo-Saxon word. Except in her case it would have been high irony.

After hanging up the phone, she gave in to the tears she had been holding back. After they subsided she merely sat . . . Maybe she could call Bill McNeil and thank him for the ride. He was probably listed in the book—*you're going nuts, Janet, you know that?* She picked up the phone and instead placed a call home. She had to touch base. Reality.

It was six o'clock on Monday morning when Janet stepped into the shower. She hadn't slept all night and was worn out. How, she wondered, was she going to make it through the day? But she would if it killed her.

Kit was the last person she wanted to see today, but she knew it was inevitable.

When Janet walked into the make-up room Kit looked up from the dressing table. "My God, you look like something the cat drug in."

Trying not to show her hurt and anger, she avoided Kit's gaze. "I didn't sleep very well last night—"

"Well, you'd better watch it, that camera picks up every little . . ."

But Janet wasn't listening. All she could hear was the voice inside that said, Where were you when I needed a friend yesterday?

Kit sensed Janet's reaction and could have kicked herself for being so self-centered. The kid from Kansas had sent up a smoke signal yesterday and she'd been too insensitive to read the message . . . "What are you doing for lunch, Janet?"

"I'm not going to have lunch, but thanks all the same."

"Now don't be a sorehead and overreact. I'm sorry about last night . . . more than that I can't be. Now, how about lunch?"

Janet looked at Kit's face. There was no doubt that Kit really was a very good friend. Except for Fayge, Kit was the only real friend she'd made since coming to this so-called mecca of the world. And Kit was right. She was acting like a petulant, spoiled child who ran to mommy or daddy in tears over the least little setback. "I'd like that . . . And Kit, I want to apologize for acting so—"

"Forget it, where do you want to meet?"

"Anywhere."

"Russian Tea Room, noon. Got to run, we're shooting on location this morning."

Janet was in a mild state of inebriation when Kit arrived a half hour late. She had been embarrassed when the waiters began to look at her questioningly—almost reproachfully, she thought—as she waited for Kit, and so she had ordered a Bloody Mary just to keep the table. She was now almost through her second drink.

Kit sat down alongside Janet and, out of breath, said, "Couldn't help it, took longer than we thought . . . I see you're having a Bloody."

"Two," Janet answered, speech slightly slurred.

"Well, girl, you've had your quota for the day," Kit said, then hailed the waiter and ordered one for herself.

"Make that the same for me," Janet put in.

Kit didn't try to stop her. Maybe it was what she needed to get through whatever it was that ailed her.

After the drinks came, Kit asked her what she felt like eating.

"A big bowl of fettucini with lots and lots of butter, Parmesan cheese and—"

"Are you crazy? Do you know how many calories are—"

"Who cares? So I won't put Suzy Parker out of business."

48

"You won't even work if you start eating that kind of dynamite."

"Who cares?" Janet repeated, taking a sip of her drink.

"I do, damn it, and you're not going to louse up that body with pasta because you've got some kind of a problem—"

"How'd you know I have a problem?"

Kit laughed and shook her head. "Because I'm psychic, born with mystic powers—" Kit broke off as the waiter came to take their order. "Two green salads with crabmeat. No dressing, just fresh lemon."

"I'd like the Louis dressing," Janet said defiantly.

"No you wouldn't. Just knock it off."

When the waiter left, Janet whispered, "I have to go to the ladies' room."

"You think you can tell the difference? The one that has Little Bo Peep on the door is . . ."

But Janet was already out of the seat and walking unsteadily toward the back.

The salads were waiting by the time Janet returned.

"You took so long I thought maybe they had a crap game going on."

"No-o . . . I . . . didn't feel too well . . ."

"Last night's dinner?"

"Didn't have any."

"Oh? Well, I think we should get down to a little girl talk," Kit said.

Janet watched as Kit squeezed the lemon over the crabmeat salad. Now that they were together it seemed difficult to begin. Yesterday the desperation would have poured out, but now she felt embarrassed, humiliated. Imagine going out and stalking a man she didn't even know. It was all so crazy . . . so . . . juvenile. Kit was so worldly and sophisticated that she would probably laugh, and the one thing Janet was sure she couldn't stand at this moment was being laughed at.

Kit snapped her fingers.

"Have at your salad. It will settle your stomach."

Toying with the food, Janet said almost inaudibly, "Tell me about Bill McNeil."

Kit finished chewing a mouthful of salad, all the while

49

looking at Janet very closely, before she swallowed and said, "He's a rat."

Janet blinked.

"But how can you say that about a friend?"

"That's just the reason why."

"But you invited him to the party."

"So? He's a rat I happen to love a lot."

Janet's shoulders slumped and her gaze stayed on the uneaten salad in front of her.

"I thought you were in love with Nat Weiss."

"I am, but there's all kinds of love. I've known Bill since . . . I guess all my life. He went to school with my brother, our families were very close."

"Then why did you call him a rat?"

"Janet, honey, let me tell you something. If you're going to survive in this world, you can't take everything so literally. I don't mean he's a rat rat. I mean . . ." She paused for a long moment, and when she went on her face had a new softness in it. "At one time I was really in love with him, but he didn't feel the same about me." Another pause, then . . . "I guess I was about eighteen when I went to the McNeil summer place in Maine. We were together more than at any other time of our lives. Well, to make a story short, we had a picnic one day, swam a lot, laughed a lot at silly things kids laugh about. There was a mild summer rain and we ran to the boathouse. I was shivering and he got out blankets and put one around my shoulders. I was really nuts about him. I turned to him, looked at those beautiful brown eyes and threw off the blanket. Also caution to the winds, as they say. Well, before you knew it there was lots of kissing and touching and fondling and then he was on me . . . or was I on him? I don't remember. When it was over, it was over. He said how sorry he was, that he hadn't meant it to happen, that he hoped I'd forgive him. Forgive him . . . that was the joke of the century. *I* had seduced *him*. He didn't even know it. He thought it was his fault. Well, anyway, that was the first and last time I ever loved anyone quite like *that*."

"You're still in love with him, aren't you, Kit?"

"Yes . . . I suppose I am . . . but he's not in love with me. And it takes two, baby . . . two."

"Is that why you see Nat the way you do?"

"Right . . . he gives me what Bill never could. Or would. And let me tell you, honey, it's nice to be *loved* . . . nice. And the thing is, Nat loves me a whole lot. Now what else do you want to know about just plain Bill McNeil?"

"Nothing."

"You don't lie very convincingly, Janet."

"Well, I was just—"

"You just fell for him. Why not say it?"

Was she so transparent? Of course she was . . .

"Well, *say* it, for God's sake."

She ran her tongue around her dry lips. "Well, now that I know how you feel, it changes things."

"How so?"

"Well you just told me you loved Bill and I'm your best friend—"

"Don't let *that* bother you, dear. I also told you he *doesn't* love me, and nothing's going to change that."

Janet had tears in her eyes. She didn't know if they were for Kit or herself or both of them.

"What the hell are you crying for? It's not an Italian opera."

"Because—"

"Because you fell, hard and heavy. Right?"

"Yes. And you're not upset?"

"That question is so stupid I'm not even going to answer it."

"You mean you're really not upset, Kit?"

"That's right, I'm *not*. Now let's hear your saga."

For a long moment Janet sat looking down at her uneaten salad. Finally she started to tell how she had bumped into Bill at the party, how embarrassed and tongue-tied she had been over spilling champagne on his new suit, then how they had accidentally met downstairs and how apparent Bill's annoyance had been over the awkward meeting. She repeated every detail and every event from that moment until now and ended with, "Can you imagine anything so stupid as going to the park and actually thinking I might meet him by chance? My God, how crazy can you get?"

"It's not stupid and it's not new. Every woman who

51

falls for a man discovers things in herself she didn't know she possessed . . . and that happens to be a good word for it too. She gets possessed, does all kinds of crazy things. After which, of course, she regrets them, hates herself for her weakness and proceeds to think of all the ways to attract him, catch him . . . For whatever consolation it may be for you, I hear tell that some men get it pretty bad too when they take the fall . . . I just haven't happened to come across any . . ."

"But Kit, I've never ever felt like this about anyone before. Believe me. I thought I'd die yesterday, I wanted to see him so badly—"

"I know that feeling all too well. Don't look so surprised, Janet. I might have a tough line and front but down deep is an old marshmallow heart. I can cry when hurt too . . . Okay, enough philosophy. You say he didn't look at you, much less ask you out, right? Well, we'll just take care of that."

"How?"

"Simple. I'm having a small dinner party for my birthday anyway, so I'll sit you next to Romeo. The rest, of course, is up to you."

"Oh, Kit . . ." She felt guilty for the thoughts she'd had this morning. "Kit, are you sure you want to do this? I can understand inviting Bill to a large party but to an intimate small one, won't it be . . . sort of awkward for you?"

"Why, because I laid him once? Darling, let mama clue you in on a few facts of life. When a man doesn't love a woman he zips up his pants and loses his memory fast. That's how sensitive and sentimental most of them are. Besides, it happened a long time ago and I doubt Bill even thought about it after he apologized. And I might not be doing you such a big favor, you know. Even if Bill decides to carry you off to his bed, I'm not so sure you'll thank me for it."

"Why?"

"Billy is what's called a one-nighter. A roll in the hay and that's it. But one thing I'll say for him, he's damn particular who he rolls with. He's very selective that way."

"You're really bitter, Kit. Why don't you say it?"

"Bitter?" She laughed a bit too loudly. "Okay, I'm going to give it to you straight. Mama McNeil had a lot to do with his not wanting to get close or involved with *any* woman. She hasn't let him breathe since the day he was born."

"Is she that difficult?"

"Not at all. She's simply adorable except for one thing. She smothered him rather than mothered him, and even though he's a big boy of twenty-five she still considers him her baby. So there you are. I wouldn't fantasize about a big church wedding and all the trimmings. I seriously doubt he's ever going to take that plunge. Knowing him, I just can't see that happening."

Janet sat silent, eyes cast down, beginning to water . . .

"Oh, God, again? Listen, Janet, and carefully. You've got the hots for Bill McNeil. Right? So be prepared for a trip to the moon. Maybe it's about time. On the other hand this very well might not be what you think . . . LOVE. It might be nothing more than a little girl from Kansas who's ready for her first step into something called life, and sex is part of it. Since you never tried it, let it be with someone like Bill McNeil. If it goes no further, at least he's a gentleman. Mama, though, isn't easy to exorcize. Don't underestimate her."

Kit wasted no time. Bill said he wasn't sure he'd be able to make it, but she didn't give up easily. Besides, she'd been around Bill's mother Violet long enough to know which guilt buttons to push.

"You're one crumb-bum friend," Kit said. "I'd have thought you of all people would have remembered my birthday. Now, don't get carried away and send me a Rolls-Royce. Just bring your sweet adorable miserable self—"

"Hey, I'm sorry I forgot, Kit. Congratulations. If you're having the immediate world I'll bring a—"

Kit quickly interrupted. "No, this year it's going to be very small and very private and I'm only inviting close friends, so forget a date. I'm getting sentimental when it comes to sharing the most important day in my life. You want the guest list? Brother Charlie and wife Carol, and—"

"It's okay, surprise me, see you Saturday."

For the next five days Janet could think of nothing but meeting Bill again, and by Saturday night her fantasies had become so real that she sat nervously next to him at Kit's dining table and wondered if her feelings for him were written all over her face, or if he could read her mind. She looked at Kit, who was laughing at a joke Nat had just told. Bill seemed to think it was hilarious, as did Charles and his wife Carol.

Janet forced herself to join in the laughter, though she had hardly heard a word. Her mind was distinctly someplace else. She was remembering that Kit had advised her to come late, wearing the white matte jersey. "Let him eat his heart out, it fits like a second skin . . ."

Whether he was eating his heart out or not, she had no idea. When Kit made the introductions he'd merely said, "We've met."

She had turned to jello on the spot, relieved that he remembered her but worried that it might only be with annoyance.

Now, sitting next to him, she was uncomfortably aware of the effect of him, not only in her stomach but between her thighs . . . She wanted to be so exciting, exotic, a brilliant conversationalist. But on the few occasions that he spoke to her, she sat there with a fixed smile, with such snappy ripostes as . . . "New York? Just wonderful . . ." In fact, the answer to almost every inquiry he made was "wonderful, just wonderful." She knew what he must have thought of her conversation . . . pure boring.

When the cake . . . thank God . . . was finally brought in, Kit blew out the candles and Nat took up his glass of champagne in a toast. "To Kit, long live the queen."

They all raised their glasses and joined in the toast.

Then came the final disaster of the evening for Janet. As she was putting her glass down, it became detached from her hand—and landed in the middle of Bill's lap. Jolted by the cold and wet, he stood up immediately and grabbed a napkin.

Janet merely wanted to die. Clearly God had decreed the end of this affair with Mr. Bill McNeil before it even began . . . "I'm so sorry, I'm really so, so—"

"It's *okay* . . ." But his tone implied otherwise. His

pants were soaked and when he went to Kit to kiss her and say "Happy Birthday," he added that he hadn't been in wet pants since he was three and thought maybe he should be excused to go home and change his diapers. Janet was destroyed. . . .

Charles and Carol had taken her home. It wasn't until five in the morning, as she lay in the dark staring up at the ceiling, that she gave way to the tears, telling herself, over and over, that she had lost him.

Nathan Weiss had been born into a wealthy family that had run a well-respected brokerage firm for over two generations now. He had cut his eyeteeth on stocks and bonds, and within a year after finishing Harvard Business School—three years younger than his classmates—Nathan Weiss was considered the boy wonder of Wall Street. If he didn't take this status seriously, he was well aware of the enormous responsibility of handling and investing millions of dollars for other people. That had been drummed into his head from day one by his father. So, much as he adored Kit, he always left her by four o'clock on Sunday afternoons to go to his club's steam room and have a massage to revitalize himself. He didn't enjoy having to leave, but he needed to be in top shape for Monday morning when the market opened.

In the beginning of their romance Kit was exasperated with him. "You're a coward—a 6-foot, 170-pound weakling." He would nibble on her ear lobe, smile, kiss her and leave. She would lie back and smile like a Cheshire cat. Nat left her feeling more fulfilled than if she'd slept with a half dozen men. Who needed them? It was the quality that kept her happy. Foolish smart-ass she might be, Kit told herself, but she at least knew a good thing, so to speak, when she saw it . . .

When he left the day after her birthday party, she lay in bed thinking that if she wasn't careful she just might let down her guard one day and find she had fallen in love all over again. No, not this girl, not Kit Barstow. Falling in love was too painful. She'd tried it once, hadn't she? Once was enough and she liked things just the way they were. Keep it light. Look at poor Janet. She'd almost died last night when that sonofabitch split without saying good-night to her. Mama McNeil certainly hadn't taught her Billy how to be gracious. And military school and M.I.T. hadn't taught him anything more than how to be an up-tight engineer. Big deal, so Janet accidentally spilled the wine. So what if the front of his pants were wet. The truth was that Bill was a spoiled, egocentric child at times. Also a louse. And poor Janet. She might have become a hugely successful model in the big tough city, but somehow she'd never acquired the thick skin that went along with it. Janet was just too vulnerable . . .

She picked up the phone and called her. "Hi, cookie, what're you doing?" As though she didn't know . . . drowning in her tears. Well, Kit knew what tears felt like too, though the world rarely was allowed in on it.

A long silence. "Nothing. Just . . . just sort of taking it easy . . ."

"Okay, so you've had enough of that . . . now, where would you like to go for dinner?"

"Kit, I'm really not hungry, but thanks all the same—"

"Listen, Madame Butterfly, dry your wings and get your little ass out of bed—"

"Thanks for being such a good friend, Kit, but I honestly *don't* think I'm up to it—"

"In that case I'll pick up some goodies from Chang Lee's kosher kitchen and bring it on down to your room. We'll read fortune cookies. Who knows what the future will . . ."

I already know my future, Janet thought. I ruined it for good last night over a glass of wine. "Kit, please don't think I'm being ungrateful but I just have to be alone to sort things out. Okay? You do understand?"

Of course she understood. The rats. Men were a flawed species—except for Nat, of course. Whoever invented the word *love* was probably some sadistic character.

"Okay, Janet. I'm against it, but if that's the way you feel, I'll see you tomorrow."

"Thank you, Kit. I'm sorry if I ruined your party."

"*You* didn't ruin anything. It was that fool stalking off like someone had stolen his teddy bear."

"I really can't blame him. I mean, after all, it was the

second time I spilled a glass on him, and *I* feel such a fool."

"So he should be happy it wasn't hot coffee, he could have wound up with a scorched pecker. Now get something to eat."

"I will, and Kit . . . thanks for everything."

Chapter Four

After a sleepless night, Janet was too exhausted to go to work so she called and said her throat was sore and that she was coming down with a cold. From the sound of her voice no one would have suspected it was less than the truth. For two days she stayed at home and brooded, not even answering the phone, although she knew it was probably Kit. What good was all the so-called glamor of her career if she was so inept that she had driven Bill away before she'd even had a chance to get to know him? She was out of her element in this city, just another pretty face that should have stayed put in Kansas. The loneliness and depression she had felt when she first came to New York plunged in on her with even greater impact now, and by Wednesday she didn't even get out of bed. There were no more romantic fantasies about Bill. Just a sense of loss . . .

At five o'clock on Wednesday there was a knock on her door. It was Kit, and she entered the room with all the fury of Madame Defarge.

Janet slipped weakly back into bed while Kit stood facing her. "*What* do you think you're doing and *why* didn't you answer the phone? Now you listen to me and listen carefully. For the first time in your life you didn't get to be pom-pom girl of the year. So you lost the contest. Grow up, Janet, throw away your shovel and pail. Bill McNeil's not worth having a nervous breakdown over. Neither is any other mother's son, for that matter." With that, Kit threw back the bedcovers and continued, "Now you get out of that bed. You look terrible and a few more days of this nonsense will make you look like the girl who came out of Shangri-la to find out that she was ninety. Out, and now."

Kit, of course, was right. She was acting like Camille. But it also happened to be the first time she'd fallen in love and been rejected, and the humiliation was almost more than she could handle. It was only Kit's top sergeant voice saying, "Okay, kid, let's get this show on the road" that gave her the impetus to shower and get dressed. . . .

When she returned after dinner her spirits were better and all she prayed for was that God would take over the job of making Bill McNeil disappear from her mind as quickly as he had disappeared from her life.

Her prayers were unanswered. She went back to work the next day, but there was hardly a moment she didn't think of him. In the midst of shooting a long sequence she barely heard the instructions being given by the photographer . . . "Lean a little forward to the left into the camera . . . walk like you're floating off the ground . . . *hold* it . . ."

The days seemed to crawl by, with the image of his face and the overpowering feelings aroused by his presence growing stronger rather than weaker. Finally, the need to have some kind of contact with him—anything at all—was so intense that Janet looked up his home number, called, then hung up the moment he said hello. She'd had no intention of speaking to him. She just had to hear his voice. The terror she felt afterward was numbing . . . did he suspect it was her? Don't be stupid, she told herself. He didn't even know she existed. . . .

At the end of the next week, however, she was on the phone again, waiting nervously for him to answer and wondering what on earth she would say to him. When she heard his voice, for a moment she panicked.

"Hello."

"May I speak to . . . uh, to . . . Jane?"

"Who do you want?"

"Jane."

"You have the wrong number." Dial tone.

She looked at the silent receiver in her hand, replaced it like a live snake grown in her hand. This had to stop, had to. The whole thing was too crazy, childish. Being in love made you do stupid things, but at least she'd have to stop these irrational anonymous calls . . .

59

When Kit saw Janet the next morning she knew at a glance that Janet was still depressed. Affecting a casual air, Kit said, "Do you know what I feel like doing?"

Janet shook her head.

"Splurging. To hell with the cottage cheese. Let's go to the Stage Deli and wrap our mouths around a little hot pastrami."

"I'm sorry, Kit, but I don't feel hungry."

"I didn't mean now. I said lunch. Listen, I've got to run. Meet you there at noon."

Before Janet could object, Kit was gone.

At lunch, Kit kept up a light banter while Janet nibbled on her sandwich. No dialogue. Janet's vagueness was getting to Kit.

"Okay, kiddo, let's have it. I mean let's talk. So far it's been a monologue."

Janet toyed with her cole slaw. When she finally looked up there were tears in her eyes. "I don't know what's wrong with me, Kit . . . I've done the most insane things . . . I astonish myself—"

"Such as?"

Shaking her head, she answered, "I'm really so ashamed and embarrassed . . . even to tell you."

"Look, Janet, you can tell me anything. I don't sit in judgment."

So she told Kit about the phone calls, the fantasies, her inability to shake Bill from her mind. "I've never done such things in my life, *never*. My family would faint. All my life I've been told how level-headed and mature I am. That's some laugh."

"So what makes you think you're alone? Listen, there hasn't been a woman since Eve who hasn't gone through all the crazy antics and depression that's happening to you. Love can make basket cases out of the sanest of us. Especially when it happens to be a one-way street and there's nothing you can do about it. It's still a man's world, honey. They still call the shots. If Bill McNeil wanted you he wouldn't have to sit and suffer while he waited for you to phone. He'd simply call and say, 'Hi, there, how about dinner?' It isn't fair, but those still seem to be the rules of the game."

Janet shook her head. "So what do I do now?"

"I think you should go home for a few days."

"I've thought about it, but how will that help to get Bill out of my head?"

"I don't know. Maybe because it's comforting to be with those who really love you . . . It puts you in touch with a good reality. Home is a very special place when you feel unloved. You know what I mean?"

Janet nodded. She remembered the Kowalskis and the love they'd given her. "You're right. I'll go this weekend."

On Thursday Janet went to United Airlines and bought her ticket, then walked up Fifth Avenue to 59th Street and stopped on the corner. She looked up at the office building across the street where she knew Bill McNeil was probably working at that very moment. Again the same feeling of longing . . . no logic in the world could exorcise the compulsion to see him. She went to a pay phone, called his office . . .

"Is Mr. McNeil in?"

"Yes, may I ask who's calling—?"

Janet hung up the receiver and walked across the street and into the huge marble lobby. She sat down on the leather bench and looked up at the large clock above the bank of elevators. It was four. She'd wait 'til hell froze if need be, but once and for all she was going to see Bill McNeil.

Kit had said earlier that it was a man's prerogative to do the pursuing, that those were the rules of the game. Well, maybe so. And maybe she was being brazen, unladylike. Certainly she was risking outright rejection, but so be it. The last month had been such hell that she simply had to take some action, never mind the consequences.

Keeping her eyes on the elevator doors she tried to think what she would say, how she would explain being in the building. The dentist . . . ? That's it, she had an appointment with . . . No, she wasn't going to play any more damn silly games, she was going to be honest, even if it meant letting him see how afraid she was . . .

At five o'clock, elevator after elevator began to disperse homeward-bound commuters. A half hour later Janet was beginning to think she had missed him in the crowd—

suddenly there he was, the first to emerge as the bronze doors of the elevator slid open. She got up unsteadily, braced herself against the wall for a moment, then took in a deep breath and started toward him. "Hi, Bill."

He looked toward the voice. When he saw her he smiled and put up his hands in a mock gesture of defense. "You don't have any champagne, do you?"

Janet blushed, then smiled back. "No, not this time. I thought you might let me take you to dinner to make up for my clumsiness. Is that a fair exchange?"

He looked at her. *Looked,* this time, in spite of himself. Long legs and a near-perfect body. A thick mane of hair the color of molasses. Velvety soft violet eyes, an unblemished, almost translucent complexion, sculptured lips, perfect nose . . . just as he'd remembered her. Why the hell had she shown up? He'd been struggling not to call her from the first moment he'd seen her. That first night when they sat together in the taxi, he'd realized that his anger over the spilled champagne had merely been a way of fighting the overwhelming feeling of desire that had hit him the moment he'd set eyes on her. He'd had his share of beauties but no one had ever affected him quite the way this Janet Stevens had. He suspected that if he saw too much of her she was the likely candidate to hook him. And that had shaken him. He couldn't afford to get involved, not now, not when he had finally won his freedom. Which was why he had been so sore at Kit the night of her birthday when Janet had walked in. And then to have been placed next to her . . . He had almost forgotten that he wasn't going to get involved, that love and marriage were out. Almost. But then she had tipped the glass over, and the shock of it had brought him out of his daze and back to his first resolve, given him time to recover equilibrium. But Kit hadn't let it go at that, she had to make a big thing out of it. She had called the next day. "You know what you are? A schmuck . . . translation—a prick. I learned it from Nat. Good word for you . . ."

Janet. Now she was standing in front of him looking so . . . so impossible to say no to. If he had an ounce of brains he'd say he had a date, but between the thought and deed he heard himself saying, "That's a very fair exchange, but I don't let ladies take me to dinner. Now, where would you like to go?"

She couldn't believe it. All the agony she'd been going through could have been avoided if only she'd had enough courage to swallow her fear and pride and chuck all the conventions. Modern women weren't quite as emancipated as they pretended to be. Not even Kit . . .

"How about the Italian Pavilion?" he prompted her.

"You make the decision."

This time they sat a little closer in the cab and when they arrived at the restaurant they were seated next to each other in an intimate booth. As they sat drinking their martinis, Janet felt a sense of unreality about it all. The heightened awareness of his nearness, of what he might be thinking, of his eyes and voice, of the soft fluttering that rose from her stomach and washed her with a feeling of weakness—it was new to her, overwhelming. Her entire being seemed tuned to his presence, as if nothing else existed, and yet it felt as if it might all be a fantasy, gone the moment she turned her eyes from him . . .

"What would you like for dinner?" he asked, taking up his menu.

"What? Oh . . . I . . . why don't you order for both of us?"

He gave their order in what was apparently flawless Italian, judging by the waiter's pleased reaction, although Janet understood none of their conversation.

As they sipped their martinis they fell into moments of silence that were broken when she spoke at the same time, their words overlapping. They smiled then laughed when this happened, but Janet felt she was acting like a fifteen-year-old on her first date, with her first crush. Why couldn't she be at least a little sophisticated like Kit? She was doing the best she could with the tools she had, but she was afraid the tools spelled Kansas.

She silently thanked God when the waiter brought their meal, giving her a temporary reprieve. One couldn't talk too much except between bites, but even then she cringed at the thought of how banal her remarks must sound. "This is the best lobster . . ." And his responses didn't help. "I know . . . it's marvelous." And so forth.

What Janet, of course, didn't know, or even guess, was

that Bill was just as uncomfortable. He was aggravated with himself because he couldn't control or deny his reactions to her. The physical was only part of it. No one had attracted him with such intensity, but there was also a fascination he felt, as if he had to know everything about her. She'd hit him where he lived, was most vulnerable, never mind what he pretended . . . right in the heart. *No* one had ever done that. He kept telling himself to be sensible, that if he took her to bed, got close to her he would lose the freedom he'd tried to guard so carefully. He wasn't about to give that up at twenty-five. No way.

By the time their coffee was served, Janet decided that asking questions might be the best approach. Clearing her throat, she began, "Has New York always been your home?"

"Yes. And you?"

"Kansas."

"Oh? For some reason . . . you don't seem like someone from Kansas."

"Why?"

"I don't know exactly. Somehow Kansas brings to mind country fairs, square dancing and corn on the cob."

"And I don't fit into that image?"

"Hardly. What brought you to New York?"

"I wanted to be a model, and living in New York had sort of been a dream all my life. I thought it would be the most fabulous place in the world—"

"You say you thought, past tense. Do you still?"

Janet hesitated, then said, "No. I think it's the coldest, most impersonal place in the world. Except for Kit and a wonderful Jewish family I met, I've felt . . . well, alone. I suppose when one fantasizes and anticipates too much the reality is always disappointing."

"Yes . . . maybe you expected too much."

"You're probably right." She took a sip of water. "Truth is I guess I wasn't prepared for a lot of things."

"Such as?"

"Well . . . people seem so aggressive. And so often they seem to *want* to be superficial, as if friendship doesn't mean too much. I'm not good at being that casual."

"Men in particular?"

Hesitating for a moment, she looked up. "Yes . . . men

64

in particular. I don't know how to play the games. And I guess I don't really want to."

It was the honesty in her eyes that impressed him most. Nothing coy or forward about her. Just a certain shyness, and total candor. Bravo for Kansas.

Janet looked embarrassed as she said, "You must have thought I was pretty brazen to show up at your office the way I did. I've really never done anything like that before . . ."

If he had thought she was being brazen, which seemed a rather old-fashioned word for it, he now knew that she was simply forthright and that it had taken real courage for her to do it . . . "I was surprised to see you—but yes, I do believe you. And I'm glad you were waiting, although I'll never know why you bothered. I acted like a heel."

"I didn't think so, I'm sure I'd have reacted the same way."

He smiled. "I doubt it. They don't grow them that way in Kansas."

The smile made her go almost limp. She took a sip of the tepid coffee.

She was saying now that it was his turn, she wanted to hear about him now . . . about his childhood . . . What was he going to tell her? The truth? Impossible.

He was conceived at a time when his mother already had three daughters past puberty and certainly didn't expect any more children. It was a shock when Dr. Humphrey had said, "Wouldn't worry too much about the nausea or throwing up. It's pretty normal."

"Normal? Look, John, if it's a tumor, say so. I have a right to know."

"Violet, you're in perfect health—for someone who's pregnant."

She was stunned. "That's impossible."

"I'm sure Eve must have said the same thing and she'd only eaten an apple."

"John! This is no time for *levity*. I still say it's impossible. I'm forty-three and going prematurely through the menopause."

"That's the time it happens. The change in the menstrual cycle is deceptive."

How was she going to explain this to the girls? It was simply too embarrassing. And by June, when Betsy turned fifteen, she'd be bulging under her maternity clothes as she stood there singing happy birthday. The very idea of it was absurd, humiliating.

In the end of June, after six miserable months, she gave birth to a beautiful baby boy of almost ten pounds. The moment she saw him all her misgivings vanished. This chubby "adorable angel" became the new love of her life. With a vengeance. She adored Betsy, Alice and Harriet, but she had always wanted a boy, and this child was like an unexpected gift. From the moment of his birth she doted on her William. For the first five years of his life he was rarely out of her sight. He was cuddled and pampered not only by his mother but by his three adoring sisters—at least until his father stepped in. Jason McNeil knew something had to be done if he was to end up with a son and heir instead of a limp wrist. When Bill turned eight, his mother and father almost came to a parting of the ways when Jason announced "Violet, our son's going to a military academy."

"Over my dead body."

"I wouldn't want to be the one to cause your demise, but unless you want to have four daughters instead of three, I'd advise you to take a good look at what's happening . . . Violet, can't you see he's turning into a . . . well, a sissy?"

"How dare you say a thing like that to me!"

"You've kept him in Little Lord Fauntleroy suits. You've never let him play ball or be a cub scout out of fear he might get hurt or catch a cold. You've never—"

"I think I've heard enough. He happens to be a very extraordinary child who loves to read and practice the piano. He's a very special and sensitive child."

"And what I'm saying is that he's going to grow up like a man and, I hope, become an engineer like me. He can't do that with four mothers hovering over him like he was some sort of fairy princess."

There was fire in Violet's eyes. "You're *wrong*, Jason. And I refuse to even discuss it."

"Violet, for God's sake, take a look. You're right about one thing. He's sensitive, all right, so sensitive that he cries at the least little thing, whether it's because he's stubbed his toe or can't have his way. And I don't much like the idea of a boy of eight years still wanting to sleep with his mama. He's going to military school."

Violet stood there, on the verge of angry tears as she looked at her husband. "I don't know why you're doing this to me, but it strikes me rather strange that you should suddenly notice all this now—"

"You're wrong there and you know it. You've taken over since the day you brought him home—in a pink blanket, I might add. Not once did you let me take him fishing or the other things fathers and sons do. I told you how I felt about the elocution lessons and the damned dancing lessons and you fought me. It's time that it stopped, unless you want to ruin him for good. Your sweet William is going to military school. Make no mistake about *that*."

Violet was in tears now. "You're taking my baby away from me, and I'll never forgive you for . . ."

The break was as traumatic for her son as it was for Violet, but after six years in a disciplined academy he became the kind of fourteen-year-old his father wanted. In spite of his mother's protests he played football, was captain of the rowing team, excelled in basketball and was an honor student. It was not the horror show Violet imagined, or that was chronicled so chillingly in Calder Willingham's *End as a Man*.

But when it was time for Bill to attend high school, Violet was determined to have her way. He was to go to public school on Long Island, and that was *that*. Jason could scream, rant and rave, do anything he wanted except deprive her of her son. This time Jason didn't protest; the die, he figured, had been cast, he no longer worried about his son's future.

The one who did rebel, though, was Bill. Violet started right in where she had left off. She bought tickets to concerts, ballets and theaters, which Bill not only resented but refused to attend. Violet regretted having let him slip through her fingers more than ever now, and her tearful urging that he should learn to appreciate the finer things of life made him feel guilty. He loved his mother, but he just didn't want to spend all his time with her and he couldn't stand being kissed and hugged and doted on. Nor did he have much patience with the fact that he never left the house without her asking where he was going, telling him to be home early, to button his coat, wear his overshoes. On and on it went, and telling himself that she was really a dear woman, despite all her nagging, only made him feel more guilty for his anger. The only thing that made life tolerable for him was that, thank God, his sisters were married now and couldn't add their protests to his mother's. That and the fact that his father stood firmly behind him, making it two against one. Violet would never know that Bill crammed four years of high school into two and graduated at sixteen because he so badly wanted to get away from her. He was the youngest college graduate of his class, having jumped another year ahead in his studies.

With M.I.T. out of the way he went straight to the top and became vice-president of his father's engineering firm. He was more than equal to the challenge and found more satisfaction in it than he'd expected. As he stood with a drink in hand at the end of a day and looked out over Manhattan from his apartment window, he would give an unconscious sigh, enjoying the heady sense of freedom that had entered his life. Finally . . .

His emancipation, though, was short-lived. Jason died of a coronary three months after Bill joined the firm. Added to the painful loss of his father was his concern and guilt over Violet, who was in a complete state of bereavement and felt that she had no one left, that she must live out her days alone in that huge mansion. Now, as she said, a mausoleum for her . . .

When his sisters suggested that she live with one of them, however, she had refused to give up her home, the home she had shared with Jason, the home that held all the echoes of her children's laughter. After the funeral, as she sat by the fireplace in her bedroom, she seemed so vulnerable, pathetic and lost. So much so that during the drive back to Manhattan Bill's conscience nudged him to the point where he simply felt compelled to move back to the house on Long Island until she recovered. That recovery lasted much, much longer than he'd ever imagined. Her state of mourning went on and on . . .

Three years of living with her . . . In his more cynical moments he was reminded of one of his father's lines about a cranky, hypochondriac aunt. "She used to enjoy ill health but now, thank God, she's complaining she feels better . . ." Violet, he sometimes felt, was enjoying ill health. And, of course, no sooner did the thought enter his head than it began to make him feel guilty again. A vicious circle . . . My God, he couldn't leave her alone in that ancient mausoleum. If anything happened to her it would be his fault. It was his *duty,* after all; she was his mother and he was single . . . But damn it, he was also entitled to some life of his own. He didn't even feel he could go away for a weekend with a girl. She was so pathetic when he came back, like an abandoned waif or something . . . "Oh, Bill, I've missed you. I'm so happy you're home. There's nothing like my wonderful son . . . I'm really so grateful to have you, my darling . . ." It made him cringe, and yet he knew how much it meant to her not to be alone.

What about living with his sisters, he'd once gotten up the nerve to ask her.

"Oh, I couldn't, dear. They have large families and lives of their own. I can't intrude on them."

Which was the trap. They had lives of their own. But what about him? . . . And that was the reason he had finally called Kit. She knew the family well, and she was one of the few people he could talk to openly.

Over lunch he poured out his fear. "Kit, I just don't know what to do," he concluded.

As Kit took a sip of her martini she saw the misery in his eyes. Maybe that was a good sign, she thought. Maybe he'd reached a breaking point and would finally change. About time . . . "Well, you've got a real problem and that ain't no lie. But the problem is *you,* buddy."

"What do you mean by *that?*"

"I *mean,* your mother's using you and you're too dumb or guilt-ridden to see through it. Well, buddy, you have two choices. Either you move back to Manhattan or you take a vow of celibacy and babysit with mama for the rest of your life."

"Using me? Look, Kit, she's frightened and lonely and—"

"And devious. She's going to see to it that you're single for a long, long time. She wants you around and not because she's frightened and lonely, kiddo."

"I think you're overboard about that, Kit." (Or was she?) "She's not really devious—"

"Really? I guess I have a better memory than you. When we were kids and you came home from school every summer she tried to gobble you up. It was your father who always kept you a couple of feet away from the sheriff. You have him to thank for the reprieve you had. He tried to give you a little backbone, help you stand up to the kind of emotional blackmail you were too young to understand. Your mother, in her sweet adorable innocent little way, wanted to keep you chained to the bed . . . her bed . . . and I think if your father were here he'd tell you to get the hell out while there's still time, if there is . . ."

"You mean just move out and leave her alone—?"

"Brilliant . . . you catch on fast. About a lifetime late . . ."

He ignored that. "And then what happens to her, please answer me that."

"Okay, I will. You have a family. You should say to darling sisters, Betsy, Alice and Harriet—I've had it, served my time. It's your turn to pay your dues."

"Kit, it just isn't that simple. Betsy's got three children, Alice four and—"

"Harriet none. So how about her moving in with mom if mom won't move off the plantation."

"Boy oh boy, I had no idea how tough you really are, Kit. Harriet has a husband, every woman wants her own home . . ."

She shook her head . . . what a joke *that* is. Sure, I'm real tough. My parents died eight years ago and I still wake up at night crying for them. Mr. Bill McNeil has forgotten he ever made love to me but I'd still go into a swoon if he even hinted that he was interested in me . . . She shook her head again and said impatiently, "Well, I guess I've been misinterpreting what you're feeling. What you're really saying is that you love living with your poor defenseless mama. What is it with you, Bill? Is it an oedi-

70

pal thing or do you just love being a martyr, acting out the part of the victim? Hey . . . you're twenty-four now and that's a very good year to pick up your marbles and tell mother that she doesn't have the right to deprive you of what belongs to you . . . your life. Just get on with it, for God's sake. She's a *lot* stronger than you think. She'll survive. Most women do. I'd get in touch with Harriet if I were you. It's worth a try."

Bill watched as Kit walked across the dining room to get her coat. He was upset at her abrupt departure, but at the same time he suspected that what she had said made sense. Tough but smart. Or maybe she wasn't so tough . . . He remembered a different Kit, before she had lost her parents in that airplane crash. But he admired the strength it had taken to live through the shock. And if her loss had toughened her, it had also given her some perspective he never could manage . . . He could do worse than listen to her.

He got up and called his sister Harriet from the telephone booth in the restaurant.

She was not overjoyed at the prospect of living with her mother. But then Bill was right. He had his life to get on with and she was the most logical choice to pick up the responsibility for their mother. She didn't have a family like Betsy and Alice and at thirty-five she wasn't about to start one. It would be easier, of course, if mama would come to live with her and Gordon but what the heck . . . It was her mother they were talking about, an old lady who had lost her husband and was living alone. It was the least she could do.

Thanks to Harriet, Bill had been freed from his bondage and had moved back to Manhattan about a year ago.

Of course the story he told Janet had many omissions and portrayed his mother as nothing less than a loving and gracious woman. About Jason McNeil he was more truthful—a concerned father, successful in business, a humorous and understanding man who had died before his time ". . . So that's about the whole story. I've been living in Manhattan for a year now . . ."

Janet was touched by his apparent selflessness. He hadn't felt that he'd done anything so noble, caring for and about his mother all that time. It was just a matter of returning what had been given to him. She felt ashamed that only a short while ago she'd said that New Yorkers were insensitive and uncaring. When she'd first met him she had been so swept off her feet that she hadn't stopped to wonder what kind of person he was. For all of Kit's sophistication, she had been mistaken about Bill, mistaken about his relationship with his mother. But then maybe Kit's feelings had been colored by her own disappointment . . . Janet was beginning to see that Bill was a man of some integrity, and his family had evidently fostered the quality in him. She was also impressed with his mother, who had persuaded her son he could no longer go on making such a sacrifice. She had insisted, he said, "Bill, you simply must make a life for yourself." He'd left, but reluctantly.

"She sounds wonderful," Janet said.

"She is," Bill answered, trying to forget her hysterical sobbing when he'd taken his suitcases and put them in the car. He swallowed the last of his coffee, then said, "Now enough of the Bill McNeil story . . ." More than enough . . . "Where would you like to go?"

What she said was, "Anywhere." What she wanted to say was, "Right smack into your arms . . ."

The night was clear, and cool. They walked slowly without speaking, but it seemed to Janet that words were superfluous, only for people who had nothing to say to each other. She felt taken over by him . . . wrapped up in him . . . It wasn't until they passed 53rd Street and Fifth Avenue that Bill roused her from silence.

"I live in that building," he said.

She followed his gaze and counted with him up to his apartment on the twenty-ninth floor, all the while wondering if he would ask her up. But he didn't. They walked on, stopping from time to time to look at the displays in store windows.

Much too soon she found herself in front of the Barbizon Hotel. For an awkward moment she stood silently looking at him, frantically searching for the right words and afraid she would blurt out the wrong thing and never see him again. She was saved when she heard him asking, "Are you busy Saturday night?"

Suddenly she remembered the airline ticket in her purse. And panicked. She wanted so badly to see him Saturday night. If she said no, would he ask her again? How many women were there in his life? It would be stupid to think for one moment that he was so taken with her that he would ever give her a second thought if she said no. And yet her parents were expecting her, and after Bill's story about his father's sudden demise she felt strangely compelled to see them, as if maybe it were an omen, a warning. It was nonsense, she knew, but the urge to go home was almost as strong, in its way, as her desire to see Bill.

"I was planning to fly home this weekend to see my family . . ."

"I see . . ."

Maybe it was her imagination, but he at least seemed a little disappointed. And then before she had a chance to answer she found herself being drawn into his arms, and gently kissed.

"I wish you didn't have to go . . ."

"Me too . . . but, well, I just feel that I really should."

"Well, you know best. This was the best evening I've had in a long time."

She most assuredly *didn't* know best, she thought.

He was looking at her intently. "I really mean it, Janet."

"Oh, Bill, thank you . . . it was for me too."

"Have a good trip," he said, kissed her again, and walked off. She lingered a moment, watching until he disappeared around the corner, and then quickly went inside. As soon as she'd closed the door to her room and sat herself down on the edge of the bed, she suddenly found herself crying. She knew she was probably overwrought after the emotional drain of the last few weeks, but tonight had changed everything. Hadn't it? No, she was still confused . . . pulled two ways now . . . She wanted to be with Bill . . . needed to see her family . . .

What to do? She stared at the phone for a moment, then picked it up and called Kit.

Kit was home, thank God.

"Kit? It's me. Janet. You sound breathless."

"I just got in and flew to the phone, but you sound like

73

Madame Butterfly when the captain said *sayonara*. What's up?"

"I'm not sure. How can anybody be *this* happy and miserable at the same time?"

"That's not so tough for you. All right, let's hear it."

Janet started relating the day's events, beginning with how she had bought a ticket and had then felt impelled to wait for Bill in his office building. Then there was the romantic dinner, and how impressed she'd been by what he'd told her about his family—so much so that she recapped the conversation for Kit. "It just proves one should never go by first impressions," she concluded. "I didn't picture him as someone whose family meant so much to . . ."

It was a rare moment for Kit, but she couldn't find her voice. She had a little difficulty squaring the Bill McNeil she knew with the Bill McNeil who had presented Janet with an image of unadulterated devotion. It was obvious he hadn't told the truth and now he had Janet seeing him as Prince Charming on a white charger. Oh well, so what if he came out looking like the guy in the white hat. Why not? In a way she admired him for not making mama the heavy in the drama. Violet McNeil was one in a long line of mamas who had trouble coming to terms with the notion that their sons grew up. You didn't have to be Jewish to be a Jewish mother. Truth to tell, except for her problem with weaning, she could really be quite a nice old lady. Sweet, even . . . But, also no question, murder on prospective daughters-in-law . . .

Kit was brought out of her reverie when she heard Janet saying, "I suppose I found it all so surprising because of the things you'd said about him."

"Like what?"

"That he was a rat, for example. Well, he isn't, Kit. He's a sensitive person—"

"Yeah . . . well, sometimes I have a quaint way of putting things. Sure, you're right, Bill's a really nice guy. I just get a little sore at him from time to time."

"Why, Kit?"

To hide the fact that he hurt me once and that I'm scared silly of giving him or anyone else an opportunity to do it again . . . "I don't know . . . maybe it's because

74

I've known him for so long I forget he's not part of the plumbing fixtures. It's only with a friend like that you can take out your frustrations. Enough. Let's get back to you. Now, what's the problem?"

"Well, as I told you, Bill asked me out this Saturday but I said I couldn't because I had to go home—"

"But the reason for that is gone, since you got up enough steam to take the initiative. So why not stay?"

"I don't know . . . something else tells me I should see my folks—"

"Really? And what's this something else?"

"My instincts, I guess, and something else . . . After Bill told me how suddenly his father died I got frightened . . . it was almost like a warning signal—"

"For God's sake, Janet, don't take everything as though it were a sign from heaven. I'm beginning to think you're more afraid of seeing Bill than this fate you're always so worried about."

"How can you say that when you know how I feel about him—?"

"I know how you feel, and I suspect that's why you're afraid."

"Honestly, Kit, that doesn't make any sense."

"I think it does. You want him and you know he's attracted to you, but you're afraid to put out because you want a commitment. The problem is that you're not in junior high, waiting for some guy to pin you before you'll let him hold your hand. When you play with grownups you wind up in bed, and take the chance that it's either the beginning or the end of a glorious affair. You're a big girl, Janet, time you learned you can't have it both ways."

Startling though it was, Kit had read it right. Yes, she *was* afraid that Bill would take her to bed once and then brush her off. Kit had warned her that Bill majored in one-nighters.

"So what do I do now?"

"That's up to you, baby. Just be sure you understand that if you have an affair with Bill it's not likely to be 'and they lived happily ever after.' He doesn't allow himself to become involved. When a girl gets too palsy-walsy he backs off. So don't say I didn't warn you if and when that happens. On the other hand, you're going to have to take that plunge eventually, whether it's with Bill or someone else, and as long as you remember that Bill is a confirmed bachelor you couldn't choose anyone better. He's a decent guy and lots of fun but you'll have to remember to play it cool, take it as a terrific experience and be willing to walk away saying it was worth the trip."

Kit knew even as she was speaking how ridiculous all that was. Janet was in love and a woman in love never walked away without scars. Well . . . at least she had been warned. (Which was more than anybody had done for her.)

There was a long silence. Then Janet asked, "Kit, I'd love to see Bill but what can I do now? I told him I was going home."

"Phone tomorrow and say you changed your mind. It's still a woman's adorable prerogative."

Chapter Five

Bill was happier than he sounded when she called the next morning. "I'm glad you decided to stay. Now, what would you like to do?"

Go to the moon with you. "Whatever you feel like."

I feel like taking you to bed. "Do you like Mama Leone's?"

I could skip dinner. "That sounds wonderful."

"Great, I'll pick you up at eight." God, he thought, now I'm doing rhymes. . . .

By eight o'clock Janet was a nervous wreck. In the last hour she had changed five times and was still not sure she was wearing the right thing. Should she dress to look demure or sophisticated? She finally settled for demure and now wore a pale lilac chiffon that enhanced the delicate coloring of her skin and brought out the violet in her eyes. She was studying herself in the mirror when the phone rang. He was in the lobby waiting for her. She grabbed her purse and wrap and ran to the elevator.

She had, apparently, guessed right. When he saw her coming toward him his broad smile told how much he approved. He took her by the arm and before she knew it they were sitting side by side in a taxi.

At Mama Leone's the maitre d' showed them to a quiet corner. The dinner was marvelous although neither ate much. The conversation was light, nothing of consequence. As they sat across from each other in the soft candlelight they were both thinking only of what lay ahead of them that evening. Bill was eager to get dinner over with and it was difficult to keep himself from simply taking her by the hand and walking out of the restaurant before they'd finished their meal. As for Janet, it seemed to her there was now no doubt that he'd take her home to

77

his apartment. It would be a hugely important night to her. It would be the first time she'd made love to Bill McNeil. The first time she'd made love to anyone. . . .

Once again they were in a taxi, only now he held her hand. Just that simple gesture made her, God help her, turn to jelly.

"Where would you like to go? There's a place on 94th that plays lovely music."

"If you like."

"Actually, I prefer my place."

"I think I would too."

The rest of the ride passed in silence. As they entered Bill's building she was conscious only of the warm pressure of his hand on hers. She wasn't aware of the echoes of voices and street noises, of the doorman who opened the door for them or the click of her footsteps across the marble floor on the way to the elevator. She snapped out of it only when she stood inside Bill's apartment.

It was startling, spacious and masculinely furnished. The walls of the living room were a deep blue. An extraordinary array of modern art hung over the leather sofa that flanked one wall, and an enormous glass and brass coffee table sat on a plush carpet the color of autumn leaves. There were two large chairs in plaid corduroy on either side of the fireplace, and bookshelves with a built-in stereo and bar occupied the remaining wall. The dining room was austerely but appropriately furnished and it looked out onto a balcony from which could be seen an expansive view . . .

Janet turned from the sight of the city lights when she heard the stereo.

"Champagne okay?" Bill asked.

She laughed. "Do you think I should? You wouldn't want to ruin another suit."

He looked very serious. "I'll take the risk if you will."

As he handed her a glass he said, "I'm glad you changed your mind about not going home this weekend."

"So am I." Wonderful boring understatement, she thought.

There was a moment of awkward silence. More out of

embarrassment than curiosity she wandered across the room to look at the modern paintings. She had taken the last drop of her champagne when Bill was beside her pouring more into her glass. She watched as the bubbles danced, then looked up at him. Only a month ago she had been sure she would never see him again. If this was a dream, she didn't want to wake up.

Taking the glass from her hand, he placed it on the table and took her in his arms. He kissed her gently and then with more urgency, and when he sensed her response his tongue separated her lips. Just when Janet thought she couldn't stand it anymore he took her up in his arms and carried her back to the bedroom.

As he set her down in the darkened room he stood for a moment with his hands cupping her face, taking in each detail in the soft illumination cast by the city lights outside.

Janet was acutely aware of the sound of her own breathing, and his. He traced the outline of her nose, eyes, forehead, the nape of her neck, until his fingers found the first button of the chiffon bodice. He kissed her while his hands slowly ventured downward until the front of her dress was open. He slid it from her shoulders to the plush carpeted floor. He unfastened the lace bra and slipped it over her arms, then held her rounded breasts and brushed her nipples first with his fingers and then with his lips and tongue. Janet gasped at the sensation, and from there on it was a kaleidoscope in slow motion. She felt, she was pleased to discover, no shame standing nude before him.

When he had undressed he held her against him, then picked her up and carried her to bed. He lay facing her, kissing her gently, caressing every contour of her body. Without words he guided her hand down to his groin and placed his hand over hers for a moment, moving it slowly up and down until Janet felt him harden and grow under her fingers. His tongue played over her lips, probed to meet hers. The taste of her was like honey. She heard the sigh of her breathing, the soft moan as his fingers teased down the front of her body and between her legs, pushing them apart. Then he moved on top of her and slowly began putting himself inside, pushing deeper and deeper still until he momentarily halted. She did not sense his uncertainty when he realized she was a virgin. Should he stop? Could he withdraw? No, not now . . . not now . . . Gently he moved forward . . . a muffled cry . . . a sharp pain for her, and then incredible release. For a moment neither moved. Then she arched her back to receive him. He responded, thrusting faster and faster until an explosion seemed to build inside her and erupted . . .

He lay still on top of her, their moist bodies clinging together. She *never* wanted this moment to end. His breathing still heavy, he kissed her and said almost in a whisper, "Sweet Janet, lovely sweet Janet . . ." then rolled over on his back. They lay there for a while, holding hands. The silence was broken only when Bill said, "I wish I had known, Janet. I wish you had told me before."

"And if I had, would you have still wanted me?" she responded contentedly.

"Oh *yes,* but I would have handled it differently."

"But I wouldn't have wanted you to. I love you, Bill—" The moment she'd said it, Kit's warning sounded in her head. She knew she'd made a bad error.

He released her hand and said, "How about some champagne?"

She merely nodded, too alarmed by her blunder to trust her voice.

He got out of bed, slipped into his robe and left the room.

Alone, she looked up at the ceiling. Well, the words couldn't be retracted. As she got out of bed she looked down at the bloodstained sheet. It didn't matter . . . Kit had said that Bill would take her to the moon and he had, she thought as she went to the bathroom to wash.

When she returned, Bill stood at the side of the bed, holding a bottle of champagne and two glasses. Suddenly she felt ashamed and began to dress.

"Hey, what do you think you're doing?"

Without looking at him she answered in a half-whisper, "I think I should leave."

Her expression caught him off balance. If he had an ounce of brains he'd let her go, but something about her wouldn't let him.

"Why do you want to?"

80

Taking a deep breath, she said, "I just think it's best. Really, Bill."

"What do you suppose I'm going to do? Put you in a taxi and let you go home alone?" Even as he heard his words he was mildly shocked. He'd never asked a girl to stay. But then, he'd never met anyone quite like Janet Stevens, and she'd zeroed in on him, scored on him, if you please, whether he liked it or not. Exactly what he felt for her at this moment he wouldn't question. He only knew that he wanted her to be with him because he felt a loneliness inside he'd never known, or admitted, before. He wished she hadn't told him she loved him . . . well, later he'd put all the pieces together again. For now . . . "Please stay, Janet . . ."

She gave him a searching look, then picked up her long satin slip and put it on to cover her nakedness. Bill watched her in the light from the bedside lamp. She seemed so small, so fragile, vulnerable. There wasn't another girl he knew who would have covered herself. She stood in front of him, her eyes lowered, and it took all his discipline not to take her off to bed again. Instead he turned to the bottle of wine and poured a glass for each of them. He held out his hand and she went to him. They sat on the edge of the bed and sipped at their glasses.

Janet averted her eyes from the stained sheet. Strange thing to be thinking about at this moment . . . She sipped once more, then drained the glass. "Awfully good champagne," she said, handing him the glass to be refilled. The wine began to work its way, and she felt more confident as they sat beside each other making easy conversation in low voices. So what if she had told him she loved him? He had become aloof, reacting exactly as Kit had predicted but—no, not quite. And now he was smiling at her, and he hadn't given her a brush-off and sent her home after her blunder, if it was a blunder . . . You're wrong, Kit, and he's no rat. He's a very nice person who simply doesn't want to become too involved. And—oh God, it would be too painful not to have your love returned. She shut out the thought, held out the glass to him. "Don't mind if I do."

"Do you think you should, Janet?" Again he was shocked by the feeling of protectiveness she'd roused in

81

him. Lord, how many girls he'd encouraged to get high just to free them of inhibitions. But Janet? This had been her first time and she'd given herself so . . . openly. No fakery, no pretense. Totally honest . . . It meant more to him than he would admit . . .

"Do you mind?" she said, still holding her glass out to him.

"No, of course not. But you know this stuff isn't ginger ale."

"So-o-o? I happen to be very fond of champagne. Even if I do spill it . . ."

He refilled the glass and watched in surprise as she drained it. A tiny smile played around her lips and eyes and then became a low laugh as she looked first at him and then at the bed. She stood unsteadily and took his hand in hers. "I'd like to change the sheet . . . if you don't mind . . . think it's only fair. I'm very neat, you know."

"Okay, if that's what you'd like—" He was beginning to smile now too.

"*Thass* what I'd like," she said, giggling as she pulled him to his feet.

Where were the sheets? he wondered. His housekeeper took care of that department.

"Why are you just standing there? Let's get the sheets . . . please."

"I would, but I don't know where they are."

"You're just saying that."

"No, really."

"All right . . . let's go find 'em . . . okay?"

"No, you stay. I'll find—"

"No, no, no . . . we'll do this together like buddies."

They were both laughing as Bill steadied her and they went down the narrow hall to search the cupboard. He opened one louvered door after another. Damn it, imagine living in a place and not knowing where the linens were?

"Aha. I think we stumbled onto something here," Janet announced. She reached into a cupboard for the sheets and back they trudged to the bedroom.

Pixilated as she was, somehow Janet managed to strip off the bottom sheet.

82

"Okay," she said, "you stand on the other side and tuck the thing under."

Together they achieved the task. It wouldn't have passed muster in the army, but Janet patted the bed admiringly and said, "Now isn't that neat. I *tole* you . . . Boy, I'm really dizzy." Having made that pronouncement, she flopped down on the rumpled sheet.

Bill got out of his robe and climbed in beside her to hold her close.

She responded eagerly, kissing him without restraint, running her hands along his smooth hard body and pressing him to her. Then she was on her back, and he was on top of her.

This time he thrust deeply, rotating gently. Between kisses she said again, "I love you, Bill McNeil," and added, "What's more, I don't care if you know it. I'm not supposed to tell you, but I love you love you love you."

He silenced her by putting his mouth firmly over hers.

She clutched at the pillows beside her head as she began to buck against him, feeling as if she was on a roller coaster going up to the highest peak. Faster, faster . . . At the highest point she whispered, "Don't let it stop." And then she passed out.

He leaned on his elbow and looked at her. God, she was beautiful. The thick lashes almost touched her cheeks. He smiled, thinking what a curious evening this had been. He'd had his share, more than his share, of sexual encounters, but never anything like this. He laughed softly to himself. He'd never forget how she'd looked trying to get that sheet on, and no one had ever felt so good in his arms. There was nothing contrived or studied or shopworn about this lady. Maybe that was what intrigued him . . . well, partly anyway. She had never been touched and, without vanity, he was happy he had been the first. There *was* something very special about her, even if it seemed an old-fashioned notion. Strange, the effect she had on him. He had resented it when she first said she loved him, but suddenly he didn't feel threatened by it. In fact he liked the feeling that he wasn't just *another* stud male servicing a female. That's what all his sex had amounted to. Just performing. Proving he could outscrew, literally and figuratively, the competition. Women compared, kept score who was the best in bed. They'd told him so.

Janet moaned and mumbled contentedly, then rolled onto her side.

He covered her shoulders, switched off the bedside lamp and snuggled into the contour of her body, gently putting his arms around her and feeling the soft velvet skin of her firm abdomen.

Janet awoke feeling slightly disconnected. Her head pounded and the morning sun glared painfully in her eyes. She'd been drunk last night . . . *very drunk*. What a stupid thing to have done. She was sure she'd made a complete ass out of herself. How would she ever be able to face him, much less explain her conduct? When she realized that he was no longer in the bed she put her arm over her eyes, feeling even more desolate.

"Good morning. Sleep well?"

She was startled. He was bending over her, and there was nothing derisive in his voice. In fact, if anything it was a voice that sounded like a smile. Still, she couldn't look at him. "I feel terrible . . . and ashamed. I must have made an awful fool of myself."

He took her arm gently away from her eyes and looked at her. "You have nothing to feel ashamed about."

"Yes I do, a lady doesn't act the way I must have last night."

"You couldn't be anything but a lady. Take it from someone who's had his fill of the other kind. . . . Feel like a cup of hot coffee? Just made it."

She nodded, then looked at Bill's face to see if anything of last night could be read into it. It revealed nothing. She asked softly, "I suppose I said a lot of things I shouldn't have . . . last night?"

"Not that I can remember."

"I hope you know I've never been that way before."

"I didn't think you had."

When he left the room she sat up too quickly. Feeling as if her head would blow up, she inched herself to the edge of the bed and stood unsteadily. She took a deep breath, then walked to the bathroom, where she used

Bill's toothbrush and took a long shower, letting the hot spray pelt against her.

She turned the shower knobs off reluctantly and reached for a towel. Bill watched from the bedroom, remembering the silkiness of her hair under his hands as she combed through it.

She came out of the bathroom with the towel draped around her like a sarong and got into bed.

"Here's your coffee. Drink it while it's hot."

She sniffed, then sipped. Ambrosia. And a few moments ago she thought she was dying. "This is delicious."

"That's the beginning and end of my culinary art."

"It's so good."

"Glad you like it."

"Mmmm . . . I do."

They sat side by side drinking the hot brew.

"Did anyone ever tell you that you look like Audrey Hepburn?"

"Oh . . . a few times," she answered, embarrassed in spite of her effort to sound flip. "Well, did anyone ever tell you that you look like a cross between Charlton Heston and . . . Gregory Peck?"

"No. What part of me looks like Charlton Heston?"

"You're making fun of me."

"I'd never do that," he said, taking the cup from her hand and placing it next to his on the nightstand. Sliding down into the bed, he lay on his side and put his leg over hers. "God, you smell so sweet." Between kisses she answered, "You . . . too . . ."

For a while nothing else existed except the wonder of exploring each other's bodies with soft caresses. Once again he drew her hand between his legs, then left her embrace and trailed his lips downward until he found the moist tender sweetness between her thighs.

He discovered places she didn't know existed as he parted the lips with his tongue. She could scarcely breathe with the onslaught of new sensations, and her heart pounded as she ran her fingers through his hair. When both sensed the moment was right, he moved up to her, thrusting himself deep inside. Janet felt herself dissolving in a warm turbulent sea, her passion rising to match his until both were spent.

How strange, she thought as they lay clinging to each other. A few short Sundays ago her day had been spent in the worst sort of despair. She'd been desperate, compulsive, walking through Central Park like some feline stalking its prey. If she hadn't defied every convention she'd been brought up with she would never have been here now, feeling so content in Bill's arms. She snuggled closer and listened to his heart beat. It was a marvelous sound.

"Bill," she asked softly, "how do you spend Sunday?"

He'd almost forgotten. This *was* Sunday, the one day his mother lived for. Damn. He wanted badly to spend the day with Janet, the first girl to sleep in his apartment around the clock, but he sure as hell wasn't going to tell her that he had to go home and see mama every Sunday. "Why do you ask?" he answered with more irritation than he intended.

Janet was startled by the annoyance in his voice. Last night he had almost begged her to stay after he'd recovered from her declaration of love, and from then on everything had been unbelievably wonderful. But now he was peeved by a simple little question about how he spent his Sundays. She simply couldn't figure him out.

"I don't know why I asked . . . I just wondered what people did for diversion. It's . . . that I find Sundays so lonely."

He laughed to himself . . . for him loneliness spelled M.O.T.H.E.R.

"Oh, people do different things, I suppose," he said, trying not to think of what lay ahead for him this afternoon.

"Like?"

"Like . . . play tennis, skate, horseback riding. I don't know. I suppose visit . . . with family."

"Do you?"

"Do I what?"

"Visit? A lot I mean?"

"Well, quite a bit," he answered reluctantly.

"I think you're lucky."

"You do?"

"Yes, I'm very family oriented. I just wish I could see mine more often. Telephone calls aren't the same."

Telephone calls . . . Lord, it was already noon and she

86

was probably waiting right now. "Janet, I'm sorry as hell, but you'll have to excuse me for a moment . . . I should call my mother, she's expecting me for lunch today and if any of us are late she worries herself sick . . . well, you know, she's an old lady . . ." He looked embarrassed.

She could have kissed his mother. So *that's* what he did on Sundays. And just a few weeks ago she'd fantasized that that was his big day for bedtime dates . . .

Janet dressed while Bill was phoning. Looking at herself in the mirror, she wondered how she was going to walk into the Barbizon with a long dress on. Everyone would know. If only she had a coat she could hike up the dress and tuck in the waistband. Well, it was either lose her reputation or ruin one of her favorite dresses. No more debates. Using a small pair of scissors that she found in the bathroom, she cut the dress to a daytime length and then launched into the surgery of her long satin slip.

She wasn't going to fool anybody by this, she thought as she surveyed the dismal results. She'd not only ruined the dress and slip but her name would be mud forever. No one would look at the ragged raveled edge of the chiffon and believe that that hem had come undone. Sighing, she went back to the bedroom.

Bill was in such a hurry to get out of there and get Long Island over with that he didn't notice her dress until they stood in front of the elevator. "What happened to your dress? Moths get it?"

Men, in *their* fashion, were really so naïve. "I could hardly go back this time of day looking like I'd come from a four o'clock wedding reception, so I had to cut it off."

"By God, that's right." That was one of the problems of living in a hotel he hadn't thought about. "No one's going to notice," he said reassuringly. "Just too bad that lovely dress had to be ruined."

"Do you think so?" she asked as they stepped into the elevator.

He answered by kissing her.

They were still kissing when the doors opened. They walked out of the lobby to the garage across the street and Bill helped her into his Cadillac convertible.

"I didn't know you had a car."

"Easier to take cabs in the city."

"I suppose . . . Bill, do you honestly think I look—"

"Fine, I swear. No one will notice."

"I hope so."

Before she knew it, Bill was stopping at the curb in front of the hotel and turning off the ignition. She didn't know what to say. Thank you for a wonderful . . . wonderful what? God, she didn't know what to say, but when she saw that he was about to get out and come round to her side she had another worry. "Thank you, Bill, but I'd prefer to go in alone. It would be less . . ."

"Of course, I understand," he said, brushing a strand of hair from her forehead. Taking her to him, he kissed her. "I'll call."

She merely nodded and let herself out of the car. Instantly a wave of loneliness swept over her as she watched the car disappear from sight. It was as though she had suddenly been set adrift in an unfamiliar world. She turned reluctantly and went through the revolving door.

With the greatest dignity she could command, Janet strode across the lobby to the elevator. But just as she had feared, she became the focus of attention. The ladies of the Barbizon were making sure they didn't miss one small ragged thread. She could feel eyes piercing through her, as if they could see everything that had happened to her since last night.

It seemed an eternity before the door swung back. The elevator operator slowly eyed her from head to toe. "Good afternoon, Miss Stevens." Her tone seemed to say, Well, well, well, Miss Kansas Corn finally got laid.

As Janet stepped out of the elevator at her floor she heard, "Have a nice day, Miss Stevens."

Her face turned crimson. She ran down the hall to her room and stood fumbling for the keys in her purse. Once inside, she leaned against the door and angrily wiped away the tears in her eyes. God, how humiliating. She threw her satin slippers across the room and ripped off her dress, then sat on the bed blowing her nose and wiping her eyes. She was weary now and felt terribly alone. God, love was pretty awful too.

She picked up the phone and called the old homestead. "It's me, mom."

"Janet, I'm so glad you called."

"Well, I just got lonesome for you—"

"It's mutual, darling . . . Do you have a cold?"

"No."

"Oh? You sound a little stuffed up. Are you feeling okay?"

"Just wonderful. How are you and dad?"

"Fine, darling. Just fine."

". . . Could you and dad come to New York for a few days?"

"We'd love to but your father's so busy and I don't think he can take the time. Dr. Sanders is on vacation."

"I see . . . Well, then I think maybe I'll come home next weekend. I want to see you."

There was a silent moment. "Janet, are you sure you're all right?"

"I'm sure. Just a little homesick, that's all."

"Well, your father and I will be happy to see you. Let me know when the plane arrives."

"I will. Is dad there?"

"No. He's at the hospital."

"I see. Say hello to him. And mom . . . I love you . . ."

After hanging up she sat with her hand on the receiver. She felt rotten, and suddenly frightened that Bill wouldn't call her again. God, he must have thought she was cheap. She hadn't exactly protested when . . . the thought made her cringe. She went into the bathroom, let the water run in the tub and lathered herself with the lavender-scented soap. Then she lay back, wondering if Bill had even given her a thought . . .

He sat at his mother's table now, having lunch with Harriet and Gordon. He ate mechanically, scarcely hearing a word that was said. It was the usual menu. Fresh fruit salad, capon, hot popovers, vanilla ice cream and chocolate sauce. The conversation too was predictable. About how busy Alice was with her children. Getting the boys ready for high school kept her hopping, and Gwen had decided she wanted to attend the Sorbonne for two years. And imagine Randy going to Yale . . . Good Lord, it had been like yesterday, Violet said, when she had sewn all the name tags into Bill's clothing and he went off to military school, then to M.I.T. If only Jason could have lived to see their grandchildren grow up. And Betsy . . . where did she get the stamina to do all she did? It was beyond Violet's comprehension. Imagine Betsy being president of the . . .

Bill wasn't listening. "Mother, I won't be able to be here for the next few Sundays . . ."

Silence. Violet sat looking at him. He had been unusually late today and vague with his excuse. But it wasn't only that that bothered her. He had been silent throughout the meal, sitting there with an abstracted look in his eyes . . . "I'm sorry to hear that, dear. But I'm sure it must be important or you wouldn't—"

"Yes, it's very important. We have a large project going on in Galveston."

"When did you say you were leaving?"

"I didn't, but on Friday afternoon."

"You'll be staying on until the following weekend?"

He had to think fast. She'd call the office to check up. She was mighty crafty that way. She always used to catch him in a lie. But he'd double-check with his secretary. "Yes, mother."

"Have a wonderful trip. And write even if it's just a card."

He had a friend who flew for Delta Airlines. Jack had mailed prewritten cards one or two times before. God, this was so damned ridiculous.

The afternoon moved on slowly as he played billiards with Gordon. By dinnertime he was ready to jump out the window. He agonized through the meal, then excused himself early, explaining that he had a big day ahead of him tomorrow and so forth . . .

She kissed him good-by as if he were leaving for Siberia, told him to take care of himself and be careful.

He promised he would and was off. . . .

Violet turned to Harriet. "You don't believe I was taken in by Bill saying he was going to Galveston, do you?"

"Why not, mother? After all, he is an engineer."

"Yes, of course, but I always know when Bill's not telling the truth. He's not very good at fibbing. Never was."

90

"Why should he have to do that?" Harriet asked, as though she didn't know.

"Harriet, Bill's carrying on with some woman and I think it's serious."

"Really? Well, why shouldn't he?"

"Because he's far too young. He has plenty of time for that."

"Mother, for heaven's sake. What Bill does is his own business, not yours, and you'd better get used to the idea. He's going to marry one day and you won't have a thing to say about it."

"Let's get back to our game of cribbage."

The moment Bill got into his apartment he called Janet, but her line was busy. He kept trying every few minutes, but whoever she was talking to was surely long-winded. . . .

The moment Janet hung up after speaking to Kit, she took up her purse and locked the door.

She was a few feet down the hall when she heard her phone, and rushed back, fumbled for the key and unlocked the door. But by the time she grabbed up the receiver the caller had hung up. It had to have been Bill. It had to . . . The only other possibility was Kit, and she was meeting her for dinner. Sitting on the edge of her bed, she debated whether or not to call him back.

At the very same moment Bill was thinking, damn, first it's busy then no answer. She must have gone out. Well, he was going to do the same. Have a few drinks. He really could use it after today.

By the time Janet decided to call, he was already in the elevator and halfway across the lobby—and so no answer.

It must not have been him after all . . .

Chapter Six

Bill worked in his office until eleven o'clock Monday night, sending out for sandwiches and coffee. By the time he came up for air it was too late to call Janet. She had to be up and out very early in the morning, so he'd have to wait until sometime tomorrow. . . .

On Tuesday he called Conover's only to be told that she was out on location and that they had no idea when she'd be back . . .

Well, he would try about six. She'd probably be home.

Six came, but still no Janet. Well, she did have a life of her own. He tried on and off until nine-thirty. She was out for the evening, the hotel operator finally said. Would he care to leave a message? No, he wouldn't care to leave a message. She seemed to lead a very busy social life, he thought sullenly . . .

Having gone to an early dinner and movie with Kit, Janet arrived home at nine-thirty, almost to the moment that Bill had hung up. She asked the switchboard if there were any messages. The operator, who had just come on for late duty, said no.

That night she slept badly. Why hadn't Bill called? *Face it, Janet. You were a one-night stand after all.* She was hurt, but if she had a shred of pride left it had to be salvaged. She was *not* going to call him. She'd made a fool enough of herself. She was beginning to wish she had gone by her upbringing. If nothing else, she'd still have her dignity . . . not to mention her virginity. She'd certainly given it away fast enough. Well, if she *ever* went beyond a casual date with another man she was going to make absolutely sure that *he* liked her as much as she liked . . . Except that none of these fine resolutions were one bit of comfort now. . . .

On Wednesday, Bill had to be out of town, and negotiations on the contract he was bidding for became so involved that he didn't get home until midnight. Damn it, too late . . . He set his alarm for six. He was going to get to Janet if it killed him.

At six-fifteen Janet picked up the ringing phone. "Hello."

"Hello is *right*," he said. "Do you know I've been trying to get you since Sunday night?"

Janet's hand began to shake. All those terrible things she'd thought about him all week . . . "I didn't get any messages."

"I didn't leave any, I thought you might be too busy to call me back—"

"Oh, Bill, I wasn't that busy. In fact I wasn't busy at all."

"Really? For someone who lives such a Spartan life, it's strange I could never find you in."

"I'm sorry. If only you had left a message—"

He wasn't going to tell her that jealousy wasn't only a woman's prerogative, or curse. All irrationally, he'd *expected* her to be there when he called. Well, grow up, for God's sake. You don't own her and you wouldn't want to even if you could . . . well, would you? God knows, *you* don't want to be owned . . . well, do you? Come on, slow up, or you'll push her right out of the ball park . . .

"Well," he said, "I guess it *was* foolish not to leave a message. Still friends?"

She laughed nervously. "Still friends."

"In that case, I'd like to take you to dinner tonight."

"I'd love to, but it will have to be a short evening. We start shooting early on Friday . . ." She smiled to herself as she hung up the phone. Imagine his caring enough to be angry . . . She wasn't kidding herself that it was love on his part, but the fact that he had been angry was a sign of something—oh, stop figuring it, Janet . . . stop fantasizing. . . .

At dinner they talked trivia, each happy to be in the other's company but somehow feeling ill at ease, as if they were holding back the words and thoughts that were really in their minds.

When they were almost through with their coffee Janet asked almost apologetically, "What time is it, Bill?"

"Almost nine."

"I hate doing this, but I really must go."

What a hell of a profession, like taking the vows, Bill thought. The evening hadn't even begun . . . finally met a girl he liked, wanted, and—

"I did say it would have to be an early evening—"

"Sure, of course. Well, how about Saturday night?"

She hesitated. "Bill, I'm going home this weekend."

He couldn't believe what she was saying. After all the fancy maneuvers he'd gone through with his mother to be free for two lousy weekends . . . The postcards already written and given to his friend Jack, the pilot, to mail. Maybe God was punishing him for lying to his mother, and maybe also for taking Janet for granted. "Do you really have to go? I mean this weekend?" He tried to keep the hurt out of his voice.

"I really do. I haven't seen them in three months."

I should be so lucky. "So when did you say you were leaving?"

"I'm taking the six-thirty flight tomorrow."

"Oh. Well, I'll drive you to the airport."

"You're very sweet—"

"That's me. Used to be an Eagle Scout. Youngest in the troop. I'll show you my good conduct medals."

But Janet heard the pique in his voice, more than a tinge of disappointment, even, maybe, a smidgin of loneliness? No, she chided herself, dismissing the thought immediately as being absurd. Wishful thinking, that's what dreams are made of . . . illusions and delusions. . . .

The next day's shooting session on location had taken longer than expected, and by the time it was over Janet was a complete wreck, filled with anxiety that she would miss her plane, that Bill might already have gotten impatient and given up waiting for her . . .

When Janet reached the agency, she dressed quickly ran a comb through her hair and hurried down the hall to the elevator. She got to the street just in time to see Bill driving off. He must have been around the block a dozen times. It was the height of the rush-hour traffic and no

94

parking was permitted. Anxiously glancing at her wrist watch, she waited and watched, praying that he hadn't given up and gone home. After what seemed an eternity she recognized his car inching down the block in the stop-and-go traffic. Finally it come to a stop at the curb. She hastily opened the door and slid into the seat.

"Now you know why I take taxis," he said, impatiently, grabbing her suitcase and putting it in the back seat.

"I'm awfully sorry, Bill, we ran overtime and there was no way of getting a message to you—"

"It's *okay*." But his tone said differently, and they fell into an uncomfortable silence.

The traffic going out of Manhattan moved at a crawl, and as Janet looked at the clock on the dashboard she asked, "Do you think we'll make it?"

"Who knows," he said tightly. "It probably takes less time to fly to Kansas than to get to the airport this time of day."

She settled back and gazed in silent frustration at the mass of slow-moving cars and trucks. When at last they arrived at La Guardia, they drove round and round the airport parking lots until they finally found a spot.

From then on it became a marathon. Carrying Janet's suitcase, Bill took her by the arm and the two ran, weaving through the crowded terminal. They arrived at the United waiting area just in time to watch Janet's plane taking off.

She looked at Bill, breathless and on the verge of tears.

He had never been able to see a woman cry . . . his mother had given him his fill . . . but it was worse with Janet. Besides, Janet Stevens was incapable of using tears as a ploy. She was exactly what she seemed to be, a lovely young woman whose exposure to the world hadn't hardened her one bit. Not yet, anyway. He liked that. He liked it very much.

"Let's see if we can get a later flight," he said.

"It's the last one."

"We'll try another airline."

"Same thing . . . Wichita isn't the crossroads of the world, you know."

"Then I suppose you'll have to call home." He spoke with quiet concern, but underneath he was not displeased with this turn of events. You can't argue with fate, he told himself. This hadn't, after all, been his fault.

"Bill, they're going to be so disappointed—"

"Sure they will, but no one's to blame. They'll understand."

"I know, but still . . ." She knew her mother and Effie must have spent the last few days preparing all the things Janet loved for Sunday's early dinner, when all her aunts, uncles and cousins would be gathering to celebrate her homecoming. As Bill led her to the phone booth and she began to dial, she was feeling miserable and guilty, and the familiar sound of her mother's voice only deepened the feelings.

"Hello?"

"It's me, Janet. Mother, I don't know how to tell you but . . . I missed the plane . . ."

There was a confused pause. Then, "Well, those things happen, dear."

"I know, but you must have worked so hard . . . I suppose Aunt Linda and the family will be there?"

"Yes. Now, Janet, you're not to feel so badly. These things happen, and more often than not for the best."

Maybe, but as much as she wanted to be with Bill, she badly missed her family. Three months was a long time.

"I promise I'll be home next week even if I have to walk."

Martha Stevens laughed. "I hope it won't come to that. Good-by, darling, and take care of yourself. I'll call during the week. Now, here's your father."

"How's my girl?"

"Oh, dad, good to hear your voice. I missed the darn plane by seconds—"

"I gathered as much. But as your mother said, there's always next week."

"I know . . . I can't wait to see you."

The operator interrupted, requesting an additional seventy-five cents, but by the time Janet fished out the change the phone went dead. There hadn't been enough time for proper good-bys. She looked at the silent black phone, then got up and left the booth.

On the drive back to Manhattan, Bill had one hand on the steering wheel, and the other held Janet's hand. It was

96

a comforting gesture, but Janet was still full of thoughts of home.

After Bill drove into the garage he helped her out of the car, asking, "You feel hungry?"

"No . . . not really."

"Well, what do you feel like?"

Confused . . . that's what I feel like, she said to herself. And mystified about who changes the plans, rearranges the destiny of a person's life. Like missing the plane by seconds, or having to take all those extra pictures today just so Oleg Cassini's latest creation could be seen in next month's *Harper's Bazaar*. Man proposed, but God clearly disposed.

Bill, a mere mortal man, repeated, "What do you feel like doing?"

"Well, I think I'd like to go back to my place and get rid of this suitcase and freshen up a bit—"

"Why bother? My place is just across the street. You can freshen up there, then we can decide."

He took her hand and guided her across the street and up to his apartment.

Feeling spent, she lay her head back against the large sofa pillows and let her eyes wander about the lovely room.

"What would you like?" he asked. "I have champagne on ice. That's sort of our drink, wouldn't you say?"

Yes, to meet and get high on and . . . "I think I'd like some sherry if you have it, Bill." No more bubbly for this girl, she thought.

As she sat listening to the clink of ice and glasses against the soft music in the background, she began to relax. Bill handed her a glass of sherry, then sat next to her and raised his Scotch and soda in a silent toast.

"I love this time of the day," he said, looking out at the gold streaks against the sunset sky.

"It is beautiful," she replied. But so different from the bold, stark colors cast by a Kansas sunset . . .

"So are you."

She peered at him in surprise over the rim of her glass. "Am I really?" Was she even *close* to being that?

"Why, do you have any doubts?"

Janet reddened and turned away. "I don't think of myself that way . . . not really. In fact, it's all kind of confusing at times——"

"In what way?"

"Well, sometimes I feel like a store mannequin instead of a person. I don't know, maybe modeling does that. You don't sort of know what's real and sometimes I feel so self-conscious about it."

How deceptive Janet's facade was, Bill thought. Who would ever guess the insecurity that lay behind her poise and beauty. Under the sophistication of the photos in the fashion magazines was the real Janet, who must have found her sudden exposure to career and city life more than a little overwhelming. No, it wasn't really insecurity, he decided, but a curious mix of naïveté and a kind of basic and honest perception of life that hadn't quite adjusted to the new world she'd come into. Still, he felt protective of her all the same. Yet . . . but did the urgency he felt to be with her mean that he was actually in love? And all *that* meant . . . He doubted it, he sure wasn't sure . . . how could he be? . . . he'd just met her. She was great, so different from the others . . . which, he decided with a kind of new-found relief, must account for the way she so intrigued him. Sure, mostly it had to be that . . .

He got up abruptly and switched the soft music on the stereo to an upbeat jazz record. As he sat down again he said, "You must be starved."

"I'm not, but I'm sure you are."

"A little. Where to?"

"You decide. But if you don't mind I'd like to wash up first."

"Sure."

Bill sat in the living room for a few minutes, then got up and walked to the window. The view was always changing and he never tired of it. Or of the apartment, or his bachelorhood, for that matter. It was comfortable, uncomplicated . . . To hell with it. As he turned away he saw his reflection in the hall mirror. Boy, he could stand a little washing up too.

Going to the bedroom, he reached in the closet for a clean shirt, tossed it on the chair and stripped off the old one. The door to the bathroom was open and he could see Janet combing that magnificent head of hair. Then, as she came out and stood looking at him, all the debates were gone from his mind. All he knew was that he wanted her. *Now*. Last Saturday night? It had been the first time, and he had played the part of the proficient guide, going through all the subtle motions to gradually awaken and heighten Janet's passion. But tonight?

He took her in his arms and kissed her without restraint, their lips and tongues meeting in breathless desire. Quickly. almost fumbling, he undressed Janet as they remained in their embrace, and with her help he was out of his pants and shorts. He pushed off his loafers with the tips of his toes, and with their mouths still meeting he peeled off his socks. Then they were lying together. their bodies clinging, and suddenly it was like a storm. Everything was forgotten except the exploring, the hungry touch of skin against skin, the building rhythm of their lovemaking. The climax left them in a breathless wash of fulfillment, and he made no move to withdraw from her. He'd never been caught up so completely in the act of love or felt what he'd just experienced. Never . . . And the moment was *Janet* . . . face it, admit it . . . the difference was Janet . . . Reluctantly, he rolled away, then drew her to him and put his arm around her shoulders.

Brushing the damp hair off her forehead, he said, "I know it's selfish of me to say this, but I'm very damn happy you missed the plane."

For Janet too it had felt so exactly *right*, as though *this* was where she belonged—and above all where she wanted to be. Wichita, Kansas, seemed very far away indeed.

They lay in silence for a while. Bill languidly trailing his hand along the curves of her body. Suddenly he said, "I have a brilliant idea, believe it or not. There's a terrific Chinese restaurant that delivers. How's that for creative thinking?"

"Brilliant, like you said."

He reached over and took the phone book from inside the nightstand. He scanned the pages, and as Janet watched it occurred to her that she was just beginning to discover the many facets of this man.

"Here it is." Turning to Janet, he asked, "Do you like almond duck?"

"Yes, sure . . . but please order what you like. I'm no expert."

"You trust me that much?"

Oh, yes, she thought, and with more than choosing Chinese food. Janet lay back. It was really something . . . just a few hours ago she'd been nearly wiped out because she couldn't go to Kansas, and now there wasn't a place on God's green earth she would rather be than right here. Suddenly she remembered her suitcase. Why pretend? He might not be in love with her, but it was obvious he wanted her to spend the weekend. She laughed to herself. Something good seemed to come out of everything . . . at least lately. Last week she hadn't even been prepared to spend the night. But this time, because she had missed a plane, she was equipped to stay for the full weekend. God worked in mysterious ways, no question.

"Bill, do you think I could get my suitcase?" she asked when he got off the phone.

"Sure, I'll have one of the doormen come up and get the car keys." As he got out of bed and put on his robe he turned to her and said, "It'll take about forty minutes for our order to come. You know what I think?"

"I'm getting pretty smart. I think you're thinking more champagne."

"And you are *right*. And I shall reward you for your brilliance." Whereupon he leaned down and kissed her properly before he went off for the champagne.

As she listened to him fussing in the kitchen, she ran her hand over the place on the bed where he'd been beside her . . . and thought how wonderful it would be if things could always be the way they'd been tonight. To be Mrs. Bill McNeil, to be able to reach out and touch him every night of her life . . . to know he'd *be* there . . . Her reverie was interrupted by the sound of a popping cork. She watched as he poured the champagne into glasses on the bedside table, taking in his relaxed air, his casual manner. Casual . . . that's probably what it was to him. If only she could say, I love you, Bill, and hear him say, I love you, darling . . . Well, she'd be careful about that this time. Don't rush . . .

"What shall we drink to?" he was saying as he handed her a glass.

"To . . . friends . . . ?"

"That sounded like a question."

"Did it?"

"Yes . . . well, the answer is, and to lovers too."

Running her fingers around the rim of the glass, she was barely able to get out, "I'll drink to that, Mr. Bill McNeil."

The next two days were filled with ordinary pleasures, things people do all the time, but the mundane seemed magical. It was the sharing, the being together that made it so. Bicycling through Central Park on a tandem bike . . . Stopping for a hot dog and sauerkraut, for ice cream cones or a bag of peanuts . . . Rolling on the grass like two silly children, strolling through the Museum of Modern Art, ambling down Fifth Avenue to watch the skaters at Rockefeller Center . . . then further on down Fifth Avenue to the New York Public Library, where they raced each other up the stairs and then collapsed at the top, arms around each other, laughing and kissing at the same time.

They strolled the crooked streets of Greenwich Village hand in hand. How different, how quaint it looked today. Somehow the frightening squalor of her first visit to the Village had disappeared. The theaters, Times Square, the Empire State Building . . . they all took on a new dimension.

On Saturday evening they shopped at an Italian grocery and she cooked dinner for Bill. After the door was closed to the world, there was only Bill's apartment. A place for lovers, he said as he lifted her off her feet and carried her into the bedroom.

On Sunday they sequestered themselves in Bill's room. Except for the kitchen the rest of the apartment became superfluous. Janet fixed breakfast while Bill showered, and as she set their breakfast tray on the bedside table she called out, "Come and get it while it's hot."

He poked his head out the bathroom door and grinned through the lather on his face. "It will always be hot," he assured her.

She laughed. "Not the scrambled eggs, idiot."

When he returned from the bathroom he slid into bed, pulling the sheet up to his naked waist, and Janet placed the tray over his knees. Patting her side of the bed, he said, "Boy, I would never have believed it. To look at you one wouldn't think you could even boil water."

"Just goes to show you. Never judge a cook by its cover."

He groaned. "A genius with puns and pasta. Especially the pasta. Last night's dinner, no kidding, was a work of art."

"I have many hidden talents."

He leered. "Okay to keep them hidden, but not from me," he said, reaching over to draw off her robe as she settled next to him.

After breakfast he put the tray on the floor and they read the Sunday *Times,* Janet the arts and leisure section and Bill the business and sports pages. It seemed so *natural,* Janet thought, like married people. For a moment she wondered if Kit and Nat had that special quality in their affair. Janet was no judge, but somehow she knew that what she and Bill had together was rare. It had to be. She knew it because Kit had given her a clue, and because Bill had shown her in a dozen different ways that he'd never been this content with any other woman. He'd never even indulged in the simple, wonderful adventures they had shared. She knew instinctively that he had revealed much more of himself than he would have liked, but his inadvertent disclosures had also told her she was definitely more than just a one-night stand. The physical part was fantastic. To feel his lean, taut body next to hers . . . but they always talked afterward.

Even now, as they lay in each other's arms with the paper strewn on the floor and the sheets rumpled at the bottom of the bed, he wanted to know about her childhood in Wichita. And she listened as he told about growing up with that wonderful but overly protective mother and three adoring sisters. The odds, he said, were against him. It was his father and himself against four females, and his father had finally liberated him by packing him off to military school—not without female voices raised in protest, he added. "Brave man, my father. That's probably one of the reasons I was a little gun-shy of women." There was just enough bitterness in his laugh to make Janet realize the truth of what Kit had told her, but she was even more aware of the closeness she felt with him because he had trusted her enough to be honest.

Her mind shifted back to the moment she had stood in that vast lobby, waiting for him to come down in the elevator and wondering if he was going to reject her. But he hadn't and now she was here. For whatever reasons . . . she was *here*. Maybe she was tempting fate and this was the wrong moment to tell him, but somehow she had to get it out of the way.

"Bill, I have something to tell you . . . I suppose I shouldn't. I know people play games with one another, tell little white lies or simply avoid admitting little things, but something's been bothering me . . ."

"What?"

"Remember the first night we met?"

"Do I?" He laughed. "I'm still drying out."

"Well . . . I know this is absolute insanity but I was so devastated about the whole thing, I mean ruining your suit and all, that I called you a couple of times to . . . apologize. I never spoke to you. I mean I did once but I guess I was too embarrassed to . . . well, to . . ."

A smile broke across his face. "So you were the one, you little minx. I ought to rap your bottom."

"You're not angry?"

He was sitting up in bed, looking down at her and brushing her hair back against the pillow, fanning it about her head. She returned his look, open and candid. And not to be resisted. He slid down and took her in his arms. That was his answer, and it was enough for her.

When Bill drove her back to the hotel Sunday evening, she stood in the center of her room feeling abruptly sad and alone, let *down*. Lovers, she reminded herself, were only on a part-time basis. She wished she could be like Kit and take it all in her stride. No tears when Nat left. But she wasn't Kit, damn it, she was Janet, who had fallen in love and was convinced this was the one and only time she ever would.

She picked up her suitcase and put it on the bed, took

out the mauve silk robe and hung it away. Nine-thirty. Call home? She picked up the receiver, but then hesitated. If she heard her mother's voice she would probably cry, and then she'd have to make up some excuses for her mother. This whole affair was turning her into a weeping, wailing mess, she thought angrily.

She sat down heavily on the bed and wondered what Bill was doing. Were men sentimental, romantic idiots like women? She doubted it, at least not any that she'd ever met. The talk she'd overheard among men she worked with seemed almost to boast of walking from one affair to the next, never looking back but always forward. Not so with women. They lived and relived the past, running through every nuance of each and every shared moment like an endless litany. Maybe Kit was right and Bill did have the advantage. All men did. There had probably never been a woman in the history of the world who had said to a man, "Darling, I want you to be my husband," and had heard him respond—and not as a joke—"This is so sudden, I thought you'd never ask." Kit might enjoy the irony in that, Janet thought, but she didn't. Frustrated, she got under the shower and washed her hair, scrubbing her scalp until it hurt.

Chapter Seven

On Monday night Bill called, asked how her day had gone and made idle conversation. But there was no mention of those magical moments. It was almost as though he'd forgotten about them. If he'd just said, "I haven't been able to get you out of my mind . . . thought about you last night and today . . ." *Stupid girl. If he'd said that it would be a declaration of love. Take what you can, Janet, because it's either that or nothing . . .*

Of course she accepted his invitation to dinner on Tuesday. And then there was lunch on Wednesday and dinner at his apartment on Thursday, with a short trip to his bedroom for "dessert," as he put it. Too short. Hurried lovemaking wasn't to Janet's taste, but then, Bill wasn't really to blame for that. She had to be up at five in the morning and she was catching a flight to Wichita at the end of the day.

Bill drove her to the airport on Friday and for once everything went according to schedule. They even had time for a long good-by kiss—which didn't make her departure any easier. As she settled into her seat on the plane and fumbled through her bag to find her handkerchief, the elderly woman sitting alongside patted her hand.

"Don't be frightened, dear. Flying is safer than . . ." Than loving someone, Janet almost answered, and continued to think of Bill across the miles from the tip of Delaware to Washington, D.C., West Virginia, Kentucky, Missouri. . . .

It wasn't until the plane began to make its descent that her anticipation began to build.

She ran across the field to the terminal, where her mother and father were watching from the window.

"There she is," Martha Stevens said excitedly.

The next thing Janet knew she was in their arms, suddenly feeling warm and at home in the excited exchange of greetings. "Oh, dad," she said as she hugged him, "I didn't know how much I missed you 'til now."

That night she curled up in the canopied bed . . . feeling she had never left. The room was just as she had known it would be. She was a little girl again, feeling so *safe*. The photograph of Clark Gable still hung above her desk. He had been Rhett Butler and she Scarlett O'Hara and this was Tara . . . God help her . . . New York was the fantasy now, and this the reality. Still, Bill was standing in the shadows of her mind, and as she fell asleep she held the extra pillow close to her.

On Saturday morning, as Effie was serving breakfast in the dining room she said to Janet, "You better eat that oatmeal . . . getting to look like a scarecrow. Good *Lord*." She returned to the kitchen and came back with a platter of sausage and eggs. "Don't believe in all that modeling in the first place," she went on. "Seeing your picture in the magazine doesn't make me all that proud . . . told your mother so. Good Lord." She could still be heard muttering as she went back to the kitchen.

"She's more proud than she lets on," Martha Stevens whispered.

There was a hush when Effie swung the kitchen door open again, this time holding a pot of fresh-brewed coffee. Looking at Janet's plate she said, "I see you lost your taste for eating. Don't see why those modeling places don't just dig up a bunch of bones. That's what you're getting to look like. Or maybe the food's not fancy enough like those New York places—"

"It's delicious, Effie, and I love it, but I really can't eat any more."

"Oh, nonsense. They want you to look like a skeleton? It's downright ridiculous, all this posing and prancing around. Why, sometimes when I see those pictures in that fancy *Vogue* magazine I don't even recognize you, looking like Theda Bara. If that's their idea of what a woman should look like, they ought to take a look at *women*. Real women. Good *wives* and *mothers*. That'd be more sensible for *you* . . . to my way of thinking."

"That's right, Effie. You give 'em hell," Dr. Stevens said, getting up from the table. He kissed Martha and Janet. "Don't wait on me for dinner. I have a feeling I'll be late, got a couple of real sick ones. If I'm not home by seven you go to the club and I'll meet you there."

The country club hadn't changed in fifty years, Janet observed as she and her mother met her father that evening. Same red damask sofas and chairs. Maybe the draperies were more faded, the Persian rugs a little worn in spots, but no one seemed to notice. That's what happened when you went away and came back. Friends she'd grown up with hadn't changed either, not really. They were older, of course. Some were engaged, some married . . . Mary Lou was pregnant and Clare had a little boy one year old. But their talk and their interests seemed so familiar, so easy and so . . . similar. And the young men she'd known all her life suddenly looked like they'd been stamped out by a cookie cutter. White dinner jackets, black trousers. The big event . . . not to knock it . . . was still going back to the high school football games to root for the alma mater. No, none of them had changed.

But she had. She wished she hadn't noticed, and in a way she disliked herself for the thought, but all at once she realized she had little in common with them. Face it. New York had seduced her in more ways than one. When she was in New York her heart was here, and now that she was here she very much missed Manhattan. More than ever she realized she had a foot in both worlds, was split between the two. And suddenly she knew she wasn't sure who she was anymore. The things that Effie had said about not being married, not having children cut deep. She *still* wanted all that more than anything . . . and yet her career had hold of her . . .

That's the trouble with life, she thought. When we get what we've dreamed of, look out . . . because it's not quite the brass ring after all. Not so long ago she'd thought she had achieved everything she'd dreamed of— living in New York and seeing her picture in the pages of *Harper's Bazaar* and *Vogue*. But that really wasn't the ultimate, was it. Love mattered more. She looked 'round the room at the young men she'd known all her life. Could she be married to any one of them? No. And she could

107

never come home again. Not really. And not to stay. She felt estranged from the people she'd known all her life, and all because she'd left and they never had. Their world was much more snug and safe, they knew who they were, so they had no need to leave. Who was to say who was better—or well—off?

That night she lay in her four-poster bed thinking how much she had changed, even since last night. Now she knew she wasn't that little girl anymore. Rhett Butler and Scarlett O'Hara . . . God, all the fantasies she'd lived with. She was Janet Stevens, and Bill McNeil was her lover, and her love. That was true, if somehow less comforting right now than fantasy. . . .

Sitting in church on Sunday between her parents made her realize even more how far she had drifted away. This morning was the first time since leaving home that she'd attended a church service. She felt less guilty than that she *ought* to feel guilty. Her family were moderate Presbyterians . . . good people who practiced the good life they preached. It occurred to her for a moment that it was curious that her father continued to worship here after his decision to be buried as a Jew. But then this was the habit of a lifetime, as it had been for her. Her father's strength was in his goodness, as Yankel's had been, and not in the religion he chose to follow during his lifetime. He was not denying one part of his heritage for another, but paying each its due.

When they stood on the front steps greeting friends and neighbors after church, Reverend Halsey held Janet's hand and said, "It's lovely seeing you, Janet."

What would he say if he knew she was having an affair? What would her family say, for that matter. . . .

Sunday luncheon was a buffet served out in the garden. Effie had outdone herself, with blueberry and corn muffins, rack of lamb with mint jelly, creamed pearl onions and emerald green peas, baked stuffed potatoes and persimmon pie. At four o'clock, lemonade and homemade cookies were served out on the terrace. Her Aunt Linda and Uncle John were there, along with her twin cousins Sally and Amy. Her cousins were fourteen, exactly the right age to be mesmerized by the very notion of her glamorous career in New York.

A starry-eyed Sally asked, "What's it really like being a model in New York?"

"Wonderful," she answered, simultaneously flattered and dismayed by their admiration.

"It must be terribly exciting," Amy put in.

"Very," Janet said, trying to sound enthusiastic.

"Are the men simply gorgeous?" they asked in unison.

"Absolutely."

"And the women glamorous just like the pictures in *Harper's?*"

"Oh, yes," Janet said, and wished she had the courage to tell the truth.

The two looked at her almost hungrily and continued to ask questions, but she answered them mechanically, her mind in a different place. All afternoon she weighed her love for her parents and her love for Bill. She wasn't sure where one began and the other left off. The only thing she knew was that she wanted to go back. This weekend had been a turning point in her life. Of that she was sure. Her family would always be cherished but her childhood would be put away. Now she wanted to go back to the life she had carved out for herself in New York. Two days ago she had arrived a girl, but today she thought of herself as a woman, ready to take on the responsibilities of making her own way in the world with all the rewards and hardships that might come her way. Growing up didn't make the heart immune, of course, and good-bys were always bittersweet. But while it had been wonderful coming back to visit, somehow she knew that when she boarded the plane she would be going home, not leaving . . .

As the plane taxied down the runway for takeoff Janet had the same thoughts she'd had for days. How had Bill spent his time? Had he missed her? Had he taken someone else out, taken her to bed? Janet closed her eyes, trying to visualize him with someone else, but her mind rejected the idea. She would never ask him, of course, but she prayed he missed her . . . missed her badly. As she had him . . .

If Janet had known the truth, she could have laughed at her anxious thoughts.

Bill had watched that Friday afternoon as Janet boarded the plane and then had waited for the takeoff. As the plane streaked into the sky he had turned and slowly walked to his car.

He missed her already. More than he wanted to. In fact, more than he'd ever missed anyone. Back in his apartment, he sat staring out into the dark. That night he didn't see the bridge and the view he loved so much. He saw the vivid memory of the past weekend. He *felt* her presence. But he couldn't touch the softness, smell the sweet scent of her. And memories, no matter how fine, were lousy substitutes. Yes, by God, face it, he was lonely as all hell.

He switched on the lamp, poured himself a Scotch over ice, turned on the stereo and sat down again. He'd never had to wonder what he was going to do on any given night. He knew dozens of people he could call, and getting a date would be no problem either. All he'd have to do was pick up the phone. But somehow that seemed offensive. What the hell was wrong with him, was he getting moral all of a sudden? Not exactly. The women he knew did everything but eat a bunch of grapes from his navel while swinging from the chandelier and he had never complained. But after Janet his former affairs somehow seemed sordid, cheap . . . demeaning to both of them.

He reached for the phone, dialed Kit's number. Out of all the people he knew, Kit and Charles Bristow were the only real friends he had. Now that he thought about it, he'd never felt close to anyone . . . it had never seemed important before. If anything, he had kept people at arms' distance, happy not to be beholden to anyone.

He was so deep in thought that Kit's voice startled him. "Kit? It's Bill."

"Hi. What's up, doc?"

"What are you doing?"

"What did you have in mind? A gin game, billiards or a roll in the hay?"

"I'm . . . sort of at loose ends."

Well, well, well, that's a switch, Kit thought. Bill

110

McNeil needing someone? She smiled to herself. Things must be picking up for Janet.

"Why don't you come right out and say it, Bill? It only hurts for a minute."

"Say what?"

"That you're lonesome."

"Don't be ridiculous. Why should I be—?"

"Because you called me."

"I called because I haven't talked to you for quite awhile."

"I see. Well, that's a right friendly gesture, especially at ten o'clock at night."

"Is it that late?"

"Okay, kiddo, we're on for a drink at your favorite pub."

Bill was down to some serious drinking by the time Kit arrived at eleven. "What took you so long?" he asked as she slid into the booth.

"Had to get my face on. What are you complaining for anyway? You did get me out of bed, you know, and I've been up since five this morning. Give a girl a break."

"I'm sorry—"

"Sorry! My God, will wonders never cease. Watch it, Bill, you might be turning into a real person."

"What do you mean by that?"

"Only that I never expected to hear you apologize to anyone. You're the center of your own little universe, and you just go your merry way without ever considering other people. And then you sit and wonder why no one's standing there to put you on your feet again when you fall down."

"And you?" he said, taking a long sip.

"I have Nat, Charlie and his wife, and a very dear friend named Janet Stevens."

And I have my *mother*, he thought . . . and Janet . . . ? "What do you want to drink?" He said it brusquely.

"Temper, temper . . . Irish coffee."

They sat silent for a long moment.

"Okay . . . now what did you call me for?"

"Like I said . . . I thought it was time—"

"You didn't say anything and you didn't think it was

111

time to meet an old friend. You've fallen on your face for the first time and you can't cope with it . . . right?"

God, was it that apparent? Bill ordered another double Scotch and sat stirring it with the swizzle stick.

"Okay, so you don't want to answer. Incidentally, booze isn't going to solve anything. Janet is still going to be running around inside your head tomorrow morning, and being hung over isn't going to make you feel any happier about it."

Taking a deep swallow, he said, "So you know about us?"

Kit laughed. "What do you think girls talk about? Of course I know. Now listen to me, Bill McNeil. You have a habit of lovin' and leavin' 'em when it gets a little too close for comfort. But Janet's no quick roll in the hay. Janet's in love with you."

"I know. I mean, I think I know . . . but that's what bothers me. She's the only girl I ever felt this way about. But damn it, Kit, even though I'm crazy about her, I still don't want to get involved—"

"You mean married."

"I'm plain scared, to tell it straight."

She didn't have to ask why, but once and for all she was going to bring it out in the open.

"Of what?"

"Losing my freedom, I guess—"

"And *what* does freedom mean? Bedding a lady any time you want? Did it ever occur to you that one day you're going to be old, that even *you* won't be able to get it up? Then what? By that time mama will have been long gone and Betsy and Alice will have a whole passel of children and no time for you. You'll just be old Uncle Bill, brought off the back burner for Thanksgiving and Christmas. Did you ever think about that?"

He kept silent, then looked up at her. "Sure, I've thought about it, and I'd be less than honest to say that marriage hadn't crossed my mind since I met Janet."

"So?"

"Well, I've only known her about two months."

"Got nothing to do with it. George Bernard Shaw fell madly in love with a woman he'd seen on a train, and he

112

knew right away that he'd love her forever. And he did. So it happens. Love at first sight."

"Okay, okay, that may be true. But I don't know if I'm in love with Janet or maybe just infatuated. She's just so different from anyone I've ever met. When I'm with her something happens to me. In fact, even when I'm not with her. And damn it, I did miss her today. Badly. I can't imagine getting through the weekend without her. I'm going to be off the wall by the time Sunday comes."

"Now honest injun, Bill, have you ever felt that way about any other girl?"

"Never . . ."

"And you don't think you're in love?"

"I honestly don't know, Kit."

"Because you don't want to. But what makes you think all women are like your mother? Give us a break, fella."

Kit had a point. And it wasn't only his mother's example. Betsy and Alice had followed right in mama's footsteps, clucking and fussing over their children and manipulating their husbands as if they were puppets on a string. Harriet was the only one who made a man feel like a man. She went along with whatever Gordon wanted. Or did she? How had she convinced Gordon to move into that big mausoleum with mama, and did Gordon see it as compromise or capitulation . . . ? Kit made a lot of sense. He certainly had been conditioned to feeling trapped by women. But understanding this didn't make him any less trapped.

"Okay, Kit, what do I do? I really want Janet but I don't want to get married. I don't want to *belong* to anyone again—"

"I think you've got your ass in a sling."

"Why? You and Nat have been together for two years."

"And that's what you'd like. To have your cake and eat it too, right? Well, I'm not Janet and she's not me. Besides, my life has been a little different from hers. I don't come out of her ball park."

"But you love Nat."

"More than you know, but like I said, I'm different . . been around the block a few times. Besides, they

113

grow them a little different out in Kansas. Janet wouldn't go for that."

Bill looked down into his drink. "Well," he finally said, "let's see how things develop. Maybe if I have time to get used to the idea—"

"Listen, if you have to brainwash yourself it won't work. Be a nice fellow and break it off now . . . for Janet's sake. It won't be easy for her, but nothing lasts forever. I'm the expert on that. There's nothing like a good man to help mend a broken heart, so set her free and let her find someone who *does* care for her . . . Now, let's have one for the road and call it quits. I've got to be rested come morning. That's my day with my special guy." . . .

If Bill was confused and unhappy on Friday night, Saturday certainly hadn't been any better. He roamed the spots they had visited the week before, but without Janet there was no fun, no real pleasure. He called Charles to see if he and Carol were free for dinner, but they were busy and so he stayed home, remembering the dinner Janet had fixed last Saturday. After ordering out for Chinese food, he found he had no appetite for it and threw it into the sink to let the disposal gobble it up.

He went back into the living room and poured himself a stiff drink. As he sat on the sofa Kit's words kept coming back to him. "There's nothing like a good man to . . ." Well, a man needs a woman too, he thought, but the idea of falling in love with Janet, of marrying her . . . He tossed back his drink and poured another. Kit was wrong about one thing. Booze helped . . . damned right it did. Didn't have to think, didn't have to feel. With a half-empty bottle at his side he passed out on the living room sofa.

When he awoke on Sunday morning it was ten-thirty. His head felt like a balloon and every muscle in his body ached. Wow, he'd really tied one on last night . . . never did that before, never *had* to.

When he looked at himself in the bathroom mirror, his eyes were bloodshot and the lids puffy. He looked like he felt, which was plain lousy. He'd better shape up and get himself together, he thought, opening the medicine chest and reaching for a bottle of eyedrops. He had to drive out to Long Island to see his mother for a few hours, then go to the airport and pick up Janet at six-thirty. The way he felt now he wondered if he could make it through the next six minutes.

By the time he had showered and shaved he was beginning to think he might survive after all. He poured himself a mug of coffee, brought it into the living room and sat down. The room was a mess. Records were strewn about and there was a large wet stain on the rug where his glass had broken. It must have fallen out of his hand when he'd passed out. The ashtray was bulging with cigarette butts. A wonder he hadn't set the place on fire. Don't drink while driving. Don't smoke while drunk . . . don't fall for a girl, you could go all the way . . . Well, he wasn't going to. That's how it came out in the light of day. He was crazy about Janet but not in love . . . not enough, anyway, to give up his life . . . yes, damn it, his *freedom*. He'd never cheat on her, he'd be as loving and caring as he was capable of and he'd be the best friend she'd ever had—and lover, if she'd let him. There would be nothing he wouldn't do for her, except marry her. Some people stayed in love for twenty years and never got married. And maybe, just maybe he could get Janet to feel that way. Oh, to hell with it. Don't try to second-guess life. Pour the wine and enjoy it while you can . . .

No man, whether husband or lover, had been as happy as Bill when he saw Janet walking down the landing steps.

During the drive back to Manhattan they talked about how they had spent the weekend. Both stretched the truth a little, he more than she. Loneliness was never mentioned, but now it didn't matter. They'd soon be snug and together. No pillow for her, no booze for him.

As soon as they stepped into the elevator in his building his lips were on hers. He carried her down the hall to his apartment, kicked the door closed behind them and put her down on his bed. This was where she wanted to be, Janet thought as she held him against her, where she needed to be. This was no childhood fantasy but what her life was really about.

Their desire had been heightened by the separation and

115

they made love eagerly, quickly. As Bill lay spent on top of her they spoke in hushed, contented voices, then made love again, more unhurried now, until Janet arched her back to receive him and they met each other with a surpassing urgency. . . .

Bill loved her, she thought as she lay beside him, his arm hugging her to him. She was as sure of that as that the world was round. She knew by the way he had loved her tonight. The words left unsaid were unimportant. They were spoken through his touch and the honest outpouring of his feelings. . . .

Bill's feelings were not quite as tranquil. He had made love as never quite before, but the intensity of her lovemaking made him vaguely uneasy. Trying to dismiss his thoughts he said lightly, "This is getting to be a boring question, but what would you like to do? I mean for dinner?"

She laughed. "You're right. And I'll give you the same boring answer. You make the decision."

"Okay. I had a little time to kill this morning so I went to the deli and loaded up the freezer."

Well, well, he was becoming domesticated, she said to herself. The first time she'd been here all he'd had was some wine in the refrigerator and coffee in the cupboard.

"What did you buy?"

"I don't remember. A whole bunch of stuff. Want to see?"

Smiling, she got out of bed, opened her suitcase and slipped into her robe while he got into his. They went into the kitchen, and when he opened the door to the refrigerator Janet stood back and laughed.

"How did you get this home, with a moving van?"

He smiled, rather pleased with himself, and that she approved. "No, hailed a taxi."

"Well, in case the Russians land in New Jersey there's enough food to last for the duration."

She viewed the assortment of goodies. A large wheel of Camembert, an enormous wedge of imported Swiss cheese, a ball of Gouda encased in red wax, Cheddar and American cheese. There were pounds of cold cuts, from ham to pastrami, turkey and corned beef. She rummaged through the shelves and found cream cheese and smoked

116

salmon, tubs of potato salad and cole slaw, a jar of kosher dills, a pint of black mammoth olives. In the freezer were pizza, blintzes, bagels, kaiser rolls and English muffins, tins of sardines from every country in the world.

She took the sardines out and put them into the cupboard, stacking them alongside the two-pound can of Hills Brothers coffee.

"I take it sardines shouldn't be frozen," Bill said sheepishly. "But at least you've got to give me an A for effort. I'm just learning."

And I'm learning a lot about you, Janet thought. This is a country mile from the Bill of a few months ago. "Suppose you go inside and fix a drink, turn on the stereo and I'll do what women were supposedly born to do. Get supper."

He kissed her and did as she said.

As Janet came into the living room carrying a large tray, he said, "Here, let me take that."

"It's not heavy," she said, placing it on the coffee table.

"That looks beautiful, Janet."

"Don't it just. And it was so taxing," she said, smiling as he looked at the platter of cold cuts, cheese and bread.

They talked and laughed, and in the contentment of the mood Bill confided in her about the postcards his friend had mailed for him as a ruse to escape the usual family visit on that first weekend they'd shared.

She told him about Effie, with all of her well-meaning complaints—eliminating, of course, the part about marriage and children—and about her starry-eyed teen-age cousins whom she hadn't had the courage to disillusion about the glamor of modeling. Which was an unpleasant reminder that the time had come for her to pack her overnight case and go home. She had to be up at six in the morning.

Taking the last sip of her wine she stood up and started to remove the tray.

"Don't do that now," Bill said. "We can clean up later. Sit down here next to me."

"I wish I could, darling, but the witching hour has come. Tomorrow is blue Monday and we working girls have got to get our rest."

He stood up, took her in his arms and kissed her into

silence. Or tried to. Between kisses she said, "I've got . . . to . . . go. It's . . . ten—"

"No, you don't. Stay . . . please."

"Can't—"

"Please . . ."

"No, I can't."

He released her gently, took her face in his hands. Almost whispering, he said, "Please, I think you owe it to me."

"Why?"

"Because you loused up my whole weekend. You weren't here."

There was an awkward silence as the surprise of his admission hung between them.

Janet was the first to recover. *You loused up my weekend. You weren't here . . .* The words still rang in her ears as she answered, "Well . . . how can I make it up to you?"

"I'll think of something," he said, and picked her up in his arms.

Chapter Eight

On Monday she was so exhausted that she merely went through the motions of being alive. They hadn't fallen asleep until after three, and when the alarm clock went off at six she had wanted to throw it out the window. Edna St. Vincent Millay had nothing on her. She was burning her candle not only at both ends, but in the middle. A few more nights like that and she'd have to give up modeling and take up basket weaving.

When she joined Kit for lunch that day she was greeted with "Wow, you look like you just came out of a wringer."

"That's the way I feel. I can't wait for today to be over."

Kit laughed. "Listen, kid, sex is great, but like anything else, overdose can be hazardous to health."

Janet blushed. Even with Kit she felt embarrassed. "What did you do over the weekend?" she asked, anxious to change the subject.

"Well, on Friday night I had a drink with Bill."

"Oh . . . ? Strange he didn't mention it—"

"Nothing strange about it. It wasn't all that important. I didn't have anything to do and I was feeling a little restless, so I gave him a call. He'd just gotten home from the airport."

"Did he say anything about me?" Janet asked tentatively.

"Yes. He said he thought you were a terrific lady."

"That's it?"

"What else did you think he'd say?"

"I don't know, Kit . . . The truth is, when I'm with him I get the feeling he really cares for me . . . a great deal. Not that he says so in those words, but—"

119

"Don't get hung up on what you want to hear . . . or think you're hearing. Guys can be nuts about a girl but have no intention of going beyond an affair. I told you that."

"Is that what *he* said?"

"No, we didn't really discuss you all that much."

Kit knew that hurt, but not nearly as much as it would hurt when Bill checked out of the affair. She couldn't just stand by and let Janet build up all kinds of romantic notions about walking down the aisle. If only Janet knew the real story of that long conversation . . .

"Listen, baby, take the goodies while they last. Look, we all go through this." Kit gave a sympathetic shake of her head. "Now, Saturday I'm having a small dinner party, so don't make any other plans."

During the week Janet and Bill had an early dinner, which left him rather out of sorts. By the time they'd finished dinner it was nine o'clock, and since Janet had to be up early the next morning the evening was practically over. He respected Janet's aversion to love on the run, her feeling that it was somehow sordid and cheap, but he couldn't help feeling as if he'd been left high and dry, in more ways than one, when he dropped her at her hotel. Still, he had to admit when Friday came the waiting had been worth it.

There was still, though, the matter of Sundays to be settled, and he made a decision. The weekends belonged to him and Janet—mama or no mama. He knew it would be no easy job to break it to his mother but he hadn't suspected just how hard it would be until he sat across from her in her living room after broaching the subject.

At first she didn't seem to comprehend. "You mean it's just this coming Sunday you won't be here—"

"No, mother, I mean from now on I can't make Sunday a standing day to come to—"

"Bill, . . . you can be honest with me. Is there a special girl?"

"Yes," he answered, surprised at his courage, then suddenly ashamed that it should take any courage.

"Oh . . . and is she your—?"

"Mistress? No." He denied it not just for the sake of

120

his mother's sensibilities . . . when the time came for them to meet he wanted to spare Janet any possible embarrassment.

"But she must mean a great deal to you if you prefer her to your very own family. Are you . . . in love?" She swallowed hard, waiting for the answer.

"I'm not sure, but I know I like her a great deal, and so will you."

"You mean you intend to bring her here?"

"Yes, I do, mother."

Her tone was suddenly adamant as she said, "Bill, I'd prefer that you didn't."

"Well, in that case, I'm afraid I won't be seeing you very often."

She looked at him and suddenly saw a hint of Jason in his determination. Jason was gone. And now Bill too . . . ? Her voice softened as she said, "Is she a really *nice* girl? I mean, the sort you would be *proud* to—"

"Yes." Jesus, this was a soap opera.

"What is her profession?"

Profession? He wanted to say brain surgeon. "She's a high-fashion model."

Silence, then a clearing of the throat. "Model?"

"Yes."

"That doesn't sound like a terribly respectable profession to me, dear."

"Modeling has changed a lot since the days of the *Police Gazette*, mother. Take my word for it, she's not only in a respected profession but she's one of the best. I wouldn't worry too much."

Violet let it pass. "Tell me about this young woman."

He hated being questioned. This was going to be like a cross-examination on the witness stand. "What would you like to know, mother . . . ?"

"Where does she come from?"

"Kansas. Wichita, Kansas."

"I hope she's not Catholic."

What the hell did that mean? "No," he snapped back, "as a matter of fact she's part Jewish."

Silence prevailed. "Jewish?"

Bill sat in shock.

What the hell was wrong with her. She wasn't anti-Se-

121

mitic. She had never been anti-anything, for that matter, unless it threatened her little world. His father's firm had started with the name of Unger & McNeil and Abraham and Rosalyn Unger had been accepted as family. She was using this as a ploy. He hadn't realized how really devious she could be until now. The echoes of Kit . . . "Your mother's devious, Bill . . ." He had rejected it before but he was beginning to believe it now . . . "Just part Jewish, mother, but you'll be happy to know that Janet's family are good Protestants . . . same as we are and much more churchgoing. Any other questions?"

Violet sat quietly. When she did not respond, Bill said, "In that case I'll be seeing you soon. Take care." He walked out, slamming the door behind him. . . .

Alone, Violet let the tears come down. He was his father's son, all right. And she was losing him again, maybe irrevocably this time. . . .

Driving back to Manhattan, Bill sat behind the wheel hating himself. Yes, his mother was manipulative, maybe even devious, but he shouldn't have hurt her so badly . . . or at least been so rough on her. Sure she'd made him mad. But she was still his mother and he loved her . . . but God, the time had come when he had to be a free adult man, belong to himself. Life could sure push you into the corners . . . trading off someone else's happiness for your own . . . He pressed down the accelerator. Hard.

The magnificent antiques Kit had acquired from her mother were gleaming in the flickering light cast by tall tapers on the rose marble mantel. Two large arrangements of exotic flowers completed the festive setting, their perfume lightly scenting the air.

Kit sat at one end of the dining room table, looking radiant with shimmering crystal beads at the neck, and Nat, sitting opposite her, looked especially handsome and happy tonight.

Bill looked from Kit, the dark-haired olive-skinned beauty, to Janet, exquisite in a dress of hyacinth tissue taffeta, heightening the effect of her violet blue eyes, her fair, delicate skin and that wondrous mane of silk.

Then he switched his attention to Charles's wife Carol

122

and wondered what it was that made their marriage work so well. The differences in their personalities were startling. Carol bordered on the shy, just pretty enough not to be unattractive, and Charles had always been so outgoing, had always had his pick of girls, was a great conversationalist and so forth. What was the chemistry that went on, Bill wondered? Better not to know . . .

Janet's thinking was not so different, though with a variation. She too looked around the table . . . at Kit and Nat, Charles and Carol. Kit and Nat seemed especially in tune with each other tonight, and now that Janet was getting to know Carol better she saw the essential gentleness of her nature and her look of quiet pride and love when she turned to her husband. And what wife wouldn't be pleased to have a husband as attractive, warm and open as Charles? They seemed to complement each other almost perfectly.

It was amazing, really, that Kit and Nat or Charles and Carol had somehow managed to find each other among the multitudes of men and women. Was it accident, something predestined, that had brought them together? And what about herself and Bill? The last time this group had been together was that disastrous night of Kit's birthday party, when Janet would have bet her life that she and Bill were never meant even to be civil together. But tonight . . .

When the table had been cleared for dessert, the maid filled the hollow-stemmed champagne glasses and Charles launched into one of his jokes. As the laughter subsided Kit stood up and tapped a spoon against her glass for silence. Smiling at Nat, she said, "Here's to you, darling. To a long life filled with joy, and a few friendly fights so we can appreciate the good things even more."

And then Kit announced, "Ladies and gentlemen, I'm here to tell you that we were married yesterday before sundown in the rabbi's study."

Complete silence for a moment, then everyone seemed to talk at one time and Charles said, "How come you didn't tell your own brother, so I could give you away?"

"No one had to give me away. Nat took me the way I am."

123

"Yes," Nat said, putting his arm around her, "but it took me two years to talk you into it."

"Don't ever say I didn't warn you," Kit replied.

Janet got up and kissed her friend. "Kit, I'm so happy for you." Kit gave her a warm hug, suddenly sensitive to the hopes Janet must be feeling about her relationship with Bill at this moment. Janet, hung up on a man who acted as though Independence Day had been created with him alone in mind . . .

Charles was shaking hands with Nat. "Congratulations. You married yourself quite a woman. And I'm proud of you, Kit, for picking the best."

"We Barstows always had a lot of class. Look at you and Carol. You couldn't have done better."

Carol kissed her sister-in-law. "Kit . . . Nat, I hope you'll be as happy as Charles and I have been."

"Even half as happy would do," Kit said, her eyes suddenly moist as she remembered what Carol had meant to Charles after the death of their parents; it was Carol who had helped him out of those long, long nights of despair.

Bill was standing in front of Kit. "You know what I wish for you, don't you?" he said, thinking of how she had always been there, strong and sympathetic, when the going got rough.

She knew he wanted the best for her. And in a curious way she had him to thank for making her appreciate what she had with Nat. *You're a taker, Bill, not a giver, but I love you in spite of it all . . . and God help Janet.*

Bill kissed her, then shook hands with Nat. "You're a lucky man." As he sat down, though, he suddenly felt a sense of loss, and envy. His two best friends were married. And where did that leave him . . . ? He looked briefly at Janet, then quickly away . . .

Janet lay snug in Bill's arms that night, but she hardly felt secure. Staring up at the ceiling in the dark, she could still see Kit standing alongside of Nat as they cut their wedding cake after the big announcement. Kit's hand had shaken badly but Nat's had steadied it. It was a sight she would never forget. Kit had revealed a side of herself that few had ever seen. The conversation still rang in her ears . . .

"I still don't understand why you didn't tell me you were getting married," Charles had said.

"Sorry, brother dear, but there's that one special moment in every person's life and for me that moment was marrying Nat. I didn't want to share it with anyone. It's crazy, but then whoever said I was sane? But tonight I want to share it with those I feel closest to. I just wish Nat's mother and father were here . . . well, when they get back from Europe we'll have a bash."

Bill felt uneasy too. Kit's words hung in his thoughts. *What the hell is freedom?* As Janet moved restlessly at his side he drew the sheet over her shoulder and looked at her in the dark shadows of the room. What he'd seen tonight between Kit and Nat reminded him of the saying that you're not really whole until it's we, not me . . . But I've never really even been *me* . . . No, I've spent my whole life being or reacting to what other people wanted me to be. He'd always been pulled in two directions, as his mother's and sisters' darling little boy or his father's successful man-of-the-world son. And now he had a choice between being Janet McNeil's husband, maybe even someone's father, or being her lover and finally his own person. Janet *McNeil?* Weddings always affected people.

The next day at work Janet was slipping into her jacket to go out for lunch when Kit walked into the dressing room.

"What are you doing here? I thought you'd be on your honeymoon."

"I am . . . have been for two years. Come on, I'll buy you lunch."

As they sat over salads in their favorite restaurant, Kit said, "I gave my notice today. I'm through showing off this fabulous body of mine . . . going to save it for Nat only."

"I'll miss you, Kit," Janet said very quietly.

"Why? I'm only giving up modeling, not going to Outer Mongolia."

"I know, but it won't be the same. For me, I mean."

"Why, do you think getting married takes you away

125

from the world? We'll still meet for lunch, for God's sake, and continue as we have before."

"Of course we will . . . Being married must be wonderful—"

"It is," Kit replied after a pause. "It's something you can't explain. Here Nat and I carried on like mad for two years and on our wedding night I felt like a virgin, an honest-to-God bride. Would you believe it?"

"I'm very happy for you, Kit. It all seemed so sudden, though. You never mentioned getting married—"

"It wasn't sudden at all, not really. Nat kept badgering me and I kept telling him I was a lousy risk."

"Why would you think that?"

"I don't know. I could have gone on with Nat for the rest of my life just as we were and never being unfaithful. It was just my own crazy fears, I guess." Kit broke off and took a sip of her Bloody Mary, uncomfortably aware of Janet's surprised expression.

"I'd never imagine you being afraid of anything, Kit. Why were you afraid of getting married?" Janet watched as her friend carefully folded the moist edges of her cocktail napkin around the bottom of her glass, then smoothed it flat again.

"I adored my mother and father," Kit finally said. "There weren't two more wonderful people in the world. I was sixteen when they went off on a holiday and died in an airplane crash. I went completely to pieces . . . wound up in a sanitarium for a year. I never told you, I guess because it's no use reliving the thing. But I was very bitter. It seemed so senseless that they should die. So damned unjust . . . I just hated the whole damn world . . . it was impossible to believe in anything. Somehow I managed to get through the next few years, but the pain of losing them hadn't softened too much. Maybe that's why I reached out to Bill that summer. Then I met Nat two years ago. I don't know exactly what attracted me to him, but attracted I was and I needed a lover, a sweet, tender lover to make me feel . . . some emotion. Nat did that. Then I got scared when I realized I was beginning to like him more than I wanted to. We broke up any number of times . . . it was all my fault. He put up with a hell of a lot of nonsense from me but he kept coming back. Don't

126

think I didn't know I was destroying the best thing that ever happened to me. But tell a drunk not to take a drink. I was crazy nuts with fear."

"But what were you afraid of?"

"Afraid to love because loving always seemed to result in pain. Losing the most important people in your life changes you. You get gun-shy . . . sure, parents die, but they should have lived a full life right into old age. That's the way it should have been. But my mother was thirty-seven and my father was buried on his fortieth birthday." She paused and took a sip from her drink. "Well anyway, Nat hung in there with me through brimstone and fire. To make a story short, the other day he gave me an ultimatum. It was either-or. He wants to start a family. I'm twenty-five and I don't want to risk losing Nat and going through life without someone to love. I guess he taught me that love can give you enough emotional ballast to accept whatever comes. It wasn't an easy lesson to learn, but Nat was a good teacher." Kit smiled. "Yes, sir, he sure was, and all those ghosts are just about gone. I'm going to have a family as soon as possible. It will be like being reborn. Literally and figuratively. It took Nat to make me see that . . . Did you know that Jews name their children for the dead? It's like the perpetuation of life. And it's just one of a whole lot of reasons I'm going to become Jewish . . . Nat and I are going to Europe. We're meeting his folks in Paris, then spending a month in London. I'm going to buy up a storm in furniture because when we come home we're going to buy a place in Westchester. Janet, I'm going to be the best wife and mother the world ever saw. Mrs. Nathan Weiss is going to lick the *whole* goddamn world . . . My God, I have to clean up my language, for the children's sake. Seriously . . . I don't need the cussing anymore because the anger is gone. Anger and love are mutually incompatible."

Kit's courage, strength seemed to fortify Janet. Love really *could* conquer all. Looking at the peace in Kit's eyes she realized that, yes, Bill had his fears too, and she understood them, thanks in part to Kit.

That evening, she felt closer to her goal when Bill said, "We're driving out to Long Island on Sunday." She knew he'd never done that before . . . taken a girl home to his mother.

Happy as she was about it, she became more nervous as the week wore on, and by the time they drove up in front of the mansion she had a stomach full of very active butterflies. Would his mother like her? And if she didn't . . . ? Kit had told her that Mrs. McNeil wasn't likely to relinquish her claim without a battle. Yes . . . it was true that she and Bill were becoming closer all the time, but if he were forced to choose . . .

Janet waited nervously in the living room with Bill for Mrs. McNeil to come down that long winding staircase. When Mrs. McNeil finally made her entrance, she was dressed in a long flowered chiffon gown. She was not the diminutive, aging creature Janet had imagined from Bill's description. She looked both regal and formidable. Intimidating, in fact, at least to Janet. This woman could change her life. *Stop it, Janet.* But the admonition had little effect. The echo of Kit's words sounded too clearly.

"Mother, this is Janet Stevens."

Mrs. McNeil took Janet's hands in hers and held them. "You are *just* as Bill described you . . . so very, very lovely, my dear, and I couldn't be more *pleased* at Bill's choice . . . I'm so happy for my son."

Bill paled at his mother's words. He had told her very little about Janet. Nothing, in fact, except that while she was a lovely person he was far from sure about his feelings or intentions. And yet here his mother was acting as though they had just announced their engagement . . . ?

Why indeed . . . Because Violet had debated with herself how best to handle the situation and being a veteran at handling such matters, had decided that no apparent offense gave the opposition no defense. To argue with Bill would only push him closer to this girl. She knew her Bill. He had, more and more, a mind of his own, it seemed, and had already made one upsetting break. Bill was not Jason, who mostly could be wrapped around her little finger except for that time he defied her and sent Bill to military school . . . Violet looked at her son, took his hand. "You're a naughty boy not to have brought this beautiful

128

child to meet me sooner. Of course you *have* been traveling a lot recently. I'd forgotten about that." Still smiling graciously, she turned from him to Janet. "Now come sit down, dear, and tell me all about yourself."

All of Janet's fears went up in smoke that moment. It was almost too much to believe that Bill had told his mother all about her, and it could mean only one thing, couldn't it? And perhaps the battle Kit had warned her about was already in the past and Mrs. McNeil had made her peace with Bill's decision? It certainly seemed so, judging by her obvious interest as she drew Janet into conversation about herself, doing her best, it seemed, to put Janet at ease . . .

It was Bill who seemed tense, even surly with his mother. He didn't relax until Harriet and Gordon walked in. Harriet threw her arms around Bill. "Sorry we're late, but Gordon got into a sandtrap and couldn't hack himself out . . . I think it took fifteen strokes."

"That's a lie, Harriet, and you know it. I was out in three . . . Glad to see you, Bill."

Bill shook hands with him, then said, "Janet, I want you to meet my sister Harriet, and Gordon, my brother-in-law."

Harriet looked like Bill. A handsome woman, tall, athletic and tanned. Her eyes and the gentle pressure of her handshake seemed to say that she knew how tough it was to meet a man's family for the first time, and her genuine and open manner put Janet immediately at ease. Gordon was no less cordial, and by now Janet was both pleased and perplexed. They were all behaving so differently than she'd expected. Even—or especially—Bill.

"Gordon, you fix drinks while I go up and change," Harriet said, starting up the stairs with her cleated shoes in hand.

Bill followed his sister. "Harriet, I want to talk to you."

"Sure, but it will have to wait for a few minutes. I need a shower."

While he waited for her to come out of the bathroom he stood by the bedroom window, looking out to the oak tree he'd climbed as a boy. He'd slept in the treehouse one night without telling his mother, he recalled, and she had frantically set their half dozen gardeners on a search of the grounds. In the morning he had finally surrendered, and now he felt a perverse combination of pleasure and pain over the amount of worry he'd caused.

"So what do you want to talk about?" Harriet asked, rousing him from his reverie as she entered the room.

"Harriet, you've got to do something about mother."

"Such as?"

"Have a talk with her. You should have been here earlier."

"Really? Why?" she asked, sitting down on the bed to towel-dry her hair.

"When I introduced her to Janet she acted like the mother-in-law to be."

"She was only being polite. For Pete's sake, isn't there any pleasing you? She could have been a stinker, you know."

"I almost wish she had. But she went to the other extreme."

"How?"

"By deliberately giving Janet the impression I had confided in her. She blew the whole thing out of proportion. I didn't tell her I was in love—"

"Are you?"

"Well . . . no, damn it. But that's the way mother made it sound. The truth is, Janet's the first girl I've ever been this nuts about. But love? I just don't know."

"Why did you insist on bringing her then? You must have known the way mother would take it."

He shook his head. "You're right." He hesitated before saying, "Harriet, can I trust you?"

"I shouldn't think you'd have to ask."

"The reason this whole thing came up with mother at all is that the only time Janet and I have together is weekends. We . . . well, the truth is we're lovers and because of her crazy profession we don't have many late evenings on weekdays. She's a model—"

"*Now* I know where I saw her face, in *Harper's*. It was like *déjà vu* when we met . . . Sorry, go on."

"The problem is that I can't get up on Sunday mornings and tell Janet, 'Sorry, the party's over. I have to go home and see my mother.' I like her very, very much and—"

130

"Then why don't you get married?"

Bill let out a long, exasperated sigh. "Every single guy over twenty is asked the same question. Kit was impossible . . . Incidentally, she got married."

"Good for her. I hope she'll be happy. After what she's been through, she deserves it . . . But you didn't answer my question. Why *don't* you get married?"

"Because I'm not ready—"

"When do you think you will be?"

"How do I know?"

"Haven't you thought about it?"

"Sure, but somehow I always think when I'm thirty."

"So where does that leave this girl? She's lovely and if I'm any judge, she loves you."

"You could tell that fast? Come on . . ."

"That's right . . . Listen, do you know how tough it is for a girl to meet a guy's family? It's like standing in the buff in the middle of Times Square. If you like her, come to a decision. A woman in love can't take the strain of an affair indefinitely."

"But that's also maybe pushing a guy into a position he's not ready for. That's not fair, is it?"

"Sorry, Bill. I'm just telling you the facts from a woman's standpoint. And Janet, as I believe you gentlemen say, is all woman . . ."

"We've only known each other a short time," he said slowly.

"Look, Bill, I'd be the last to push you. I think you're right to be cautious. Marriage is a big step, and once you've taken it you'll never be the same, not ever. So give yourself time, but don't take forever. And don't keep your Janet dangling. That's not fair either. And it could be fatal."

Bill was noticeably uncommunicative on the drive back to the city, and Janet became more and more uncomfortable. But she was stunned when he pulled up in front of the Barbizon to let her off. She'd assumed that he would take her back to his apartment to spend the night, that the introduction to his family had been a sort of declaration. She received his quick good night kiss silently, feeling abandoned, let down as she got out of the car and watched him drive off.

When she let herself into her room it seemed stark and impersonal, as if it too were rejecting her presence. Bill had seemed so remote, she thought as she sat on the bed, much as he had that first night. Only it had been worse today.

She couldn't imagine what she'd done . . . if indeed she'd done anything. His family had accepted her with warmth, so it couldn't be that. He was so damned unpredictable. Last Sunday he'd all but begged her to stay, and tonight he had been cold, distant . . . rejecting. Was he trying to break off? She shuddered as she looked about the room. It seemed to close in on her. God, how she needed Kit. She must have said or done *something* to cause such a drastic change in him. But what? . . .

The next day she went to a photo session with her mind in a total muddle. The photographer was less than patient. "Relax, relax," he shouted. "You look like a wooden statue. Hold it . . . hold it . . . For God's sake, Janet, *hold* it."

She had walked from the room, surprising the photographer with what he took as a show of temper. But she had needed a moment to compose herself, to damp the panic that had lain just below the surface ever since last night. She stood in the hall, her breathing shallow and her heart pounding. *You can't bring your problems to work . . . Damn you, cry on your own time.* After a few minutes she had gone back and apologized.

By the day's end, when she had packed up her tote bag and stepped into the elevator to go home she was exhausted. Tonight of all nights, she prayed she'd be able to get a cab. She stood on the curb anxiously scanning the oncoming cars, when she suddenly heard Bill call out to her.

He was smiling when he came across the street to her. "I almost missed you," he said. He bent and kissed her, and when she didn't respond he drew back and saw the obvious hurt in her eyes. She was no good at dissembling. It said flat out that she loved him, and that, of course,

132

was what had made everything so hard for him. But it had been even harder to spend the night without her.

"I acted like a heel yesterday," he said. "I'm sorry."

"Yes, you did." Her anger helped control the pain she felt. "And I don't know why."

"We all have our moments . . . don't take it seriously. I'm not like that too often—"

"What got into you?"

"I don't know . . . Let's forget it, and have a drink and something to eat."

In spite of herself she didn't resist when he took her arm, then hailed a taxi and helped her into the back seat. Strange, that constant going forward and backward between love and anger, she thought, that small thin line separating the two.

After the first drink she felt a little better, although there was still a painful residue. As she sat and looked across the table at him, she knew she couldn't continue to let his unpredictable moods influence her life the way they had, leaving her like last night, sitting alone in a hotel room, not knowing whether they were on or off . . .

Janet said, "Bill, I'm going to look for an apartment."

He looked at her in surprise. "Why?"

"Because I hate hotels. And because I want a place . . . where I can . . . entertain, have friends . . ."

"I don't know why you need an apartment," he said, suddenly feeling threatened, as if he might be losing her. "It's a lot of responsibility. And besides, you can always use my place—"

"No. It's not the same. I need a *home*, Bill. Not just for friends but for me. I feel like a gypsy, living the way I am. So transient . . . no roots."

He reached over and took her hand. "Janet, you're still upset with me, aren't you?"

"Not as much as I was . . . I suppose we all have problems, I know it's sometimes hard to talk about them—"

"Thank you for understanding, honey."

That's me . . . I know, understanding little Janet . . . the sweet perfect little ass. She looked at him, but kept silent.

"Really," he went on, "it means a lot to me that you're

133

that much of a friend." *Friend* . . . that was a bull's-eye, right on target. Better slow down and let it ride, Janet, unless you want to start a fight and lose him right now. So what if he'd been out of sorts? It was only after the first few dates that people could get to know each other, she reminded herself. He couldn't deny his feelings any more than she could deny hers. They'd simply have to give each other time. Squeezing his hand, she smiled and said, "You're right, that's what real friends do, try to be understanding." *But how long?*

"Right . . . now, about the apartment. Suppose we look this weekend?"

"Would you? I'd like you to help me find a place. I want you to like it, too."

"Absolutely. We'll find a place. Together . . ."

But somehow they never got around to looking for an apartment. Instead, life fell into a pattern. Janet began staying at his apartment two or three nights a week, as well as on weekends. Many of her clothes hung in his closet and in time she almost forgot they *weren't* married. She cooked dinner for him, and loved doing it. Gradually she came to feel there was more reward in her life with Bill than in her career.

As for Bill, he had never known such contentment either. The bachelorhood that had been so all-important seemed to fade in the distance. It was as though they'd been together forever. He loved the feeling of having her there to greet him when he went home, the sounds of her preparing dinner and the quiet togetherness of their evenings. The more time they spent together the surer he became that their affair might go on for years. Janet had, after all, given him reason to think so.

Chapter Nine

That autumn was an especially happy time for them, with warm clear weekends spent in Central Park or discovering new sights and shops, and with rainy weekends spent taking in a movie or just relaxing at home.

One day early in November, when winter was just setting in, Bill called Harriet and asked if anyone was going to their farm in Maine that weekend. She wasn't sure, but if Betsy or Alice asked her about it she'd tell them she'd lent it out to a friend. Leave it to Harriet. . . .

It was snowing when Bill and Janet drove up to the farmhouse. As they brought their bags inside they found that Ned, who had been with the family more years than anyone could remember, had left an ample supply of logs for the fireplace. His wife Lucy had carefully dusted every surface, stocked the larder and filled the house with pots of chrysanthemums and huge vases of pine branches and juniper berries. As a finishing touch she had prepared some mulled wine. When she left she gave a last glance around, thinking that it was a perfect setting for newlyweds—completely unaware that Harriet had told her this was a honeymoon only to insure Bill and Janet some privacy. Harriet hadn't known how else to handle the situation, and while she wondered what explanation she would give if Janet was no longer in the picture, somehow she suspected that it wouldn't be necessary, that what was now a deception might soon become reality.

After dinner that evening Janet lay in Bill's arms, looking into the fire. The mulled wine, fragrant with cloves, cinnamon sticks and slices of lemon, heightened their mood of quiet contentment and added a sweetness to their kisses. In the aftermath of their lovemaking, they lay on the fur rug in front of the fireplace, watching the shifting play of light on each other's bodies and feeling as if this moment might last forever. . . .

The next morning, after a breakfast of ham steaks, country fresh eggs and biscuits, they dressed and went out into the snow. The earth lay blanketed in soft winter white and the snow-laden branches of pines and firs shimmered in the winter sun of a cloudless blue sky.

The stillness was absolute, as if they were the only people on earth, and the awesome beauty of the morning immersed Janet in a happiness she simply had never known.

Bill found an old toboggan in the barn, and they trudged up a hill behind the house, startling a deer into flight with their voices. As they careened down the hill, snow flew up around them, stinging their faces, and they broke into exhilarated laughter when the sled came to a halt and tipped them over.

Bill wiped the snow from her face and lashes. She looked, he decided, like a rosy delicious apple, her cheeks aflame from the cold, crisp air. God, she was beautiful . . . "This is the best fun I've had in my life," he whispered, "and it's because of you . . . I can't even imagine what it would be without you. These last months have, as they say, opened up a whole new world. I mean it. I hope you never leave . . ."

It was the best for her too. Better, deeper even, than their physical lovemaking. Which was saying a great deal indeed. All right, he still hadn't said the magic three little words, but hadn't he in effect said them . . . ?

"I won't, Bill," she replied softly. "You can count on it."

For a moment there was silence between them. He had never said such things to her before, and while they were true he was momentarily alarmed by the deep trust he saw in her eyes. He still had no intention of marrying her, but God, he *did* love her. To lose her now would be . . .

He helped her to her feet and righted the sled. "Game for another try?"

"Game . . . bet I can beat you up the hill."

"Sure you could, I'm carrying the sled."

"Leave it and we'll slide down without it. It's even better by the seat of your pants."

136

She broke loose sooner than he. The snow wasn't as solidly packed as she'd thought and Bill was gaining on her. She picked up a handful of snow in her mittened hand and threw it at him. It landed on his chin.

"You want to play rough, huh?" he said, ducking her next snowball and scooping up his own ammunition.

Now there was a quick volley of snowballs as she inched her way to the top of the incline. Breathlessly, she called out, "See, I told you I could beat you."

"That was dirty pool."

He reached out and wrestled her to the ground, and they rolled together down the hill. When they reached the bottom he was on top of her, pinning back her shoulders, and the echo of their laughter reverberated in the silence.

"See . . . I told you you couldn't beat me," he said, his breath steaming against the cold air.

"Okay, you win."

He gave her a victor's kiss, then pulled her to her feet.

After lunch, Bill harnessed the chestnut gelding to the old sleigh he had ridden as a child. They wrapped a fox-skin rug over their legs and rode through the countryside, completely absorbed in the enchantment of the snow-covered scene.

"Oh, Bill, let's drive over there," Janet said, pointing beyond a stand of birches to a small village in the distance.

"It's really nothing, Janet," he replied quickly, "just a nowhere little village with a country store as its one claim to fame."

"I love country stores. Please let's go."

She didn't notice his uneasiness as he pulled the reins to the left. . . .

When they reached the general store Bill hitched the gelding to the iron post in front of the feed and grain barn and then helped Janet out. He saw her excitement as she looked about at the old village, and he had to admit it was picturesque, like something from another time. That was why he'd always enjoyed coming here, no matter what the season.

When they entered the store there was a group of men chatting around the black pot-bellied stove. The store's proprietor, Mr. Swanson, saw Bill from the corner of his eye and got up and walked behind the counter.

"Well, if it isn't Bill McNeil. Congratulations to you and the missus. Lucy told us the good news."

There was total shock on Bill's face. He had known it would be awkward to bring Janet in here, but he had hoped they would assume he'd met Janet at the ski lodge, that she wasn't staying at the farm with him. After all, these were country people and they would be scandalized by the truth. But this! Obviously it was Harriet's doing, a way of sparing Janet the inevitable embarrassment of gossip. Which was something he should have thought of himself—though he certainly wouldn't have handled it the same way. Harriet's damned decency had put him in a touchy situation with Janet. Hell, he should have known better than to leave the farm today. But . . . done was done. He tried to smile and mumbled a thank you.

Seeing Bill's discomfort, Janet averted her eyes as old Mr. Swanson continued, "So you went and took the plunge—that's a mighty fine lookin' woman you took it with. Now, what can I do for you?"

You already did it. "We're going to look around, if you don't mind."

"You do that," Mr. Swanson said, going back to his game of checkers.

Janet's embarrassment was so apparent Bill didn't know what to say. He took her hand and walked into the adjacent room, where patchwork quilts, handmade sweaters, socks, knitted mufflers and an assortment of calicoes and woolens lay on the shelves.

She let go of his hand and wandered about, trying to focus her attention on the items, but all she could think of was the shock on Bill's face a few minutes ago. That look had said it all. That was the reality, and the hope and security that had built up over the last months together had been nothing more than an illusion. She had been living a lie, with no one to blame but herself.

"Janet . . . I'm sorry about—"

She ignored his outstretched hand and walked out of the store. Bill followed her, unable to look her in the face as he helped her into the sleigh and secured the rug over

138

her legs. He unhitched the reins and they rode back in silence. Cold silence.

As they approached the house she said, "Let me out here. I want to be alone." She walked slowly to the front door, oblivious now to the beauty she had seen this morning. When she let herself in the door she stood trembling against it. She had deluded herself for nine months but now it was over. She wasn't cut out for love affairs that went nowhere, and this man had said nothing to deny that that was *exactly* what this was. . . .

When Bill came back to the house after putting the gelding back in its stall he went directly to the bedroom to find Janet. But the door was locked.

"Janet?" he called out softly.

There was no response.

"Janet, please let me in . . ."

He heard the click of the lock, and as he slowly opened the door he saw Janet's suitcase on the bed. She continued to pack without a glance in his direction.

He went to her and took her hands in his. "Janet . . . I'm really sorry about what happened today. I *tried* to avoid it . . ."

As she looked up at him he saw the streak of dried tears on her face, but she was calm now and she resolutely withdrew her hands from his. "*You* have nothing to be sorry about. You never promised me anything. You can't help it if you don't love me and I'm not going to try to understand what made me fall in love with you. All I know is that I'm not going to go on this way. I ignored Kit's warning. She told me you would never be really serious with anyone. I didn't believe her. I do now. I'm going back to New York. End of speech."

"Janet, please, sit down . . . I want to talk to you—"

"It won't change anything. Your feelings will stay the same. Mine too."

"Will you at least let me try to explain mine?"

She moistened her dry lips, looked at him . . . and at herself . . . *You* have no pride, Janet Stevens, none at all . . . explanations and words, that's all this will be—

"Please, Janet. I think after what we've meant to each other at least I don't want you to go away hating me. I really couldn't stand that."

She sat down in the chair next to the dresser.

"Come sit next to me." But she stayed in her chair, her only answer a look that was both skeptical and reproachful.

"All right . . . I never *tried* to mislead you."

"But just this morning, what did you *mean* by asking me never to go away?"

He ran his hands through his hair, lit a cigarette and slowly blew out the smoke, watching it dissipate before he answered. "I'm in love with you. So much so that I was beginning to let my big fat guard down . . . something I promised myself I'd never do—for *your* sake, believe it or not, so help me God—"

"Never mind God just now . . . Why did you think not letting me know you loved me would protect my feelings?"

"Because I don't want to get married, not now. I just don't think I'm ready. In fact, until I met you I completely rejected the idea. I like being a bachelor . . ." He hesitated, it wasn't coming out right. It sounded so damn cold, calculating. "Let me explain—"

"You don't have to, I understand. Kit told me all about your mother, how she held on to you, tried to possess you, so you got the feeling marriage would be a trap—"

"Yes, but meeting you has changed me a lot . . . But I still have to have some time, Janet—"

"For what? To still convince yourself that marriage won't be a bondage? When people fall in love they want to *belong* to each other, Bill, not *own* each other. They want to share all the love they have . . . to build a life. And when two people fall in love they shouldn't have to be afraid and hold back. I never withheld myself from you. I tried to give, to be patient and understand why it was so difficult for you. I'm not going to push you into a commitment. It's not only wrong but it would be demeaning to me, and I have to think of myself too . . . You said you needed time. Well, since I'm involved too, just what kind of time are you talking about?"

He got up, took her in his arms and held her against him. She did not respond.

"Please, Janet, be patient with me. I've never come this far. I told you I love you. Believe it. We'll work it out,

140

but let's go on as we are for a little longer. This is a new feeling for me. And that's the truth."

She swallowed hard. Giving him up wasn't so easy. In the heat of anger it was one thing, but as she looked into his face she saw pain—honest pain. He *had* come a long way. He *had* finally said it. *I love you, Janet* . . . Yes, all right, she'd give him time. At least now she could say, without feeling it was one-sided, "I love you, Bill . . . I suppose I have from the first time we met. That's the kind of idiot I am."

There were tears in his eyes as he kissed her. The first she'd ever seen there. The first he'd allowed anyone to see since he was a child.

They spent Thanksgiving separately, Janet in Wichita and Bill on Long Island. Separate, but equal in their loneliness for each other. After the holiday, Janet flew to meet him at the airport.

"My God, I missed you."

"Me too, darling . . . me too."

Their lovemaking that night was better than ever.

The best ever.

Since they weren't going to spend Christmas together either, she prepared a special dinner for the two of them the night before leaving for Wichita. He gave her a gold and diamond bracelet and when he opened the small box she gave him he found a pair of gold cuff links made in the form of a calendar. A small ruby was placed on November 5th, the first day he had said he loved her. Neither one would ever forget how painful it had been for them that day in Maine. They had thought it was the end, but now it seemed like just the beginning. Now it was easy for him to draw her inside his arms and say, "I love you, darling, and beautiful as those are, they're nothing compared to you . . ."

That night after they'd finished making love, he said, "I wish you didn't have to go home."

"Me too, darling."

"Then stay," he said, knowing she wouldn't.

"Come home with me," she challenged, knowing he wouldn't . . . knowing he couldn't.

As if reading her thoughts he gave a short laugh and

141

said, "If we ever have kids, I'm going to teach 'em to fly right out of the nest."

"What do you mean *if?* Of course we are, and going home for Christmas with our children is going to be wonderful. All right, this year is a little difficult for us, but *next* Christmas..."

Marriage ... it was taken for granted now, she thought as she lay beside him. "After the first of the year," he had said before he'd drifted off to sleep. "We'll talk about it then."

Chapter Ten

When Janet walked into Kit and Nat's New Year's Eve party there were many of the same people who had been there that night she'd first met Bill. That was almost a year ago now, and Janet felt none of the awkwardness she had felt that time. So much had changed.

Bill was at her side as the New Year was ushered in. "A happy New Year, sweet, sweet darling. I love you."

As Kit embraced Nat, she glanced over his shoulder at her two friends. Well, well, she thought, Bill was real flesh and blood after all. His feeling for Janet wasn't being kept a secret. Kit squeezed her way between her guests until she had her arms around both of them.

"Happy New Year," she said, giving them each a kiss.

"And to you, Kit," Janet said.

The two women looked at each other. "It's going to be the best, Janet. I want you to stay after the immediate world moves out."

By three in the morning Kit closed the door on all but Janet, Bill, Charles and Carol. Coming back into the living room, she kicked off her shoes and said, "Okay, now let's really have a party. This is going to last until dawn. We held back on the Mumm's, kept it just for the *mishpocheh*. Translation for the *goyim*—it means *family* in Yiddish."

Nat laughed. "She's taking a course at Berlitz. In fact, she's teaching me Yiddish words I never heard of."

"You'll learn, darling. Wait until I start conjugating my verbs. Now start popping the corks, honey."

With champagne served all around, Kit raised her glass to her guests. "Are you ready for this surprise? Just the two of us, Nat and yours truly, made a pair of twins. Got

143

the little package right here." She laughed and patted her stomach.

There was silence, then an eruption.

Charles put his arms around her. "Twins? You're some woman, sister Kit."

"Thanks, but Nat claims he had a little to do with it. He's right."

"When am I going to be an aunt?" Carol asked.

"In four months."

"You mean you're five months pregnant?"

"Right. I remember the night it happened in Paris. Nat and I don't fool around."

"But you don't show."

"You should see me without the draperies. I wanted it to be a surprise so I wore this caftan."

This was indeed the beginning of a happy new year, Janet thought. Kit was pregnant—with twins, no less—and there was also the memory of Bill's words the night before she'd gone home for Christmas. After the first of the year, he'd said . . . Maybe it was the excitement of Kit's announcement, maybe it was the champagne. Whatever it was, she could no longer hold back the undeniable realization that she and Bill were going to be married. It was really only a matter of time. This seemed the moment. The stage was set. She took a sip of her champagne, then another . . . *"I've* got a secret too . . . Bill and I . . . are getting married . . ."

Kit looked from one to the other, too stunned to say more than "When?"

"In . . . March?" Janet said, looking at Bill.

The color had drained from his face. "But, Janet, I thought we agreed to—"

As though she hadn't heard, Kit broke in with, "You sly dog, holding out on us, your best friends?"

"Yes, well . . . Janet and I do intend to get married. But we're going to wait for a while," he said firmly.

It seemed everyone was talking now. Kit saying, "Wait for what?"

"That's what I asked two years ago," Nat chimed in.

"That was different . . ."

Amid all these voices Janet sat silently staring at Bill.

144

Different . . . ? How about stupid, trusting—those were the words for her.

Her voice shook as she stood. "I've changed my mind. You don't have to wait anymore, Bill. Because as you've just made quite clear, there isn't anything to wait *for*." And she grabbed her coat and ran out of the apartment.

The impact of her words left Bill standing in shock before he went after her. He walked to the elevator, Janet wasn't there. He hoped against hope she'd be waiting for a taxi downstairs, but when he opened the door to the street she was nowhere in sight.

He ran a few blocks, then hailed a cab. It was almost five o'clock when he arrived at the Barbizon and was told, no, Miss Stevens had not picked up her key.

He waited. By eight o'clock New Year's morning he was frantic. Where had she gone? She'd have known he would come here, so she must have gone to another hotel. It was the only logical answer. He went to the phone, looked through the directory and called the most likely hotels, but the answers at the Plaza, the St. Regis and the Waldorf were all the same . . . no Janet Stevens registered. He could have gone on and on, but what was the use? New York had a million hotels. The only one who might know where she was now was Kit . . . or the police . . . or the hospitals. His stomach was turning over as he dialed Kit's number and heard the anxiety in her voice when she answered the phone.

His own voice was drum-tight as he said, "It's me, Kit. Have you heard from Janet?"

"No," she said after a pause.

"I've been at her place waiting in the lobby since five o'clock."

You poor thing, what a terrible ordeal for you, she thought. "You idiot s.o.b.," she said. "We haven't been to bed either. I called too. Nat and Charlie have been out looking. Now go home and live it up with your precious freedom . . . and to hell with you."

She banged down the phone, nervously paced the floor. It was freezing cold outside. Sure, Janet had her coat on, but in this weather . . . Could Janet have done something crazy? No, she wasn't going to concoct trouble . . . but for God's sake, Janet, where are you? . . .

After leaving Kit's, Janet ran for blocks, slipping and sliding on the icy pavement, oblivious to the blinding tears and the cold that penetrated her cloth coat and the soles of her thin silk pumps. Exhausted, she finally huddled in a doorway, leaning breathlessly against the wall and then sliding down to sit on the cold concrete.

Now there were no more tears, only the numbing realization that Bill had never intended to marry her. If he hadn't misled her before that day in Maine, he certainly had afterward. Except why blame him? In her heart, didn't she always know it would end this way? She was at least as much to blame. She'd wanted him so much, she'd refused to face the reality. Yes, all the signs had been there, but she hadn't wanted to see them. It's over . . . over . . .

When she got up from the shelter of the doorway she had no idea how long she'd been there. She walked unsteadily along the deserted streets, barely able to lift her arm to flag down a taxi. She remembered little of the ride home or how she'd gotten up to her room.

She lay now under the covers, shivering with cold. Her face was on fire, her head pounded. Every bone and muscle in her body ached.

When the phone rang, the sound jarred her nerves. She lay motionlessly, praying it would stop. And then she fell into unconsciousness.

When Janet opened her eyes everything was white—like the snows of Maine, except it wasn't beautiful. She had no idea where she was, and didn't care . . . all she wanted to do was sleep, for the rest of her life . . .

A hand gently closed around hers . . . Yes, she was at home in her four-poster bed and her mother was here . . .

Then a voice. Her father's. "Janet, it's Bill."

No, it couldn't be Bill. He had only been something she had invented . . . a dream . . . She closed out the thought, fell into a deep sleep.

Kit and Bill walked out into the hospital corridor and waited as they had been waiting for the past three days.

The anguish in Bill's face was etched. It was, Kit thought, the first time in his life genuine suffering had touched him.

Which was why Kit was able to take any pity on him. She remembered how he had looked, red-eyed and disheveled, beside himself with fear and grief as she had opened her door and let him in. He'd sat heavily on Kit's sofa. When she'd looked at him her feelings were mixed with sadness and, she admitted, a certain satisfaction. He was overdue . . . Life had never touched him in any deep way. Rather it seemed to have washed over him. It had been *kind*. Too damn kind . . .

His hand had shaken as he'd accepted a cup of hot coffee from her. "What do you think happened to her . . . ?"

"I don't know."

"Good God, Kit, I feel so damn helpless, I've been calling her room . . . I walked the streets knowing I'd never find her but . . . I finally called the police, the hospitals . . . I don't know what to do."

All right, she believed his feelings now . . . "Well, we'll keep trying. I left word at the hotel to call as soon as she comes in."

He winced. "If anything happens to her—"

"Keep a good thought. Drink your coffee while it's hot."

He wasn't listening. He stared up at the ceiling. "I'm a fool but not a complete idiot . . . she's the best thing that ever happened to me and I threw it away. Destroyed it. I took advantage of her love—"

"Well, at least you can admit it, which is a comforting thing for you—"

"No, it's not. I feel like there's a big hole inside me. It's after twelve now, she's been missing since four this morning."

They'd sat in silence, each with their thoughts.

And then the phone had rung. It was the hotel, reporting that Janet Stevens was in her room. . . .

When they were let into Janet's room, they found her unconscious.

Bill sat on the edge of the bed and held her very cold hand in his. He wanted to die.

Kit phoned for an ambulance . . .

After they'd got Janet settled, Kit went home to Nat but Bill took a room at the hospital. For three days he hardly ever left. She had pneumonia. If he'd ever prayed, he did so now.

After five days Janet regained consciousness. She was still in an oxygen tent but her breathing was more even and her vital signs improved. The first face she saw was Kit's.

Whispering, she said, "Thank you . . . I love you, Kit."

"And I love you, baby."

"You shouldn't be here in your condition."

"You're worrying about me?"

"That's what friends are for, isn't it?"

"I'll buy that. The doctor says you're coming along great. Be good as new in a few days," Kit said, hoping she sounded more convincing than she felt.

"How long have I been here?"

"Five days."

"I must have been really sick."

"Yeah, you were a sick cookie, all right."

"Kit, would you call my mother and father?"

"Do you want to worry them now that you're on the mend?"

"Maybe you're right, but I'd feel better . . ."

"Okay, if you want."

"No, on the other hand . . . I have to grow up, Kit. I'm not very strong, just fell apart . . . Do you think I'll ever put the pieces back together?"

"You can bet on that . . . Now let me do the talking, Janet. Bill's been here with me. He hasn't left the hospital. You know I'm the world's champion cynic and show-me girl, but I'm telling you, he loves you, Janet. More than you can believe. And who would blame you? But if you believed him too much before, don't go to the opposite direction now. You should have seen him New Year's morning when he came to my apartment. He was a destroyed man. We had a long talk and for the first time I really felt sorry for him. I know he's hurt you a lot. But will you see him?"

Janet wondered if she should risk it. In his fashion, maybe he had loved her. And it had been her self-delusion that had led her on too . . . But how much was her

148

illness influencing him now? Was he here only out of guilt? Mostly?

Kit could guess the questions in Janet's mind. "I don't want to persuade you, Janet, one way or another, but he's outside waiting for an answer. What shall I tell him?"

"To come in."

When Bill came into the room and sat by her bed she was as shocked by his appearance as he had been by hers. He was gaunt and hollow-eyed. The ordeal he'd gone through no longer needed to be questioned. And when he looked at her now he was ridden by the same thought that he'd lived with for the last five days. *He* had brought her to this . . . There were dark circles under her eyes and the outline of her body, even under the blanket, seemed near-skeletal. Her once shiny hair was dull and limp.

He took her limp hand between his, but it was impossible to speak at first. Finally, his voice low and intent, he said it. "Janet, I love you. I admit it's a lousy way to come to one's senses, but it's taken *this* to make me realize that without you I just have nothing. Honey . . . please, please say you'll marry me . . ."

She looked at him, said nothing.

When she did not respond he said, "God, Janet, I know I've hurt you, hurt you terribly. Nothing I say can make up for that or show you how I feel. Just give me the chance to *show* you."

She was so *tired*, so weary. "We'll talk about it when I'm well, when we're both feeling less emotional . . . it's been a bad time . . ."

He got up and held her frail body very close and kissed her. "I love you, Janet. I never said that to anyone before, except you. You know that, at least. I love you. Just give me some hope that you'll—"

"Not today."

He replaced the flap of the oxygen tent and walked out of the room, feeling dead.

When Kit saw him, she knew that if, as they said, the eyes were the mirror of the soul, then Bill's soul was in hell.

"She won't marry me, Kit."

"Did she say so?"

"No, but she certainly didn't say she would. I'm afraid,

149

Kit, very afraid she won't. Well, it seems I got what I wanted . . . my damned freedom."

"Nothing stays the same. Janet's been hurt and unsure of you for so long she's very afraid. Can you blame her? All right, if you really want her, fight for her."

Chapter Eleven

Each day found Janet just a little stronger. Bill was with her constantly.

Her room was filled with flowers. He had special food sent in, and they had dinner together every night. He bought her presents and silly little gadgets, hoping to make her laugh—and they did. When she was able to get out of bed she walked down the hall on his arm. She was, finally, beginning to look a little more like herself.

When it came time for her to leave the hospital, Bill persuaded her to come back to his apartment rather than return to her hotel. His housekeeper would be with her in the daytime and he would spend as much time with her as possible.

She was too weary to resist, to think of another alternative, but as she lay next to him in bed that first night she *did* feel as if she'd come home. Yes, she'd been put off by the guilt he felt over her illness, but she was also beginning to see that the suffering they'd been through—he no less than she—had, in its fashion, bonded them more closely.

Over the month of her convalescence she had not been able to make love. Her feelings were too mixed. It wasn't easy on him and she knew it. He didn't say a word, though, and showed his love in a thousand other ways. Not once did he ask her to marry him. This time, though, there was no need to question his motives. She knew he was waiting for her. This time she was not deluded. She had gone through her testing . . . she was a woman now. And a woman knew that when a man slept next to her consumed with desire but restrained his feeling for her . . . well, that man was in love. . . .

This day she especially felt the strength inside her.

After Bill left for the office she called Kit and asked if she and Nat could come to dinner.

She planned the evening carefully, preparing escargot, beef Wellington, stuffed artichokes, scalloped potatoes, green beans with slivered almonds, and chocolate soufflé. She laughed at the menu. It was far from well-balanced, but oh, the sheer delight in feeling alive.

Bill called several times during the day to tell her not to overdo it, but her efforts had left her feeling more energetic and optimistic than she'd felt in months. By the end of the day, when she heard Bill's key in the latch and ran to greet him she didn't feel the least fatigued.

"God, you smell delicious," he said as he kissed her.

She took him by the hand and led him to his favorite chair. "Let's have a drink, just the two of us before they come. Let me fix it this time. Okay?"

"Fine." She was looking more like herself every day, he thought as he watched her preparing their drinks, and tonight she looked radiant. He sensed a curious mix of calmness and excitement in her, but he wasn't about to question its source. If she was happy . . . well, that would have to be good enough for now. He had been afraid to bring up the question of marriage again, afraid he'd long ago blown his chances. Now, come what might, he'd not ride roughshod over her feelings again by pressing her too closely on anything.

As she handed him his drink and seated herself on the ottoman by his chair he glanced through to the dining room where the table was set with crystal candleholders and a centerpiece of pink roses and baby's breath. "You worked so hard—"

"A labor of love, you should forgive the expression. You know, I think I'm happiest when I'm cooking . . . Maybe I should have been a chef instead of a model."

"Is the kitchen the *only* room where you can be happy?"

"Don't be devious," but he was pleased to note that she smiled when she said it.

And then Kit and Nat Weiss were being announced from the lobby.

When Kit walked into their foyer she was preceded by

her now enormous belly. "You've got to enlarge the door for the twins and me . . . My God, Janet, you look scrumptious."

As Nat shook hands with Bill he was relieved to see that he too had recovered from the ordeal of Janet's illness . . . though perhaps not completely. Bill was still waiting, just as Nat had waited for Kit to give in . . .

As soon as they were in the living room Kit opened the conversation with the apparently inevitable subject of all mothers-to-be. "These kids are going to be wrestlers. They kick up a storm every time Nat comes near me and that, dear friends, isn't easy with my . . . shall we say, girth? I think they're jealous of the man in my life."

"You never looked so great, Kit," Bill said.

"Well, I never felt like this. It's so fabulous not to have to count calories. Nat loves me fat and pregnant. At least so he says."

"I'd love you in any shape, I say it, I mean it."

"Good, because next time it could be triplets."

"Don't knock it, my mother couldn't do that. All she had was me, which was some big deal."

"With a son like you she didn't need another."

"You're prejudiced."

"Better believe it. You'll pardon my bluntness, Janet, but when do we eat? I'm starved and I've got to feed these kids."

Dinner was served by a maid Janet had hired for the occasion, and each course brought another round of compliments. The conversation was the usual easy banter among these four friends, but there was no longer any undercurrent of tension between Janet and Bill. Kit and Nat exchanged knowing glances as the dessert was cleared away. Bill was clearly hooked. He couldn't take his eyes off Janet.

They sat around the table after dinner, their talk sporadic now, but only Janet was silent.

When a lull came in the conversation she looked at Bill, a shadow of uncertainty in her smile as she cleared her throat and said, "I'd like to propose a toast . . . To the man I love. Now . . . and always . . ."

Bill looked startled, and although he spoke in an off-hand manner there was an intentness in his eyes as he said, "Is that a proposition or a proposal?"

"Most definitely a proposal. Is it okay . . . ?"

Without hesitation Bill got up and went to Janet. Holding her face cupped in his hand he looked directly into her eyes. No surprise, no evasion this time. "*Thank* you, darling."

Kit and Nat looked on with pleased smiles. "My God," Kit said with a laugh. "I feel as if I've just witnessed a miracle. And about time, too. *Mazel tov*. When's the lucky day? Or is it too early to ask?"

"As soon as possible," Bill said, glancing down at Janet from where he sat on the arm of her chair.

When the party broke up and they stood in the foyer saying good-by, Kit put her arm around Bill and quietly said, "This is the greatest news I've heard in a long time. My only, my best wish for you is to be as happy as I am."

He could only nod his thanks.

She gave him a hug, thinking of all she had shared with these two. "Okay, Nat," she said as she slipped into her coat. "Time to put the kiddies to bed. I'll talk to you tomorrow, Janet. And I love you both."

That night there was a newness to their lovemaking, as if all that had gone before had merely been a preamble to what they would now share. All the pain and love of the last year only brought them together with a greater tenderness in each kiss, each caress of the hand. Bill found himself finally *knowing* that Janet was the most important person in his life.

He held her against him in the darkened bedroom. "Darling, let's get married tomorrow. We can fly to Mexico—"

She smiled. "But don't you want a real wedding?"

"I don't really care, but if it's important to you I guess I can wait . . . if it's not *too* long."

"I'll have to call my parents first and break the news. They still don't know about us."

"You mean you never told them anything?"

"No—"

"Why?"

"I guess I was afraid to," she answered reluctantly. "I

154

couldn't very well tell them we were lovers, and I was never sure enough about us to know what to tell them."

"Well, you can be sure now. If you think I'm going to let you get away again, you're mistaken. You're hooked, for life."

"So are you," she answered, snuggling closer.

He didn't flinch this time, he wanted her more than ever.

The next day they drove out to Long Island to see his mother. As on Janet's few previous visits, Violet was the essence of charm, until Bill said, without preamble, "Mother, Janet and I are getting married."

Violet sat there, all aplomb out the window—or rather out the mouth, which in Violet's case was now wide open. *This* wasn't the way she had imagined Bill would tell her—when the time came she'd assumed he'd come alone and break the news gently. She was shocked that he hadn't given her the respect due a mother . . . Ignoring Janet, she insisted on speaking to her son in private. He grimaced, clenched his hands in his pockets, but he knew he had to get this over with. Excusing himself, he followed Violet across the hall to the library.

The moment Violet shut the door she went off like a rocket. "This is the most deceitful thing you have ever done to me, Bill. I think you'll agree that your sister and I received her openly and graciously when you called and announced you were bringing a young lady here last summer. You *assured* me it was *not* serious and you've said nothing to indicate otherwise since then. How long has this hoax been going on?"

The muscles in Bill's face tightened. "Hoax? . . . Mother, I don't have to account to you for one damn thing—"

"Is that so? Well, my son, I just happen to be your *mother*. Therefore, please show me sufficient courtesy to answer this . . . how long have you known about your intentions?"

Lord, she sounded like a bad Victorian play . . . "Over a year," he lied, remembering it was only a month since he'd pleaded with Janet to marry him.

"A *year* . . . you've been deceiving . . . I will *never*

forgive you for this, Bill, and I will never give you my blessing—"

"Oh, really, mother . . . well, I'm getting married, with or without your blessing. And let me tell you something, mother . . . I came very close to losing Janet because of you—"

"How *dare* you say that? I scarcely know her. Those times you brought her here I was surely gracious. And you accuse me—?"

"It happened long before that, mother . . . my God, you've tried all my life to dominate me so I wouldn't ever be able to think of anyone owning me again . . . yes, *owning* . . . do you understand anything I'm saying?"

"Oh, yes . . . I'm quite bright, you know . . . bright enough to know you're an ungrateful son I have mistakenly devoted my whole life to—"

"And you're like a damn noose around my neck—"

"Just the way *she'll* be one around yours . . . and you know why . . ."

He stood as though rooted to the ground. This was unbelievable. Without another word he opened the door and hurried across the hall to the drawing room, where he found Janet nervously twisting her handkerchief.

His face was pale, strained.

"What happened—?"

"Just get your coat, we're getting the hell out of here."

"Bill . . . please, tell me what happened."

"Not now, I just want to get out of here."

Bill was helping her into her coat when Violet came into the room. The two women looked at each other, and Violet's was a look that Janet had not expected, revealing as it did a hostility that the woman must have felt all the times they'd been together . . . Violet, no question now, was indeed the stumbling block Kit had warned her about . . .

Bill took Janet by the arm and was starting to leave when Violet said coldly, "I'd like to speak to Janet."

"She doesn't have anything to say to you."

"You're wrong, Bill," Janet told him, her quiet voice sounding more confident than she felt. "I think your mother and I have a great deal to talk about."

He hated subjecting her to this, but maybe it was better

for her to know now what his mother was like. Fore-warned might be forearmed . . .

"All right, Janet, if that's what you want."

"Kindly be seated," Violet commanded.

Janet sat while Bill stood.

Ignoring him, Violet seated herself across from Janet. "I am quite shocked, Janet, that a young woman as well brought up as I assumed you were would be a party to my son's deception, to letting me think your relationship was a casual one. You've known for one year that you were to be married. How could you have done this, Janet, and expect me to embrace you as a daughter-in-law?"

Janet's heart pounded as she looked at Bill, then at Violet. Finding her voice, she said, "Mrs. McNeil, we didn't deceive you. We've known each other for longer than a year, but Bill had no intention of marrying me until a very short time ago. You must believe that. I know how you feel, and why. Bill is your only son and your young-est. Sometimes it's very difficult for parents to realize their children have grown up. When I spoke to my family about getting married my father asked if I didn't think I should wait. I'm going to be twenty-two in July, and he thought I shouldn't rush into marriage."

"I think your father was quite right. I believe you're both too young. Bill has never had the kind of responsi-bility that marriage requires—"

"That's what you'd like to have me believe," Bill inter-rupted, "but twenty-six isn't exactly adolescent, mother. You'd better get used to the idea—"

"Please, Bill," Janet said quietly. "Mrs. McNeil, I'm sorry to have brought this . . . this rift between you two . . . but we do love each other and I know you want Bill's happiness. I promise you, I want the same thing. I'd like so much for us to be friends. If you can give me the chance, I think I can come to feel about you like a second mother. There should certainly be no contest between us. Bill will always be your son, maybe even more so than in the past. I want you to be a part of our lives—a very special, important part."

Mrs. McNeil sat with her hands in her lap and looked at Janet, suddenly knowing there were no ploys she could use against the honesty and generosity of this girl—not

157

without losing her son. There was really no contest, and in spite of herself Violet felt the beginning of some admiration for Janet, who might rightfully have been offended by her accusations, taken Bill by the hand and left. Instead, she had handed Violet an olive branch, and Violet knew that if she didn't accept it she would lose her son. No, she didn't welcome the prospect of being Janet's mother-in-law, but in that moment she was forced to acknowledge that she had lost Bill irrevocably—or would unless she accepted Janet. After a long pause she looked at Janet and said with all the dignity she could muster, "Very well. In that case, I do give my blessing."

Janet got up from her chair and knelt beside her. "Thank you . . . oh, *thank* you. That means so much to both of us." She kissed Mrs. McNeil, and Violet was momentarily confused by the sudden feeling that Janet was indeed more of a friend than an enemy. She had been geared for so many years to resist *anyone* Bill might marry, but she couldn't help liking, even admiring this young woman. If he was hell bent on getting married . . . well, at least it seemed he had made a wise choice.

That's what she told herself.

Although Bill said nothing to Janet, he was more than a little nervous at the prospect of meeting her parents when they flew to Kansas that weekend. His fears, though, were put to rest the moment he met the Stevenses.

Janet ran to her father's arms. "Oh, dad, I'm so happy to see you." She was beaming as she introduced Bill and the two men shook hands.

"Well, this is a proud and happy day for us . . . You enjoy golf?" asked Dr. Stevens, not too easy himself.

"Depends on my handicap." They laughed.

"That puts us in the same league."

At dinner all the talk centered around the impending wedding.

"I know it's going to take a lot of work," Janet said apologetically, "but Bill and I want to be married on March the seventh, which is only two weeks away."

"That's plenty of time," Effie pronounced as she served the coffee.

158

They all looked at one another, suppressing their amusement.

"If Effie says so," Dr. Stevens said, smiling as he saw her determined expression. He recalled now that Effie had given up the man she loved to care for a sick father, and by the time her father had died her beau had grown tired of waiting and married someone else.

Janet had similar thoughts in mind as she got up and kissed her, saying nothing, the two women not needing words after all these years.

"Oh, well . . . nothin' so hard about givin' weddin's. Just like any big party."

"You're right, Effie," Martha agreed.

"Always am," she answered, recouping her starchy facade, and disappeared into the kitchen. . . .

Saturday night they attended the country club dance, where Janet showed Bill off. The last time Janet had been here she'd felt estranged from her childhood friends—and even more so from herself. But like her friends, she had found a measure of peace, in her own way and her own world, and now she took enormous pleasure in her friends' excitement as they clustered about her and Bill.

"For heaven's sake, Janet, you really kept this a secret . . ."

"I want to be the first to give a shower," said Mary Lou.

"Thanks, darling, but there really wouldn't be time. We're going to be married two weeks from tomorrow."

Why the hurry, Mary Lou wondered, unless . . . But as she watched them on the dance floor, she was sure it wasn't that . . . They were, no question, a beautiful couple and obviously very much in love. Bill hadn't taken his eyes off Janet the whole evening. . . .

After breakfast on Sunday Bill and Dr. Stevens played golf while Janet, Martha and Effie made out the guest list and planned the menu. They would be married in church and then have a reception at the country club.

"Do you think it can all be done in that length of time, mother?"

"Of course."

"What about the invitations?"

"I've already checked, and Mr. Jenkins will be able to

have them printed up by Tuesday. Mary Lou, Effie and I can address them and have them in the mail by Wednesday. Now, come on upstairs and let's you and Effie and me take a look at your grandmother's wedding gown."

As Mrs. Stevens took the gown out of the box, Janet saw it was even more beautiful than she'd remembered. Her mother had worn it too, and Janet would be the third generation to wear it. Martha fastened the tiny buttons down the back and then stood back to admire it. The full skirt billowed and rustled as Janet moved. The silk taffeta had been carefully preserved and had turned from stark white to golden cream. The lace yoke was as lovely as the day her grandmother had worn it, and not a seed pearl was missing.

Martha's eyes went moist at the sight of her. "You look just like your grandmother, darling. She would have been so proud. Oh, my . . . how she did love you . . ."

"And I her. I remember the first time she took me to New York. I was about six, wasn't I?"

"About that."

"I remember staying at the Waldorf-Astoria. It was all so elegant and she was so grand, I thought of her as royalty."

"She was, rather. Do you know I didn't speak a word of English until I was three? She was going to make sure I never forgot I was French. My father knew it was no use to fight her, so he used to tell me stories about his English and Irish ancestors on the sly." Martha laughed, shaking her head, remembering. It was a time for memories. A once-in-a-lifetime time . . .

"She sure must have seemed out of place in Kansas City," Effie said as she pinned the bodice of the gown.

"I'm sure she was, and it must have been difficult to adjust. Kansas City is a long, long way from Paris."

"I guess you're right." Effie nodded. "Kansas didn't much take to foreigners back when your papa brought her home as his bride. Still doesn't, for that matter. Bet they'd never seen the likes of her. And she was one stubborn lady, especially toward the end. Never forget it."

"You mean about not selling her house?"

"That's what I mean . . . here, Janet, turn around so I can fit the back."

160

Janet did. "What about the house, mother?"

"Well, when my father built it, Kansas City wasn't what it is today. But eventually the city began to spread out and all kinds of building went on around my mother's house. By then my father had died and she was living in the house alone except for the help. Nothing I could say would persuade her to come and live with us in Wichita."

"How well I remember that," Effie agreed.

"Well, there she was, living in what was practically a chateau surrounded by all those tall buildings in the busiest part of town. The real estate agents made all kinds of offers, but she wouldn't even let them inside the gate. She ignored them and the buildings . . . just went on caring for the house and tending her rose garden. Everyone thought she was an eccentric old lady. She just laughed at them, didn't care what they thought . . . she was a truly extraordinary lady . . ."

"That she was," Effie said. "Take a look and see if you think I should take a tuck here at the bust line."

"No, it's perfect," Martha said.

"All right. Now the veil."

The heirloom veil was made of six yards of lace and tulle, with a Juliet cap that framed Janet's face so perfectly that Effie indulged in a rare smile. "That young man of yours is in for quite a surprise. You're about the prettiest bride I ever did see. No, *the* prettiest."

Rarer still for Effie, she held Janet close for a moment, then abruptly released her and cleared her throat. "Well, I'd better get downstairs and start doing things. There's going to be a passel of folks traipsin' in and out all day. People . . ." And with that cryptic allusion, she took herself out of the room before anybody, God forbid, could spot the liquid in her eyes.

After Bill and Janet left on Sunday night the marathon began. They were the first customers in Cartier on Monday morning. Bill wanted her to have something extravagant in platinum and diamonds. She wanted a simple wide gold band.

"There'll be other occasions," she said when he persisted. "But this is the most beautiful ring I'll ever own."

"I know, but it just seems so plain—"

"Not to me."

He shrugged. "If you like it."

"I *love* it."

Bill wasn't too keen on the idea of wedding rings for men, but he couldn't bring himself to tell her. He settled for a narrow gold band, grateful that Janet didn't press for lovers' bowknots.

When they left the jeweler's he went to the office and she to Bonwit Teller, where she met Kit for a shopping spree.

The lingerie department was her first priority.

"What do you think, Kit?" she asked as they surveyed the negligees strewn about the dressing room.

"The one you're wearing. I love the set, especially the gown—sexy as hell."

Janet viewed herself in the mirror. It was white satin and lace, gorgeous but . . . "Do you think it's a little too sexy?"

"Nothing can be too sexy. Take it. Bill will be hanging from the rafters."

"*Okay*, sold. What about the others?"

"I'd buy every one of them . . . except I don't know why you need so many. You won't have them on that long . . ."

By one o'clock Kit was exhausted from watching Janet try on clothes. "Listen, Janet, I've got to slow down. These kids have got to be fed."

"Gee, I'm sorry. Come on, we'll have lunch."

As they sat in the restaurant, Janet was so preoccupied with all the things she had to do she almost forgot about eating.

"You'd better eat, sweetie, or they'll carry you down the aisle on a stretcher."

"God, Kit . . . did you ever think it would happen?"

"Truthfully? No. But you're irresistible, kiddo. I understand he's even crazy about your folks."

"And they thought he was wonderful. The whole thing's like a dream, I didn't know anything could be so perfect—"

"The biggest surprise of all is Mama McNeil. Talk about miracles."

"She's really been a darling, Kit. There was only one complaint."

"Oh? What was that?"

"She wanted us to wait so she could entertain for us . . . but when I explained, she took it well. The thing I'm a little nervous about is meeting Bill's whole family tonight at dinner."

"Don't worry about them. Alice is a little ding-a-ling, oblivious to everything but her children. She'll be adorable, congratulate you, then bend your ear about Randy making the rowing team at Yale, Gwen being a French scholar and the twins budding Johnny Weissmullers. One word explains her . . . boring. Betsy is something else. After she birthed three kids, she traded in marital bliss for tennis, bridge and membership in every women's club in Long Island. I don't know if she realizes or cares, but Tom has cheated on her for years. Harriet and Gordon are the real winners. I always wondered how they got into the family. Anyway . . . you've apparently already charmed the only one in the family you had to worry about, so put your mind at ease."

Tuesday and Wednesday were also hectic, and she had a dozen last-minute things to do before leaving for Kansas on Thursday morning.

Bill wasn't too keen on letting her go. "I'm going to miss you like all hell," he said.

"I hope so," she answered, nibbling playfully on the lobe of his ear as she got into bed with him.

"I don't see any point in your going home. *I* have to be there in a week."

"Darling, we went over this. I've got to, you know I do—"

"I don't know anything of the kind. All we have to do is be there three days in advance to get our blood tests and license."

She laughed. "Well, a little abstinence will make you want me more on our wedding night—"

"The hell it will," he answered sullenly. "You may regret this. I could get used to doing without you . . ."

"Do you think so?" she whispered, getting on top of him.

As their lips met, all thought of tomorrow, of any time but this moment, was forgotten.

Exactly as he had feared, the next few days seemed to stand still. It was the nights that drove him out of his mind, and by Sunday evening he told himself he should have insisted they go to Mexico. Being alone gave him too much time to ask questions. There were moments when the idea of a large wedding seemed frightening. Yes, by God, tonight he made up his mind he couldn't be separated from Janet any longer. Her presence was what constantly reminded him that he wasn't losing anything, he was gaining . . . if he ever needed her, it was *now*. He'd already spoken to her that day, but he just wasn't going to wait it out. He couldn't . . .

"Janet," he said, sitting now on the edge of the bed, speaking to her in Wichita, "meet me at the airport tomorrow. I've taken about as much of this stupid separation as I'm going to. The company's in between major projects right now anyway, and this is as good a time as any to give a chance to those take-charge types I hired, see how they handle it when the buck stops at their desks instead of mine. Why the hell I didn't think of this before, I'll never know."

She couldn't believe it. "Oh God, darling, I'm so pleased . . ."

Hanging up, he smiled at himself, then laughed out loud, thinking that for a guy who'd resisted marriage he'd sure made a three-hundred-and-sixty-degree turnaround. By God, he was *happy* . . . well, wasn't he? . . . of course he was . . . and he'd stay that way, even if it killed him . . .

Now the time seemed to be flying. There was scarcely a moment for them to be by themselves, what with all the affairs given in their honor. Which didn't exactly displease Bill. Since he obviously couldn't be sleeping at Janet's side in her parents' house, it was a little easier to get through the lonely night when he was woozy from too much champagne.

Janet, however, was not quite so fortunate. Sleep eluded her and she lay awake in the dark, thinking about the future she would share with Bill . . . that soon the

164

pillow she hugged to her side would be replaced with her husband . . .

Kit, Nat, Charles and Carol had arrived three days before the wedding, and Bill's family arrived en masse the following day. Martha Stevens had reserved rooms for them at the local inn, making sure that each of them received flowers or fruit baskets with cards of welcome.

That night they all gathered at the Stevens's home for a buffet dinner, and by the time they finished the meal and went into the study to view the wedding gifts, Violet was decidedly impressed and taken with Janet's family. She'd imagined the Stevenses would be middle-class midwesterners, simple, provincial and folksy, but to her relief Martha was elegant, poised, warm and accomplished, her charm altogether infectious. She was totally taken with Dr. Stevens, who was not only urbane but a *gentleman* . . . somehow she saw a hint of Jason in him. Breeding, Violet thought, could not be acquired . . . one was born with it. Violet didn't miss a thing—the antiques were magnificent, and handed down, *not* bought. Tonight she approved more than ever before of Bill's choice. Janet would indeed be an asset to him. In fact, when all was said and done, he'd picked a girl much like *herself*, whether, of course, he realized it or not . . .

Well, it would be her little secret. She would never let him know, but yes indeed, Bill, it turned out, was a very sensible young man after all. . . .

The moment had arrived.

When Bill saw Janet moving down the aisle, her arm on her father's, he was deeply moved. If he had thought she was beautiful before, she was absolutely extraordinary now. And in that moment, all the doubts that had secretly plagued him about giving up his freedom were stored away deep within his subconscious. She was magnificent, this Janet Stevens. Soon to be his wife.

One hundred guests shared his opinion.

She took her place alongside him, and the two looked quietly, adoringly at each other as the minister began. The ceremony was a long one, the explanation of the union explicit . . . Abruptly Bill felt a moment of acute anxiety, which Janet sensed . . . and she too became nervous.

Finally the part he had been waiting for . . . "I now pronounce you man and wife in front of God and this assembly. You may kiss the bride."

Relieved it was over, Bill did just that. In fact, he did it for so long that there was nervous laughter from the guests.

Walking back down the aisle on her husband's arm, Janet looked at Kit. The smile said *thank you*.

Bill whisked his bride into the waiting limousine, and the long entourage followed.

At the country club, the reception line was long and tiring, but no one would have guessed it from the happy faces of the family as they stood accepting congratulations and best wishes . . . they were the perfect couple . . . the most handsome . . . their lives were sure to be joyous, everyone agreed as Bill and Janet moved out to dance alone on the dance floor.

She looked near-ethereal with the bouffant gown billowing about her and the veil draped over her arm. The perfect couple . . .

Now the pictures were taken. Janet wanted a replica of her grandmother and grandfather's daguerreotype and she stood poised slightly behind Bill, who was seated. This was her tribute to her grandmother, who had not only passed on her name to Janet but also a gown befitting this momentous occasion in her life.

At five she and Bill left the festivities and went upstairs to the country club's reserved rooms—he to his, and she to hers—to change. Dressed in her pink silk suit she looked at herself in the mirror, then at her mother, who had come up to help her dress and to spend a few minutes alone with her. In that moment all the childhood years in Wichita came rushing back to her. How wonderful the dreams, and memories, were. But the future that lay ahead was another gift of life, and she faced it with no doubts. Bill had stood by her side today as she knew he would the rest of her life . . . Leaving the room, she walked out into the hall, where Bill was waiting for her. Her hand in his, they proceeded down the staircase to where the guests and family all waited. She paused halfway down the stairs, throwing her bouquet to one of her favorite cousins. There were tears in Martha's eyes, and a tightness in Dr. Stevens's throat and visible weeping from Violet. Then a flurry of excitement as the two dashed out with the traditional throwing of rice . . .

Sitting in the car alongside her, Bill took Janet in his arms and kissed her. This was his *wife*. "I love you more than those words can say, Mrs. McNeil."

"And I you, Mr. McNeil."

The bridal suite looked like a bower of flowers. They toasted each other with champagne. Lovemaking that night was better, more deeply felt than before. The difference, Janet was certain, was in knowing that they *belonged* to each other, and the feeling was a kind of exaltation . . .

Later he said, "Darling, how did you ever put up with my nonsense?"

"Who knows?"—she said it with a straight face, then smiled—"but that's the past . . . I want to spend the future doing just what I promised your mother I'd do—making you happy. And I assure you, it will only be doing what comes naturally." Whereupon she kissed him, long and soundly. "Can't, in fact, wait to get started . . ."

"You already have . . ."

The next day, in a flurry of last-minute good-bys, the two families waved to the newlyweds from the window of the airport.

Violet and her family were to take the evening flight to New York, and as Martha stood with Violet at the boarding gate the two women embraced.

"It was the loveliest wedding, Martha, and you've made us all feel so welcome. Thank you."

"Oh, my dear . . . Janet has been blessed with a family such as yours."

Violet was rarely given to sentimental tears but now she gave in to them. "You'll have to come to New York so we can return your hospitality."

"We will, Violet, and you're always welcome here."

Martha was filled with a sudden loneliness as she watched Violet and her family walking across the airfield. Her husband took her hand, as if guessing her feelings. At this moment she regretted not having had more children, that their only child was to be settled so far away from them. But perhaps there would be grandchildren. And if God was good to them, maybe she and James would live to see great-grandchildren.

and lugh ... roueveu to ... ... seen over ... ...
them. But perhaps there would be any better. All
they were roiling, maybe she and Bill would
to accept ... conditions. She ...

Chapter Twelve

When Bill carried her over the threshold to his apartment she remembered the first night she had spent here. On that night she would never have possibly believed this would be her home and Bill her husband. There was still a feeling of unreality about it all, and the month they had just spent in Bermuda had done nothing to bring her down to earth. But now that they were back, life soon settled into a comfortable pattern.

Each morning she fixed breakfast, then saw Bill off to the office. After her household chores were finished she would dress and sometimes meet Bill for lunch. Then she would shop for groceries, prepare dinner and wait for Bill to come home. Their evenings together were the best part of her day. Now there was a security about it all, with no doubts to be suppressed and no feelings that went unexpressed.

They spent Sundays with Violet McNeil—at Janet's insistence, though Bill wasn't too keen about it.

"Janet, my mother's going to expect us every Sunday. I'm warning you."

"I think it's the least we can do. She is your mother and we have a duty—"

"I don't want to do things out of duty. Besides, if we start out this way she's going to sulk and feel neglected if we miss a week. I don't want to be put in that position. Not again."

"Let's indulge her a little. It means so much to her."

"You're going to regret this, honey. Set a precedent and people take you for granted. My mother is going to be an albatross—"

"We'll work it out . . ."

And so they went.

169

They had just opened the door on their return from the first of their Sunday visits when they heard the phone ringing.

It was Nat, telling them that Kit had just gone into the hospital in labor. Charles and Carol were with him but he wondered if they might not come too.

They found him pacing the hospital corridor. Charles, who was pacing in the opposite direction, was little comfort, and Carol had long since given up trying to calm either one of them. If her husband acted this way over his sister, God only knew what he'd be like when her time came.

Janet and Bill did their best to ease the tension, but finally they too fell into silence.

They waited . . .

Meanwhile, Kit in the delivery room refused to take anything. Not Kit, she wanted to be awake when her children saw the world for the first time. At the end she let out a scream, but the pain carried more than its own reward as she saw her newborn babies being held up and smacked on the buttocks. Drenched in perspiration she laughed euphorically. "Welcome to the world, my precious darlings . . ."

At long last the doctor came out of the delivery room. He looked from Charles's anxious face to Nat's, not sure which was the father until Carol intervened.

When Nat heard the news he braced himself against the wall for a moment, then let out a war whoop. "By God, I don't know how Kit knew we were going to have a boy and a girl."

Janet's thoughts were very different, though on the same subject. Like a few million women before her, the gift of a newborn child to another woman stirred the most profound yearnings in her, at this moment striking her like a living thing . . . a living person . . . She looked involuntarily at Bill, then quickly away, as though not to give her message away before he was ready to receive it. . . .

"Did you ever see anyone so happy as Nat and Kit?" Janet asked as she curled against Bill that night.

"Never. With the exception of thee and me."

"Think of the times they'll have with their children, watching them grow up and become their own people. When I went shopping for a gift for the baby shower, I looked at all those tiny things and suddenly realized how easy it would be to spoil a child . . ."

Bill had withdrawn imperceptibly at her side, and she was unaware of the effect her words had had on him until he said, "Slow down, Janet. I think I know where this is going, and the answer is that I don't want to share you with anyone. Not for a few years, anyway. Let's hold on to the freedom to do what we want. Children are wonderful, sure, but they can also tie you down . . ."

Janet felt terrible . . . and scared . . . Yes, she had assumed that children would be part of their marriage. Yes, of course she had. And he'd never indicated he didn't, and yet here he was, saying wait a few *years*. She felt as if the breath had been knocked out of her, as if they were suddenly back on the rocky ground of their early relationship. Bill and his freedom . . . She was grateful of the dark so that he couldn't see what she was feeling.

The next day she sat in Kit's room admiring her babies.

"Are they fantastic?" Kit said—rhetorical question, Janet thought, if she'd ever heard one—"I'm so nuts about them I can't wait from one feeding time to the next. And Nat's passing out cigars like Havanas are coming back in style. You should see the way his mother and father are carrying on. It's like the second coming of . . . what's wrong, Janet?"

"Nothing, why do you ask? I'm just listening . . . no one's more happy . . ."

"What's wrong, Janet?"

When Janet finally told her about the previous night's conversation with Bill, Kit shook her head knowingly. "He's still on the freedom trail, right?"

"Something like that. It wouldn't bother me so much if he'd just said we should wait a while. But he was so set against it, talked about years . . ."

"Well, screw him . . . I mean literally and figuratively."

"A woman can't plot to have children, Kit, and you

know it. Or at least shouldn't. They have to be wanted mutually."

"Agreed . . . but Bill still has the same old problem. You just take the initiative. Ever hear of an accident?"

"I can't do that. Children have to be wanted—"

"Listen to me. There'd be damn few kids around if it weren't for a few little mishaps. Whether or not a child is wanted in the beginning, the minute it's born something happens. It's *your* flesh and blood. Tell me, do you think Bill could resist holding his own child?"

"I don't know, Kit. I just feel a baby has to be something we both want."

"Okay, keep working on him."

"How would you feel, having to beg Nat?"

"Not too good, I guess. . . . Look, you're only married six weeks, for God's sake, Bill will change his mind, take it from me." And in the midst of her own glow she believed what she'd said.

"I hope so, Kit." . . .

Janet sat alone in the kitchen on Monday morning after Bill left for the office.

The previous day they had attended Mark Weiss's circumcision and then gone to a reception at the proud grandparents' Sutton Place home, where everyone had made the customary fuss over Mark and his twin sister Deborah. Janet had been uncomfortably aware of Bill's eyes on her as she'd picked up one of the infants . . .

Now she sat at the breakfast table, stirring her coffee and feeling . . . empty, at loose ends. What was she going to do today? For the first time she almost wished she had a job again to occupy her time. Apparently there were to be no children in her future . . . .

Bill had made that clear enough. And Kit had announced she and her family were moving to Westchester, which would leave another void in her life.

She picked up the phone and called Bill.

"Hi, darling," he said cheerfully.

"Hi," she answered, trying not to let her voice betray her feelings. "How about lunch?"

"Sweetheart, I'd love to, but I have a business lunch. Meet me at the office and we'll go to dinner."

"Okay . . . have a nice time."

She sat for a long moment, then went slowly down the hall to the bedroom to get dressed, but couldn't make up her mind what to wear. Momentous decisions . . .

By noon she found herself sitting alone in the same restaurant she and Kit used to go to. Echoes of conversations came rushing back at her as she picked at her salad. *Bill will never get married, Janet . . . but I love him so, Kit . . . I'd be the happiest woman if . . . I only want Bill, that's all I want . . .* She paid the check and hurried out of the restaurant.

She walked for blocks, then browsed through Bloomingdale's. There wasn't a thing she wanted . . . not true, Janet. You want the works, marriage *and* a baby. Not now necessarily, but at least eventually. At least the hope of it . . .

She walked to Rockefeller Center, sat on a bench. Just what was she going to do with her life? She wasn't an idiot. She'd worked and been a success at it. She would do her damnedest to be the same in her marriage. But she was a *woman* too, and needed, craved a woman's fulfillment. All right, enough of that now . . . The apartment didn't require much attention. And truth to tell, she didn't much like the apartment. Well, she liked it, but it was so relentlessly masculine. She wondered what Bill would say if she suggested they refurnish it. But even if he said it was okay, what then? She couldn't make a lifetime project out of furnishing an apartment. What did other married women without children do with their time? Well, her mother was president of the garden club, did charitable work, was involved with the League of Women Voters, the historical society, the March of Dimes . . . you name it, she did it. But Janet wasn't interested in any of those things. Maybe later, but now none of it appealed to her. And besides, what did it matter what other women did? She was herself and her desires were her own. Sure, she could develop a circle of friends, play bridge, go to lunch, shop for clothes, but that seemed so, so meaningless. . . .

That night at dinner Janet was so quiet Bill wondered if she were feeling well.

"You okay, honey?"

She nodded. "Yes."

"What did you do today?"

"Just . . . Bill, I want to go back to work."

He put down his fork and looked at her. "You mean modeling?"

"Yes . . ."

"I'm sorry, darling, but I really don't want you to."

"You *don't*? Why?"

"Because it's too hard on you, the hours are crazy. I'm kind of surprised you'd even suggest it—"

"You didn't seem to mind before we were married."

"Well . . . I do now."

"Oh? It's not dignified enough? I don't do lingerie, so you wouldn't have to be embarrassed—"

"Janet, this isn't like you—"

"How do you know?" She was shocked, surprised at the anger in her voice.

He took her hand across the table. "You miss Kit, don't you?"

"Yes, but she has a life, her children and her house . . . I don't know what's wrong with me, Bill," she lied.

"I do," he said.

She looked up quickly. "Do you?"

"Yes . . . it's adjusting to marriage. I'm told all women go through that. It's not the same for men, they go back to their jobs . . ."

She'd never felt so much anger, never known it was in her. He didn't understand it at all. It was okay for *him* to go back to his job, but not for her. That was some equality. Everything had to be *his* way, when *he* was ready for it. First, no marriage . . . then no baby . . . now no work.

"You're wrong, marriage hasn't been . . ." She bit down on her lip. "Well, if not a model, at least I'd like to take a sales job—"

"Why?"

"Because I'd like to *do* something, to feel worthwhile."

"Sure . . . well, I can understand that . . . how about becoming a guide at the museum—?"

"Because that's *not* what I want to do."

"Well, for God's sake, what do you want?"

She looked at him, too angry now for words. Hadn't she just told him what she wanted?

She grabbed up her pocketbook, walked out of the restaurant, hailed a cab and went home.

When he got back to the apartment he found her sprawled across the bed. What had he said to bring *this* on? Damned if he really knew. He did know, though, that it bothered him to see her like this . . . . He took her in his arms and held her close. He heard himself saying, "I'm sorry." Though just what he was sorry for was still a mystery.

"No you're not," she said, fighting back tears of frustration. "You've got our lives all arranged, haven't you, Bill? But it's all got to be *your* way. You deny me the one thing I'm happy doing, the one thing I know how to do, after you marry me and after you tell me we won't have any children. What about me? What am I supposed to do while you're running around all day being—"

"What am *I* supposed to do, give in to every one of your—"

But she had gone to the bathroom, slammed the door. Well, he wasn't going after her. He took a blanket out of the closet and threw it on the living room sofa. Two whole months of wedded bliss . . . He poured himself a Scotch. No, damn it, he didn't want to be saddled with children, if that was what really had Janet upset. Didn't he have a right to *his* feelings? Damn it, he was just getting accustomed to being a husband and now she wanted him to become a father and . . .

His second drink eased the anger . . . the old fear . . . a little. The third found him taking on a sort of boozy, self-satisfied perspective. He sat on the sofa, drinking more slowly now. Okay . . . let's take a look at things . . . why had Janet gone off like a rocket? That wasn't her style, she wasn't spoiled, didn't throw tantrums. All right, now be *honest*, he instructed himself. True, you've been married only a few months, but it isn't as though you rushed to the altar after a whirlwind romance. You lived together almost a year before you got married. Sure, Janet's going to be only twenty-two this birthday but she's a mature woman. Up to now her life has been me or her profession, so what she wants now is to settle into a marriage . . . start a family. I wouldn't care if we never had kids but I suppose a family is a part of marriage and I guess I'd like to have kids eventually . . . Still, when I think about it something happens to me . . . I want to head for the hills . . . But look at the change Janet has made in my life. It wasn't all that great being a bachelor, was it? *Was it?* . . . Well, it had its compensations, . . . but no one gave a damn. Right? Right . . . Your life was empty, sweet little Janet filled the void . . . Now let's take a look at me. I'm twenty-six. I'd be twenty-seven if we had a baby right away and they say that's about right if you're going to have fun with your kids . . . Much as I loved my dad we couldn't do a lot of things together. Not fair to kids, or parents. My mother was too old to have a baby, no wonder she thought I was the little Lord Jesus . . . Right . . . little Janet's right . . . what am I holding out for? Should be grateful I have a wife who wants to settle down instead of being like some of the wives I hear about . . . Ted's always bitching about his marriage, just the other day he said, "I want a kid in the worst way but she doesn't want to louse up her precious figure, three years I've been asking."

The more an alcoholically reborn Bill thought about it, the more attractive the prospect seemed. In his fantasy he saw himself taking his son fishing, skiing, hunting, to baseball games at Yankee Stadium . . . Damn right, and no son of his was going to military school . . . he'd see *his* kid every day—Suddenly he was brought up sharp. Poor Janet, he'd said a lot of lousy things, not, of course, that he really meant any of them . . . he just hadn't understood. Right? Right. Kit was right. He was a selfish s.o.b. . . . And now suddenly he wanted the baby maybe more than she did. He wouldn't tell her tonight, though . . . it would only make her feel she'd forced him and he didn't want that. He'd apologize, but he'd wait for the rest for a week or so, when things had simmered down . . . He took another sip, feeling much better. . . .

He was about to get up and tell Janet how sorry he was when she came into the living room. Her eyes were still swollen from crying. "Bill," she said quietly, "I went too far . . . God, I love you so much . . ."

He got up and put his arms around her, burying her head against his chest. "I just hope you can forgive me. *I* said a lot of things I shouldn't have."

Oh yes, he felt much, much better.

The next morning, the blow-up seemed all but forgotten. Before she had apologized to him last night she had told herself it was time to grow up, to respect the fact that he had a right to his feelings and to be happy with the love they shared. The lovemaking that night was a delicious way to make up, to come to one's senses . . .

She was smiling as she poured him another cup of coffee. "Darling, I've come up with a brilliant idea."

"I was sure you would." Her excitement heightened her color. God, she looked beautiful. She *was* beautiful.

"I'm going to take ballet lessons again, brush up on my French at Berlitz, be a volunteer at a hospital . . ."

"You think you'll find time for me?"

"You just keep on acting like you did last night and I may never let you out of the house."

Which wasn't, of course, exactly what he most wanted to hear.

Janet had come to her senses.

That afternoon Janet came home with a package from Capezio and eagerly took out her new leotards and ballet slippers to put them on. Looking at herself in the mirror, she almost laughed as her childhood fantasies came back to her. She was seven, nine, twelve, fifteen . . . and she was the black swan in Madame Colette's recital. She hadn't exactly been Dame Margot Fonteyn, but the applause still rang in her head . . . Well, enough memories for now. Time to start dinner.

The phone rang just as she was putting a spinach casserole into the oven. She closed the oven door and picked up the wall phone.

"Hello?"

"It's Kit. How's the bride?"

"Kit! I'm so happy to hear your voice."

"Likewise, cookie," Kit said, wondering from the sound of Janet's voice if she'd made points with Bill on the baby parade. Her thoughts were interrupted as Janet asked, "How are my gorgeous godchildren?"

"Let's not get started on that subject unless you've got forty-eight hours. They're positively heavenly—especially *after* those 3 A.M. feedings. How's Bill?"

"Do *you* have forty-eight hours?"

"It's all paradise, I take it."

"And more."

Should she ask? No. "Are you busy this weekend?"

"No, nothing special."

"In that case, Nat and I would love to have you come out and see the old homestead. Stay for the weekend."

Janet paused. "Gee, Kit, I promised Bill's mother . . ."

"For Sunday dinner, right?"

"Right."

"Listen, sweetie, I've warned you before and I'll do it only one more time. Don't let her hook into you, Janet."

"She doesn't really. To tell the truth, she's been great, and she loves seeing Bill. She's an old lady, Kit. One day a week doesn't seem too much to give her a little happiness."

"You're a pushover, Janet. No use trying to reform you. So what's the answer?"

Janet hesitated. She very much wanted to visit Kit. Still . . .

"Let me talk to her and I'll get back to you."

"You do that, Florence Nightingale."

Janet had butterflies in her stomach when she called her mother-in-law . . . "It's sort of a housewarming at Kit's, mother . . ."

A heavy silence. "Well," Violet finally said, "if you think it's more impor—I mean, I wouldn't want to stand in your way . . . not for the world, you know that, Janet. I did plan a sort of rather special day but . . . Alice's daughter Gwen is getting ready for her coming out and I . . . well, never mind, you go and have a good time, and for heaven's sake *don't* worry about us . . ."

There was no rancor in Violet's tone but when Janet hung up she felt terribly guilty. Why, she wasn't exactly sure. Maybe because Violet had been *nice* about it . . . ?

Violet . . . sweet Violet . . .

At dinner she told Bill, "Darling, Kit wants us to spend the weekend with them, but I spoke to your mother and it
178

seems she's doing something special for Gwen, sort of a precoming out party, I gather."

"I see. And you're having all kinds of problems deciding between Long Island and Westchester?"

"Something like that . . . yes."

"As far as I'm concerned, it's Westchester. My mother's not having a big shindig. I know all her little old tricks. She's got it down to such subtlety that you're in the palm of her hand before you know it. From now on I'm going to make the ground rules. We'll go when we feel like it. She has Harriet and Gordon for company and the others are usually around to entertain her on weekends."

"You should call her, Bill . . . more often. She's getting old and I don't want you to have any regrets later on, to feel you neglected her."

He smiled and shook his head. "How did I get so lucky. You're some kind of angel—"

"I wasn't such an angel last night."

"Yes, you were. Later, anyway. Well, not exactly an angel. Sort of half and half."

"And what do you mean by that?"

"Half angel, half sex cat. And all for me . . . I love both."

"You know, I think I'm blushing. Somehow I never think of myself as *sexy*—"

"That's why it ends up so good. You don't think, you just let it happen naturally."

Kit and Nat had made the move to Westchester in near record time, having hired movers even before they took title to the house so they could get settled as quickly as possible after the twins were born. There were still packing crates throughout the house, but Kit had already dragged out enough things to make the place begin to look like a home. Janet knew it would be no time at all before Kit had it looking as if it came straight out of the inspiration of the best interior designer in the business. The furnishings were country antiques, things that Kit and Nat had found during their trip to England. Knowing Kit, Janet thought, she'd probably had Nat up at dawn, honeymoon or no, depleting the English countryside. They had found the perfect fabrics, china and crystal, and every detail, right down to the silver vaults, was testimony to Kit's taste.

The house was Tudor, one hundred and fifty years old, situated on three acres of lush green lawn. The nine bedrooms were spacious and sunny; Janet especially adored the old marble washstands and the fireplaces.

For all its veneer of wealth, this was a house that its new owners would use not as a showplace but as a home to be loved and lived in, Janet thought as she lingered in the nursery.

Bill watched her face, seeing the longing as she looked down at Deborah through the netting surrounding the cradle. Well, he had to admit—if only to himself for now—that he was as taken with the twins as she was. Soon, he thought. I'll tell her soon. . . .

By four that afternoon, Nat's parents arrived with so many presents that it looked like Christmas and Chanukah all rolled into one. Charles and a now pregnant Carol arrived a short time later, and after cocktails they all moved into the dining room.

Dinner was marvelous. Kit had engaged a cook while in England, and the woman had brought her recipes along with her baggage.

"She's great . . . how did you manage to lure her away from king and country?" Janet asked.

"Coin of the U.S. realm, I guess . . . I predict she'll be here three or four years at the most, make her bundle and go back to Devon-by-the-Sea."

Later they retired to the enormous living room. The four women sat at one end, planning a shower for Carol's baby, while the men sat at the other end, going over the minor stuff, such as stocks and bonds and the price of oil. But Bill's interest was really focused on more personal matters tonight.

"How does the commuting affect you, Nat? Doesn't it make for a pretty long day?"

"Not really. I gave up going into the market early. Who needs it? Listen, the best time of my life is now. I'm going to have breakfast with my wife in the morning and take the time to be with my kids. That's what life's about. I'm going on thirty-four already, and I want to enjoy every cotton pickin' minute. You put it off today, you never make it up tomorrow. There's no price tag on some things . . . those kids upstairs aren't traded on the stock exchange."

Janet sat close to Bill on the drive back to the city.

"Wasn't it a terrific weekend, darling?"

"One of the best I've ever had. But you know why?"

"Why?"

"On account of you, *us* . . . You know something else? When I looked across the room at you and realized you were my wife, I had the most incredible feeling—"

"In what way?"

"That we belonged together. Like the perfect meshing of gears."

" 'Gears'? . . . well, all right, the image isn't so romantic but I'll accept the sentiment . . . also, I happen to love you very much, Mr. McNeil."

"It's mutual, Mrs. McNeil."

He drove the rest of the way with one hand on the steering wheel and the other holding tight to hers. . . .

Bill had just finished undressing that night when Janet came out of the bathroom. He took her hands in his and stood looking down at her. "The time, Mrs. McNeil, is now."

"What? What time . . . ?" But suddenly she knew, and had the grace to say nothing, to let it be his moment.

"We're going to make a baby. Isn't that the phrase?"

Her eyes appropriately widened.

"And I want it understood that this has nothing to do with that fight we had the other night . . . No, you didn't convince me or intimidate me, and seeing the twins this weekend had nothing to do with my decision. I made up my mind long before that. *I* want a child . . . I want to have something that's part of us. You're going to be the mother of my son and he's going to grow up to thank me . . ."

He really did want a baby . . . and that *was* a surprise. She kissed him over and over again. All over . . .

Chapter Thirteen

They were on the balcony, looking out over the city and the bridge beyond, when he asked, "What's your pleasure for your birthday, honey? It's three weeks away but I thought you'd like to celebrate it with your folks or maybe fly to Mexico. You're only going to be twenty-two once, you know."

"I know, almost over the hill."

"True, but you didn't answer my question. We need to make reservations if we're going anywhere—"

"You know what I'd really like? To give a party at our home. I think it's about time."

"You're sure?"

"I'm double sure."

The next day the first person she called was Violet—who was of the opinion that *she* should be the one to give Janet a party.

Janet thanked her, and then thanked her again, and finally said, "It's an old French custom, handed down from my grandmother, that the one celebrating her birthday should give it—"

"Well, I'm not up on French customs and I never heard of anything so . . . quaint, but if that's what you want . . ."

"It is. Bill and I can't wait to see you."

Betsy was just as surprised as her mother had been that Janet would throw her own birthday party, but she accepted readily. Alice accepted with no comment on the custom and Harriet was openly delighted. Kit, of course, needed no explanation. She'd be there with all bells on. Nat's mother thanked Janet for including them, and Carol said she and Charles wouldn't miss it. A clean sweep. Almost.

When she placed the call to her parents she was not going to take no for an answer. "Mother, there isn't going to be an epidemic in Kansas just because daddy goes away for a week. And I want Effie to come too."

"It will be easier to get your father than her."

"Let me talk to her."

"Hold on." Janet waited.

"Yes, Janet," Effie said in her usual crisp manner.

"You're coming to New York with mother and dad for my birthday. And this is one time, Effie, you're not going to have the last word."

"Don't be impertinent, young lady, and of course I'm coming. Do you think I'd miss your twenty-second birthday after all I went through?"

"I love you, Effie."

"Of course you do. Now here's your mother."

From that moment on Janet was busy with the preparations of her first dinner party.

"What do you think, Bill? Since there will be eighteen of us, should we have one long table, or two round? Which would be the most intimate?"

"I don't know."

"You're no help at all."

"Well, I'll help in other ways." He was standing close behind her, his hands moving over her breasts and his lips grazing her neck.

"Don't distract me. I'm *thinking* . . ."

"Oh, let me distract you."

"You're not serious about this at all."

"Of course I am," he said, kissing her as he turned her to face him and drew the zipper of her robe slowly downward.

After consulting with Kit, she decided on one table rather than two, and the catering company delivered it along with gilt Vienna chairs. This was the first time she would be using her wedding gifts. The most prized among them was a fine Limoges service for twenty-four, that and the magnificent Baccarat crystal candelabras and matching epergne and the heavy lace cloth, which had been wedding presents from one generation to the next going back to her great-grandmother's time. They would

183

be handed down to her daughter, Janet thought . . . and suddenly she found herself about to cry.

Bill walked in just then and saw her wiping at her eyes. "What's wrong?"

"I'm just so incredibly happy, darling."

"And so naturally you're crying." He shook his head and pulled her to him. "Now let's stop all this happy crying or your folks will think I beat you. Better go put some powder on your nose. We have to pick them up at the airport in forty-five minutes."

The morning of her birthday she was awakened by a kiss from Bill.

"That's probably the best early morning birthday gift I'll ever get," she said, reaching out to him.

"No question," he said, placing a breakfast tray over her legs. "I'm not exactly what you call a great chef, but accept the thought. It's better than the eggs, I assure you."

"Oh, Bill, you're a fraud. I'll never tell, but you're more sentimental than I am."

"No, birthday girl, you get the Nobel Prize for that . . ."

At exactly eleven in the morning the caterer came with her assistants, followed shortly thereafter by the florist and housekeeper. Everything was sailing along smoothly, Janet thought as she put on a pink silk dress and left the apartment to meet Bill, her parents and Effie for lunch.

Bill was late, and while they waited for him they chatted over cocktails in the dimly lit restaurant. This, Janet knew, was a day she would long remember. She had Bill and her family around her, and the evening to come would seal the contentment she felt, would allow her to share it with those who meant most to her.

Bill rushed in, apologizing for being late and explaining he'd been tied up in a conference.

Martha laughed. "Don't apologize, Bill. Your father-in-law certainly doesn't. He's stood me up so often that when he *is* on time I get suspicious."

"I can understand that, mother. Daddy's not a bad-looking old gent," Janet said, giving him a wink.

Her mother gave an exaggerated sigh and put on a look of forbearance. "Well dear, it's the risk a woman takes when she marries a handsome brute like your father, or Bill."

Bill and Dr. Stevens exchanged amused glances. "I suspect the ladies are putting us on," Dr. Stevens said, "not that I don't love every word of it. Now, let's order something to toast the birthday girl."

Bill signaled the sommelier and ordered a bottle of Mumm's.

After they had toasted Janet's health, Dr. Stevens shook his head and looked at Janet fondly, but the humor she saw in his eyes made her wonder what he was up to. "Twenty-two years old already . . . Seems like yesterday I was pacing the floor waiting for you to . . ."

Janet smiled at what she knew was coming.

"James, dear, you weren't pacing." This from her mother.

"I wasn't?"

"No, Janet was three hours old when you came rushing down the hall into my room dressed in your surgical garb."

"You even remember that, do you?"

"I certainly do. You stayed with me for about five minutes, then rushed out to answer a page."

"Is that what I did?"

After so many years together, her parents knew exactly which buttons to push for which response, but it was a game they played with a good-natured seriousness, as if making fun of themselves at the same time they were reaffirming all they had shared over the years.

"Well," Dr. Stevens went on, "here's to my beautiful daughter . . . Happy I'm not late for this occasion."

"Thank you, daddy. Me too."

Effie had been silently taking it all in, but now Dr. Stevens said, "Let's hear something from Effie."

"Oh . . . well, I don't set much store in just being *pretty*. Got to be a real person and Janet's that. Didn't think anybody'd be good enough . . . but you found you a country fair husband." Her pronouncement complete, she sat back and folded her arms, but her face was mottled from the embarrassment of paying a compliment, however sincerely felt.

Bill looked at his watch. It was quarter of two and he

had to get back to the office. He kissed Janet, said his good-bys and was gone.

As they lingered over coffee, Dr. Stevens said, "I agree with Effie—you have quite a fine young man, Janet. I suppose it's the hope of every parent to see his child settled in life. You two have your own special world now. Nothing compared to that, is there? I don't know why I'm asking. All anyone has to do is look at your face."

Janet smiled and looked down at the table. "I didn't know it was that obvious . . . I still have to keep kicking myself to make sure I'm not dreaming."

It was two-thirty when Dr. Stevens motioned to the waiter for the check. "Well, I'd say this is the longest lunch I ever took—"

"It's been good for you, James. Now we'd better let Janet go. I know she has a lot of last-minute things to do before tonight."

Indeed she did. She had to stop at Godiva's for chocolates, then race over to a Madison Avenue gourmet shop to pick up some fancy frilled toothpicks for the hors d'oeuvres and some other odds and ends, and then to her dressmaker on 57th and Fifth Avenue to pick up her gown. By the time she hailed a cab for the ride home she was ready to collapse.

After depositing her purchases with the caterer, she was walking through the living room on her way to take a bath when she saw the roses Bill had sent. "Twenty-two for the love of my life," the card read.

As Kit might say, she'd buy that.

By five she was dressed in her mauve silk gown and waiting nervously for Bill. There wasn't a picture, a pillow out of place, but she walked from room to room and back again, inspecting.

When she heard Bill's key in the latch she ran to him. "Darling, the flowers are lovely. Thank you."

She looked flushed, radiant, and Bill had the feeling there was something somehow different about her, not disturbing but . . . different. But all he said was, "No more so than you. Now, I'd better take a quick shower if I'm going to be ready for my debut as a family host . . .

186

too bad you're all gussied up, we could have taken a shower together."

"Is that a standing invitation?"

"Hey! I'm not touching *that* line!" he answered as she led him by the hand into the bedroom.

His suit, shirt and tie were laid out on the bed, black socks were actually *tucked* inside his shoes.

Once he'd showered and dressed, they stood together surveying the living room. Their turf.

Janet's heart skipped a beat when the bell rang and Bill opened the door on the McNeil family.

Violet was regal in a gray lace dress and pearls. She kissed Bill first, then turned to congratulate Janet. "Happy birthday, dear. You look lovely."

"Thank you. I'm so pleased you're here. And Betsy, darling . . ."

After all the greetings to the McNeil clan, they walked into the living room and settled down with cocktails.

The Stevenses and Effie arrived a few minutes later, Mrs. Stevens wearing a striking emerald green satin dress and Effie the same dress she'd worn to Janet's wedding.

The rest of her guests arrived shortly afterward, and as Janet greeted them she thought it was beginning to look like a fashion parade. Kit was wearing flowing black chiffon, her raven hair swept back into a soft chignon. Carol's pregnancy had given her a lusty glow highlighted by her demure white maternity dress, and Mrs. Weiss, in a rose satin taffeta, wore star rubies for her elegantly coiffed white hair. All this finery set the stage for a very special evening.

Soon there was a buzz of conversation as the drinks and hors d'oeuvres were passed . . . "You look like a combination of the Cheshire cat and the Mona Lisa," Kit told Janet.

"I don't know what I look like," she said with a laugh. "All I know is what I feel—which I guess is what they call wedded bliss. I must be looking really loopy, because my father said practically the same thing to me this afternoon."

"The *miracle* is the way Bill is acting. Like an old professional husband. I'd never have believed it. But the shockeroo is Mama Violet. I could be wrong but I think

187

she really likes you. It goes to show, I guess, don't ever try to second-guess people . . ."

Their conversation was interrupted by Betsy. "Congratulations, Kit. I mean about the twins."

"Thanks," Kit said, instantly extracting a dozen snapshots from her evening purse. She had brought them deliberately, knowing what a yawn it would be once Betsy got started on her own children.

After viewing a few, Betsy lost interest, as if Kit's children were the product of a mere amateur in the motherhood game. "They're very sweet . . . Pardon me, I want to say hello to . . ."

"Be my guest," Kit said under her breath as Betsy drifted away.

When dinner was announced and everyone took their places, Janet sat at one end of the long table, looking from her guests to her husband at the opposite end. It was a sight to be remembered, the two families united, her best friends together . . .

Bill opened the festivities. "This is to my wife, who's made me—I confess—the happiest man in the world." He got up, walked down to Janet and handed her a small box from his pocket.

When Janet took off the wrappings and opened the box she almost fainted. Inside was a ring with a ten-carat square-cut gem. As Bill slipped it on the ring finger of her right hand she glanced at her wide gold wedding band. Of the two rings the band was still the more beautiful—to her, anyway—and the dazzling jeweled ring was but a small part of all Bill had given her.

"You like it?"

She was almost speechless, but managed ". . . I love it . . . you most of all."

Violet was looking distinctly uncomfortable during this exchange, which wasn't lost on Kit. The Queen Mother had been dethroned. Sad woman. Children were just on loan. Enjoy them while you can, she thought.

Harriet's thoughts ran parallel to Kit's at that moment. But what her mother was feeling now was nothing to what Harriet and Gordon were putting up with living in that big house with her, hearing the same complaints from mama over and over. And over. "I didn't shut my eyes last night. Do you think Janet is deliberately keeping Bill away? Sometimes I wonder . . . since he got married . . ." And it went on and on. Harriet knew if it weren't for Janet, Bill wouldn't call even as infrequently as he did . . .

When dessert was cleared away, Janet got up from her chair and faced her guests, her eyes sparkling. "This is just the happiest birthday of my life. And I can't imagine a better time to announce . . . that Mr. and Mrs. McNeil are going to have a baby."

Ignoring the cheers and customary huzzahs, Bill got up, went over to her and kissed her soundly. "You held out on me, lady."

She gave him an arch smile. "Not really . . . only on the announcement. . . ."

And later that night, lying in bed beside her . . . "How long have you known? I mean how far along are you?"

"One month."

"By God, I didn't know I was that good. Must have taken the first time."

"Some man," she said, winked and pulled herself on top of him.

Chapter Fourteen

As the months went by, Bill watched the changes in Janet as though observing a miracle in the making. The more she showed, the prouder he became.

When he arrived home one evening from the office to find her in a maternity dress, he whooped, turned her round and round. "That's the best-looking thing I've ever seen you in."

"You really think so, do you?"

"You bet." He put his hand under the tunic. "Here, let me feel that little guy—"

"It *could* be a girl."

"Maybe . . . but remember my virility . . . just one time and—"

"And aren't you lucky I wasn't that fertile before? It does take two, you know."

"I know, and I also know we're going to celebrate."

"But I cooked—"

"Put it away. I want to show off my son's mother."

When Janet was going into her sixth month, they began looking for a place to live. The apartment was out of the question, but nothing they saw really suited them. Bill was getting quite upset about it but Janet kept trying to appease him, telling him something would be available soon, that it wasn't all that crucial.

On a crisp Sunday in November they drove out to Long Island to spend the day with his family. Janet loved this time of the year, with the trees displaying their fall colors. Living in the country . . . but she knew Bill would never move from the city, so she pushed the thought down, didn't mention it.

As they sat in the living room after lunch and watched the fire glow, her eyes wandered beyond the French doors to the garden, where Gordon and Bill were taking a stroll.

"You look a little sad, Janet," Harriet said.

"No, not really, I was just thinking how beautiful the country is in the fall."

For a moment Harriet remembered the house she had given up to come and live here. "It is lovely, isn't it? By the way, how's your house hunting going?"

"We're having trouble finding something we like."

"Really?" Violet asked, and the wheels in her head started turning. "What are you going to do if you don't find a place soon?"

"I don't know. Make do until——"

"Ridiculous. You can't bring a baby home to Bill's bachelor apartment. One bedroom, one bath . . . that's nonsense with all the space here."

Janet quickly wished the subject had never come up, while Harriet was beginning to wonder if Bill's marriage might give her a reprieve.

"It's sweet of you to offer, mother, but Bill wouldn't like commuting," Janet said, knowing that was only part of the truth.

"Nonsense. He did it before and never complained——"

"Complained about what, mother?" Bill said as he and Gordon came into the room.

"Commuting."

"What are you talking about?"

"I was saying you never minded commuting to the city when you lived here."

"Yes?"

"Well, Janet was telling me what a difficult time you're having finding a place——"

"And?"

"I suggested that you come out here and live. My word, there's enough room for six."

Long pause. "Thank you, mother, we appreciate it . . . but every woman needs her own home——"

"Every woman, Bill?" Harriet's tone was light but she gave him a sharp look.

"Well, I guess it's different with you——"

"Yes, sure, I know what you mean. Oh, the joy of being so free, with no family to tie one down."

He wished he could crawl into a hole. Harriet had saved his life and now, thanks to him, she was in a tight spot. A spot called mother . . .

"Tell you what. This summer we'll bring the baby out and stay so you and Gordon can take a long vacation."

"You've got it all arranged. How nice. But I suggest you check with Janet first, dear brother . . ."

He looked to Janet for her reaction.

"Yes, it sounds . . . just fine," she said slowly, knowing the conflict Bill was feeling. Not to mention herself . . .

Violet's eyes became extra bright.

"This is wonderful news . . . to have my son's baby right in this house . . . that is, yours and his, Janet . . . Well, now that that's settled, let's all go in to dinner."

Bill hounded every real estate office in the city with new determination, but the houses they saw were either too old and run-down or too new and boxy, with rooms the size of telephone booths. The one he did like wasn't for sale, but it could be leased for six months. He didn't, though, much like the notion of moving around, so that was out. He wanted a permanent place. His place.

And now it was getting down to post time, so to speak. It was February and Janet was in the middle of her eighth month.

"I don't know what to do, honey—"

"Suppose we buy that one on West Ninety-fifth—"

"I hate it."

"But if we remodel it could be—"

"A crummy old house remodeled. It's dark, no view . . . nothing. Just a lot of money down the drain."

"Then I guess the only thing to do is stay here until something comes up."

Lousy way to bring home a new baby, he thought. The nursery furniture couldn't be delivered because they had nowhere to put it. And the layette was stacked in its original boxes . . . "How can we manage with a nurse and all?"

"The nurse will be here only two weeks and she can sleep in the living room."

192

"And where will the baby sleep, in the bathroom?"

Janet laughed. It seemed he was taking it much more seriously than she was.

"What's so funny?"

"You. The baby will sleep in the living room until the nurse leaves, then we'll move the bassinet into the bedroom and . . ."

Not much of a solution, Bill thought. But . . .

Janet looked at the clock on the nightstand. It was five in the morning and the pains had been coming at ten-minute intervals since three-thirty. She shook Bill gently awake.

"Darling . . . I think it's time—"

He bolted up in bed. "You mean it's started?"

Jumping out of bed, he started to dress in a rush, his hands fumbling at the buttons on his shirt.

Janet lay back watching, amused. Bill was having labor pains.

He groped in the closet for her fur coat. "*Okay*, let's go—"

"Not until you kiss me."

He gave her a quick, apprehensive kiss, then helped her out of bed.

"Bill, let's have a cup of coffee before we go."

His mouth fell open. "Are you having labor pains or were you just kidding?"

"I am and I wasn't, but it's not that bad—"

"Then get into this coat right now or I'll have a nervous breakdown."

He called downstairs to have his car brought around.

"Okay. Is there anything we forgot?" he said, glancing nervously around the room.

"Yes, call my mother and *yours*."

"No . . . not my mother—"

"I promised. She wants to be at the hospital when the baby's—"

"I'll call her later."

"No, Bill. I want you to let her know now. I promised."

"Okay, when I get to the hospital."

Janet's cheerfulness did nothing to set aside his fears,

and not even Janet's mother was able to calm him when she joined him at the hospital. Mrs. Stevens had been staying at the Plaza Hotel for the last two weeks, coming to their apartment every day to relieve Janet of cooking and household chores. Now she kept reassuring him that Janet was just fine. She'd gone through her pregnancy with a minimum of discomfort and that was the best sign of all.

It still didn't help and he kept right on pacing the corridor.

Violet made her entrance at ten, with Harriet and Gordon. Bill found his mother's presence was only an irritation. Hardly a relief.

"Now, son, you've *got* to calm down. Having a baby is the most natural thing in the world. I went through four births. Of course, yours was the most—"

Bill was walking away down the hall before she could finish. He didn't want to be reminded now of all times how much she'd suffered bringing him into the world. Not, for God's sake, *this* morning.

He went into Janet's room for the umpteenth time and held her hand. "You all right, darling?"

Although the pains were coming more frequently, she managed a thin smile.

"Fine, dear . . . fine . . ."

The nurse spared him the ordeal of seeing Janet during the worst of her contractions by asking him to leave.

At eleven o'clock the doctor came out of Janet's room and told Bill she was ready to be taken to delivery.

"Is everything all right?"

"Everything is going along smoothly. A first baby for someone as small as your wife can be difficult, but she doesn't appear to be having any problems at all."

He walked alongside Janet as she was wheeled down the hall, and when they reached the wide surgery doors he bent down and kissed her. With the doors swinging closed behind her, he stood praying everything would go all right. He couldn't manage a smile when Martha Stevens took his hand and gave it a sympathetic squeeze.

Violet sat twisting her handkerchief and remembering how she had suffered at Bill's birth. Six hours for a first child was *nothing* compared to the twenty it had taken to bring Bill into the world . . . Well, Janet was a young girl . . . midwestern stock . . . and today's methods were different . . .

At twelve-thirty the doctor came out, looked at Bill, then broke into a smile. "Congratulations. You're the father of a seven-pound baby girl."

"A girl?" But the disappointment was short-lived in the excitement of the moment.

"And Janet?"

"Like a pro . . . about the best patient I ever had."

When he was finally allowed to see Janet, he stood at the side of her bed, holding her hand and looking at her as though she were somehow sainted.

She looked at him, realizing he had gone through an ordeal almost as great as hers.

"It really wasn't all *that* bad, darling. Look what we've got for our few labor pains. Did you *see* her? Isn't she adorable?"

That adorable little baby actually looked like a red lobster. "She's just . . . beautiful."

Janet smiled, knowing he had never seen a newborn baby before and that he was disappointed at not having a son. But he'd feel differently in a few days.

"Darling, will you call Kit?"

He didn't think he was up to doing *anything* right now, but he reached for the phone by her bed and dialed.

Kit let out a war whoop. "Janet got her little girl." He glanced at Janet as he answered Kit's barrage of questions. Odd, he thought. Janet had never said anything to him about wanting a girl. They were so sure it would be . . . oh, well.

When he went out into the corridor to give Mrs. Stevens a moment with Janet, his mother pulled him aside and spoke to him in a confidential tone. "Bill, I've given this a lot of thought. Since you're my only son I think it's appropriate that family names be handed down to your children. If you'd had a boy it would have been Jason, but since it's a girl, why not Violet? I'd be *so* proud . . ."

Bill flinched, annoyed at her intrusion and yet also realizing that *she* thought she'd just offered him some sort of honor . . . But one thing was for sure. If there was one name he could not stand it was "Violet." "Mother, we never discussed girls' names . . . and besides, I'm afraid it would probably hurt Janet's mother's feelings. I'll talk to Janet about this." And that he did immediately.

As soon as Mrs. Stevens had left Janet's room he went in and sat at her bedside. "Sweetheart, since we never considered having anything but a boy . . . don't misunderstand, I couldn't be more pleased, but we never thought about a girl's name."

"You're right, dear, but I did, just in case."

"Oh? Well . . .?"

"If it's okay with you, I'd love to name her after my grandmother."

"That's who *you* were named after. You suggesting Janet Junior?"

She laughed. "No, Bill. My grandmother had more than one name. Janet seemed more appropriate for Wichita, Kansas. But her real name was Nicole Jeanette Antoinette Buchart."

"You mean you're going to put all that on one little helpless baby?"

"No, of course not. Just Nicole. Would you like that?"

Nicole . . . Would they call her Nikki . . . or Nicky . . . or Nick? No, he'd insist on Nicole. No nicknames. Nicole McNeil, Nicole McNeil . . . "I think it's beautiful, honey."

"You're not just saying that—?"

"No, I love it. And you too, mother of Nicole McNeil."

Four days later, when he drove his wife and daughter home from the hospital, the baby had changed so much he couldn't quite believe it. She *was* adorable, Nicole McNeil, and any disappointment had long since evaporated.

When they arrived at the apartment the nurse was waiting and took charge immediately, but Janet was so eager to take over that the woman was paid for her two weeks and let go after a few days.

Motherhood, as the song said, was what came naturally to Janet, but fatherhood kept Bill in a state of high anxiety. When the bassinet was brought into the bedroom it was put on his side of the king-sized bed. He'd insisted.

196

He slept hardly at all, listening to the baby's breathing, and he often woke with a start and got out of bed to check that the baby's covers were in place.

He became convinced that Dr. Spock was a sadist. Whoever heard of feeding a child on schedule—two, four and six? It hurt him to hear those hungry cries. His sisters had breast-fed their children on demand, but Janet was firm about following the pediatrician's instructions. She believed with Spock that even babies had to begin to learn that the world wasn't altogether their oyster. They had to learn to begin to take some frustrations to grow up into healthy human beings. You could coddle and smother to death in the name of love but out of self-indulgence. Like Violet with Bill . . .

One night Bill was so upset he held Nicole consolingly, pacing the floor with her in his arms and rocking her.

"To hell with the rules, this is cruelty." Holding her close, very close. With the baby in his arms, he went to the kitchen and heated the bottle. He was getting really good at this, he thought. Had his own father had a chance to do this? No, probably not, everything considered.

As the baby sucked contentedly, he brought her back to the bedroom and sat in the chair with her as she drained the two ounces. He burped her, then watched as she fell asleep in the crook of his arm. He put her down carefully, then got into bed.

Janet watched him closely. This was the man who had once rejected the idea of having a child? He'd certainly reversed his tracks. He phoned two or three times a day to see if everything was "going all right," came home early from the office in time to see the baby have her six-o'clock feeding. He chickened out on bathing her, afraid she would be too slippery with soap suds to handle, but stood by and watched as Janet took over. Watched, or supervised?

Chapter Fifteen

By the time Nicole was six weeks old, Bill was a more relaxed father. But what worried him now was the way they were living. Janet's days were full from early morning to evening and she was doing the best she could in their cramped quarters, but there was no denying that the apartment was beginning to look like a Chinese laundry. The bathroom was cluttered with diapers, and the bathinette left almost no room to turn around in. Clothing was strewn over the bathroom towel bars and over the three collapsible wooden racks that stood in the dining room in front of the sliding doors. He was happy that Janet wasn't complaining, of course. But even so, this couldn't go on much longer, and going to his mother's for the summer was no solution. It wasn't even a reprieve, except for Harriet and Gordon.

Maybe they should think of going into a larger apartment . . . but that was a hell of a way to raise a child, he thought, recalling the freedom—he'd blanked out for the time being the distinct *lack* of freedom—of being raised in a large house. Well, there had to be something in this big city for them. Maybe Janet was right, if they bought the townhouse and remodeled it, it might not be too bad. True, it was narrow, dark, squeezed in between two big apartment houses. But they might be able to do something with it, and it had a little garden in the back . . .

He called the agent and, to his dismay, was told the house had just been sold.

A few days later Janet received a phone call from Kit.

After comparing notes on motherhood, Kit said, "I saw a house that I think you'd love, Janet."

"Where?"

"Not far from me."

"Oh, God, Kit, that would be terrific, except Bill would never move out of the city—"

"Tough. He has more to think about now than just himself."

"But I don't want him to be unhappy. He has to be considered too."

"I know, you're still so grateful because he indulged you *once*. Remember, dear, that baby is his too, you know."

Janet laughed. "If only you knew. Sometimes I wonder if he remembers I'm the mother. You should see him with Nicole."

"Well, talk to him anyway. The house is fabulous."

Knowing how he felt about moving to suburbia, Janet decided not to make an issue of it. She brought it up casually, without reference to Kit. The answer, as predicted, was an unequivocal *no*.

When Kit called back a few days later, she asked Janet if she'd spoken to Bill. Not wanting Kit to make him the villain again, she answered, "We've both decided to wait. Something's bound to come on the market . . . besides, lots of well-adjusted children grow up in Manhattan—"

"Okay, good luck. Hope you find the house of your dreams . . . or should I say, Bill's."

Bill was going over a problem with his chief engineer when his office intercom buzzed.

He picked up the phone. "Yes, Bonnie?"

"Mrs. Weiss is on the phone," his secretary reported.

That's all he needed . . . "Okay, put her on." Kit rarely phoned him at the office unless it was to bawl him out. And he was right.

"Bill, I'm mixing in where angels ought to fear to tread, but I think you're a selfish twerp."

"Now wait a minute, Kit—"

"No, you wait. Your apartment needs a sign saying 'gypsy fortune telling.' "

"That's not my fault. You know I've been looking. Can I help it if we can't find a place—?"

"Yes."

He shook his head angrily. "There's a housing shortage, in case you hadn't heard. Besides, Janet's not complaining."

"Of course not. Which is her problem. She doesn't have the heart to ask you to move to the country because you're so mad about the Rockettes and Rockefeller Center, and you might have to miss going to your club to play squash on Thursday nights—"

"I haven't played squash for—"

Gotcha, she thought when he broke off. "Well, there's a place not far from us. Be a sport, sport, and buy it. Not only for Janet but for your Nicole, who you adore so much, *and* for yourself—"

"You know, Kit? I agree, this isn't any of your business."

"Yes and no. Let me remind you, there were many times *you* made your business mine. So I figure if *I* don't tell you, no one will."

"Thanks a lot. You're a real pal. But don't worry, we'll find a place *here*."

She slammed down the phone so hard he jerked the receiver away from his ear.

As he turned to his engineering problems his mind kept running over the conversation with Kit. Maybe she was right. When you had a family you were supposed to give up things . . . the family came first . . . a child should be raised in the country . . . He found himself calling Kit back.

". . . Where did you say that house was?"

"About a mile from us. It's really lovely."

When he arrived home that night and saw the condition of the apartment he became even more determined to get them into a decent-sized house. He sat in the kitchen, watching Janet prepare dinner. "Darling . . . ?"

"Yes," Janet said, turning over the steak in the broiler.

"I've been thinking about it, and I've decided we should buy in the country after all."

Janet wasn't sure she'd heard right, but when she looked at his face she threw her arms around him. "You sure?"

"I'm sure."

200

"Now I can tell you . . . Kit said there was a house not far from them—"

"Really? Kit told you that? So it must be in Westchester?"

"Yes. Would you like to see it?"

"Okay, why not?"

"Oh, Bill, thank you."

She called Kit immediately. ". . . I didn't say a word, I swear. It was all *his* idea."

"Well, I'll be damned. That's one thing about our Bill. When he comes to a decision, he takes action. Yes, sir, Bill's a man of action . . ." Providing the nudge was hard enough and in the right place, she added silently.

"Can you believe it? We'll be neighbors!"

"You know how much I'd love that. But maybe you won't like the house."

"If you do, I will. Can we see it tomorrow?"

"It's vacant, so you probably can. I'll call the agent. And since you'll be here, stay for dinner. I'll call in the morning and give you all the information."

With Nicole bundled up, they drove to Westchester in relative silence. Janet's discomfort now bordered on guilt.

When they stopped in the driveway, Bill helped Janet out and took Nicole. Kit had been waiting for them. Today she wasn't one of his favorite people. If she hadn't gotten into the act . . .

As glowing as Kit's description had been, it hadn't done the house justice. Before entering the rambling, ten-year-old house, Janet stood looking at the magnificent fieldstone facade and the heavy shake roof. When the double oak front doors were opened she found herself standing in a square stone foyer that led to a large octagon-shaped living room. The garden could be seen from every window. There was so little partitioning that one room seemed to flow into the next, giving the house a sense of openness.

They walked through the library, exclaiming over the ebony bookcases on either side of the fireplace, and then down the long loggia separating the main part of the house from the bedrooms. The master suite was enormous, with sliding doors opening to a terrace. There were double marble washbasins in the huge bathroom, two dressing rooms, and an adjacent sitting room. The other four bedrooms were not as large but they were just as bright and airy. But the pièce de résistance was the kitchen. It was Janet's dream of what a kitchen should be. There were oak cabinets, red brick tile floors, terra-cotta drainboards, built-in stainless steel ovens, a table-top stove with six burners . . . it was a cook's joy. Imagine the things she could create. And the laundry had every built-in convenience. It was overwhelming.

They went back to the living room and looked out of the windows. Beyond was the pool. It was early spring and the trees had blossomed into a profusion of delicately colored flowers and the daffodils and iris were altogether a beautiful sight to behold. So far Bill had only wandered about, showing little enthusiasm. Should she hope? What was he thinking? Yes or no . . .

"You're sure you want this house," he asked tonelessly, "or should we keep looking?"

"Not unless you want to . . ."

"Well, it's really for you, Janet . . . A house is a woman's domain—"

"Oh, Bill, I do adore it, darling—"

"Then it's yours."

She looked at Kit, then at Bill and the child in his arms. She thought of how much he had given her . . . "Thank you, darling, this house means so much to me, but are you sure—?"

"I'm *sure*." His smile was a little thin, but she felt reassured . . . she *needed* to . . . knowing how hard a decision it was to give up Manhattan . . .

Three weeks later the William McNeils were living in Westchester with only the furniture from Bill's apartment. It was just enough to furnish the den. The king-sized bed that had seemed so enormous in their apartment looked like a postage stamp in the master bedroom. They agreed that Nicole would sleep with them until the nursery was complete, but even the clutter of things that had crowded them out of their apartment looked lost in the huge bedroom. Janet urged the decorator to *please* have the draperies hung, and they were installed just in the nick of time.

Janet's mother and Effie arrived to help Janet with the preparations for Bill's birthday celebration, and Dr. Stevens joined them three days later.

Effie took over the kitchen immediately, and soon the house was permeated with smells so familiar to Janet. Effie baked and decorated Bill's birthday cake, made her special bean casserole with brown sugar, ham with cloves and pineapple, molded salad, corn muffins and peach cobbler. The only thing that annoyed her was the extra help Janet insisted was necessary for the large gathering they were expecting for Bill's birthday. "Faddle, they only get in the way."

The gathering of the clan was on a Sunday. Bill's family arrived en masse, with all the children. The senior Weisses drove to Westchester with Charles, Carol and their son Brett, now a year old. And of course Kit, Nat and the twins were there.

They spent the afternoon outside, enjoying the clear, warm June day.

Betsy called everyone's attention to her son Gary, the Olympic candidate from Brookline, as he executed a perfect dive into the pool. Alice kept out of the sun because it caused skin cancer and wrinkles, so she said.

Harriet and Gordon had brought their putters and were out on the lawn practicing. Of all the McNeils, only Violet seemed subdued. As she sat looking at the house her son had bought for Janet, she couldn't help remembering that Janet had promised to spend the summer with her on Long Island . . .

Nat and his father played gin rummy while Martha and James Stevens chatted with Mrs. Weiss, agreeing that grandchildren were almost more rewarding than children as they watched Bill showing off his daughter. Children were clearly the focus of everyone's attention today. Charles and Carol took turns teaching Brett how to swim and Kit was keeping a close eye on the twins, who were into everything.

Janet took snapshots and kept the motion picture camera going. This day would be recorded for Nicole's grandmothers, aunts and uncles, cousins and best friends . . .

They ate dinner on the veranda after the younger children were fed and put down for naps, but when the birthday cake came Bill got up, went to the nursery and picked up a sleepy Nicole.

While everyone sang "Happy Birthday" he blew out the candles, took a bit of frosting and touched it to Nicole's lips. Nicole was duly appreciative, crying for more.

What a day this had been, Janet thought as she snapped a picture. A day that seemed to end too soon.

Bill took Harriet aside as the party began to leave. "I want you and Gordon to take your holiday, go away for a few months . . . mother's going to stay with us—"

"You don't have to do that, Bill. Janet will go nuts with her around every day."

"It was her idea . . . and I agreed."

"We'll see."

At first Violet refused when Janet extended the invitation for her to stay the summer. She reminded Janet of what Bill had said, that no house could tolerate more than one mistress, and her feelings had been very hurt at the time.

"I'm sorry about that, mother," Bill said, taking up the lance for Janet. "But you forget you wanted us to come and *live* with you. This is different."

"How so?" she answered, pursing her lips.

"This will be a vacation for you."

"Well, you also said you'd come to my place for the summer."

He looked up at the ceiling. "Now that we've bought the house, there's no need for your generous offer. And there's too much work to be done on the house to take off for the summer."

"Indeed. Well, Janet's a very lucky young woman. You've been a very . . . giving husband for her."

Strange, Bill thought, nothing was good enough for her daughters. Their whims were indulged by their husbands. But it was a little different for Janet, even though his mother knew as well as he that he wouldn't even be talking to her now if Janet hadn't intervened that day he'd announced his intention to marry.

"You're very fortunate to have a daughter-in-law like Janet. What am I supposed to do, deny my wife and my child the things I'm capable of giving them?"

"Bill, I simply do not understand why you persist in debating everything I say."

Oh, for God's sake. If it weren't that he knew how badly Harriet needed to get away from mama, he'd call the whole thing off. "I'm sorry, mother. I didn't mean to do that . . . Now, have your things ready and I'll pick you up next Saturday."

"I don't know, Bill. How will Betsy and Alice feel about my spending such a long time with you when they've asked . . . and I never like leaving my home . . ."

They'll be thrilled to get off the hook, they only asked out of duty, he thought . . . "I'll call and explain how much we'd like you to enjoy Nicole. They'll understand, mother. I guarantee you."

"And you, Janet?"

Well, finally . . . "I'm looking forward to it, mother."

"Well . . . if you really insist—"

"We do."

Harriet was indeed grateful that the yoke was being lifted, but she knew Janet was in for a less than tranquil summer . . .

Her prophecy, unfortunately, more than proved out. Violet found fault with *everything* . . . the bed was too hard so she sent for her own and had Janet's stored. The food was too hot, too cold, too soggy, too lumpy. There were never enough towels in her bathroom and the air conditioning gave her a *dreadful* headache and dried up her sinuses. She couldn't understand feeding a baby canned vegetables . . . "In my time it would have been unthought of . . ."

The instant Nicole cried she picked her up and rocked her (like mother like son?), which caused Nicole to expect to be held every time she let out a whimper. "There, there, grandmother's little darling . . ."

In the evening she monopolized Bill's time with her reminiscences. "Oh, yes, things were so different then. I remember when . . ."

205

Bill tuned her out. Or tried. Janet had less luck . . . with her all day long.

She also chastised the housekeeper, Sarah, for not cleaning under the sofa and in the *corners* . . . Sarah finally told Janet, "I'm sorry, Mrs. McNeil, but I've taken as much as I intend to."

Janet was approaching that point too. But she couldn't walk away as Sarah could, nor did she want to complain to Bill and increase his obvious irritation with his mother. All she could do was keep her frustration to herself and pray for the summer to be over.

By the time September came, Janet had lost ten pounds and Bill was in a knot. Harriet had never been so welcome as when she returned from her holiday to pick up Violet and go back to the house on Long Island.

The moment Violet said good-by, Bill shut the front door and leaned hard against it. Silence, peace, as though a presence had been exorcized, the house depossessed.

Even Sarah came back.

Months slipped away. Once again the landscape changed. It was autumn. The falling leaves of red and gold covered the earth. The air was crisp with the season's change.

And then it was time to go to Violet's home for Thanksgiving. For the first time in Bill's life he knew what Thanksgiving meant. It was impossible to believe that only a little over two years ago he had sat here in this selfsame place, pining away for Janet and not even fantasizing that a Nicole McNeil might even exist. How much had happened in that short span of time . . . It was, indeed, a rhetorical point.

In December the McNeils shopped together for gifts, the lists becoming longer and longer . . .

Alice's son Gerald had married a girl from Ann Arbor, Michigan. And Betsy's daughter was announcing her engagement on Christmas Day. Betsy was annoyed with brother Bill and sister-in-law Janet when they told her they'd have to miss this momentous announcement, but

206

by this time Bill was a bit weary of his family. He was taking Janet and Nicole to Kansas for the Christmas holiday.

A fir tree laden with ornaments and tinsel stood in the corner of the large living room, just as it had for Christmas at the Stevenses for as long as Janet could remember. Ten-month-old Nicole sat in her father's lap on the carpeted floor and looked dazzled by the ornaments and blinking lights.

Her white organdy dress made her round cheeks glow. Her eyes were the color of blue star sapphires and her hair, just enough now to be tied up with a thin red velvet ribbon, promised to be the same color as Janet's. She jabbered inarticulate things to her father, waving her hands and kicking her legs excitedly.

Janet snuck up and took a picture, then joined them on the sofa. Taking Bill's free arm, she snuggled close to him. "Do you know, two Christmases ago I cried an ocean of tears because I missed you so. Then last Christmas I had you. And look what I have *this* Christmas."

"Funny, I was thinking the same thing this morning."

By two o'clock on the day before Christmas the house was filled with family and friends. Presents lay heavily stacked under the tree. It was a time for eggnog and mulled wine, for a lavish dinner of orange duck, mince pies and hard sauce, chestnut dressing and plum pudding. A time for Christmas carols, and a time for love.

The whole week passed in such simple pleasures, and then it was New Year's.

Cheers and laughter, kisses and tears, a new year of promises was welcomed in, a year that could hardly surpass the previous one but that held every sign of being a very good one indeed for the William McNeils.

Except signs could be deceptive—as the ancient gods had taught even the rulers of the earth.

Chapter Sixteen

When they returned from Kansas on January 3rd, Harriet called.

"Bill, mother's rather ill."

Bill couldn't quite take it in. He'd spoken to Violet at Christmas and early on New Year's Eve. She'd sneezed a bit and coughed slightly, but when he'd questioned her she assured him it was a simple cold.

Yet Harriet's voice sounded strangely ominous. "Don't you think I should have been told, Harriet?"

"I didn't want to spoil your holiday . . . she's been taken to Mt. Sinai Hospital—"

"How long has she been there?"

"Since yesterday."

"What's wrong with her?"

"Well, as you know, she had a cold during the holidays and it seems to have worsened. This morning the doctor found she has a little fluid in her right lung. We're all at the hospital—"

All . . . the whole family? "I'll be there as soon as I can." He hung up, unable to control his trembling hands.

Janet looked at him. His face was colorless.

"What's wrong, Bill?"

"My mother's in the hospital. I'm going into the city. Chances are I'll stay."

"I'm going with you."

"What about Nicole?"

"She can go to Kit's. I'll send her over with Sarah."

While Bill packed his suitcase Janet called Kit. She was terribly sorry to hear the news, and of course Nicole could stay as long as need be.

Bill's sisters, their husbands and children were there when Bill and Janet arrived at the hospital.

"Mother's been asking for you, Bill," Harriet told him.

He followed her down the hall and she waited outside while he went into his mother's room. He was shocked to see his mother lying so still. The shallow breaths she took under the oxygen mask seemed to come much too slowly. He observed the intravenous in her arm, the distended blue veins in her almost fleshless hands, the white hair that lay limp on the pillow. He was grateful that she was asleep so she could not see the tears in his eyes. Quietly, he moved the chair close to her bed. Watching her at this moment, all the antagonism, the anger . . . whatever had happened between them through the years seemed of no importance. When his mother was well and able to defend herself he could challenge her, but this was the first time she'd ever been in a hospital, and somehow he was more shaken than he dared admit . . .

It seemed forever until Violet opened her eyes. She looked happy to see him sitting at her bedside . . . Dear me, he looked like a little boy sitting there . . . he would always be that to her, anyway . . . she would simply never get used to the idea of him being a husband and father . . . the one regret she had was all those years he'd spent away from home, especially those childhood years away at military school . . . dear Jason, you thought you knew best but I should have been stronger and not let you take my child away . . . of all of my children, he was the dearest to me, but I forgive you, dearest Jason . . .

Shakily she removed the mask, and as she did so Bill said, "I don't think you should, mother . . ."

She smiled. "It's all right . . . well, did you have a nice holiday, darling?"

Swallowing hard, he answered, "Yes . . . How are you feeling?"

"Quite well . . . really . . . I missed you so . . ."

"I would have been here sooner if I'd known you were ill."

She reached out and he grasped her hand between his and held it tight. How well he remembered the times when those same hands had been young, and strong . . . had held him close to her as she sang him back to sleep

209

after those childhood nightmares that had made him cry out in the night. Lord, he remembered, though he couldn't have been more than four and five . . .

The door opened slowly and the nurse came in. "You must be Mr. McNeil. Your mother has described you well, in fact she's spoken of little else but you." Looking at Violet, the nurse said, "Now, it's time to get you ready for a little back rub, and let's please put on the mask . . . you'll have plenty of time to visit later."

Bill stood, looked at his mother for a long, silent moment. "I'll be right outside, mother."

It was eight in the evening when the family returned to their rooms at the Waldorf to freshen up before dinner. Bill, though, decided he'd just use room service. Dinner was a silent affair. Janet had tried very hard to reassure him that his mother wasn't so critically ill and that, in fact, the family all seemed to think that she was much improved since yesterday. He nodded, but something down deep kept nudging him that it wasn't true . . . maybe it was only his own fears, his guilt . . .

Janet held his hand in the dark that night, and he fell asleep quickly. But at two he woke up with a pounding headache. Quietly he got out of bed, went into the living room and poured himself a drink. By God, he'd been some great son, hadn't he? Always so impatient with her, always taking everything she said literally . . . Damn it, she'd seemed so vulnerable today . . . Well, one thing he had made up his mind about. When she got well he was going to be different, stop acting like a spoiled child. Treat her like the lady she was . . .

The week dragged on, the waiting became unbearable. Watching his mother deteriorate left Bill feeling totally helpless, but he persisted in telling himself that she was going to survive.

Bill was awakened from a deep exhausted sleep by the sound of the telephone. He looked at his watch. Five in the morning. He looked at the receiver. Pulse racing, hand trembling, he picked it up. "Yes . . . ?"

"Mr. McNeil, this is Dr. Goldberg. I think that you

210

should come to the hospital. Your mother is asking for you."

There wasn't any need to question the doctor. "I'll be there immediately."

Janet sat up in bed and watched as Bill began to dress, fumbled with the buttons on his shirt. "Darling, who was that?"

"The hospital called."

"I'm going with you—"

"No, I think it would be better if I went alone."

She lay back. There were moments, she knew, that no matter how close they were couldn't be shared. Some things had to be done alone.

He almost ran down the hall to Harriet, who stood in front of Violet's room. "I'm glad you're here, Harriet . . ." He started to open Violet's door when Harriet said, "Don't go in, Bill." There was a pounding in his heart. From the look on Harriet's face he knew he was too late. Always too late . . . Barely able to form the words, he said, "What happened?"

"Her heart simply gave out."

He gave way to it then . . . the guilt, the recrimination.

"Don't beat on yourself, Bill . . . you loved her and she knew you did—"

"No, I'm afraid I was selfish . . . she was an old lady, but she was my mother and I didn't even get to tell her I loved her. Which is hardly her fault . . ."

For all her own grief, Harriet stood like a fortress. Death always, she knew, evoked purifying feelings of remorse, anguish. Making the dead sacred, saintly and pure of heart, the living suddenly became the offenders, the evildoers, guilty for all the sins of omission. It always seemed to come down to what we should have done, what we could have done . . . what we didn't do . . . if only we could relive it, it would all be different . . . But not so, Harriet thought, because the living never think about the ending. It's easier to condemn oneself after . . .

Harriet, Gordon and Bill made the funeral arrangements. There was little to do, inasmuch as Violet's affairs

211

were well in order. It was her wish that only her family should see her put to rest near her beloved husband.

The small group of black-clad mourners stood in a gentle snowdrift and saw the casket lowered into the ground. Bill especially thought how as long as she had been here they were a family ... she was the mortar that held them together. Now they would go their separate ways, seeing one another only on special occasions ... there'd be no more holidays on Long Island bringing together the McNeil clan ...

They left the cemetery, each with his and her own special memories ... the embraces of childhood which mama had given them ... a soothing kiss after a skinned knee ... a smile when a splinter was painfully removed ... the echoes of a tearful good-by. A train whistle, the waving of a handkerchief in the hand of a mother watching her only son depart for school ... a silhouette in black standing so long ago in this same cemetery, witnessing what all widows must ... a lonely lady, even in the midst of her children. The circle of life ... today the world stood still, but tomorrow the wheels would start to turn again, and with time the painful memories would at least fade. ...

Bill felt no relief until he went back to Kit's, and held his child in his arms. She was his confirmation of life. Right now he badly needed it.

That night Janet tried to comfort him, holding him like a child until he fell asleep.

Nothing lasts forever, Janet thought wryly, realizing that her thought was hardly original. But how true ... Not happiness, not grief. Somehow, though, there was that blessed in-between time that made forgetting easier. Thank God.

March was a very special month. Janet and Bill celebrated their second anniversary, and Nicole became one year old. Her birthday party was for only a few— Harriet and Gordon, Kit, Nat and the twins, Janet's mother, father and of course Effie, who baked the same kind of cake she'd made for Bill the year before. Nicole sat in her highchair near her father, banging on the metal tray with a spoon. Bill wiped the frosting from her face as

212

she reached out her arms to him. He could have sworn she said "dada" as he took her on his lap. A brilliant girl, no question.

"Janet, I think she's talking . . . say 'daddy,' Nicole."

She said some inarticulate thing that Bill, of course, insisted was "daddy."

"Did you hear that?"

"Yes," Janet said, snapping a picture of Nicole putting the spoon up to Bill's mouth. Bill put a tiny piece of cake in her mouth and she cooed appropriately.

Tonight was Bill's turn . . . He undressed her, changed her diaper, washed her hands.

"You're my princess, you know that, don't you? Say 'daddy.' " But she yawned, closed her eyes and in a moment was fast asleep. A brilliant girl, no question. . . .

The days fled, replacing one another like leaves in a gentle wind, like turning pages in the calendar. . . . It was June. That too was a special month. Bill became an old man of twenty-eight. . . .

The first week in November they went up to Maine. If possible this year was better than the first.

Nicole was twenty months old and getting increasingly marvelous. No question. She took her first step to her father's outstretched arms, and the first word she said *was* "dada." A brilliant girl, no question. Not to mention smart.

She fell in love with their new Irish setter, Duffy, and wouldn't go to bed unless he slept in her room. The best of all was the snowman her father made, but the supreme moment in her young life was when he hitched the gelding to the sleigh and they drove into the village.

Bill was openly preening when he held Nicole and led Janet into the general store. "You remember my wife?" he said to Mr. Swanson.

"Yup, pleased to see you again, Mrs. McNeil, and this is the young one. Pretty little thing. Anything I can help you with, don't hesitate."

Janet bought six yards of calico in various colors for pinafores which she would sew this winter. As she touched the fabric, her mind shifted to another place, another day . . . a lonely Sunday afternoon, and then Orchard Street. The country store's display of two magnificent patchwork quilts completed the memory, bringing her mind back to the store just beyond Fayge's . . . dearest Fayge . . . pastel satin comforters . . . white goosedown feathers floating about in back of a dimly lit room . . . Quickly she left the past as Bill said, "Don't you think it would be a good idea to buy these sweaters for Christmas gifts?"

Janet looked at the handmade cable-stitched sweaters. "I think that's a fine idea."

They purchased those and a jug of molasses for Effie . . .

After Nicole had been put to bed they sat by the fire, remembering as they looked at the dancing flames how tempestuously they had made love their first time here. But none was better than what they had known the previous night.

Life, time was like legerdemain, Janet thought. Now you see it, now you don't. The magical week was over, it was time to go home again. Magical . . . yes, that seemed the word for it . . . Only last month Kit had told her how amazing she found their marriage . . .

"You know, you two are almost too good to be true. Especially after your, shall we say, stormy courtship. Now you never argue—hell, I don't even detect a little old frown, never mind an occasional *spat* . . . I don't know whether to congratulate you or warn you that maybe you're living a bit of a fantasy. The couple that *never* fights together . . . All right, enough from Kit the Cassandra . . ."

Fantasy? Well, if that's what this was, she didn't want to wake up to reality. Not now, not ever, Janet thought determinedly.

A month later and it was time for another Christmas in Kansas, and this year Nicole was old enough to be caught up in the excitement of Christmas Eve.

Her eyes were bigger and bigger as she watched her grandfather set up the electric trains he had bought her, complete with overalls, red handkerchiefs and caps for the three of them.

Nicole took over as engineer, but when she switched the generator off, making the trains come abruptly to a

214

halt, she was frustrated. "Daddy, make the train go, daddy."

Bill turned the generator on and explained they wouldn't work if she kept playing with the switch—and somehow managed to catch her just in time as she reached out to test this new fact.

Janet was ready with her camera, and thought of the news she would tell him later on. He was going to be a father again. . . .

She told him as she lay in his arms that night. He immediately sat up and turned on the light. "Impossible."

"Evidently not. It must have happened last month in Maine."

"But your diaphragm?"

"That's what *I* asked. According to my doctor it must have tipped over, or slipped or something."

"You're kidding. I mean—"

"I mean I don't know what happened, but I *do* know I'm pregnant."

"Wow! I sure married one fertile lady."

"I guess you did. Between your virility and my fertility . . ."

"What a present . . . listen, Janet, I'm telling you now, it had better be a boy or else."

"Or else, what?"

"Well, I'm just warning you, it better be. I already have one perfect daughter, and that's a tough act to follow."

"Okay, if you're that set on—"

"Stop talking and turn off the light."

"It's on your side."

"Oh . . ." And the light went off and the room was silent, but their lovemaking was more eloquent than any words might have been in celebration of the occasion.

In August Janet gave Bill exactly what he'd demanded the previous Christmas—she was delivered of a baby boy weighing just under nine pounds.

Bill preened like a male peacock, even handing out cigars to complete strangers in the hospital corridor. And when Janet suggested naming the child after his father, he was ready to buy her the moon. He could see it now, in big bold type on the office door . . . "MCNEIL & SON." It

215

had started that way. First Jason, then Bill . . . now it would be Bill and Jason once again. God, wouldn't his father have been proud?

And the mother of the wonderful boy child? Well, she'd done her job . . .

Chapter Seventeen

The next years moved on steadily. No sudden shocks, mostly the rhythms of conventional living.

Alice's children married, as did Betsy's.

Kit's family had increased too. Chairs had been added one by one to her dining room table after the birth of Mark and Deborah. Joel, Jeremy and the youngest, Rebecca, known to her peers as Becky . . . Kit was now the mother of five. When she looked around her table at her husband and children she never forgot to say to herself, Thank you, God, for blessing me . . . I'm not sure I rate it, but I'll take it . . .

Janet settled into the life of a suburban housewife. Her apparent contentment was a quality Bill both envied, and, face it, resented at the same time. Changing events were so *normal* . . . matter of fact . . . all in a day's work. No traumas . . . no special upset that Nicole was growing up and would soon be ready to start nursery school. It didn't seem to bother *her* a bit. Well, it did him. . . .

After the children were put to bed they went to the den and settled into their favorite chairs. Bill read the paper, Janet worked on her needlepoint. From time to time she interrupted his scanning the column of the stock market report, but he scarcely heard—though he was careful to nod his head as though he hung on every word.

". . . if you could have seen how excited Nicole was . . ."

Bill poised his index finger on a quotation for U.S. Steel and looked up at her in sudden interest. "Sorry . . . I'm afraid I didn't hear. Who did you say was excited?"

"Nicole."

"Oh? What about?"

"Going to nursery school."

"What nursery school?"

"The one Kit's sending Mark and Deborah to. Of course they're in kindergarten, but Nicole will be in the same group as Joel and—"

As though he'd been struck by lightning he said, "You're sending Nicole to *school?* For God's sake, she's only three."

Janet was shocked by his outburst. Suppressing her own anger, she said quietly, hoping not to upset him more, "Kit sent the twins when they were two . . ."

"I don't give a damn what Kit did. Nicole's not going to be regimented. If she's in the way I'll take her to the office . . ."

Regimented? And then she remembered, and understood . . . remembered what had happened during *his* childhood . . . being carted off to a military academy . . . It wasn't Nicole . . . Bill was reacting to Bill . . . a hundred years ago. It was a little frightening . . .

"Nicole's not in the way, Bill," she answered quietly, "quite the contrary. But she needs other children to play with. She's very sad when the school bus passes the house in the morning. The other day she asked Mark if he wouldn't take her—"

"Why the hell didn't you discuss this with me before?"

"Well, darling, that's what I'm doing now."

The hell she was . . . that decision had been made by Kit and herself. Who was she kidding? "Okay, Janet. Since you're now kind enough to tell me about this, the answer is no. Nicole's entirely too young to be sent away to school."

Janet bit on her lower lip. She'd had no idea he would carry on this way. Still, she did understand. Better take it easy . . . "She isn't exactly being sent away, Bill. She'll be at school from nine to eleven-thirty. But most important are her feelings. She'll be very lonely without Jeremy and Rebecca to play with . . ."

Leave it to her to push him into a corner . . . in her sweet, compassionate way she sounded as though the sacrifice was all hers . . . like it was only for Nicole's sake. The hell it was. Whatever Kit did, Janet followed suit. He wished to God he'd never moved to Westchester, especially this close to Kit. Janet couldn't go to the bathroom without her. At this moment he wanted to pull

218

up stakes and buy a place in Manhattan . . . at least he'd be able to take Nicole to school and back. If they were living in the city he might understand Janet's feeling that Nicole needed the company of other children, but here . . . damned if he did. Nicole seemed to be happy enough playing with the baby and more than content with the things she and Janet did together. Well, what was the use of arguing? He'd look like a heel if he tried to stop Janet. And it was inevitable that Kit would tell him he was a selfish s.o.b. Eight would get you five that she'd get into the act. She always did . . . Wasn't she responsible for their moving to the suburbs? You bet. Talk about mothers-in-law? How about friends? . . . If only she'd butt out . . . she dominated everyone, especially Nat, or so it sometimes seemed to him. But damn it, what's the use of arguing the thing? Janet was going to have her way, didn't she always? . . . "Okay, where the hell is this school?"

The day Nicole was enrolled Bill went with them. Something very personal happened to him when Nicole quickly let go of his hand and sat on the floor next to a little boy, speaking to him as though they'd been buddies from day one. Soon they were sharing crayons, and Bill felt even more pushed out when she pecked him on the cheek and said, "Good-by daddy" so fast and went back to her work of art. For a week Bill stayed home from work in the morning so that he could drive Nicole home at noon . . . he wasn't about to trust her to the care of some stupid bus driver . . . He'd read about how they sometimes careened off the highway. The fantasized horrors got to be so extreme he could hardly work at the office in the afternoon. Never once did he hear his own mother's voice in his, but it was there . . .

At the end of the year he had saved enough of Nicole's crayon sketches to all but cover the walls in his office. More than once he looked up from the drawing board to see her extraordinary work, all thumbtacked to a special bulletin board he'd bought. By God, she was really good, for a four-year-old. He especially, no surprise, liked the one captioned "Daddy." The composition was at least as good as some of the nutty art he'd seen. And her description of it to him one night, as he held her on his lap, was more proof that she was turning into the brilliant little girl he was always sure she'd be . . . the sky was blue and the tree was green, the moon was yellow and the house was white. Red, purple and orange flowers grew along the path leading to the front porch . . . He laughed at the baggy suit on the spindly-legged man with the thick brown hair, a round face with two large brown eyes and a curved smiling line below the nose of two dots.

"Do you like it, daddy?"

"I love it, princess, but you best of all," he said, holding her closer. "Just don't grow up so fast, baby . . . stay a little girl for just a while longer. For my sake, okay, princess?"

And though princess had said she was willing, time was not . . . Somehow, when he wasn't looking, she was already turning six, and once again he was going to school with Janet to enroll Nicole, except this time in first grade. Today was even more painful. He'd allowed Nicole to slip away, had been deprived of her baby days.

Janet couldn't help but think again about the generations overlapped . . . Bill reacted exactly as his mother had when he watched three-year-old Jason climb aboard the bus on his way to nursery school for the first time. Just as he had with Nicole, and as his mother had with him.

Later that afternoon he sat in the office unable to concentrate on anything. Swiveling his chair around, he stared out the window to the bridge beyond. It wasn't that the view was so impressive—in fact, he scarcely noticed it now. He just felt so *empty*. The children seemed to notice him less, both Jason and Nicole had their own playmates, and on weekends went to someone's house to stay overnight. Matter of fact, Janet didn't seem to need him very much either. He seemed someone moving around between the lives of his children and wife . . . hell, no one noticed he was there too . . . that *he* needed attention . . . well, he didn't mean to sound sorry for himself . . . What the hell, he didn't want to sound like his mother . . . not that she hadn't been entitled at times . . . But he was a man, and a man didn't complain. Not then, after six years in suburbia, and not even when the same thoughts still plagued him after ten years.

No, Bill didn't complain . . . not openly . . . and his stiff upper lip kept Janet in the dark, assuming the marriage was basically okay . . . After all, she didn't have much time to dwell on it . . . taking the children to the orthodontist, to dancing, tennis and swimming lessons, and then there was the PTA, and at election time getting involved in who the next assemblyman, senator or congressman would be. That was the least she could do, she figured, for their children's welfare, their future. Still, for all her involvements, her first priority, she reminded herself, was Bill. By four every afternoon she was home to supervise dinner, refresh herself and get ready for his homecoming. He was, after all, her husband . . .

They were considered the ideal couple. Especially envied was the apparent *permanence* of their marriage, based on its predictability . . . Janet's weekly routine worked like a clock that kept perfect time. It wasn't always so easy, and sometimes she'd have liked to have skipped a beat, slept late, violated the routine. But she owed it to Bill, to the marriage, she would remind herself. And he did seem content, although at times she thought he seemed rather remote, unusually quiet.

Monday was pot roast. Wednesday was men's night at the club. And Saturday was men's *day* at the club; after eighteen holes of golf, Bill would shower, and immediately after dinner the men would settle down to a game of poker or gin rummy. The women had dinner at one another's homes on Wednesdays and Saturdays, chatted about the latest fashions, exchanged gossip, discussed the latest fad diets . . . then out came the bridge tables. After the children were driven to school there was tennis in the morning—Kit and Janet were partners for doubles—a quick sandwich at noon, and then it was time to pick up the kids.

Janet spent a great deal of her time chauffeuring. It was like reliving her own childhood back in Kansas. Sometimes she laughed at herself. She still had that midwestern mentality. For all the supposed sophistication of living in Westchester, she was no different than Mary Lou back in Wichita.

The McNeils . . . theirs was a charmed life. Ask anyone . . .

Anyone except, for example, Bill McNeil. He was jealous of Janet's tranquility, and decent enough to be angry
with himself for begrudging her it. But after ten years of
being submerged by . . . no, not *by* . . . *in* . . . in
Westchester . . . he felt himself, almost literally, being
strangled. He needed air . . . needed to get away . . .
they all did . . . And so it was that one night after dinner
he took out the brochures on Hawaii and made the earth-
shaking announcement as he passed them around, "I
bought tickets today, it's sort of my surprise . . ." And
having said that, he handed the tickets to Janet.

She looked at the date and then at Bill's face. Reluctantly she said, "Darling, these are for March."

"So?"

"Well, we can't very well take the children out of
school—"

"Oh . . . right . . . well, how about April, Easter vacation?"

"Mr. McNeil, you've got a date. April 15."

On the fifteenth of April, at precisely 9:45, Bill
checked the nine pieces of luggage plus Janet's carry-all
equipment, and then they boarded TWA to fly off into the
wild blue yonder. Bill settled into his seat. The only annoyance was when their plane was held up for two hours
in San Francisco because of poor visibility. Also, Jason
wasn't being too cooperative. After exploring all the airport shops, having purchased enough bubble gum, Her-
shey bars and comic books to last until he was ninety, he
got tired and even sullen. His persistent question . . .
"When are we going to leave, dad?" drove Bill nuts. His
own patience growing a bit thin, he informed his son that
he expected it would be when *they* were ready. Janet, of
course, kept her cool throughout, reminding him that
Jason was, after all, pretty tired, and still a little boy . . .
Well, damn it, *he* had feelings too, even if he wasn't a
darling sweet six-year-old . . . Oh, God . . . what was
the matter with him? . . . jealous of his own son . . . ?

At nine-thirty Honolulu time they debarked, walked into the terminal to be greeted by fragrant leis, steel guitars and merry voices singing out *aloha*.

Leaving most of their gear and keeping their suite reservation at the Royal Hawaiian, they took off again to Maui. But as far as Bill was concerned, a day of traipsing through the flower-filled paths, exploring the island, smelling the sweet perfume of hibiscus was very much for the birds, and he suggested it might be an idea to get back to the excitement of Honolulu. Jason supported his father wholeheartedly on that one. He couldn't wait to get back to the giant waves and the surfboard. So back they went.

After the children had been kissed goodnight, Janet and Bill danced until three in the Monarch Room of the Royal Hawaiian, then went to see the last act at the Haymarket, their eyes slightly out of focus now as they watched the grass skirts swaying back and forth on the hips of the dancers. The four Mai Tais Bill had consumed made Polynesian dancing seem the only way to go . . . They also, with the dancing, made him ready for love. He could hardly wait to get Janet back to the room . . .

That same morning he was up at eight. Leaving Janet asleep, he met the children in the sitting room and the three of them went to breakfast. Boy, they *were* gorgeous kids, he thought as he looked at them over the rim of his coffee cup. The thought was interrupted by Jason's, "Dad, could we rent a boat today?"

"That's a good idea, Jason. How do you feel about that, Nicole?"

"Oh, I'd love it, daddy."

"Okay, we'll go up and tell mother."

Janet was yawning away the last vestiges of sleep when Bill came into the room.

He kissed her. "How'd you sleep, honey?"

Smiling, she answered, "Just great . . . after you simmered down."

"Was I simmering?"

"Among a few other things. I'm not complaining."

"Well . . ." beaming . . . "how'd you like to go boating today?"

"Darling, would you forgive me if I didn't? I might—pardon the small joke—only rock the boat . . . Frankly

223

I'd just sort of like to be lazy on a chaise and soak up the sun."

"You're sure?"

"Sure . . . you'd better have the hotel pack a box lunch if you're going to be out that long."

"Good idea . . . we'll meet you back on the beach."

When the children saw the fourteen-foot sailboat they were delighted, and judged it, simultaneously, "terrific."

Bill laughed as he helped them aboard. "Okay, matey," he said to Jason, "let's haul anchor and head to Tahiti. Crew, rig the mainsail. First Mate Jason, hang onto this rope; Second Mate Nicole, grab onto this one," Bill said, tossing the ropes to them. The sea was calm and mesmerizing as Bill switched on the ignition, starting the auxiliary motor.

Three miles out to sea a gentle wind filled the sail, and Jason was thrilled that the boat was able to glide now on its own power. "Okay, matey, take over," Bill said to him, and stood behind as the little boy steered a straight course.

At noon Bill said to Nicole, "How about some chow, mate?"

"Okay, captain," she said, and handed her father and Jason their box lunches. As the two children sat devouring ham sandwiches and Cokes, Bill munched on a cold chicken leg with one hand while steering with the other.

"This is the best fun we've ever had, daddy," Nicole said.

"Mr. Christian's the name, if you don't mind, and don't throw those boxes overboard, Jason. The sea's not a garbage can."

"Okay, sir . . . but I got to go to the bathroom."

"Head." But Jason had already disappeared, missing the nautical equivalent . . .

Abruptly the winds shifted, shocking, startling Bill. The little vessel twisted and turned nervously. "Okay, crew, you're confined to the galley, and keep your life jackets on. In fact, I want you to sit on the floor."

More annoyed than frightened, they went below.

Giant waves now began to break over the sail like huge fangs, and Bill was beginning to pray for the Coast Guard. Fighting the wind, he managed to lower the sails and start the auxiliary motor, but he seemed unable to steer the boat properly. Lord . . . he'd sailed all his life but the waters of Maine weren't the erratic tropics. He kept wondering what he'd do if the boat capsized, which at this moment he felt was a real possibility. The rush of water made it almost impossible for him to see what he was doing. Wiping his face with his hands, he had a moment of visibility before the next giant wave hit, and there was Jason, crying and standing in the open door of the cabin below. As loudly as possible, the boy yelled out, "Nicole hit her head and she's bleeding."

Switching the motor to automatic, Bill rushed below. Nicole was lying on the floor, unconscious. Lifting her head gently, he implored her to wake up, to speak to him . . .

Slowly she opened her eyes, but there was no recognition in them. And he wanted to die. As the boat twisted, turned, he held the child with one arm while his other arm went about Jason.

It was Jason who intruded on his sense of helplessness. "Daddy, I think it stopped."

Bill looked at his son, then realized that the boat was calm and quiet once again, the sea having calmed as abruptly as it had erupted. Quickly he put a pillow under Nicole's head, ripped a blanket from the bunk and covered her.

"Okay, Jason, take care of your sister, we're heading home." A moment ago he wouldn't have counted on that being possible.

Bill carried Nicole ashore, hailed a taxi and sat in the back seat, Jason at his side, as the driver sped them to Honolulu's General Hospital.

After Nicole was taken to emergency he called Janet, who wasn't in her room and had to be paged.

They'd been gone for so much longer than Bill had said. Instinctively she knew something had happened. When she heard Bill's voice on the phone she was sure.

"Janet . . . don't get upset, but we got into a rough sea and Nicole had a little accident . . ."

She thought her knees would buckle. Swallowing hard, she asked what had happened.

"Well . . . she hit her head . . . but I'm sure—"

"Where *are* you?"

"General Hospital . . . emergency."

She found Bill waiting with Jason in the hall. "Where is she?" She tried to hold back the tears, but they were spilling down her cheeks.

"She's been taken upstairs."

"How badly is she hurt?"

"The doctor told me she has a slight concussion."

"Concussion?" She bit her tongue . . . not wanting to express the anger that was mixed in her fear for Nicole . . . plain old swimming wasn't enough . . . he needed to show the children what a free spirit he was . . . never mind if they were maybe not ready for it . . . and the echoes of his mother's words came through . . . "Bill's too young to take on the responsibilities of a family . . ." She knew her son . . . it seemed he still *was* her son . . .

But Nicole, not Bill or herself, was the concern now. She found her lying in bed with her head bandaged, and for a moment she was afraid she was going to faint. She put her cheek against Nicole's as the child reached out to embrace her.

"Hi, mom."

"How are you, darling?"

"Great, mom. I just got a bump on my head."

Janet silently thanked God. "Are you sure, you're not just saying that?"

"No, mom, really. Boy, it was sure rough and poor daddy had a terrible time . . . Jason told me. But daddy's a great captain."

Laughing out of relief, Janet said, "You're a pretty fair skipper yourself, darling."

The doctor confirmed that it was a mild concussion, and after a few days of observation Nicole was allowed to go back to the hotel, apparently as good as new. Bill and Janet, though, had sustained scars less easily healed, though they tried to dismiss the resentment and anger they'd felt at the time . . . she feeling he'd foolishly jeopardized the lives of the children, not to mention his own life . . . he resenting the guilt her silent accusations made him feel . . . especially since he knew damn well there was more than a little justification for them . . . Well, Janet told herself, motherhood being what it was, her reactions were probably stronger and more protective than her wifely understanding, which wasn't altogether fair to Bill. And Bill was hardly proud of himself when he heard his young son having to defend him with, "It wasn't daddy's idea, it was mine and it's not his fault if a storm came up . . ." God . . . nice try, Jason, but I guess I *am* supposed to be the adult . . .

Janet decided it was time to back off, not to pursue the subject, to try and mend fences . . . Life, after all, did have to go on.

And for the McNeils, it proceeded to, back in the old rhythms . . . the pages of their family story turning, turning, almost as though moved by the wind.

Chapter Eighteen

Nicole, they realized with a shock, was being graduated from eighth grade, and was going on to high school.

Listening to the principal's speech, Bill's thoughts drifted back . . . It truly seemed that that exquisite little girl had been born only yesterday . . . one year . . . two . . . three . . . God, how had he misplaced them? In his mind's eye he was teaching her how to ride a bike, feeling what he'd felt when she fell off and he'd run to help her up and put her back on, and after a while how she'd been able to say, "Look, dad, no hands . . ." She'd been only five . . . at six he remembered how she was outswimming him across the pool . . . On father-and-daughter Girl Scout excursions *he* was the one who came home with a case of poison oak . . . And then there was her first piano recital. She was only eight, played the Schubert Serenade. God, he was proud of her . . .

A montage, changing color and form. A million pictures to review, to remember, try to put in order. And here she was *thirteen* . . . Where had all the time gone? For him too . . . ? (Janet was left out of these reveries.)

He glanced over at Jason, now ten, tall and handsome for his age. Bill wanted to shout out to him . . . Son, don't let the years go so fast. It was only yesterday when he'd umpired the Little League baseball game. Yesterday when the two of them had gone trout fishing. A year had passed since they went to Colorado, just Jason and himself, going down the rapids, while Janet took Nicole back to Kansas for a week . . . The years had sped by while he wasn't even looking. Well, he was looking now. Taking a good look. He was forty and a little frightened. At least he was still hard as a rock, and Janet didn't seem to notice the gray hair around the temples. And in bed? As good as ever . . .

He was brought out of his reverie as the parents got out of their seats and walked to congratulate their children.

"You were gorgeous, princess." Bill smiled, kissing her on the cheek and holding her just a little tighter, as though he could prevent time . . . her . . . from marching on.

All the bittersweet memories were gone by the time Bill got home and changed for the children's swimming party. He was to be the chef, making a big production out of fixing hot dogs and hamburgers. Gallons of soda pop were consumed, there was no hold on the potato chips.

By six the party was over, and Nicole went to her room to prepare for the evening party at Linda Mason's.

When her father saw her come into the den in her long white organdy dress, he just sat staring. Again the years came rushing at him. There was a peculiar sensation at the pit of his stomach, recalling how he'd walked the floors with her when she had colic, changed her diapers, helped ease the pain of cutting her first tooth . . . the sound of an electric train whistle as it went over the trestle, he could still hear the laughter, she had been only two . . .

"How do I look, dad?"

"Like my beautiful little princess. Come on, I'll drive you."

"Oh, thanks, dad, but Mark Weiss is taking me."

He was disappointed and slightly annoyed. She and Mark seemed to have been going steady ever since the days when they'd played doctor and nurse . . . Well, they'd known each other all their lives, and it was a little stupid to think they could be serious about each other at this age.

"What time will you be home, honey?"

"I don't know, dad. About twelve maybe."

"No maybe, Nicole. I want you home at the witching hour, or you'll turn into a pumpkin. Courtesy of old dad."

Bill had more than a little difficulty concentrating on bridge that evening. In fact, he did the unpardonable—trumped Nat's ace.

"Why the hell did you do that?" Nat exploded. "I had a grand slam going."

"I feel like a drink. Sorry . . ."

Kit looked at Janet, both knowing that Bill was having a rough time accepting the fact that he was, in his fashion, losing Nicole. Kit thought, things sure as hell reverse themselves. Bill was his mother reincarnated . . . one word—possessive. He of his daughter, as Violet McNeil had been of her son. . . .

Later that evening, as Kit and Janet sat having coffee in the kitchen, Kit said, "I think Bill's a little pushed out of shape."

Janet gave her an ironic smile. "A little? It wouldn't be so bad if he'd just talk about it, but he locks it up inside. He can't admit that Nicole has become a big girl and he's having a very difficult time accepting it."

Kit laughed. "Ah, sweet irony of life. He's going through the pains his mother suffered."

"Something like that."

"Well, I'm going to let my brood fly. When they're all gone it will be just Nat and me and I won't mind a bit. You wind up like you began, with just the two of you. So you enjoy parenthood as long as it lasts, then sit back and enjoy being a couple again."

Kit made sense, Janet thought.

Two days later the four McNeils flew to Europe for their summer vacation.

By the time they had seen Westminster Abbey, the changing of the guard, the Tower of London, Bill was ready to push on to Paris. The sidewalk cafes, the Champs Élysées, the Louvre, the Eiffel Tower were okay, but the French were a pain in the ass, as far as he could see. Rude, arrogant, avaricious.

Rome was a little better, but he got bored with the cathedrals and museums, and the pasta in Manhattan was better. Besides, he'd seen it a couple of times with his mother and father when he was a kid. The Coliseum hadn't changed a bit . . . same pile of rocks.

Janet knew his lack of enthusiasm had nothing to do with Rome, Paris or London, knew he was going through a rough time accepting the fact that his children were growing up—which was a sure reminder that he was growing no younger himself. Well, what could she do to cheer him up? . . .

He was in bed, staring up at the ceiling, when she came out of the bathroom in a sheer black nightgown. The black lace bodice revealed her nipples.

He sat up in bed, looked at her. "Take that damn thing off. It makes you look like a . . ."

She ran back into the bathroom, locked the door and tore the gown from her body, her hands shaking. She had thought, hoped, it might make him feel better, perk him up. Instead it apparently had made him feel impotent.

As though he needed that damned thing to get a hard-on. And then, gradually, his anger quieted and he berated himself. Sure . . . she was trying to lift his spirits, and he felt like an ass for the way he'd reacted. He might just as well have slapped her. Right. He felt better.

He got out of bed and tried opening the door but she had turned the latch. He knocked.

No answer.

"I'm sorry."

He waited.

"Janet, please open the door."

No response. He went back to bed, wishing he'd have an attack of appendicitis, like when he was a kid at that damn military school . . .

Janet took a look at herself in the bathroom mirror. It had been so contrived. No wonder Bill had been offended. Gimmicks, fantasy, sex talk—he had never indicated any interest in them before, and certainly they had never been necessary. His fortieth birthday had been traumatic to him, and in his present state of mind her prank had probably planted some doubt about his appeal for her.

It never bothered her, but she knew some of the women at the club had more than once made a play for him, showing him by a smile, a gesture, that they wouldn't at all mind being seduced. In fact, a few had been very obvious. Westchester had its share of husband-

and-wife-swapping. But she would have bet her last dollar that Bill had never cheated on her . . .

She washed her face, took a deep breath and came back to the room dressed in a simple white silk nightgown. He looked up at her as she sat on the edge of the bed.

"I was just teasing, honey . . . I'm sorry if I offended you—"

He reached for her hand. "It wasn't you, Janet. At another time I would have loved it. It's so out of character—not just what you did but the way I reacted . . ."

"Do you want to talk about it?"

"Well, it's just that I feel sort of . . . crummy. I mean the kids growing up and all. You know when I really felt it?"

"When?"

"The day of Nicole's graduation. I tried acting like a damned kid myself. Fixing the hamburgers and the hot dogs and putting on a big jolly show about it. But I felt like an old futz, standing there with that apron over my swimming trunks and that crazy chef's hat. Looking at all those kids swimming, their young bodies . . . Well, I just felt old, over the hill."

"If this will make you feel any better, do you know what your daughter said to me?"

"What?"

"That her father was the most handsome man she'd ever seen in her whole life. And Linda said to Nicole, 'If I didn't like your mother so much I'd make a play for him.' "

A broad smile, in spite of himself. "She did? You mean Linda, a fourteen-year-old girl?"

Janet laughed. "Don't you remember being fourteen? It's a betwixt and between age, when you don't know how to handle all your new feelings."

"So is forty."

"It shouldn't be, especially when a man looks like you," she said, winking and tilting her head. "I believe you know what I mean?"

He knew. Off came the white silk nightgown, and he proceeded to show her—and himself. Before dropping off to sleep, she whispered, "You're getting better with age. Keep it up."

At nine the next morning Jason came into the living room of their suite at the Excelsior Hotel. He found Nicole dressed and ready for the day's excursion but the door to his parents' room was closed. That was unusual, he thought, especially when they had planned the day for sightseeing. "Where are the folks?"

"Sleeping."

"How come? We were supposed to go to the Catacombs early."

"The Catacombs have been here for thousands of years."

"But we won't. I'm going to wake them up."

"I wouldn't do that, Jay."

"Why? Everything closes down here at two for their crazy siestas."

"I know . . . that's why the Italians have so many children."

"What's that got to do with the folks and us?"

"You know all about the birds and bees? Parents know about it too."

"You mean, *mother and* . . . ?"

"That's what I mean . . . Okay, baby brother, let's go down to breakfast, hop a bus and strike out on our own."

"They won't know where we've gone."

"I'll leave a note."

Janet blinked the sleep from her eyes, then looked at the clock. It was late, already eleven-thirty. She hastily put on her robe and went to the sitting room, expecting to find the children and apologize for spoiling their day, but the room was empty. Then she saw the note propped up against the lamp. "Dear mom and dad, when in Rome do as the Romans do. *Molto amore.* Will be back at three. Love, Nicole."

Janet blushed. She had been the one who'd fought for sex education in the school, she reminded herself. Well, fighting for a principle was one thing, but when it got down to a personal level and your children knew *all* about what happened behind closed doors . . .

She showed the note to Bill.

He laughed. "Couldn't have said it better myself. Get back into bed, wench."

For the rest of the trip Bill was wound up like a mechanical man. He took Janet go-go dancing until the place closed, followed by capuccinos on the Via Veneto. The next night he took the family to an Italian nightclub. Didn't understand a word but he laughed nonetheless, caught up in the spirit of it. Go-go-go . . .

In Venice, he sent the children off to explore the Doges Palace while he hired an old-fashioned gondola, complete with curtains. They made love as the gondolier broke into a robust *"O sole mio."* They laughed over how hackneyed the serenade was, but couldn't have cared if the gondolier had sung the Italian national anthem. This was the only way to go in Venice. Go-go-go . . .

Bill came home feeling, he told himself, a reborn man . . . He beat everyone at golf, his handball improved with the lessons he took, and he decided Janet and he should drive in to the city more often to go dancing and take in the shows. Suburbia was getting a little boring, a little too predictable. Same thing week after week. Wednesdays, poker. Sundays, swimming and barbecues. Saturday nights, dinner at the country club. Boring. He decided they had to spend more time in the city. Janet went along with it.

It was the first week after their return and he had asked Janet to meet him in the city for lunch. Lunch turned out to be champagne, caviar and chicken divan, all served in a suite at the St. Regis and followed by four hours in bed.

It would be great to spend next Saturday night in the same room at the St. Regis, he told her. After they had dined and danced, of course.

She smiled and agreed, but wondered if this room wasn't going to become a home away from home. Uneasily, she packed an overnight case and left the children with Kit for the weekend. . . .

No doubt about it, Bill was reliving his youth . . . or trying very, very hard to. But time, as they said, stood still for no man. Including Bill McNeil. . . .

This year Janet gave Bill's birthday party at the country club. He would have been grateful had she not given him that honor. He was less than enthusiastic about blowing out forty-one candles . . . it looked like the night Mrs. O'Leary burned down Chicago. But like it or not, birthdays rolled on.

And so did anniversaries. Difficult to believe, thought Bill . . . the years were slipping away so fast . . . so damn fast. . . . Nineteen had come and gone, and this time he felt a shiver go through him. He'd fought against it, he really had, but try as he might, the idea, the *fact*, of marriage, of being, as they said, "hitched," weighed, pulled heavily. But as always he was a man given to overlapping guilts, and to acting them out in a fashion hardly likely to give Janet an opportunity to know and help resolve them. Never go to bed mad, went the conventional wisdom . . . and so when really angry—the anger turned inward to become guilt—conventional wisdom also prescribed especially dedicated lovemaking . . . as though the flesh could cure all the ills of the heart . . . Well, for all his restlessness, Bill was really not a very unconventional man, and so this night he pursued it with a special passion, the better to blind himself—and Janet—to all their misgivings. Love conquers all. . . .

Chapter Nineteen

Love conquers all? Not quite. Certainly not Bill's increasing dislike of the commute between New York and Westchester. Or the overwhelming restlessness he would feel after dinner as he sat in his den trying to read the afternoon newspaper.

One evening he put down the paper and watched Janet as she worked on her tapestry—which she did almost every night now . . . it was her unknowing escape, though they didn't discuss such notions. How could they . . . ? Good Lord, he thought, it took so little to make her happy. Didn't *she* get bored, doing the same things over and over? Even watching her pull that piece of yarn up and down through the tiny holes in the canvas drove him nuts.

"Janet?"

"Yes," her eyes still intent on her needlework.

"Now that the children are grown up I'd like to move back to the city."

She looked up at him, said nothing.

"What do you say, Janet?"

What did she say? She shook her head, slowly, startled by his abruptness. "You mean just like that? Nicole is graduating from high school in June. We can't pull her out of school now, and she'd be pretty upset about being split up from Mark Weiss. And Jason's on the football team. What about all the friends they grew up with? It wouldn't really be fair to the kids to uproot them now."

"Janet, I wasn't too keen about moving to the country, but I did because you wanted it, because it seemed the best place when the kids were young. But it's different now. And as for Nicole and Mark, I thought we'd gone through that and she wasn't going to see so much of him.

She's too young to be so serious. The move would be a good thing for her."

"Would it really? And us? We've made our lives here—"

"Well, times change and so do people."

"Of course they do. I believe that's called life, and I'm not fighting it . . ." She thought of adding, Are you? Then thought again and said nothing.

It was the way they were. . . .

In the weeks that followed, Bill tried to pretend that everything was fine, that everything would continue as before. The perfect family, living in complete contentment. But the perfect family caught on to the pretense. Conversation around the dinner table became stilted and at times there was total silence.

It was Nicole who finally brought the issue out in the open. One night as they sat through yet another silent meal, she looked at her father, then at her mother. The tension between them was obvious, and she was beginning to feel anxious about it. To her knowledge her parents never fought . . . But then, it wasn't normal for married people not to. They must have kept their arguments behind closed doors. So she could only assume that something serious had happened, something they couldn't resolve and that was making them act indifferently to each other. And it was getting worse all the time, affecting all of them now. If they were upset, why didn't they just say so, maybe even talk about it? After all, she was eighteen and Jason was old enough to try to understand. And what he didn't understand wouldn't hurt him.

Finally she spoke up. "I don't know if the two of you realize how . . . well . . . how uncomfortable this is for Jason and me . . . we've been sitting here night after night as if we're waiting for the roof to cave in. What's going on?"

Silence, as everyone but Nicole carefully avoided looking at one another.

"Well," Nicole said, "are we going to talk about this?"

"I'm sorry, but it's between your mother and me," Bill told her. He wasn't going to blame Janet and make *himself* look like a martyred husband. Children have to have some illusions. Still, it was damned hard not to think of Janet as selfish, thinking only about herself and the *family* . . . He'd made plenty of sacrifices for the family— eighteen years of commuting, eighteen years of suburban life that had been regimented down to the last boring minute.

Nicole was exasperated now. "But things that happen in this family aren't just confined to the two of *you*. Not when it affects *us*."

Bill glanced at Janet, then quickly looked away. "Since you insist . . . I think it would be good for us to move back to the city, and your mother disagrees."

"And *that's* why we've been under this much strain? All because of a house?"

"It has nothing to do with a house."

"Then what?"

"It's a question of . . . cooperation."

Nicole stared at him, her expression changing from surprise to disapproval. "In other words, your idea of cooperation is for *you* to make the decisions, uproot our family and move where you want. Suppose you decide on Tahiti? Should we all give up a life we've known so *you* can be a beachcomber?"

Bill was shocked at Nicole's tone. "You've never spoken to me like that before and I very much resent it, Nicole."

She reddened . . . there was, after all, no one she loved more than her father. Everyone knew that. "I'm sorry, dad, I really am, but I just don't understand. This is our home, and you always seemed to love it here as much as we do."

Janet sat absolutely still, feeling as if the earth were crumbling beneath her. Why hadn't she seen it before? From the very beginning Bill had played the role of country squire so well that he'd even managed to convince himself for a while. Certainly he'd convinced her. But the truth was that he'd made the move to Westchester only for the sake of his family. That was the *role* he was expected to assume, and he'd played it for eighteen years. Now he could no longer manage it. The feelings he'd suppressed had reached the boiling-over point. Whatever he felt surfaced and he couldn't control it.

Jason looked as bewildered as Nicole. "I'm not going to take sides with who wants what," he said, "but I'm not going to move and give up my friends . . . if you and mom want to move to the city, then do it. But I'll live with Aunt Kit." He got up, ran to his room, locked the door and stared at his trophies. Stared hard to keep back the unmanly tears.

Janet went after him and knocked on his closed door. "Jay, may I come in?"

"No, mom, I want to be alone—"

"Please, darling."

When she walked in he was sitting on his bed and angrily wiping away his tears. Janet sat next to him, not quite knowing what to say. Bill's feelings counted, but so did theirs. There had to be something that would satisfy them all . . .

"Okay, mom, you're here. What do you want to say?"

"Just this, Jay . . . people change . . . time changes them. But we're still a family. I'd like you to come back inside so we can work this out—"

"Work what out? Didn't you hear dad?"

"Yes, but people have to make compromises, Jay, and find the solutions."

He didn't move.

He looked so much like his father, Janet thought, the same chestnut hair, the same planes to the face, although the eyes were a deep blue like hers and Nicole's. He even had some of his father's stubbornness, though in recent years it had often been turned against Bill. Jason had grown up idolizing his father, just as Nicole had, but when he reached adolescence there had been sudden and unexpected tensions between them. Or maybe not so unexpected. It was probably the all too common rift—temporary, she hoped—that opened between father and son when the son began to be his own person and sensed that his father was resisting the change, as if it were a threat, a challenge.

She bit her lower lip. "You want us to come to an amicable agreement, don't you, darling?"

Without looking at her, he got off the bed and followed her back to the dining room.

As Janet sat down she said, "You're right, Nicole,

we've spent the best part of our lives here and have a million wonderful memories. You and Jay have made friends you'll have all your lives. But you're both getting grown up and you'll soon be making your own lives, whether you realize it or not. I've thought a lot about this"—she looked at Bill—"and I hope we can agree that maybe the best solution for everyone is if we keep the house until Jay graduates. After that, I feel my place, my life, is with your father."

Which meant two years, Bill thought, two more years taken out of his life while he sat around waiting for Jason to go to college. And Janet no doubt thought this was just a whim that would be forgotten during all the holiday parties, the birthday and anniversary celebrations that were part of the good life in suburbia. And then there'd be engagement parties, weddings, grandchildren—always some reason to delay giving up the house. They'd just slip into old age in Westchester. He felt like a steel trap had snapped shut on his life. . . .

It was a terrifying—and very familiar—feeling.

Janet could sense his discontent as they lay in their darkened room that night. "Bill, I know you're not happy about this. But tell me truthfully—what else could we have done? You can't just pull up stakes when you have children. The time will pass quicker than you think, and before we know it Jay will be at M.I.T. Then we can do what we like. . . ."

What *we* like? That was a joke, he thought. *I feel my place, my life, is with your father* . . . How *gracious.* . . . He'd compromised for eighteen years and kept his mouth shut. She'd had her way in everything all these years . . .

As though reading his mind, she said, "Bill, I do know how you feel . . . but the years were good here and I think we ought to be glad the children had such a place to grow up in. I'll be more than happy to go back once they're both in school."

Thank God she hadn't said, *for your sake.*

She kissed him. "I love you, Bill."

"And I love you," he said, returning the kiss. And he meant it, in spite of all the resentments. Of course he loved her. But husbands and wives weren't born with the same needs, same desires. They were separate people, with hidden, secret wants, and not even children, however well loved, could bind their parents' lives together, help them bridge the gap. Even more frightening, Bill thought, he had changed but couldn't even pinpoint why or when it had all begun . . . well, it had happened. When the children were young they had been the pivotal point of his life with Janet. That was no longer true, and as much as he tried to fight his discontent he felt as if he'd lost his bearings, as if there were no center to his life. It never occurred to him that the maternal center, pivot of his life, was also gone . . . and with her passing had begun the acute withdrawal pains he was feeling more and more. The long arm of Violet McNeil was alive even in death. . . .

As Janet sat alone at the breakfast table early the next morning, she knew she could no longer rationalize away the change in Bill. No denying that he was different, and maybe understandably so. He was facing middle age and somehow seemed unprepared for it. The move to Manhattan was only a partial solution to what he was feeling. How did she make him realize that these could and should be the best times of their lives?

They'd passed through the years of their children's adolescence with the least amount of trauma. No school or emotional problems. No drugs. A few anti-war demonstrations but thank goodness neither of them had ever been hurt.

Now she and Bill should have been able to sit back and enjoy the togetherness they'd have in the approaching years, savor them as the best part. But she knew Bill didn't share her thoughts. He was afraid, as if middle age were a void, and it didn't help that everything was so youth-oriented these days. Oh God, if only she were wise enough to know how to scatter his fears . . .

It was only seven in the morning when he joined her in the kitchen. The children were still asleep. As he sat down to breakfast she said, "Bill, I'd love to go to Maine. I think it would be so good to get away together, just the two of us. Would you like that?"

Would he like that? Well, after the tensions of the past weeks, it might help to try and recapture some of the old

241

magic they'd once had there . . . especially that first weekend before they were married.

"Okay, let's go tomorrow."

Janet closed her eyes. Everything was going to be all right. Wasn't it . . . ?

There was little conversation between them as they drove to Maine. All they seemed able to talk about at all were the children. It appeared they'd lost whatever mutual interests they'd once had. God, through the years there were so many . . . Well, hadn't there . . . ? Yes, she told herself. But gradually their lives had taken on a predictability that had somehow cut their rapport to such earth-shaking issues as what color to paint the living room, whether or not to send Nicole to a different orthodontist, where to buy Jason's new skis . . . and on and on and on. Well . . . this weekend would be their time together, to rebuild some of the closeness that had once been theirs.

Janet moved closer to Bill, took hold of his right hand as she looked out at the passing scenery. This holiday was what they needed. No question. Married people should get away from everything and everybody, especially children. She hadn't understood that well enough through the years. It had seemed so important to do things as a family, but today she knew otherwise. There was a time and place for . . . Well, once they got to the farm it would be a new beginning . . .

They did all the things they'd done before when they were lovers, tried so hard to relive those times . . . but they would not come back to life. The sparks didn't fly . . . the pulse didn't race. God . . . they were like two robots going through the motions. Both knew it and both were miserable and afraid. Nothing stayed the same and nothing could change that fact. It wasn't anybody's fault, of course. Something had happened to their lives, without either knowing when, or how, it had happened. The air was very chilly, even for Maine.

Chapter Twenty

Bill sat in his office, thinking back to last month's trip to Maine. He'd lost whatever he'd once had with Janet—the trip had proved that. The kids were almost on their own now. And what did he have left? He was forty-five years old in a world meant only for the young. He was obsolete. Read the ads . . .

It hit him hardest when he realized most of the men in the office were in their late twenties and early thirties, none of them married, none of them with a care in the world. And the secretaries were . . . what? About twenty. He'd been the youngest in the firm when he had joined after graduating M.I.T. In fact, he was referred to as "the kid." But the men of his father's time had either died or retired. Youth had taken over, the world belonged to them.

He looked at the phone for a moment before picking up the receiver and dialing.

"Janet?"

"Yes?"

He paused and cleared his throat. "Listen, Janet, I have to work a little late at the office—"

"All right. We'll wait for dinner then."

"No, I think you'd better not. Go ahead without me. I don't know when I'll be able to get away."

He didn't notice the slight hesitation before she said, "Well, I'll see you when you get home."

His hand lingered on the receiver after he had hung up, as if holding onto the tenuous link between them. In all the years they'd been married he had never cheated on her, never wanted to. He didn't intend to now, but the routine—the same things day after day, night after night—it was killing him. He felt almost as if he were being unfaithful to Janet by not going home as usual, but the monotony and the emptiness were more than he could face tonight. He just didn't want to go home . . . and the feeling, unrecognized, was not so different from the one so many years ago when it was his mother's home he was avoiding . . .

In the elevator he observed the faces of those around him. They'd be meeting a date or going to a singles bar. That had become a big thing . . . singles. Young and single. Your own person . . .

He walked out into the crisp early evening and eventually stopped at a bar on Third Avenue. He doubted if anyone was much past the age of consent. The girls there were nineteen, twenty. And the fellows? Thirtyish.

Ordering a Scotch and soda, he sat at the bar and listened to the banter around him. The world had surely changed . . . twenty years ago Janet had walked into his office building and apologized for being so *brazen*. These days no one would think twice about it. There was one long gap between the fifties and seventies. It was a time of no-holds-barred. The girls were as emancipated as the guys, many of them even insisting on paying for the drinks. He laughed to himself. "I don't let girls take me to dinner." That's what he'd said to Janet when she'd offered to make amends for spilling champagne on his precious suit . . . That seemed a million years ago.

He watched, fascinated, as a girl sashayed up to the bar, sat down and spoke to the young man next to her as though they were old friends. Bill wouldn't have known the difference except that the young man introduced himself. Did Nicole do that sort of thing, he wondered? No . . . No . . . ?

He was out of place, beyond his depth. Leaving his drink on the bar, he turned and left. The girl who took his place at the bar watched him disappear through the door, shrugged and thought . . . better luck next time. One damn attractive man. . . .

On his way home something seemed to compel him to gravitate to his old apartment building. He parked the car and looked up to what had been his window. That had been a damn nice time in his life. The apartment, perfect

... for a bachelor, of course. He tried not to remember how he'd fought against being "owned," but his efforts at this moment were futile. The past rushed back, the memories springing undeniably to life. He'd fallen in love with Janet ... which, of course, was what had made him so ... vulnerable. But the truth was—face it—that marriage made him feel as though he were in a jail cell ... hard to say exactly why, but he did, he just *did* ... Yes, he still loved Janet ... of *course* he did ... but he was losing himself. What did it profit a man to gain the whole ball of wax ... marriage, children ... and lose his soul ... all right, all right, he was being melodramatic, but really, the more he thought on it, the more it seemed that things *had* been all Janet's way. He was the one who rolled over, gave in to get along. He tried to close his eyes to the children and only remember how it was before they were born ... but no, damn it, he hadn't been ready for a family when Janet had cried her eyes out only two months after they were married. But he'd gone along again, even deluding himself that fatherhood was what he wanted. Why? To prove he was everyone's good boy? (He couldn't substitute "mother's" for "everyone's," not even now.) He had to prove to Kit he wasn't a selfish s.o.b., so he forced himself to buy the house in Westchester. He had to prove to Janet he was a good husband so he ... But, forgive the thought, what about him? Nobody gave a damn about the way he felt. He'd been weak, no question. You bet ... otherwise he'd have had the guts to say what Jason had said, except in reverse ... We're moving back to the city because up to now every one of you has had it your way. You say you don't want to move? Fine, Jay, you can go live with Aunt Kit. And as far as you're concerned, Janet, you don't really give a damn about me, if you did you'd see I'm dying inside, choking on all this domesticity ... you're making me feel old, pushing me to the edge, over it ... I want a divorce—

Bill bolted upright behind the steering wheel, and held on. Perspiration ran down his face but he felt chilled. Although secretly he'd held the thought for a long time, never before had he allowed himself to go so far as to acknowledge it. He turned on the ignition and looked once again at the building that housed the memory of his bachelor days. He had to get away. This place was no good for him. Too many memories . . . too damn many. . . .

Nicole and Jay were in their rooms, doing homework.

Suddenly he got up and fix himself a drink, stood in front of the windows and looked out to the dark night. The thoughts he'd had earlier reverberated in his mind. Mostly they translated down to being free . . . like he'd been before . . . Janet glanced over to him. She sensed the tension across his shoulders, even with his back to her.

"Bill . . . come and talk to me."

He turned around and looked at her. Slowly he walked back to the chair, sat down, switched off the television, took a sip of his drink.

"What's wrong, Bill?"

He shook his head. Nothing.

Janet only wished it were so. "If something's wrong, don't you think it would help to discuss it? We don't do much of that . . ."

Silence.

"Please, Bill, don't keep on shutting me out."

She was pushing him again, just like she always had . . . "I'm . . . I'm going to bed. I'm really pretty beat . . ."

"Darling, please give me a chance . . . give *us* a chance . . . talk to me about it?"

He sank back into his chair, took a long pull on his drink. "Janet, I love you . . . I always have and I suppose I always will . . . That's what makes this all so difficult . . ."

Her heart was suddenly pounding. "What's difficult, Bill?"

"Janet, I don't want to hurt you and I don't quite know how to say this—"

"Say what? Are you sick or—"

"No . . ."

"Then what is it, for God's sake?"

He began again. "I fought this, believe me, I really have—"

246

"Fought what?" Except even as she asked, she was terrified that she knew.

He couldn't do this without another drink. Janet watched as he poured out half a glass of Scotch, then sat down again. "Janet, I don't want you to hate me . . ."

She was becoming very frightened. "Why should I hate you?" What else to say?

Almost under his breath, he said, "Because . . . I want a divorce."

She sat like a statue, as though not having heard what she'd been so afraid to hear. Rejecting it, pushing it away, she told herself, he's going through a phase, it happens to men his age, everyone knows that . . . the forties blues . . . he isn't serious. Now don't, for God's sake, start screaming and carrying on. Isn't that what the books said about such situations? As a rule of thumb . . . *rule?* . . . what rule? There were no rules in this stupid game . . .

"Bill, maybe you should take a little time off—"

"Janet, you don't seem to understand. I didn't ask for a divorce impulsively. Getting away isn't the solution. I'm sorry . . . truly sorry . . . but I need to be free . . . it has nothing to do with you . . ."

Nothing to do with her . . . ? Her outrage broke through the calm of shock. "It doesn't? Who *does* it have to do with? I'm your *wife* and your leaving has nothing to do with *me?*"

"What I mean is . . . it's nothing that you've done. I just want to be—"

She lost control. "Yes, I *know* . . . God, you've said it enough before, one way or another . . . you want to be *free?* You selfish fool . . . you have two children and almost twenty years of marriage and you want to be *free* . . . ? Free for what? To sleep with every little available piece . . . is that the kind of freedom you want? Well, you were never anything but a bachelor who accidentally got married. You're a selfish man who's willing to destroy your family. No, you insist on it. I put my life into this marriage. I'm not complaining . . . it's a fact . . . I made the best home I could to make you, us, happy—"

"Please, Janet . . ."

"You'd like me to be calm? Was it the house, or living in the country? I don't think so. Not really. This is something that's been coming for a long time. I knew, but refused to face it." And then she sank to the lowest, hardly able to believe the demeaning words were coming from her . . . "What is it? Some twenty-year-old secretary you've been—"

"No, damn it, there isn't anyone like that. I'm not leaving this marriage for the reasons most men do. I told you . . . you're the only woman I ever loved or ever will—"

"You don't know the meaning of love. Where is the love in walking out on your family like this, then telling me how much you love me? You're a lying . . ." She couldn't finish it, slumping down on the couch. "Bill McNeil, you never loved anyone except yourself. And I wonder about the yourself part."

He went to her and knelt at her side. He took her in his arms. "You're wrong, very wrong. I do love you, but I just don't want to . . . I *can't* . . . be married any more. I feel like I'm choking, I can't take it—"

His words, his nearness, seemed to wrench at her, and she pushed him roughly away. She was off the couch now. "And neither can I. Get out of this house . . . now . . . tonight . . . please . . . just get *out*. . . ."

She went to their room, opened the closet and dramatically threw his clothes on the floor, feeling, in spite of herself, a bit foolish. "Go on, pick up, pack up and take your damned wonderful freedom. Choking, are you? Well, *so am I* . . ."

Nicole and Jason had come running out of their rooms and now stood behind their father in the bedroom doorway.

"What's happening?" Nicole was crying.

Janet wasn't going to be kind. She had no intention of sparing Bill, no intention of prettying things up so he could look wonderful in the eyes of his children.

"Ask your father, who loves you so much."

She did.

Bill felt numb inside. "Mother and I are separating for a while."

Oh, no. She wasn't going to let him get off that easily. "That's not true, Nicole. Your father wants a divorce."

"Oh, God, no. It isn't true, daddy . . . is it?" When he

didn't answer, Janet said, "The burdens are a little too great for your father—"

"I don't believe that. I know what this is, it's because of the house. Daddy wanted to move back to the city and we didn't. Well, it doesn't make any difference. A house isn't that important ... we'll move—"

"It's not the house, Nicole," Janet said. "Don't *you* feel guilty ... your father wants to be a free man. Free of us so he can recapture his precious youth. You're a big girl now. You can stand the truth. No lies, no subterfuge. You're too smart for that anyway. I won't insult you with pretense ..."

"Don't do this, daddy ... please, what happened to us? We were such a good family."

Bill put his arms around her and lay her head against him. "We still can be, honey. It doesn't mean we won't see each other. I'm still your father and I love you—"

"Then *why?* Why are you leaving?"

Janet couldn't listen to this any longer. "Because, Nicole, it seems we're in his way!"

Jason had been silent all this time, but now he broke in. "I think it's all crazy. I don't care ..." He looked at his father, with all the hurt of his young years suddenly alive in his eyes. "You ... I think you stink. I *hate* you ..." He ran to his room, before anyone could see his tears.

Nicole followed.

At least at this moment, Bill wanted to go down on his knees and plead with Janet to forget what he'd said. She'd lived with him so long she could read his feelings, and this time she wasn't going to make it so easy for him. How could there ever be a marriage between them now? It would only be a compromise ... That's what he'd done by marrying her. Compromised. Well, now it was at least out in the open. Let him live without a family, see what his terrific freedom brought him. He'd been too tied down, had he?

She pulled out his suitcases and started stuffing his clothes inside, but with the job only half done she turned abruptly and left the room.

Slowly he came into the living room and stood looking at her, suitcases uneasily in hand. "Maybe you're right,

249

Janet . . . maybe I do just need to get away by myself and think things out."

She didn't look at him, didn't answer . . .

"If you need me, I'll be at the Plaza."

She clenched her hands until the nails bit into her palms. I need you *now* . . . I need you, you selfish . . . But she couldn't beg for what he couldn't offer, for what he couldn't be.

"I love you, Janet . . ."

When she heard the door close, she was stunned, shattered, as if he had taken the reality of her life with him when he walked out the door. The reasons for his leaving were only theories to her . . . He loved her, she *knew* it. He'd never thought of another woman, she knew that too. And the children . . . no doubt how he felt about them. None of it made any *sense*. Or it made too much sense. More than she dared, or was able, to face.

By two o'clock in the morning she was no closer to the answer. Finally she went to her room and lay staring up at the ceiling. What time she fell into exhausted sleep she didn't know. Nor was she aware when she woke up that there were tears streaming down her face. The reality was simply too much for her to come to grips with.

When Nicole came into her room and saw her mother's face, her own anger and confusion were put aside. She sat now on the edge of the bed and held her hand, but Janet made no response. She was listless, hollow-eyed.

At a time when her mother needed her most, Nicole felt unable to say any of the comforting things her mother needed so much to hear. No words seemed enough.

"Mother, I have some hot coffee. Please drink it."

Janet looked at her daughter, her eyes and voice dull when she finally spoke. "Why, Nicole? Why do you think your father did this to us?"

"I don't know, mother, unless he's sick or something. I mean seriously, and doesn't want to tell us—"

"He isn't sick . . . just obsessed." And he always was, she thought to herself. Maybe a psychiatrist could figure it out. How could a man with a family like theirs just walk away?

"Please, mother, take a little something. The coffee . . ."

250

Janet's sobs became near-hysterical. "All right, what did I do, where did I fail?" She felt as if she wanted to die. If it weren't for the children . . . Her thoughts were so apparent that Nicole left the room, frightened, and called her Aunt Kit. . . .

Kit was shocked at Janet's appearance. If only Janet were angry enough to scream or break something, but she just lay placidly, inert.

"Look, Janet. I'm not going to fill you with all the bromides . . . about how this has happened to a million other women and you'll get over it. I'm not going to say this is a little whim, that Bill will reconsider and come crawling back on bended knees. He's an adolescent forty-five-year-old man, carrying his special monkey on his back. He always had it, I'm afraid he always will . . . But I'm worried about you. The hell with him. This has been a terrible shock, but you're going to have to pull yourself together, reach down, get on with the business of *your* life—"

"I want to die, Kit."

"*No*, goddamn it. Not Bill or a thousand Bills are worth that—"

"But he has been my life. How do I go on without him—?"

"Like you would if *he* died. You have your children and they're suffering as much as you are. It's tough but—"

"What did I do wrong, Kit?"

"Why do people have that terrible habit of always assuming they're guilty for everything that happens to them? Why are you so anxious to make yourself the scapegoat? *You* didn't do anything, and you know it. You're quite a gal, honey, but you don't run the world . . . you're not responsible for the making of Bill McNeil . . . that happened long before you met him . . . now I want you and the children to come over to my place and stay until you get over the initial shock—"

"Thank you, but I want to stay here. This is where my life was . . . we were so happy, Kit—"

"So you had almost twenty years that were good and now you have to move on. It's called phase two."

"Just like that? If only there'd been a woman, I could have understood it. But how do I fight this?"

"You can't fight selfishness, delayed adolescence, whatever . . . Besides, don't kid yourself, if Bill had another woman the hurt would have been worse. Now come on, get up, take a bath, dress and we'll go to lunch." It was a feeble attempt, but anything to get Janet moving . . .

"I just want to rest, Kit . . ." She said it as if she would never get up. . . .

For once Kit felt helpless, unable to do more than just sit with her through that day.

In the following week Kit sat in Janet's room watching her disintegrate. Janet had simply given up. She could barely summon the strength to make it to the bathroom. She hadn't slept or eaten. Her weight dropped abruptly, her eyes were hollows. Kit struggled with the notion of calling a psychiatrist. Instead, she decided to risk trying a little of her own homegrown therapy.

Kit walked into Janet's room and jerked back the covers. "I want you to get the hell out of that bed and now. You've wallowed in self-pity long enough. Your children have suffered just as much and you're only adding to it. Damn it, you're going to be the strong one. You have to be. The props have been knocked out from under them and the only one they have is you. Now, enough is enough." She prayed Janet might rally.

Janet looked at Kit, expressionlessly, then slowly managed to swing her legs over the edge of the mattress. She stood unsteadily, holding onto the bed for support.

Kit stood close by, but she made no effort to help. Janet had to do this on her own.

Janet walked toward the bathroom, and Kit followed her to turn on the water taps and let the bathtub fill. She added scented bubble bath and watched as Janet feebly let the nightgown fall, then immersed herself in the soothing water.

Thank God, Kit thought. At least a beginning.

From then on, Janet obeyed her like a puppet. No, like a zombie. But after a solid week of near catatonia, at least she was responding.

Kit picked out a suit, waited while Janet went through the motions of dressing, and then drove her into the city.

They had lunch in the restaurant where Janet had first confided to Kit so many years ago about her love for Bill. Kit had deliberately chosen this restaurant. If life was ever going to become real again, Janet would have to come face to face with the ghosts of the past.

While they had their drinks, Kit said, "Nat and I think that what you need is a little sea change . . . There's a cruise going to the Caribbean. It could be just what the doctor ordered."

Janet began to tremble, recalling that glorious honeymoon in Bermuda, the things they'd promised each other. How could she have guessed then that Bill would ever leave her? The tears came. "I don't feel up to it, Kit."

"If you don't make that first step, honey, you never will. Are you going to let that s.o.b. louse up your whole life? You listen to me. You have to start picking up the pieces and put your life back in order. A trip restores the spirit. Read the ads . . ."

"And what do I come home to, Kit?"

"Your children. That's one thing Bill left you with. We'll take it a day at a time. Now eat something. You look like a cadaver. Then we'll go pick up the tickets."

"What about the children? I don't think I should leave them, Kit—"

"That's not a good enough excuse. In fact, it's a cop-out. Obviously they'll stay with us, just as they have for the last week. I think what they need is to get away from you too."

"You're so good to me, Kit."

"Fine, and don't forget Nat—"

"I know. If I envy anybody anything right now, it's your marriage, Kit. I don't know too many people who are happily married or whose marriages have even survived, but yours is the best. What a father Nat is. He adores those five children and you're the best wife and mother. I just can't understand why mine didn't—"

"Because as I told you long ago, it takes two. I do, though, have to say that Nat is an unusual man and, yes, I think I have one of the few really happy marriages."

Janet looked at Kit. "It's so hard to understand what

makes people become what they are . . . it's a foolish question, Kit, but how is it Nat never seemed to go through the middle-age thing like—"

"Because he *knows* who he is and he's an intelligent man who takes life as it comes, lives every day as if it were going to be the last and hasn't time to waste on nonsense. If you live, you grow old. It's as simple as that. Nat accepts it. Bill doesn't." Or probably can't. . . .

Chapter Twenty-One

Janet didn't go on the cruise immediately. It was a month before she felt strong enough to face it, to face anyone except Kit and her family. She had tried to explain the divorce to Jason and Nicole, but beyond making repeated assurances that they were not in any way to blame, there was little she could give them by way of explanation. The fact remained that Bill had gone off, had left his children as surely as he'd left her. He had rejected them all. How do you explain that to kids who'd grown up idolizing their father? She couldn't, after all, really comprehend it herself.

She and the children spent as much time with Kit, Nat and their five children as possible, escaping the reminders in their own house, escaping the long, pained silences when they were alone together. Kit's children helped divert Jason and Nicole from their confused hurt, and Nat's joking even brought a faint smile to Janet's face from time to time.

But it was Kit who began to give her some perspective as they sat talking long into the night. "Janet, face it. In some ways Bill is a great guy, but somehow he's just never really matured. It's as if he's finally going through an adolescent identity crisis in middle age because he never really dealt with his feelings about Mama McNeil and that whole scene."

Janet grimaced. "That sounds like pop psychology. Somehow it's just too easy an explanation—"

"Not really. Bill had two ways of dealing with Violet. Either he bent over backward to go along with what she expected or he just completely withdrew. And that's pretty much what he did in your marriage. First he conformed—because he really does love you, in his fashion—and then he made the great escape. To *freedom.* Whooppee."

Janet gave her a look. "And that explains it? That excuses his behavior, walking out on us as if we were nothing—?"

"Nothing excuses it," Kit said. "It's heartless and cruel and he's a rat for doing it. If anything, what I'm telling you is that there's probably no resolution now short of separating and making your own lives, getting on with it. Bill has to grow up, resolve things for himself, learn how to deal with problems instead of simply withdrawing from them."

"Fine. And what do *I* do in the meantime? What do my children do?"

"Janet, I think your kids will weather it okay. It isn't easy for them, but Nicole has some understanding, some intuitive sense, at least, of what makes Bill tick—and loves him anyway. When he was giving her a rough time about seeing Mark she remembered something I once let slip about how Violet put up a stink over you before you and Bill were married. Nicole asked me about it, asked if maybe Bill was acting about her the same way his mother had been about you."

"Nicole said that?" Janet shook her head in surprise. "It seems everyone but me is able to see him so clearly . . . Well, one thing I'm glad of is that Nicole can have Mark to turn to now. Things don't look so easy for Jason, though."

Janet had lived through that month in a haze, sorting and resorting all the facts, never quite able to put them together in a pattern that made total sense of what had happened . . . The pain . . . the nagging, disabling pain . . . dulled the senses, the intellect . . . but at least she had been functioning, however mechanically, and she had finally let Kit persuade her to go on that cruise after all . . .

Now, as she stood in the middle of her stateroom and heard the popping of champagne corks, the laughter and the toasts to love, to the future, she wondered if it hadn't been too soon to take this trip. She began to tremble as the memories rushed in on her, dragging her down, drowning her. Her hand unsteady, she took out two tranquilizers and reached for a water glass. Kit was well-intentioned, but she probably shouldn't have gone along with her advice. Not yet . . .

She managed to get dressed and then stand in line to be greeted by the captain, smiling vaguely as she shook hands. When she went to her assigned table, she was suddenly glad that she hadn't followed her first impulse to ask for a table for one. She was sitting here with nine strangers to whom she didn't have to say more than a casual good evening. Not that it chased her nervousness or discomfort, but at least she wouldn't stand out as some oddity the way she would have if she'd taken a table alone.

The woman seated to her left was at least in her seventies, was garrulous and hard of hearing. A considerable plus, relieving Janet as it did of any need to do more than nod.

She wasn't quite so fortunate, though, with the man who sat to her right. He was paunchy, talkative and much too interested in her.

"Peter Gerard . . . call me Pete." There was a hint of alcohol on his breath. He made small talk, his remarks punctuated by short, sharp laughs, then started quizzing Janet about herself. She wasn't up to an interrogation.

Her answers were hesitant and she spoke without looking at him. What she wanted to do was tell him to leave her alone. His familiar and overeager manner was somehow repulsive, and she felt embarrassed, claustrophobic and finally she panicked. When she stopped answering altogether, he put his moist hand on hers before she could draw it away.

"Hey, what's the matter, Jan? You're on a cruise, lady. Time to relax and enjoy yourself. Get to know people. How's about I pick you up at your cabin tonight and we go dancing?"

"Please—" Janet pulled her hand away and sat in miserable silence.

"What did *I* do—?"

"I think the lady wants to enjoy her meal in peace. You're making it rather difficult."

Janet glanced across the table at the man who had spoken. He was looking steadily at "Call Me Pete," who suddenly shoved his chair back, threw down his napkin and left the table.

"He probably did a little too much bon voyage celebrating," the man said.

No response from Janet.

"My name is Allan Blum."

"Janet McNeil."

He noticed the wide gold wedding band, but decided the look in her eye said single. It also said upset and uneasy. "Is this your first trip to the—"

"No."

Nervous . . . unsure . . . all the symptoms were there. Was she taking a holiday alone or getting a divorce? He flipped a mental coin. It came up divorce. What man in his right mind would ever allow someone as lovely looking as this lady to take a separate vacation?

"I'm from Chicago."

"Yes."

"Yes . . . well . . . and you?"

"New York . . . You'll have to excuse me. I left something in my room."

She fumbled with the lock for what seemed an eternity before she finally entered her stateroom. Quickly she swallowed another tranquilizer. Tonight had been awful. Sitting among strangers had made her feel more alienated and alone than if she'd sat by herself. Now she wished she had. At least there would have been no need for stupid, superficial conversation. And that awful Pete. God, he was like a caricature of so many of the men she'd met when she first moved to New York, the ones she had escaped by moving to the Barbizon. Maybe Pete Gerard today lacked their superficial polish, but he was in a sense what they might have become. Middle-aged, self-styled studs, panting after their youth. Just like . . . No, Bill was different . . . he wasn't that far gone . . .

She undressed and got into bed.

At three o'clock she woke up with a pounding headache. God, how she wished she'd never come. . . .

Janet glanced at the travel clock on the nightstand. Ten in the morning. She wasn't going to get out of bed.

Besides, she'd missed the second sitting for breakfast anyway. What did it really matter?

For the rest of the day she stayed in her cabin, thinking in spite of herself of all the fun and fancy freedom Bill was having . . . She wouldn't be surprised if he'd slept with twenty women by now . . . The fantasies built to such a pitch that she picked up the water glass and threw it against the wall, watching it fragment into a dozen pieces. "Like my life," she screamed silently into the silent room.

By evening her anger was out of bounds . . . I wasn't enough for you? Well, I'll *show* you. . . .

I'll show you, she repeated to her reflection in the mirror as she piled her hair on top of her head and curled tendrils in front of her ears. She observed herself in the mirror. Don't lose your confidence, damn it. You're beautiful . . . terrific . . . and don't you forget it . . . Forget it? She didn't even believe it.

She decided to wear the most provocative dress she had, a white clinging matte jersey, long-sleeved and backless. At the plunging neckline she pinned a diamond brooch. She hastily applied a little more lipstick and then slammed the door as she left the cabin.

As she entered the dining room, she walked determinedly with her head high and her shoulders back, her pace and manner that of royalty. She was aware of the admiring looks, and rather pleased that her playacting seemed to be working . . . if only for a few minutes. At least her days of modeling had prepared her for this. And it was surely what was needed by a lady whose self-esteem had been knocked six feet under.

Thank you, Mr. William McNeil, prematurely aging bachelor, recently out of bondage.

Allan Blum, her earlier rescuer, got up and helped her into the chair next to him.

She rather formally nodded her thanks and began to attack the salad. From the corner of her eye she noted that Pete Gerard was sitting at the other end of the table and pointedly ignoring her. Good.

"I was beginning to wonder if you were feeling all right. You weren't here for breakfast or lunch," Allan said.

"I'm fine, thank you." Cool. Chilly. And purposely so.

259

But somehow she felt a bit redeemed, her self-image restored slightly. It was nice to have someone miss you, even if it was a stranger . . . whatever his name was . . .

"Thank you, by the way, for getting me out of that embarrassing situation yesterday." She spoke as if performing a duty which, once dismissed, closed all further need for conversation.

Her attitude was not unnoticed. It said hands off. But Allan's legal experience had taught him never to take the opposition *too* seriously. Patience, strategy could change one's attitude . . . No question, he was attracted to Janet McNeil . . . which was putting it mildly. Who could not be, really? Early to mid-forties, lovely face and figure . . . and altogether a lady. She was angry, and he could guess why. It usually happened on the first trip after a recent breakup. He knew and recognized the symptoms. After all, that was his specialty. Divorce. *What you need is a change of scenery and an ocean voyage* . . . That was the usual prescription offered by friends and family . . . solved all the problems. Like hell it did.

"I have Dramamine in case you need it—"

"Thank you, but so do I. And I don't think I'll need it—"

"You must be a good sailor . . ."

She didn't seem to hear. Her attention was on the waiter as he removed her salad plate and replaced it with the entree.

"I said you must be a very good sailor."

"Pardon me." She cut into the Jerusalem chicken.

He wasn't getting anywhere with these meaningless remarks. But then he knew as well as anyone what post-divorce depression was like. It was a time when you couldn't reach outside your own grief and anger.

He made no further attempt at conversation—if you could call it that—until dinner was over. They both seemed to stand at the same time.

"Would you join me in an after-dinner drink?" he asked.

"No, thank you. I'm going to the movie."

"I see." He smiled. "It's quite good, slightly antiquated but always appropriate for cruises. Deborah Kerr and Gary Grant in *A Time to Remember*. Shipboard romance,

260

that sort of thing. But I enjoyed it last night myself," he said as she walked away and headed for the theater.

Shipboard romance . . . Everything, even the damn movie was conspiring to bring back memories. She sat in the darkened theater, not seeing Cary Grant on the screen but Bill McNeil. Who, my dear ex-husband, are you with tonight? She got up and left before the tears began.

Escaping into the ladies' lounge, she blotted away her smeared mascara, applied fresh lipstick, then stood wondering what to do now. She wasn't about to go back to her stateroom and admit defeat. But she felt defeated nonetheless. A ship full of happy voyagers with a dozen things to do, and she felt alone . . .

She walked slowly from salon to salon and then to the cabaret, but it was filled to capacity with an audience applauding the antics of Shecky Greene.

Janet moved on.

For lack of anything better to do, she went into a small lounge where a trio was playing music sane people could dance to. Janet was seated at a table for two against the wall.

Her depression deepened as she sipped her daquiri and took in the other people in the lounge. Widows of all shapes and sizes were dancing with men much younger than themselves; young divorcees were being held close by older men, many of them balding and running to fat. She cringed. Was this what a single woman had to settle for?

She was about to leave when she looked up, and into the face of Allan Blum.

"May I join you?" he asked.

She looked at him closely for the first time. He was no more than in his early forties. Tall, very good looking, she admitted, with a mass of reddish hair and nice green eyes. All right, just what did she have to lose? He was a whole lot more attractive than the types she was looking at gyrating out on the dance floor.

Deborah Kerr would have said . . . "Of course, why not?"

He took the chair across from her.

"Did you enjoy the movie?"

"Yes . . . very appropriate, as you pointed out."

He looked across the table and watched her take the last sip of her drink.

"I'm going to have a Scotch and water. May I order another for you?"

"Thank you . . ."

The waiter brought their drinks.

"You're from New York?"

Fascinating conversation. . . . All right, the obvious answer. "Yes."

"I love New York. It's a cliché to say it, but the place really is stimulating. We have a branch of our firm there as well as in Chicago."

An exciting piece of news. It deserved . . . "Well, I guess it's a nice place if you like it." She took a sip. Come to think of it, maybe it didn't deserve *that*.

"You're not having a very pleasant trip, are you, Mrs. McNeil?" he said quietly.

It was so sudden, and personal, she felt caught off guard. It's none of your business, she wanted to say. But she replied, "Not very."

No sooner had she said those two small words than she wondered why she was bothering. Men didn't happen to be her favorite part of the human race this year.

"Forgive me, but you're going through a transition and it's *always* rough, Mrs. McNeil—"

She looked at him, moistened her dry lips. "I don't even know you, Mr. . . ."

"Allan. Allan Blum."

"Yes . . . well . . . I don't know you and I think you're asking some rather personal things—"

"I'm sorry, but I think I know just what you're going through. I think I can empathize—"

"Really! Are you a fortune teller, or a psychiatrist?"

"Neither. I'm an attorney. I not only specialize in divorce, but I'm also a victim of my own expertise, you might say. So I understand. You're uptight and on the defensive, and the hardest thing in the world right now is to relax and allow yourself to have a little fun. Even though it's the best thing you could do for yourself. It could even be pleasant . . ."

She took a sip. What a bitch she'd turned into. At least

he was trying to be pleasant and, so it seemed, he was a gentleman.

"I'm sorry, I was rude . . . And you're right. It's just not easy."

"I know. I went through it three years ago. My wife thought fifteen years with me was enough. She married my best friend. Fortunately, we didn't have any children and that made it a little easier."

"I have two, thank God . . . it gave me something to live for or I think I would have lost my sanity—"

"I suspect it's better to have children. It was tough being replaced by another man, I assure you . . . made me feel like, if you'll excuse the expression, horse manure."

"Makes you feel like that when you're not replaced by anyone else too."

"What did yours do, go into the priesthood?" Not very funny, he thought. Even for a divorce lawyer.

"Something like that. Except his monastery is Manhattan, without taking any vow of celibacy. You see, he wanted to be free and good-by to almost twenty years and two children. I think it's better your way. At least she left you for someone. Mine left for nothing."

Allan shook his head. "Unbelievable," he said, and meant it.

"I thought so too."

"I simply can't understand anyone leaving someone like you."

"Well, you don't know that much about me. But I . . . I tried . . . I really did—"

"That I believe." And he really did.

"Since we've become . . . so confiding in so short a time, tell me, what makes a man walk away from a marriage for no apparent good reason?"

"Well, you hear about it all the time, not that it makes it more palatable, but some men—and women—are petrified of growing old, feel like they're going to miss the boat, and become obsessed with holding on . . . or rather out . . . How old is your husband?"

"Forty-five."

"That's about when it most often happens. The seven-year-itch or the twenty. No one really knows the answer.

But you'll pick up the pieces and one day someone will walk into your life out of the blue . . . You're much too young and far too desirable to live alone. You'll marry again—"

"*Never . . .*"

"A very long time, as I'm sure you've heard."

"What about you?"

"I'm partial to the notion of one special person to share my life with. When she comes along, I think I'll know . . . Now, let's dance. . . ."

The day the ship lay at anchor in Kingston, Jamaica, Janet and Allan stood at the rail watching the young Jamaican men dive for coins in the wondrously pellucid, clear blue-green sea. The money was retrieved and brought to the surface within moments. Laughing, they shook the water from their heads, held up a hand and called out, "More!"

Allan threw a handful of coins and quickly they dove back and out of sight.

Janet said, "Aren't they wonderful?"

Allan wanted to say, yes, and so are you. Instead he said, "I think it's time for us to take the launch." With a lady like Janet, you didn't rush. He took her arm, led her down the gangplank and helped her into the small boat.

Kingston could never have been adequately described in the travel folders. Statuesque Jamaican women with twisted turbans and ropes of colored beads strode majestically in bare feet. Shopping for the food their families would eat that night, they bartered not so differently from the ladies on Hester Street whom she remembered. Janet and Allan stopped at a bazaar where musk oils from the East and perfumes from Paris were sold. She allowed herself to accept a bottle of Patou's *Joy* that Allan assured her . . . more than once . . . was only the gesture of one shipmate to another, a remembrance of good companionship on this brief excursion . . . No, you surely didn't rush this lady . . . Further on, the bazaars became more exotic, and she bought earrings and beads for Nicole, Kit and Kit's daughters, Deborah and Becky. She had no difficulty selecting an ivory bracelet for her mother, but Effie was a problem. After a dozen items were eliminated she finally gave up and settled on a colorful petticoat which she knew Effie would never wear. For Jason, Nat and the boys she bought wristwatches.

The day was an enchantment. As they sat on the wide terrace of the Jamaica Inn, sipping a rum-and-fruit drink, Janet felt the first complete sense of peace she'd known since she started this . . . was odyssey too strong a word? Ironically, the realization of it made her momentarily uneasy.

The waiter came by and asked if they'd care for more drinks.

Slightly light-headed, Janet looked at Allan. "Should I risk it?"

"Live dangerously. Besides, you're in good hands, if I do say so myself."

She was beginning to have few doubts about that. "Well, all right, and then I think we should have lunch."

As they lingered over coffee, Janet said, "You know, Allan, it occurs to me that I've been burdening you with my problems for over a week, but I really know very little about you . . ."

Allan laughed. "Well, to be perfectly immodest, I'm afraid my story would read like a Jewish *Gone With the Wind*."

"Really? Well, I'd love to hear about it. Family sagas are my favorites."

"Maybe that's because you're a romantic . . ."

"About some things, I suppose . . . anyway, start properly . . . at the beginning."

Allan not only knew his family tree, but was rather fascinated by it. His great-grandfather, Julius Kahn, had arrived on the shores of Louisiana from Alsace-Lorraine two years before the outbreak of the Civil War. Julius's wealth was not quite large enough to finance the Southern cause, but the funds he contributed were considerable nonetheless. Julius was integrated into the upper strata of Jewish society, where he met and married Amanda Langer. It was a lavish wedding, and the house in the French Quarter that he gave his wife as a wedding gift was considered one of the Quarter's true showplaces. Not many weeks after being carried over that imposing threshold, Amanda was able to whisper in the silence of their bed-

265

chamber that Julius could be proud, that she was expecting a child. Nine months later they became the parents of a blonde, blue-eyed little girl that they named Evelyn. In the next few years Andrew and Charles were equally welcomed. It was a home of love and devotion, and of spirituality too. Julius, in fact, was one of the first and largest contributors to New Orleans's new Reformed Temple. Julius Kahn was also an astute student of human nature, as well as of history. When the first shot at Fort Sumter rang out, Julius understood that it also signaled the end for the glory of the old South. Inevitably, he felt, the Confederacy's cause was doomed. Democracy and slavery *were* incompatible. And separatism could only be the death of the Union. He'd had quite enough of being separate, thank you, before reaching his hard-won status in America. By the end of the war Julius's Confederate dollars had long since been converted into francs and marks, and were deposited in a secure Swiss bank. Disposing of the few holdings that he still retained, he moved his family north to Philadelphia.

When Julius and Amanda Kahn's daughter Evelyn was seventeen, she met and married Samuel Blum, whose family was three generations removed from Germany. David Blum was their only child, and he and his wife Louise were the parents of Allan and his two older brothers, Lawrence and Philip. Louise and David Blum gave their sons not only material wealth, but imbued them with pride and respect for an ancient heritage. For David Blum and his wife, Judaism was a code of ethics that a man applied to his daily life, not only on the Day of Atonement; it was a living, ongoing covenant between man and God.

It was not until Allan joined the army that he seemed to forget some of his earlier training, and it was a particularly sad moment for his parents when he told them that he was marrying outside the faith. Out of his love for them he did, he admitted, regret that Joyce Porter was not Jewish, but reminded them one didn't always have a choice in the matter of love and he prayed—literally— that they would accept her. In the end, out of their love for him, they gave their blessing.

Unfortunately, there was more than one time during his marriage that he had occasion to recall his mother saying,

266

"Your father and I don't want to play God or sound all-knowing, but the beliefs of two people do tend to make a far stronger bond . . . there are no promises that marriage will be perfect, even with people of the same faith, but at least the chances for understanding are greater. . . ." The words had especially come back to him during his last confrontation with Joyce. Indeed, the sounds of her attack . . . "I'm through with you, you damned, despicable Jew . . ." still were an ugly resonance in his head. That part of the "romantic" saga he omitted. It didn't fit. And it was hardly what Janet wanted to hear . . . or he to tell her . . . If their friendship grew and a good reason for it came up, he might tell her. Perhaps . . . another time. He had to smile to himself. A male Scarlett O'Hara . . . he'd do it "tomorrow."

"Well, that about sums up four generations of Blums," he finished crisply.

Looking at Allan sitting across from her, Janet thought of Yankel Stevensky and the four generations that had come from him. He too had left something of his stamp on her. She *felt* it, especially at this moment . . . "That's quite a story, Allan. May I tell you something that's strangely parallel in our lives?"

"Please do."

"Well, my antecedents weren't as elegant or romantic as yours. Hardly. But my great-grandfather was Jewish—"

"Were you brought up in the faith?"

"No, my parents were Protestants. But my father, like me, as I discover more and more, has an inbred sense of *Jewishness*, rather than Judaism. I'm sorry to say I know so little about it, and that I never knew the religious part, but I have a strange sort of pride in the fact that that wonderful Jewish heritage *is* a part of me. You know . . . the greatest warmth and generosity I think I ever had—especially when I most needed them—was from a lady I'll never forget . . . Her name was Fayge Kowalski. That lady taught me something about goodness that I hope I never forget. . . ."

The rest of the trip was pleasantly, but not romantically, spent with Allan. He'd been very good for her, but she'd established from the beginning that there was to be

267

a distance, and he respected her feelings . . . much as he regretted the constraint.

The last night they strolled once again around the deck, then stood at the rail looking out at the midnight-blue sea.

He put his arm around her, which she allowed, but she drew back when he leaned over to kiss her. "Allan, you've been terribly nice, you're a wonderful person and I'm truly grateful for your company . . . but you know, I didn't come aboard for a single lady's fun and games. I hope I made that clear in the beginning, but, please, don't take offense . . . you've been so . . ."

"Gentlemanly?"

"Yes, and as I said, I'm grateful—"

"Well, I'll accept that, but you should also know that I had every bad—or good, depending on one's point of view—intention in the world of trying to go to bed with you. Truth to tell, I thought about it the first time I saw you. I'd *still* like it . . . I'm not, I hope you agree, exactly Jack the Ripper. And further truth to tell, it hasn't been exactly easy being this close to someone you like for two whole weeks and . . . well, tomorrow it's homeward bound and I'd hate to think this is going to be the end of it, of us . . ."

"Allan, as you well know, nothing in my life has been resolved . . . obviously I can't become involved . . . I mean . . ."

"You mean you still hope some miracle will happen and your husband will have a change of heart and want to come home."

"I guess I'd be less than honest if I said differently."

"Don't hitch your hopes to that, Janet. It can only lead to more disappointment."

"Maybe . . . but one thing I know, this trip hasn't been wasted. I've had a lot of time to think and I'm going to see if we can't salvage something. I find it impossible to believe, when two people had as much as we did, that it can be over just like that—"

"And your pride?"

"Pride? You can't spend your old age with pride. I'm going to try, Allan."

"So . . . then this is good-by for us?"

"I think so. But I'll always remember how kind you were."

"Well, that wasn't what I had in mind. But if you ever want to be in touch, let me know. Chicago isn't very far away, and then, of course, I'm in New York a lot. Hold that thought, if you can . . ."

Chapter Twenty-Two

Kit was at Kennedy Airport to meet Janet's flight back from Florida. She was shocked—and pleased—when she saw the change in Janet, but she said nothing until they were in the car on the drive back to Westchester.

"Okay, Janet, I can't stand the suspense. What happened to you?"

"Why?"

"Well, my God. I mean you were walking a pretty thin line the last time I saw you, and now you seem almost ... content. Did anything *happen?*"

"A lot of things. Mostly in my head."

"Oh? Such as?"

"Making a stab at getting Bill back."

Kit paused. That wasn't what she'd been hoping for. "Well, Columbus took a chance and found America. Too bad the queen almost cut off his head. If it doesn't work out you could get hurt bad, Janet."

"I already am, so what have I got to lose?"

"Not much, when you put it that way. Anything else interesting happen aboard?"

"Well . . . I met a man. Very nice. But that's as far as it went. How he ever put up with me, God only knows. I was bitchy as all get out in the beginning . . . Now tell me about the children."

"Nicole is very sad and Jason's very mad . . . Not to change the subject, what about this man?"

Janet shrugged. "What's there to tell?"

"You tell me. Did he try?"

"Yes."

"That must have charged your batteries a little."

"That wasn't why I took the trip—"

"But still it helps to restore a lady's morale."

"I guess, but in my case it didn't work. You know something, Kit, you can't run away. In fact, it's depressing when you look around and see nothing but lonesome women all literally in the same boat, all trying to prove they're still marketable. I wonder how many tears were spilled at night in those luxurious staterooms? How did they feel when the blonde wigs and the false eyelashes came off and they took a good look at themselves? It's no fun to have to start all over again . . . I wonder where I begin—"

"It gets easier after the first fallout."

"Maybe, but right now I'm going to concentrate on how to get my marriage back together."

"Mazel tov."

Kit drove into Janet's driveway and helped her out with the luggage.

Janet's heart suddenly began to pound as she opened the door. Bill wouldn't be home. Not tonight, and maybe never. The thought made her shiver. She wasn't prepared for the shock of coming back to an empty home, to the memories. She'd thought she was past that. Presumptuous thought . . .

The two women stood in awkward silence in the foyer.

"Well, I'm home . . . Kit, how can I thank you . . . ?"

"Big deal."

She put her arms around her friend. "You've bailed me out of so many things, but seeing me through this is something I'll never forget—"

"You're going to make it, baby. Now I've got to run. Talk later."

Janet took the suitcases to her room, and was just starting to unpack when she heard Nicole's car in the driveway. She hurried to the front door and opened it, tears starting to her eyes when she saw her daughter. "Nicole, darling, oh, God, I missed you—"

They weren't sure whose tears were whose as they embraced. Then, arm in arm, they walked into the house.

As they sat on the sofa, neither knew what to say, how to begin.

"I loved the postcards and letters . . ." Nicole finally said.

"I'm glad."

"Did you have a good time?"

"I missed you and Jason very much. In fact when we got to Nassau I wanted to fly back, but then I thought, no . . . I needed the discipline of realizing I was going to be alone. It was a test, I suppose, to see if I could make it—"

"You did, mama . . . you survived."

"Hmm . . . well, I get a gold star for that. Now tell me about you."

Nicole hesitated. "I spent a couple of weekends with dad." She watched for her mother's reaction. Nothing.

"How is he?"

"Not very happy, mom. I think he has a lot of regrets . . ."

"Did he say so?"

"No . . . he didn't have to. The tone of his voice, the look in his eye. The way he kissed me when he said good-by."

"Well, I'm sure he misses you."

"I think he misses us *all*. Incidentally, he took an apartment. I was surprised when I saw it."

"Why?"

"Because it was furnished—and not too attractively either. I think he misses not having anything that belongs to him."

"Really? Well, no one exactly forced him to leave."

"I know, mom, but I can't help it . . . I just feel so sorry for him. It's as though he doesn't care—"

"That's strange. I'm a little surprised he's unhappy now that he got rid of his responsibilities. And I assumed he'd like living in an apartment. The way he used to . . ."

"No, he couldn't wait to get out. I don't know, mom. Honest, he really seems sort of . . . well, lost."

"I'm sure."

"You're not angry about my seeing him, are you?"

Janet saw the uncertainty in her daughter's face and suddenly felt guilty for adding to the conflicts she must already be feeling. Her voice was softer, contrite, as she said, "No, darling. He's your father and it's right and natural that you should love him. I'm sorry for the things I said about him the night he left. I was a little out of my mind, I guess."

272

"That's understandable. I mean when a husband suddenly springs it on his wife that he wants a divorce, you can't expect to be cool and calm about it."

"Still, I attacked him in front of his own children, and that was wrong. Hindsight is always . . . but I wish I had handled it better."

"Nobody's perfect, mom, especially not in a situation like that. It's been tough for all of us, dad included."

Janet was tempted to tell Nicole about trying a reconciliation, but thought better of it. What if it failed . . . ?

"Your father and I will try to act like mature people. We have you and Jason to—"

"Oh, thank you, mother, that's one thing dad was worried about. I mean, how you two would be about Jay and me—"

"Well, he needn't have."

Jason had been at the Weisses when Kit came back from the airport, and went home immediately to see his mother. He had never missed her as much as in the last weeks.

He let himself into the house and went to her room, swooped her up in his arms and held her off the ground. He looked so much like Bill that for a moment she did a double-take.

"Hey, you look great, mom . . . In fact, you're the best looking girl I ever did see . . . did you have a good time?"

"Not so bad . . ."

"Thanks for the watch . . . Incidentally, I made first string. Hey, I'm really glad you're home, mom . . ."

"Me too, and I don't intend to leave for a long time."

"Great. Now how about some chow?"

"I don't know what we have in the house except frozen food. Let's go out to dinner."

"No, I want to have dinner at home. Scrambled eggs, anything."

Janet went to the kitchen, looked through the freezer and found chicken crepes, cannelloni, pizza, spaghetti and meatballs.

Jason came in and sat at the table, watching her. His

273

mother was beautiful. How could his father possibly have left her? He must have been crazy . . .

When she turned and saw him, she noted the set of his jaw, and decided it was better not to bring Bill up. It was different with Nicole, who spoke about her father almost as much as Jason seemed to want to avoid such discussions. It was as though Bill didn't exist for him. He was very angry with his father, very protective of his mother, and . . . in the ways of the young . . . sternly unforgiving.

Attempting to keep the tone light, she said, "Decisions . . . now, we have—"

"How about cheese omelets with green chiles."

"Sounds good. By the way, I didn't congratulate you on making first string. I think it's great." And then, while beating the eggs, she asked, "Anything else happen while I was away?"

"Not much . . . I gave my car back to what's his name."

"You mean your father."

"So I've been told."

"Jason, it doesn't solve anything to be so bitter."

"Really? You mean you're not? And you can forgive him for what he did?"

"In a way, yes."

"That wasn't the impression I got when you left."

"Well, I've had time to think about a lot of things and I realize your father's going through sort of a special time in his life . . . trying to get back his youth—"

"That's very nice, but I'm his *son, not* his father, and as far as I'm concerned if I never see him again it will be too soon."

"Jason, please don't say that."

"Why? It's true. You know, mom, I could forgive him if he was a drunk or a gambler . . . they're sicknesses . . . but to just walk away from us when we need him most, for no reason . . . well, it's something I'll never understand . . . He never loved us, he couldn't have—"

"That's not true, Jason. Take my word for it, your father does love us. He's just terribly confused about himself—"

"Well, I don't know too much about psychiatry."

"You don't have to be a psychiatrist to have feelings and a little understanding. What was his reaction when you returned the car?"

"I don't know because I wouldn't talk to him."

"That must have hurt him—"

"Hurt him! He didn't worry too much about hurting us."

"You did it to punish him—"

"You bet. I don't want anything from him. I bought a motorcycle with the money grandpa sent me for Christmas. And I'm *not* going to M.I.T. I'm still going to be an engineer, but not with a degree from his damned alma mater and for sure it's not going to be McNeil & Son . . ."

Janet poured the eggs into the omelet pan, thinking Jason's wounds might well be the hardest to heal. He felt so abandoned by Bill, he'd thought of him as an idol who could do no wrong in spite of the usual adolescent tensions between father and son. Now he found his father was just a mortal man with all the human frailties and he couldn't accept that. There was still another side of the coin. Now that Bill had left, Jason was assuming the posture of the man of the family and felt he was protecting his mother. His father had left her and he couldn't and wouldn't forgive that. No, *sir* . . .

"Darling, go call Nicole. The omelets are ready."

That night Janet took out the albums which had accumulated through the years. They represented, in their fashion, the sum total of her life, the happy times, those special moments, almost twenty years there in those albums. Yes, indeed. Those years were too precious not to try to salvage. For her children, and not least for herself.

At eleven o'clock the next morning Janet called Bill at the office.

"Janet?" He sounded shaky, but no more so than she felt.

"Yes."

"What's wrong?"

"Nothing. I just got home and I thought we should talk."

He wiped the perspiration from his forehead with his

handkerchief. "My God, you scared me. I thought something had happened."

Something did happen . . . "Are you busy for lunch?"

"No."

"Would it be convenient if we met?"

After all those years . . . would it be convenient, she was asking.

"Sure, I'd like that. Where?"

Like old times. "Maxwell's Plum?"

"Wonderful."

"Twelve okay?"

Is it okay to leave you, Janet, would you object? "Twelve would be fine."

They sat opposite each other in the dimly lit room, remembering other times. The conversation was guarded, stilted, Bill thinking Janet hadn't changed much through the years. In fact, maturity had added to her beauty. So if he was this much in love, what had pulled them apart? A good question . . . He sure as hell didn't know, and that was the only thing he was sure of. How could you still love someone but not want to live with them? He felt *owned* . . . and yet Janet had never made those kinds of demands. She expected him to be faithful, sure . . . but all women wanted that, never mind what the modern ones claimed, and the truth was he'd never thought of being anything but a faithful husband. Maybe he should see a psychiatrist. And if he did, what would he learn? *You had a mother who suffocated you and you never got over it.* He really didn't much like himself, but how did he fight down these feelings of wanting so badly to be his own person, not to be beholden . . . ?

"You look wonderful, Janet."

"Thank you."

"How was the trip?"

"I had a nice time . . . You look . . . happy, Bill."

He didn't look happy or content in the least. She had never seen him with this haunted look. Nicole was right.

"Do I? Well, starting over isn't easy—"

"Oh? I thought it was for a man."

"What makes you think men don't go through . . . adjustments?"

And change of life . . . it's called male menopause. Up to now she'd never really believed it, taken it seriously.

"I'm sure they do. Well, people don't adapt so easily to change. Sometimes, I'm told, what we think will make us happiest turns out the opposite. Fantasy and anticipation don't stand up to reality too well . . . I remember I said something like that when we first met. . . ."

She'd meant that rather long speech as a springboard for him to launch into his misgivings, if he had any. But if he had any second thoughts he apparently wasn't about to admit them.

"That's true," he said. "Now tell me about your trip. Nicole said you met . . . someone . . . a very nice man . . ."

She looked at him. Wasn't it strange, he didn't seem a bit jealous. Quite matter of fact about it. But then that could also be a defense. She hoped. But then it hit her that it was typical of Bill. He had that marvelous facility of avoiding subjects he didn't want to face . . . "Nicole told you that? I'm afraid she's trying to make you jealous." The next words were said with more confidence than she felt. "Now I think I should get on with the reason I called. Pride at this point between us is ridiculous. You and I have a lot of years invested and I can't honestly believe that our marriage didn't mean anything to you—"

"You're right, Janet. It did mean a great deal—"

"Then what happened that suddenly made you want out of it?"

He shook his head. This was very tough. Honesty was not charitable; it was cruel, devastating. But this demanded the truth, so help him God . . . please.

"Before I answer, crazy as this will sound—I love you, Janet, so it wasn't that. As for it being sudden, it wasn't that either. I know you sensed my frustrations in Europe. Maybe it began then or long before. Between my mother's possessiveness and my father's sending me off to a military academy, I always felt as if I was in jail . . . like I was their *property*. Oh, who the hell really knows? I don't. But the result was that as I got older I began to feel as if I'd been shut off from myself, as though Bill McNeil got lost somewhere. I started to rebel, I guess, against the conformity of . . . marriage." Quickly he

277

added, "Not to you, but the whole *thing* of it . . . the sort of finality of it. Wednesdays at the club for cards—I hated knowing I'd see those same faces week after week for the rest of my life. There were no surprises. I knew what to expect for dinner every night. The drive back and forth to Manhattan began to seem endless and each mile became longer each year. Then I got to hate taking the train in the winter. I got so sick and tired of the same conversations coming home that I used to hide behind a paper. After all these years, Janet, this is very hard to say, but I simply wasn't cut out to be a suburban husband."

She'd become angrier with each word, with the triviality of his complaints when compared to what he had destroyed, and it was only with difficulty that she held herself in check. "But you seemed so happy."

"That's how it appeared. You even get good at deceiving yourself. The truth is I was expected to act like Nat and all the others."

"Since I wasn't aware of all this, tell me, what could I have done to make life different for you?"

"Nothing, because it wasn't *you*. It was me and I take all the blame."

"Let's not talk about blame, let's try to understand how we failed each other. Maybe then we—"

"*You* didn't fail, Janet. Unfortunately you just married the wrong man. You should have been married to someone like Nat, who loves what Kit loves. You want Westchester and I want Manhattan. I look for surprises, you want permanence, the expected . . . our needs are different, don't you see?"

"I was willing to come back to the city with you, Bill."

"Not really. You were doing it to please me and I didn't want it on those terms."

"Bill, I would have gone anywhere with you. For God's sake, you must know that."

"But you wouldn't have, Janet. Not really. The children came first. Wait until Jay gets out of school, you said."

"Wasn't that fair? Couldn't you have stood it another two years?"

"Maybe . . . but deep down I knew if I stayed I'd get

278

sucked into the undertow, settle in, compromise . . . you begin losing your edge when you feel you're being put aside—"

"And you feel I did that?"

"Yes, I guess I do . . . not that I ever stopped you. But the children came first. Period."

Janet took a long sip of wine. "All right, Bill, you say you love me, and you know I love you. I'm going to tell Nicole and Jay they're simply going to have to understand my first priority is my husband. I want us to go back together, Bill . . . life without you is—"

"Wait," he said, swallowing hard. "I know you'll never understand, but I can't be more than I am, which is a variety of louse. That's a fact of life I'm stuck with. So are you. The truth is, I don't *want* to be married anymore . . ."

She sat staring at him, feeling as if the wind had been knocked out of her. Finally she asked softly, "You don't even want to make an attempt? Don't I count? Don't you think you owe me something? We had so much together once, you know we did . . ."

The pain in her eyes was almost more than he could stand. He wanted so badly to take her and hold her. "We still do . . . but Janet, darling, I want my life back . . . I'm terribly sorry our marriage did this to someone as wonderful as you. But what it amounts to is, one person shouldn't have to keep another's life going at the expense of his own. Or hers. Life shouldn't be a tradeoff . . . that sounds cold, I know . . . I wish I could put it better . . . it's just my feeble attempt, I guess, to say I'm not marriage material. Twenty years late. I'll provide for you and the children, and I hope you and I can be, well, sensible and mature enough to stay good friends . . ."

When had she heard that said? In the very beginning of their relationship . . . *Here's to friends . . . friends* and *lovers.* It was the first night she'd slept with Bill.

"You want us to be *friends* . . . sensible and mature," she said, past caring about his feelings now. "We might even sleep together on occasion when you have nothing better to do. Like lovers? *Friends* and *lovers.* Remember? We started out that way. But let me tell you what you can do . . . go fuck yourself, Bill McNeil. Is that shocking coming from wholesome, sweet Janet, former Miss

279

Kansas? Well maybe, but I've changed too. I'm not quite as ladylike as I used to be. You can go to *hell*." She was nearly screaming as she picked up her wine glass and poured its contents into his lap. Then, with everyone looking on, she ran out of the restaurant.

How she got home she'd never know. She had humbled herself, begged. But what hurt worst was that he didn't want her. Suburbia was out, Manhattan was his mistress. Always had been . . .

For three days and nights she scarcely got out of bed.

She told the children nothing of her meeting with Bill, but they were beside themselves, thinking she was having a nervous breakdown.

Kit was as concerned as they were, but she wasn't going to stand by and watch Janet fall apart day by day. Not again. In feigned anger, she said, "He just didn't want to be married. Get that into your head, Janet. He told it to you straight . . . it was boring . . . not stimulating enough. Bill's a guy who needs a lot of excitement, even if he doesn't know what excites him."

Between tears Janet said, "I despise him, Kit, and to think I lived with a stranger for almost twenty years. He wanted back *his* life. But how do I pick up the pieces of mine?"

"It seems we've been through this one before. I remember having to haul you out of bed at the Barbizon a long time ago. Now you get the hell out of bed right now and stop feeling so damned sorry for yourself."

"You're right, Kit . . . I just made up my mind not to delay the divorce any longer . . . I want to get the damned thing started. This being separated is agony, but I keep hoping . . . and that's stupid. Imagine, after he *said* he no longer wanted me—"

"That's a wise decision. Bill hasn't made a move to do it yet . . . Damned if I understand him. He's nuts . . . doesn't want you and still can't seem to let you go." Like the little boy tied to his mother's apron strings, she thought.

Chapter Twenty-Three

Gradually the days passed and became weeks. With Kit's prodding she began playing tennis and going to the club. She despised it, but loneliness drove her . . . The first Saturday night dinner dance was the worst. If it hadn't been for Kit she would have stayed home. It could hardly be a secret that Bill had walked out on her. How could she face anyone? "Screw them," Kit said. Some joke . . .

She felt as if she were on autopilot for most of the evening, as if she had dressed in the right thing, smiled at the proper moments, made the appropriate comments—all without really being there. She tried to assume an I-don't-give-a-damn air. But the whole evening was unreal.

Their old friends stopped at the table, saying how nice it was to see her. And mechanically she smiled. Then Richard Conners, one of Bill's old golf foursome, stopped by the table and asked if he could have the pleasure of a dance. Sure. He'd never asked before, but why not? Respond appropriately and politely, Janet.

As they moved across the dance floor, they passed Richard's wife, Buffy, who was dancing cheek to cheek with George Hamlin.

Suddenly it seemed Richard was holding her closer, and closer. She seemed to wake up from a trance when Richard whispered in her ear, "I've always been crazy about you, Janet. God, the times I wanted you, thinking how great it would feel to have those gorgeous long legs wrapped around me. Of course you were married to good old Bill, but now it's different. Let's meet for lunch tomorrow and then go to a—"

She swung her arm with all her might, and it landed square in the middle of his nose. The blood ran down his face and onto his white dinner jacket.

Suddenly there was a hush. The music continued but all eyes were on her. Quickly Janet weaved through the crowd and out to Nat's car, where she sat shaking.

Within minutes Kit and Nat were sitting beside her.

"What *happened?*" Kit asked.

"I want to go home." She didn't trust herself to say more. . . .

Kit came over the next morning. By now Janet could bring herself to tell her the things Richard had said.

"Why, that rotten old—"

"I wonder if I'm going to get a phone call from his wife . . ." Even the thought of it made her feel like throwing up . . . she could imagine how ugly and distorted it might get . . . "How do you think he's going to explain what happened, Kit? I know I'm going to become the heavy in this."

Kit laughed. "So you think darling adorable little Buffy is going to call you? Buffy . . . is that a name for a woman close to fifty, I ask you? Have no fears, darling. They've been playing around for a long, long time, and not with each other. They'll pretend to have a fight. It's part of the act, but she'll forget about it by lunch at the motel after a little roll in the hay with dear dignified George Hamlin the Third."

Janet was as shocked as she looked. "Where have I been? I'm a member of this community too. How come you know everything?"

"Because you're not interested in gossip and I happen to have big ears. You learn a lot when you play golf and bridge."

"Has anything like that ever happened to you, Kit . . . I mean since you've been married?"

"Once or twice, but from the look in my eye they knew they'd get their balls chopped off."

"But when a woman's single every man thinks he can . . . my God, it's so degrading. I'm sending in my resignation. I don't want to belong to the club . . . I'm a member of a different club now." The outcasts.

In the three months since Bill had taken to his freedom, more than once he had wanted to call and ask Janet to take him back. Which was why he still hadn't
282

asked her to go ahead with the divorce. That step was so *final* . . . Having been married for so long had changed him considerably more than he'd realized the night he'd left . . . Yes, he had hoped that being apart might help him sort out the pieces, but now it seemed as if he had only meant it as a temporary measure. He had just wanted to be alone for a while. With, he now realized, the assurance that Janet would always be there in the background. But he'd asked for a divorce and it looked as if he was getting it.

He sat with a drink in his hand, looking at the large legal envelope on the coffee table. This afternoon at the office he'd received the preliminary papers from Janet's attorney. She was going ahead with . . . Well, why not? Hadn't he spelled it out that afternoon in Maxwell's Plum? But down deep, he also felt crushed. Time to pay the piper, in more ways than one. . . .

Getting back into action hadn't been as great as he'd thought it would be. At times his loneliness pushed him to drink too much. The little fillies at the singles bars bored him and while he found rock dancing sort of fun it was hardly, as alleged, a turn-on. There had to be something *wrong* with him. Those young broads would have given any normal man a hard-on, dressed in their tight jeans, sandals with four-inch heels and those revealing, glittering tops. Nothing was left to the imagination. An hour or so of that and he'd had enough. Boy, life had sure changed since the fifties . . . and so had he.

He called his sister Harriet more often. She was far from the comfort he apparently needed. She told him that what he'd done went beyond her understanding. Kit would have nothing to do with him, and Charles . . . well, he was a married man. All the people they knew had come through Janet. His only companion now was his damned feeling of guilt. There were times he couldn't think of one good reason why he'd left her. If she had been the least bit difficult maybe he could have justified it. But he knew he'd been somehow wrong, and it was a very bitter pill, indeed, to swallow. He even wondered if maybe he was a latent homosexual. Having deliberately gone to those singles bars to prove he wasn't hadn't accomplished

283

anything. Women simply turned him off. He, Bill McNeil, ex-stud . . . *ex* . . .

The first time he picked up a girl and brought her to the apartment he got only as far as taking off his pants, then looked at the young blonde standing nude with her thick long hair hanging loose to the waist and felt literally sick . . . Janet came flooding into his thoughts, and he said more sharply than he meant, "Get dressed . . . here's twenty dollars for a taxi."

She turned red. Getting into her clothes, she told him he was sick, a fairy, and to hell with him . . . Bill McNeil, some stud. When he heard the front door slam he walked to the bar and proceeded to drink himself into insensibility.

The next encounter wasn't much better. The moment he managed to get the girl in bed he had an erection. Great. Return of the stud. But when he tried going inside, his manhood suffered an abrupt relapse. The stud goes west . . .

She did everything possible to excite him, maneuvers that would make the average man do handstands, but memories of Janet stood firmly in the way.

After she left he lay in the dark staring up at the ceiling. What in God's name was wrong with him? Maybe he'd become impotent. But he knew that was untrue. He really knew . . . what he wanted was Janet.

There was a special excitement with her . . . nothing contrived, no gimmicks. She had spoiled him as a lover. He couldn't accept it and he couldn't do without it. *Why* couldn't he take being married? No doubt about it, he should see a psychiatrist.

He called Nicole, but Janet answered.

"Janet?"

She froze. "What do you want?"

"To see how you are."

She slammed down the phone. She was *not* going to be civilized, sensible and mature.

He didn't blame her. What would have happened to *his* ego if *she'd* walked out on *him*?

He dialed again, and again Janet answered.

"Don't hang up, I want to speak to Nicole."

"She's not home."

"Janet, don't turn the children against me, please—"

"I haven't. Strangely enough, Nicole happens to feel very sorry for you, and I *don't* discourage it."

"Thank you . . . may I please speak to her?"

"She's not home, I'll tell her you called."

"Jason?"

She dropped the receiver on the bed and walked down the hall to Jason's room. "Your father's on the phone."

"Tell him to go to hell."

"Jason, don't talk like that. Speak to him."

"When hell freezes."

It was useless . . . She went back to her room and picked up the phone. "Jason doesn't want to speak to you."

Pained silence.

She didn't really love him anymore—at least she was trying hard not to—but she felt a deep sadness for him in spite of herself. He was so mixed up, confused, but he hadn't been a bad husband, or father . . . a good one, in fact . . .

"I'm sorry, Janet, I don't know how to make it up to him, or you . . ."

"It's a little late for that, Bill . . . I mean for us."

"I suppose . . . I'll see you Saturday."

For a moment she was taken off guard. "Saturday?"

"Yes, at Nicole's graduation."

"That's right . . . yes."

She sat for a long time, staring at the silent phone, then went to the cabinet and took out all the picture albums. This was the first time she'd been able to do this since she'd come home from the cruise, her head filled with optimistic foolishness about a reconciliation. And then she'd been plunged into a depression even deeper than before the trip. She must be recovering, she thought, if she could bear to go through these albums now. Maybe it was because she no longer hated him. Maybe it was possible . . . except, miraculously, she no longer gave a *damn*. At this moment Janet wasn't sure if she didn't need some professional help herself.

It wasn't easy for them to sit together watching Nicole in the long procession of graduation robes.

The memories of her childhood were imprinted in Bill's mind as though it were yesterday. There had never been a child so loved, so enjoyed. But he couldn't have it both ways. He had savored the years of her childhood, but now she was a woman and he was entitled to his life, wasn't he? Of course. Then why this feeling of emptiness? He felt the eyes of former friends on him and Janet. The speculations were apparent in their expressions. "How do you suppose they feel being together, Peter?" "I imagine it's got to be awkward . . ." "Lelia told me she heard Janet was violent when she found out about his affair . . ." "Lelia's a gossip, you can't believe everything she says. I never heard that he fooled around." "Well, I believe Lelia. I understand he has some little secretary . . ."

This time the pictures Janet took were different from the ones of past years. Now it was Nicole and Mark Weiss holding each other around the waist. Jason with Kit's other children, his arm finding its way to Becky's shoulders. The other two boys, Joel and Jeremy, were goofing around and making faces at the camera. Deborah, who was away at a college work-study program, was the only absent member of the Weiss family.

Nat said, "Janet, let me take a picture of you, Nicole and Jason."

Janet handed him the camera. "Okay, Nat. Then you'll take one of Kit, all the children and me."

Snap. Bill felt excluded, was excluded. He stood back watching, then went to Nicole and took her in his arms. "You were beautiful, princess."

Her tears said it all. "Thank you, daddy. I love you." She turned and called out to her mother, "Mom, I want a picture with dad."

How she had managed to give Nicole a party with Bill being there she wasn't sure, but she wanted her child to have this special day. People needed memories and this was a real milestone in Nicole's life. Her childhood was gone.

Bill stood by, feeling . . . unnecessary as he watched Janet being the gracious hostess she'd always been. But the thing that hurt most was being ignored by Jason. At the graduation, Jason had sat on Janet's other side and had never even acknowledged his father. Inevitably, though, they met . . . "How are you, Jay?"

Jason had looked his father up and down, turned and walked away to join his friends. That was when he'd begun to feel like a leper, and the party had hardly improved things.

Kit hadn't been able to resist a shot as she passed him an hors d'oeuvre. "Take this one, *boy*, it has ground glass in it."

Nat was the only civil one. Janet's parents were understandably cold. Even his sisters were on the edge of hostility. He was a pariah, he couldn't wait to get out. But he'd stay if it killed him. To leave now would only add more malicious gossip and Janet had taken the brunt of that alone. He'd never thought of that until this moment, he realized. He'd been spared the gossip and the speculative looks, even though he'd caused them.

When all the guests had finally left, Bill let out a sigh of relief. He wandered through the house, recalling the memories stored away in these walls. He looked at the bed he and Janet had shared in love . . . a bed that went back to those early days when they'd first met. It had been his bed and then it became theirs . . .

He turned from the window when he heard Janet come in.

Surprised at seeing him there, she stood stock still. They faced each other in silence.

He wanted so much to hold her, to tell her how sorry he was and how today had affected him, but it was better left unsaid. The chance for that kind of communication was gone. He couldn't give her the pain of thinking he was reopening their relationship when the truth was there was no chance of a reconciliation, much as he wished things were different. That *he* were different . . . He studied her eyes. They were indifferent—and crazy as it seemed, *he* was terribly hurt, never mind that he was to blame for all this.

"You looked lovely today—"

"Thank you."

"You did a great job. Nicole's quite a young woman. In fact, she's like you, full of sweetness and understanding."

"No thanks to me. Besides, I'm none of those things . . . not any longer. Nicole happens to be a lovely girl who's had a rough time trying to put *our* broken pieces together. She loves us both and hoped we would . . . Well, no matter. It's Jason I worry about . . . he was devastated. It still doesn't make any sense to him, what happened . . . I tried to explain there was nothing gained by dwelling on it . . ."

A long silence. "I wish there was something I could say—"

"It's all been said . . . but at least something good comes out of everything. My children are truly remarkable."

He swallowed hard. She said *my* children. Well, she was right, they were. "I'm seeing a psychiatrist . . ."

"I'm glad . . . for your sake. Now let's keep pretending the way we've done all day. Stay . . . Nicole's been more nervous than she's let on. It would mean a lot to her if you were here for dinner. Now, that's mature, wouldn't you say?"

There was a bite in the words, and why not? Today she must have vacillated between despair, anger and pity. He remembered another day when she'd even set aside her pride and pleaded for him to come back.

Nicole fixed a plate for Mark and the two went into the living room and sat on the floor.

"Well, how does it feel to be a grown-up lady?" Kit asked. "I can't believe it . . . I used to change your diapers."

Nicole smiled. "I'll bet mom's got pictures of that too."

"Wouldn't be a bit surprised," Mrs. Stevens said. "Photography was your mother's hobby for eighteen years, that and designing her own clothes."

"What are you going to do this summer, Nicole?" Dr. Stevens asked.

"Mark and I are going to bicycle through Europe."

Dr. and Mrs. Stevens stopped eating. They had heard of young people living together, but Nicole!

The Stevenses were not the only ones who were

uncomfortable about that announcement. Bill was furious. He got up and poured himself a straight Scotch. He didn't give a damn about all the free love that went on. Nicole was different. She was his daughter and, by God, he was going to speak to Janet. He might not be a husband, but he was still a father . . . never mind that Janet said they were *hers*.

Waiting until the conversation picked up again, he tightly asked Janet if he could talk to her in the den.

She led the way and settled herself into his favorite chair as he closed the door. "What do you want to talk about?"

It took a moment to compose himself. "Are you going to let Nicole go off with Mark? Just like that? I guess Nicole still loves me, but I think subconsciously she's doing this out of spite, taking out her anger on me. She's never really forgiven me for what I did." He drained his glass and poured another. "Would you like one?"

"No, thanks. That's plain crazy. You sound like an analyst . . . Now let me refresh your memory. I was someone's daughter too and *we* had quite an affair before marrying. Why do you think it was different then? For me, I mean."

"Because I loved you, Janet."

She laughed at the irony of it. That didn't make any more sense than anything else he had done, or said.

"Nicole and Mark have been going steady since they were children. It's no secret, and at least they're more honest than we were. This seems to be a time of more openness. And, not incidentally, Mark happens to love Nicole, every bit as much as you loved me. As a matter of fact they're thinking about living together."

"Then why don't they get married?"

"Oh, my God, I can't believe this whole conversation. I think I will have that drink."

As he handed her the glass she said, "Of all the ridiculous things you've ever said, that's it. You have a pretty lousy memory, Bill. We lived together for a year before you were ready to get married."

He couldn't answer that one. "It was just different . . . that's all. But at least we were discreet. Nicole tells everyone she's going away with—"

289

"Mark's like his father was with Kit. He'd marry Nicole tomorrow if she wanted to."

"And she doesn't? She'd rather *live* with him?"

"Yes. Even with Mark she's a little gun-shy. She wants to be absolutely sure. Can you blame her?"

He narrowed his eyes. "You seem to have discussed this with her pretty thoroughly."

"I have. In fact, I gave my blessing. I don't believe in deceptions, *secret* reservations. It doesn't make for a lasting marriage, as we know. Going together and living together are two different things. I want Nicole to be completely sure too. When people just sleep together, whether it's for a night, a week, a month or a year, they still can play games. But when you live together it's impossible to pretend three hundred and sixty-five days a year. Let them have their fights, let them see each other at their best and at their worst. If they can make a relationship after that, then they're ready for marriage."

Bill sat down heavily. "I can't believe this is you talking, Janet."

"Well, believe it. I've changed. Life does that to you, if you let it."

"Would you . . . live with a man?"

"You mean without marriage?"

"Yes."

"To begin with, I don't want a man in my life. But if I did, that's the only way I would do it. Marriage for me is *out*. I wouldn't go through that again, not if I were promised the Taj Mahal."

Bill was angry, and shocked. "It's strange how guilty you felt about us."

"I just told you . . . I'm not the same person, and neither are you, if only you'd admit it . . . If this conversation weren't so bizarre I think I'd cry. Or laugh. What about *your* love life? Sex without marriage is fine for you but not for me? The world's moved on, Bill. Women aren't accepting the double standard anymore. I'm at least trying not to."

"You had a little love affair on the ship, didn't you? Either that or you're having one now. That's what you're saying . . ."

She would not tell him that no man could bed her if he

died from wanting, but let him think she was the femme fatale. Laughing, she said, "You sound like an angry, jealous husband, Bill."

"You didn't answer—"

"I don't have to. What I do is my business. We're getting a divorce, remember?"

"I also remember I love you and you were my wife for nearly twenty years . . . I'm going to tell you something, Janet . . . love affairs begin to show on a woman."

Incredible . . . if he could have managed it, she'd have been his mistress for years . . . "So does marriage." And with that she went back to join the others.

Chapter Twenty-Four

Janet sat listlessly on the edge of the bed. The house seemed too silent with Nicole away and Jason taking a summer course. She'd never felt so *alone* . . . Yes she had, come to think of it . . . it was when she'd first come to New York. And her thoughts moved back to Orchard Street and a particular Sunday afternoon, and to Fayge . . . Once again she felt the desperation that began that day, but at least then she had something to occupy herself with . . . her weekdays were filled with modeling. But now? How was she going to fill her days? There was no one to cook for . . . no one to care for . . . no incentives, no demands, no *life* . . . Kit could hardly become the whole of her existence; she had a life of her own. And although they'd shared so much together, Janet couldn't hang onto her just to fill up her own void. Her problem wasn't Kit's . . .

She got up, went to her closet to take out a dress . . . and an errant thought struck her. Well, not so errant, really. Or quite all *that* sudden. Once or twice it had occurred to her before, but she'd pushed it aside. Well, maybe now was the time . . .

She slid back the wide closet doors and looked at her wardrobe. She'd not bought a thing without Bill's approval. Mostly, in fact, she'd dressed for *him*. Quickly she took armloads and threw them onto the bed. There were practically enough things right here to open a shop . . . Yes, by damn, that's what she was going to do . . .

She picked up the phone, dialed Kit's number. "Hi . . . are you busy today?"

Kit looked at the calendar. "Nothing special . . . feel like lunch?"

"No. I'd like you to come over if you can."

"Be there in about forty minutes, hon." No questions asked.

Kit walked in to find Janet's bed strewn with clothes and a rare smile on her face. "What are you doing? Going into competition with the Salvation Army?"

"In a way."

"Really? Let me congratulate you. This is the first time I've seen you smile without cracking the plaster cast. What's up?"

"I'm excited."

"Best news I've heard since the fall of Berlin. What brought all this about?"

"I feel alive for the first time since Bill walked out. Not like something dead that was flushed down the drain . . . I'm going to open a next-to-new shop in New York."

Kit looked at the bed. "I take it you're going to stock the joint with your cast-offs."

"Right. I want to make a clean start and the first thing is to get rid of the reminders. There's not a thing in that closet Bill didn't approve of. If he didn't like it, I didn't buy it, make it or wear it. Now, do you want to go into the city with me or not? I'm about to become an entrepreneur."

"You got yourself a deal."

A week later, with the help of an agent, Janet found a small store on 49th Street off Third Avenue. The building was an old four-story apartment house and the first apartment above the street was being leased as a boutique. She adored the Victorian horseshoe-shaped marble fireplace. The windows would have to be remodeled and enlarged for display, but that was no obstacle.

This was it. She could see it now. There'd be something for everyone. Feather boas, handmade jewelry that she'd sell on consignment for some of the independent young jewelry makers, beaded bags with fringe, silk camisoles dating back to the turn of the century . . . It was going to be kicky and kooky. Her dresses weren't exactly in that category, but she could easily restyle some of them and it wouldn't hurt to leave the others as they were for conservative customers. She'd have to find a source for more almost-new clothes, and maybe she'd even hire a dressmaker to make up her designs. Thank God she knew about fashion. Those early years had not been wasted. She also had imagination. The dresses she'd designed over the years were proof enough of that. God, the things that could be done. It would be great . . .

She brought Kit to take a look at the empty store. "Do you like the idea?" she asked when she finished outlining her plans.

"Love it. How are you going to decorate?"

"Above the mantle a tall Victorian mirror with maybe cupids. I thought purple carpeting, white wicker furniture and lots of Boston ferns. Different colored old silk parasols hanging upside down on the ceiling and electrified for light fixtures. How does that strike you?"

"Great!"

"The dressing rooms could be like gazebos . . . I thought a three-paneled mirror inside would be more unique than one solid—"

"Yeah, that's really jazzy. I admire your enthusiasm, but I'm hungry."

"Oh, gosh, Kit, I got so carried away I forgot about eating."

"Let's go."

That night Janet at last slept peacefully. She had found something . . . *fulfilling* . . . in her life, and for the first time since parting from Bill she was happy. Well, if not *happy*, at least she'd restored a measure of self-respect . . . she'd settle for that. For now.

Added to her pleasure she found a young woman in her twenties by the name of Renée Bouché (who later confided to Janet she was Reva Berkowitz).

Renée came to her from an employment agency, and her credentials were the best. She could use a needle the way a sculptor molds a piece of clay. There was nothing Renée couldn't alter. Her dream was to have been a designer, but with nine children in the family there'd never been quite enough money. So Renée's great dream of becoming another Coco Chanel had been lost in the alteration department of Gimbel's.

She adored Janet from the moment they met, and the feeling was mutual.

294

Janet and Renée worked doubletime on decorating the shop, readying their merchandise and establishing contacts for future sources of clothing and jewelry. By the middle of July the shop was open and off to a modest but promising start.

Life was beginning to take on a semblance of sanity for Janet. She loved the drive to and from the city, especially now that she'd traded in her old Ford station wagon for a brand-new sports model Mercedes-Benz, copper brown with beige leather interior and a sliding sun roof. It sort of went with the new shop. Both signs of Janet's coming out, as it were. Well, better late than . . .

Tired but content, she drove into the driveway and parked the car. There was always that one bad moment before going inside, but she pushed away the thought and walked up the stone path.

When she opened the door her new housekeeper Annabelle said, "Evening, Mrs. McNeil. It's so hot I thought a nice seafood salad would tempt you."

"It sure would. Thank you. Any phone calls?"

"A few. I've got them written down on your desk. And you got some mail."

"Thanks, Annabelle. I guess we'll put dinner on hold for about an hour, okay? I'd like to shower, and then eat on the terrace."

Going to the den, she sat at her desk and looked at the calls. One had been from a real estate agent who had been hounding her to sell. She crossed that one off. A call from Jason. She'd return it after dinner. Her attention went to the mail . . . Taking up an envelope, she looked at the return address. It was from Allan Blum. Good Lord, she couldn't remember if his eyes were green or blue. But she did remember . . . It read:

Dear Janet,

I'm going to be in New York on the week of July 30th. I hope very much that you'll find time to allow us to renew our all too brief—by my lights, anyway—acquaintance. Please let me know; my time will be rather tight since I'll be there on business. I'd hate, though, to think of being in the city without seeing you.

I trust things are going a little more smoothly. As I said

295

when we last met, in times of stress it especially helps to have friends. I hope you'll consider me one of yours.

Please do write and let me know if you will be free.

Allan

She held the letter in her hand, and read it again. He hadn't signed it "sincerely," "cordially," "fondly." Merely "Allan." Without being immodest, she felt she knew why. He apparently didn't feel he could say what he wanted to say, which was "love," but he'd settle for no shabby substitutes. She liked that.

The next was a letter from Bill's attorney, asking that she come to the office to sign some papers. Her courage sank with this one. In spite of her determination not to allow herself any self-pity or idle dream that a miracle would happen, still, she was badly shaken. Getting up from the desk she poured a brandy and drank it down. Composing herself, or at least trying to, she took up the next letter, which was from Nicole. It helped.

Dearest Mother,

I think the closest thing to heaven must be the countryside of France. Today we're in the Chateau country. The vineyards are indescribable. Mark and I lie in our sleeping bags and look up at the stars. They never seemed so clear or so near. It's almost as though you could reach up and pick one out of the sky. We have our own special one.

A few days ago we were in Grasse. The mixtures of perfumed air are, to put it mildly, heady. If anybody would appreciate the silk factory in Lyon, it would be you.

While we were in Paris we stayed at a small pension on the Left Bank. Both of us almost forgot we weren't French. I bought a crocheted bag for groceries and we shopped for food every day. Mark looks hysterically funny with a beret, and imagine a Frenchman coming up to us and asking in French where to find a certain street. I was so proud of my French ancestry. I answered him in French. I guess seeing it this time is so much more meaningful than when we were here last. The only extravagance I allowed myself was a new dress I bought in a lovely shop on the Rue de la Paix, to wear to the ballet. Thank God, Mark had enough sense to bring a suit. We would have looked pretty ridiculous in our jeans, sandals and striped jerseys sitting in the first tier. And, you'll never believe this, but guess what ballet company was here? ... Balanchine's. Is that crazy? We had to come to Paris to see that? But, *c'est la vie*. It looked better on this side of the Atlantic.

You're not the only gifted member of the family, mom. I seem to have taken up the same hobby, documenting everything on film. Enclosed are snapshots of the synagogues we visited. While everyone else was viewing cathedrals . . . well, we decided to look for the treasures of our heritage. It's become Mark's favorite adventure, tracing the old houses of worship.

On Saturday we walked into a synagogue in the Jewish section of Paris, unaware that a *bar mitzvah* was in progress. It was fascinating and unlike Mark's, which was so . . . elegant. But the simplicity of this one made it even more poignant, more effective, I felt. Added to the fascination was hearing the service conducted in French *and* Hebrew. I just wish I knew more about my Jewish genes. Well, I'll learn, Mark assures me. Still, I'm so grateful for the little you used to tell Jason and me about our great-great-grandfather. Suddenly the name Yankel Stevensky sounds just right. It's wonderful to know about one's roots . . . it's also made Mark and me feel even closer, if possible. Like you, I feel very drawn to the part of us that's Jewish.

Hope you received my birthday gift. Forgive me, I got so carried away I didn't even ask how you were getting on. But from what Aunt Kit writes, you're doing great. Keep it up, mom. We love you, and give a big hug and kiss to Jay. We'll see you the end of August. 'Til then, with all our love,

Nicole and Mark

As she reinserted the letter in its envelope, Janet was smiling. I'm afraid, she told herself, you're always going to be a romantic. When all's said and done, nothing is quite like your first love . . . For Nicole, she devoutly hoped the first would also be the last.

Quickly she went to the bedroom, undressed, and stepped into the cold shower . . .

At seven she got into bed and called Jason. She gave him Nicole's hello and news, he asked about the shop, she told him how well it was doing and what fun it was . . .

"I miss you, mom," he said. "Can't wait to come home. Another month seems like a long time. You're sure you're okay?"

"You bet, Jay. Keep busy, darling. The time will pass and before you know it you'll be back forgetting you ever

297

left." Why did she say that? Why should he forget he ever left . . . ?

When she hung up her sense of aloneness was so great she almost called him back, but she thought better of it. After all, he was her son . . . God, the nights were rough . . .

But she did allow herself to call Kit. "I got a letter from Nicole and Mark. Talk about love in bloom."

"I know, I got one too. Aren't they great, and *frugal* . . . they're eating like peasants and Mark's acting all French, carrying a baguette of bread under his arm . . . uh, what else is new aside from our kids?"

". . . I got a note from Allan Blum. He's going to be in town the end of the month and wants to have dinner. But I don't know, Kit—"

"You're going, Janet."

"Why? I don't even know what we'll talk about." Or what color his eyes are . . .

"You'll find something to say, and if you don't, he will. Now you *go*. You can't keep living like a hermit and that's what you're doing. Crawling into a hole can get to be a habit. If you don't start breaking it now you'll wind up being a recluse."

"Then you think I should—?"

"I already answered that. Now don't forget my party on Saturday."

Janet wasn't enthusiastic about the prospect of a Westchester party. She'd turned down every other invitation . . . but for Kit? She couldn't say no. "I haven't forgotten."

On Saturday night she went through the motions of dressing. After she finished she looked at her reflection. Even the new dress from Bonwit's didn't lift her spirits. Whether anyone else thought so or not, she felt like the fifth wheel. She was a woman alone now, a woman whose husband had walked out on her. And in so doing had taken so much of the meaning of her life with him. Would she ever get accustomed to *that*?

The party was in full swing by the time she arrived. The pool and landscape were bathed in moonlight and illuminated by lanterns. The food was lavishly displayed on the long buffet tables.

Kit looked marvelous. Her deeply tanned skin and black hair—now with the beginning of a gray streak which she refused to color—were highlighted by the flowing white caftan she wore. Nat was in high spirits and was, as usual, the perfect host. And everyone was surprised and pleased to see her.

"The only complaint we have about you, dear, is that the girls miss seeing you. It's like you dropped off the edge," said Mary Chase.

The girls! "Well, as you know, I opened a shop in New York—"

"I heard. Lucky you. I'd love to do something like that. Sounds so exciting being a career woman. Tennis, bridge and parties are such a bore."

My God, where had she heard that before? Wasn't anyone satisfied? What went wrong with marriage? What are we all looking for? Why doesn't it . . . love . . . last? Janet had a headache.

She slipped away unseen and went into the den, closing the door behind her. She turned off all the lamps but one. In the semi-darkness she lay her head back against the sofa pillows and sat wondering if she'd ever feel like a whole woman again. The shop served its purpose, but, face it, it wasn't the complete answer she'd hoped for. It was the nights, those awful, lonely nights. Lately she'd begun having nightmares. She could never remember them in the morning, but she awoke from them drenched in perspiration and with a violent headache. Her days were sometimes little better. The memories were revived and relived. Certain songs reminded her of where they'd been, what he'd looked like, what they'd talked about. She avoided passing Bill's office building; it was too painful to look back and see herself sitting on that leather bench one late afternoon so long ago. She couldn't go to certain restaurants because she remembered the times they had celebrated in them, could still see Bill's expression as he'd poured the wine and proposed a toast.

God, who needed snapshots? All the pictures were imprinted on her mind and she couldn't burn or discard them. It still didn't make any sense. If they'd fought . . . if they'd had violent disagreements . . . if they'd had huge conflicting opinions she might be able to see or un-

299

derstand *why* . . . But none of that had happened in their marriage. They were a loving, devoted couple, enjoyed the same things. She tried hard to please him—why are you *doing* this to yourself, Janet? You've gone round and round like a dog chasing his tail. All the things you're telling yourself may be true, but as Bill put it, life got to be monotonous for him, no excitement, no challenges . . . What went wrong? I guess I was . . . too complacent, too much the contented hausfrau . . . too damn placid. I should have been more aggressive. But then I was afraid he'd think I was dominating him like his mother, and I did a complete about-face. Well, not altogether. *I* was the one who made him move to the country. *I* was the one who wanted children. He didn't. Sure, after they were born he adored them. But what would have happened if we had stayed in the city and waited until he was ready to become a father? Maybe I took him a little too much for granted. Never really considered his needs seriously enough . . . I should have moved back to the city when he asked, but the children came first, and so did I. You stupid, how many times have you tried figuring it out? There are no answers . . . maybe Bill's got the right idea, looking for them on some psychiatrist's couch. Maybe I should . . .

Her thoughts were interrupted when she saw the door open and Guy Rogers walked in. He was holding a highball glass in his hand. The room was so dim he didn't see her at first, and he seemed startled when he discovered her sitting on the sofa.

"So you couldn't take it either . . . the party, I mean." His words were slurred.

"I think it's lovely but I have a headache."

He sat down next to her. "I've had a headache for seventeen years . . . Do you feel like a drink?"

"No, thank you."

"It could help . . . the headache. I'm going to fix one." He poured straight Scotch into the glass, filling it almost to the brim, then sat down next to Janet again. "Marriage stinks, Janet, stinks. Sandra, that frigid cold bitch . . . wasn't always that way. Oh, no, she wanted to screw all the time before we were married. Didn't mind the things we did then. It was okay. Would you believe it, Janet, I
300

have to use a condom. She doesn't want me to get her all messy. She's so meticulous I can't even smoke a cigar in my own den. She fluffs up the pillows the minute I get up. I'm like a boarder she tolerates . . . I'm a goddamn money machine, is what I am. After the boys were born she needed separate beds, then separate rooms, she got migraines. Couldn't stand me in the same room. Who the hell does she think she's kidding?" he said between long pulls on his drink. "My life stinks."

"Why stay married if you're so miserable?"

"Because . . . I've got responsibilities, can't walk out on my kids. I owe 'em . . . didn't ask to be born . . . She plays good mother as long as they don't interfere with her pleasures, but she can't really cope with the teen-age boys . . . I got to be around . . . boys need a man . . . a father." And the tears came rolling down his cheeks.

Janet was shaken, her heart went out to him. The world was one shock after another . . . everybody thinking everybody else was so happy, no one knowing what went on behind the doors of other people's lives. She had always thought Sandra and Guy were so somehow suited to each other. That was the impression Sandra gave. "Guy's the dearest, sweetest . . ."

A facade. What haunted her at this moment was the difference between Guy Rogers and Bill McNeil. Guy lived with a woman for the sake of his children. Bill asked, "Do you sacrifice your own life to perpetuate the happiness of someone else? Is that fair? . . ." *You're damn right you do, when you have a family.*

Guy Rogers put his head on Janet's shoulder. "God, Janet, I'm so low . . ."

She knew what that feeling was. It had become her closest companion.

Out of pity she held his hand gently, even patted it. What he was going through was something she could identify with.

His speech slurred, his breathing labored. "You're the loveliest thing, Janet, so damn kind, good . . . if only I had someone like you." Suddenly he was taking her in his arms. "I need you, Janet . . . I need someone like you . . . let me love you, Janet . . . love you . . ."

She felt his fingers sliding down the zipper of her dress,

301

his hand reaching inside, holding her breast, fondling the nipple. The room began to swim as his other hand found its way between her legs, separating them. It happened so swiftly—quickly she stood, wrenched herself away from him. "You're drunk, Guy, so I'm going to forget this, but . . ."

He held her close again, this time tightly. "I want you, Janet, need you. Please be kind . . . let me make—"

She tried pushing him away, but his hold on her was too strong. She began to panic, groped for the heavy crystal ashtray on the table and hit him on the head. Staggering, he looked dazedly at her.

Running from the room, she went to the bathroom and threw up. For a while she sat on the edge of the tub, trying to compose herself, and when the worst of her trembling had passed she left the house, got into the car and drove home. But when she found the safety of her bed she began to cry . . .

That was end of parties. Pete Gerard, Richard Conners, Guy Rogers . . . No more. She'd had *enough* . . .

The next day she called Kit, told her what had happened and what her decision was.

"Janet, don't say that about not going out. He was drunk, you have to learn how to handle it."

"Handle what? I don't make a play for anyone. I want to be left alone. The truth is, Kit, I'm just not cut out to be the gay divorcée. That's all right for some women but not for me. No more parties. I can't take it and I'm not going to. In fact, I just wrote a note to Mr. Allan Blum. He can go to hell too. Who needs it?"

Chapter Twenty-Five

Thank God she had the shop . . . that was all she wanted, it was enough . . . at least that's what she told herself. It was her haven, actually her home. And Renée was a godsend . . . her sense of humor was especially therapeutic . . . Janet even found she was still capable of laughing, mostly at the stories Renée told about her Jewish mother.

Somehow she'd manage to get through the next months. Another four weeks and the children would be home. . . .

At five-thirty she slipped a silk jacket over her shoulders, said goodnight to Renée and was ready to leave . . . when the door opened and in walked Mr. Allan Blum.

She stood as though transfixed. He'd received her letter, so what was he doing here?

The look on her face told him too clearly what she was thinking. Well, he wasn't going to let that put him off. "How are you, Janet?"

"Fine, thank you. How did you find out about my shop?"

"I called your house and your housekeeper told me."

"Oh?"

"I'm glad to see you, Janet. I came to ask if you'd have dinner with me."

"I'm sorry, I have other plans—"

"Janet, you'd never win an Academy Award for acting."

"Why should I have to act? You're right. I have no plans, I'm going home."

He smiled. It was a warm smile, not at all condescending. "I wish you'd reconsider. I'm only going to be here for a few hours. It's just for dinner, Janet."

Her high dudgeon began to subside. You've turned into a bitch, Janet . . . a real pluperfect one . . . He's a nice man. And so, knowing she'd been unkind, she answered, "All right, but it will have to be an early evening."

"I'll settle for that. In fact, I'm taking the 10:40 plane back to Chicago tonight."

Janet relaxed.

Somehow Allan Blum was the first man she'd felt at ease with since Bill. True, those days on the cruise had been laced with stilted moments; she had weighed each word so carefully. Allan's openness, though, made her feel at ease . . . with him nothing seemed threatening. Looking across the table at him as she took a sip of her drink, she decided he really was quite handsome. Strange, they'd spent two weeks on a ship together and in her bemused state she honestly hadn't been all that aware. But tonight she was, and not only of his looks . . .

"How have things been going for you, Janet?"

"Well," she said, "some things have worked out, others not."

"Like to talk about it?"

She felt she was speaking to an old friend as she said, "Bill's seeing a psychiatrist."

"That, if you'll forgive me, sounds like a step in the right direction."

"You're a lawyer, Allan, I'm sure you have clients who get help for their problems . . . do your . . . well, do you know of marriages sometimes saved by outside help?"

"Sure . . . sometimes. But not, I'm afraid, too often. When a marriage is over, well, it tends to be over. Of course there are exceptions, I just wouldn't bank on them. Sorry to sound like a lawyer but—"

She sighed. "Obviously that's not the answer I'd have liked . . . my divorce will be final next March." She swallowed hard. "Well, on to happier things . . . I had to do something with my life so I opened that crazy little shop. It really saved my sanity, and I find I love it."

"I'm glad, Janet . . . and what about the things that haven't worked?"

"Well, I discovered it's not easy becoming a divorcée—in more ways than one."

304

"You mean about men, obviously."

"Yes."

"I hear that complaint all the time. There's a big difference being a divorced woman and a widow. A divorcée is fair game for every frustrated husband. But somehow a widow takes on an aura of virginity. Even now men still feel a widow is saintly, they have a certain respect—"

"I'm glad to hear that . . . I mean about divorced women. I was beginning to think it was just me."

"You'd be surprised how many women deliberately go out and look to have affairs . . . they'll sleep with anybody to prove they're still desirable. Others reject men totally. Divorce, no question, is a destructive thing."

"Do men go through that?"

"Sure, they go through the same symptoms, especially if the wife walks away."

"Did you?"

"No . . . not quite. I mean I didn't feel the urge to bed down every available lady. I went through all the usual emotions, anger, jealousy . . . you name it. But when it simmered down, I began to realize that it wouldn't have been any good if Joyce had stayed. That might have been even more destructive. It's important to have a sense of your own worth and I wasn't going to let anyone wipe me out."

"I was completely wiped out. I felt worthless, hated myself . . . in a way still do."

"I'm sorry to hear that, because, of course, you shouldn't feel that about yourself . . . quite the opposite. Just give it time, Janet . . . How is the divorce going? Sometimes people do everything they can to annihilate each other. Any special problems?"

"No . . . actually Bill's been very decent. He's setting up trust funds for the children and . . . God, I just realized this must be like being back in your office, listening to a tale of woe—"

"I wouldn't have asked if I weren't interested."

"Thank you, it's been . . . well, very nice to be able to let down to someone . . . I mean, parents and friends are well-meaning but overprotective . . . let's change the subject, all right?"

Allan glanced at his wristwatch. "My God, the time has

305

gone by so quickly . . . I have to catch that damn plane. I hope next time we can make it a longer evening."

She smiled. "That would be nice . . . and Allan, forgive me for being so rude to you earlier today . . . it was just that I was so surprised, shocked, actually, when I saw you—"

"Don't apologize. You've had a rough go of it. Like I said before, divorce has turned more than one woman against the male species. But bitterness is so destructive . . . please don't let that happen to you, Janet. Men aren't all out of the same mold . . ."

"Thank God for that. It could really destroy one's faith in the race . . . You might just have made me a believer again."

"That's about the nicest thing you've said to me thus far," he said. "Look, I don't want to sound pushy, but if you're not busy Saturday night, I'll be back in New York and I have tickets for the ballet. How does that sound?"

"Wonderful."

Driving home, she marveled about how good, how *un*-threatening it felt to be with Allan. With him there were no games, no innuendoes, no double-meanings. He was strong enough to be open, and Lord knew, just speaking to him had really helped her . . . Yes, Allan Blum was indeed a very considerate man.

Saturday night, as she dressed, Janet realized that for the first time in ages she looked forward to a night out on the town. Allan made her feel human again . . . he had the capacity to help restore her destroyed image, for herself . . . Applying the finishing touches on her make-up, she looked at herself in the mirror, and briefly recalled the first date she'd had with Bill . . . all those long years ago. Good God, what a baby she'd been. She shook her head, remembering how she'd debated whether to look sophisticated, or demure. Silly little Janet, trying so damned hard to make the *right* impression . . .

At six on the dot Allan picked her up at the shop. He told her she looked radiant, and she smiled appropriately, almost feeling as good as he said she looked.

Later, in the darkened theater watching the first act of "Giselle," she felt Allan's hand on hers, and although she pretended not to notice—*he* had no pretense, she was a woman and therefore entitled to be less than perfect—the feel of his strong hand greatly pleased her. It wasn't until the end of the act that he released it. She didn't complain.

During intermission they had champagne. Clicking her glass with his . . . "I hope this is the beginning of more of the same, Janet."

"I do too, Allan." And though the exchange was prosaic, the feeling when she spoke was distinctly not.

When the performance was over they browsed about Lincoln Center. Again, like the words they'd spoken, it was familiar, but the sharing of it with Allan was a lovely, relaxed moment . . .

"You feel up to Rumpelmayer's?" he asked.

"That sounds deliciously wicked. You're on, sir."

As they sat among the after-theater crowd, Allan said, "You know what would make me very happy?"

"No," she said, breaking off a piece of pound cake, acting more indifferent than she felt. Much more . . .

"I wish we could spend tomorrow together, here in New York . . ."

And once again her mind darted back to the past . . . a lonely Sunday afternoon that had led her to Orchard Street and Fayge . . . Sundays in Westchester, just as lonely now. "I think that would be very nice, Allan. In fact, I have an overnight case packed."

"Really?"

Ignoring the inference, she went on, "When the weather's bad I stay in the city. Driving back to Westchester can be dangerous to health and welfare. My bag's at the shop and I could pick it up. Incidentally, where are you staying?"

"At the Plaza."

"Okay. In that event I'm sure they'll put me up overnight at the Pierre."

"A deal."

Allan—unlike Bill—enthusiastically showed her a special Oriental collection at the Metropolitan Museum. Later they took a cab to the Frick Museum, then on to the Morgan Library, and last of all they sat quietly discussing wonderfully unimportant small things in the poolroom of The Four Seasons. Finally, unbidden and unwanted, the day came to an end, and Janet drove Allan to Kennedy Airport, where she waited for his plane to be airborne, then drove back to Westchester, full of the sensation of his brief kiss good-by. She had to smile . . . a good-by kiss and she was reacting, in her fourth decade, like a teen-ager. Good Lord . . . didn't anything *ever* change . . . ? Well, she wasn't complaining. Not now . . .

He called every few days "just to say hello . . . I'm thinking about . . ." Each call left her with a good feeling. And more and more lately, his business brought him to New York. Each time she saw him she felt even better about him . . . about them . . . ? It wasn't love, she instructed herself, but whatever it was, it felt awfully good. . . .

Chapter Twenty-Six

At the end of August, Nicole and Mark returned from Europe, and Jason was home from summer school.

Janet let Renée run the shop with the help of a girl friend. For the first time since Bill had left she fussed over dinner, making a production out of it. Tonight Kit's family and hers would all be together.

Flushed with excitement, she sat at her table watching the people she loved so much. Allan had been right. Time *was* a friend . . . it was healing. Bill's absence was no longer an acutely felt thing . . . the heavy weight of it had been lifted. Life, contrary to her expectations, very much did go on. . . .

After the Weisses went home, Nicole lay at the foot of Janet's bed, showing her all the pictures they'd taken in Europe. She poured out her love for Mark.

"How important it is when two people share an experience like you've had. Still, I'm a little selfish. You'll never know what it means having you home, darling."

Nicole got off the bed and stood by the window, then turned around and looked at Janet. "Mother . . . I've decided to go to Columbia. Mark and I are taking an apartment . . ."

Why do we always think of our children as *children?* They grow up and make a life of their own. Hadn't she done that? Nicole had told her before that they might live together. How stupid she'd been to hope she would come back from Europe and live at home . . . Strange, she'd never given a thought to what *her* mother must have felt the day she left home for New York. Raising your own children makes you understand your parents better . . . sometimes very late in the day.

"Will you stay 'til the semester starts, Nicole?"

"I don't think so . . . Mark and I want a place of our own. I'm just happy Jay will be here."

"Me too. But that'll only be for a little while. This year he'll be a junior. Well, no matter . . . welcome home, darling."

When Nicole moved her things out Janet knew that was the end of a part of her life. This would never be home for her daughter again. Birthdays, holidays, visits, of course, but now home for Nicole was Mark, and rightly so. But there was no denying the emptiness Janet felt. She *should* be growing old with a husband. She needed Bill at this moment almost more than at any other time in her life. She needed *someone* . . .

Janet sat behind the steering wheel of her Mercedes, waiting for the garage door to open. She drove in quickly and immediately closed the door with the automatic genie. Somehow she still hadn't conquered that small fear of coming home alone. Hurriedly she took the grocery bags and let herself into the kitchen. Now, in the familiarity of her large kitchen, she felt relatively safe. Putting the bags on the drainboard, she walked through the living room to the entrance hall, reached for a hanger and was about to unbutton her coat when the front doorbell rang. There was a moment of mild panic. Nobody came to her door at nine-thirty in the evening. Apprehensively she called out, "Who is it?"

"It's me, mother."

A sigh of relief as she let Nicole in. "What brought you to Westchester in the middle of the week?"

"Mark and I wanted to visit the family, which includes you . . . Where have you been all afternoon? I called the shop and Renée said you had left early."

Janet smiled at Nicole's reprimand. The roles seemed rather reversed. That was a question she must have asked her daughter a million times in the past while Nicole was climbing over the hill, growing up. "Well, darling, it was one of those days. I . . . I just decided to play hooky. That little hobby of mine is a great diversion, but I needed to get away and . . . Well anyway, I went marketing and then decided to stop off for an early dinner on the way home and take in a movie. It's the maid's day off, and I thought it was about time I had one too. Besides, I hate cooking for myself. So. That's the sum total of all my wickedness."

Nicole sat on the large sofa and looked at her mother's face, wondering if the moment was right to tell her why she'd *really* driven to Westchester. But somehow she couldn't seem to get up the courage . . . not just yet. Playing for time, she asked, "Do you have any vodka?"

Janet suddenly knew this was not going to be the casual visit she'd expected. Nicole seldom drank; it had to be serious. "How do you want it?"

"Over ice . . . why don't you join me?"

"Okay, think I will."

She handed Nicole her drink and sat down across from her. "How's Mark?"

"Fine." Then there was a long period of silence.

"It seems you're having a little difficulty telling me why you're really here. It doesn't have anything to do with you and Mark, does it?"

"God, no, mother."

"What then?"

Nicole took a slow sip. "Mother, as you know, dad's been living in that furnished apartment, but he isn't happy . . ."

Janet frowned. What did that have to do with her? "Then why doesn't he get a place he likes?"

"That's what he wants to do."

"Well, what's holding him back?"

Swallowing hard, Nicole said, "The furniture."

Again a frown from Janet. "The furniture? I don't understand what this is all about. Why doesn't he call in a decorator and furnish? He did it before we were married."

"That's just the point, mother—"

"Nicole, just *say* it."

"Well . . . daddy feels as though he has no anchor. He wants to surround himself with some familiar things, things that have memories. What I'm trying to say is, if you don't mind, could he have the den furniture? It would mean so much to him . . . as though he had roots of some kind . . ."

It was too unbelievable for words. Bill missed his furniture! Things from his bachelorhood days. He even needed that to round out his present life. Having that furniture would definitely, of course, bring back his youth. She forced herself to sound calm. "Of course, if the furniture means so much to him, why not? It was his."

Nicole smiled. "Oh, mother, you're the most understanding woman in the world. And daddy will be so grateful—"

"I'm sure. You tell him I'll arrange to have the things sent as soon as possible so he can get settled . . . In fact, tell him I want him to have his bedroom set too. I think that will be very comforting for him . . . like old times."

Nicole didn't hear the sarcasm under Janet's light tone. Wasn't tuned to it. "Oh, mother, you're marvelous. I only hope I'm like you—"

"Thank you, but forget my virtues. After all, I ended up with this lovely house."

After Nicole left, Janet stood in the center of the living room and listened to the silence. Her eyes wandered around from one furnishing to the next. Everything had been selected together, with love. Tonight Bill's presence was overwhelming. She looked at the sofa and in her mind's eye saw him stretched out on it. The echo of his words rang in her ears . . . "You did a hell of a job" . . . "By God, I'm the luckiest man in the world to have a wife like you" . . . "Sure as hell love you." That was eighteen years ago when they'd moved in. Only eighteen years. When . . . at what point had he realized the love was gone? My God, how fragile the string was. It could be severed so quickly. And the lie, that dreadful lie . . . 'til death do us part. *But then, my love for Bill changed too, didn't it? . . . it certainly did after I'd been discarded like an old shoe.* She was unaware that tears were streaming down her face. She poured herself a full tumbler of vodka, then slid slowly to the floor, bracing herself against the sofa. Having taken the first drink, she poured another. "I hope you suffer every moment of your life as I'm suffering now," she said into the silent house. Her hand shook as she picked up the bottle to refill the glass, but the vodka was gone. She threw it against the fireplace and watched the glass shatter into pieces . . . *like my life* . . .

Unsteadily she got up, stumbled to her bedroom, fell across the bed.

312

It was two in the morning when she lay spent. All the tears were dry on her cheeks.

Slowly she got up and went to the bathroom, washed her face and got ready for bed. She wished she had a sleeping pill. She'd taken them until the doctor warned her, "Janet, I'm not going to renew the prescription. It's going to be tough for a few nights but you can't go on using them the rest of your life." Why not, doctor, what difference does it make?

Usually she folded the quilted bedspread carefully, but in the early hours of this morning she yanked back the corner and slid into bed under the electric blanket. Her body was chilled. She lay in the dark staring up at the ceiling, the thoughts of the past months running through her head like a broken record. *Enough, Janet. Chew it up and spit it out . . . he's out of your life, can't you get that through your stupid head? You've gone through this a million times . . . the same old thing about what you should have done, what you didn't do. Well, Bill, you've taken plenty, now you want the roots? You want your furniture back so you can relive your wonderful past? I'm only sorry I hadn't thought about it in the beginning. I don't want one thing, not any part of it. You're going to get your furniture and your paintings. Now I'll do something for myself. You're still in every nook and cranny, but no more . . . Everything will be sent to auction and I'm going to buy what I want . . . this is going to be my house once and for all . . . I will no longer allow you to be a lingering—haunting—part of the future.* Each time he sat in a chair, or lay on that couch . . . well, let his conscience take care of it . . . she'd waste no more time on such draining emotions as resentment, anger, bitterness. . . .

Looking at his things, Bill felt they didn't represent his bachelorhood days at all, but rather a part of the past that he still shared with her. He'd even, for God's sake, taken to sleeping on her side of the bed. . . .

With the hanging of the last of the new draperies, Janet felt Bill was finally exorcised . . . a ghost of her own making, finally gone from her existence.

She walked from room to room of the newly furnished

house. It looked just the way *she* wanted it to . . . whites and beiges . . . tubs of green plants, the walls covered with pastel prints and contemporary paintings, the wood pieces antique. At long last she, too, belonged to herself.

That night when she slept in her new bed, past memories were, finally, put to rest.

Jason ran off the football field, sweating from practice, but he paused when he looked up at the bleachers and saw a lone man sitting there. Jason watched as the man got up and approached him.

"How are you, Jay?"

Jason didn't answer, only continued to look at his father's face. His hair was streaked with gray.

"I know you're still angry at me, Jay, but couldn't we at least talk?"

"We've nothing to say to each other."

"I think we do. In spite of what you think about me, Jay, I'm still your father, and I love you."

"Really? Well, you have a strange way of showing it . . . really weird."

"Can we sit down and talk, please?"

Jason shrugged. "Did your shrink tell you it would be good for you to have a heart-to-heart with your son?"

Bill winced. "Let's sit down."

They sat on the first wooden bleacher, Jason remaining stiff and silent.

"Jay, I know you can't understand or forgive my leaving your mother but—"

"No, I can't, can you?"

"Not altogether . . . no. But I'd like you to understand there are some people who should never get married." That wasn't what Bill had wanted to say, at least not in those words, but Jay was making it damned hard for him.

Jason rubbed at the stubble on his cheeks. "Then why did you marry mom?"

"I'm going to be honest with you, Jay . . . I didn't want to."

"But you *did!* . . . Why?"

"Because I loved her."

"You loved her! I don't *get* any of this . . . I really

314

don't. It's a little too complicated for me. The point is, you *did* marry her. How come?"

"The problem was I fell in love with her. At first I fought against it, but then I realized that the only way I could . . . well, have her was to marry her."

"You should have fought a little harder. It would have been better if you hadn't gotten married. You've hurt her, hurt her badly, and I'll never forgive you for that. I'm sorry, but that's how it is. And I'll tell you something else, since we're being so man-to-man honest. I thought you were the greatest person a guy could ever have for a father, but you sure turned out to be a dud . . ."

And so saying, the deep hurt buried in him now welled up and he found himself crying.

Bill held him close.

"Why couldn't you have loved us, dad . . . why?" He put his arms around his father's shoulders.

"Because I'm a pretty weak and selfish man who was never able to find himself . . . Jay, I don't deserve your love. I'm sorry I hurt your mother, she's the best thing that ever happened to me."

Jason wiped away the tears. "Then why don't you try and make it up to her by coming home?"

The only way to answer that was with the truth, painful as it was. "Because it wouldn't work . . . Let me try to tell you why. You see, things don't just happen today or yesterday. It happens very early on. I'm not blaming my parents anymore for what I am. They did the best they could. There comes a time when you have to stop putting on blame, come to terms with the good and the bad in yourself and try either to change or learn to live with the things you don't like in your character. The problem is that I never did that. Without going into all the heavy psychological reasons, the result was that I felt trapped, even in a good marriage. I didn't know who the hell I was, and I was afraid I'd never be free enough to find out."

"Are you happy now, living alone?"

"I don't know, Jay. Maybe I could be if I didn't feel so much guilt. If we could be friends—no, more than that, father and son—maybe then I'd have an easier time finding myself. I want you to forgive me, but more than that, to love me. I miss you, Nicole and your mother. It's asking too much for your mother even to like me, but you're my son. I want to do things with you . . . have you come and visit. I've been very damn lonely without you, Jay—"

"What about other women, dad?"

He looked closely at his son. "Occasionally, Jay, that's all. But it doesn't mean anything. I'm an adult male and so are you. Men need women from time to time. That's the nature of the beast."

Jason sat looking out to the empty ball field. He had tried hard as he could to hate his father. But now, as they sat together, he could only remember the good things, the things he'd shared with his father . . . Little League ballgames . . . the time they'd gone down the rapids. His father hadn't left his mother, not really . . . He wouldn't have been able to stay married to anyone. Was his father to be blamed for the things in his past that had loused him up? Jason didn't honestly know the answer, but there was one thing he no longer questioned. He knew his father was a weak man, he loved him. And weak as he said he was, it still, Jason sensed, took a lot of strength to do what he had done today. Jason had rejected him, and if his father hadn't cared he wouldn't be trying to make it up now.

"What do you say, Jay?"

"We'll give it a try, dad."

Bill held the boy tightly around the shoulders. "Come on, Jay, I'll drive you home."

"Thanks, dad, but I've got my motorcycle."

"Okay. How about this weekend?"

"I'll call and let you know."

Driving back to his apartment, Bill felt more lonely than ever. He couldn't live with them and he couldn't seem to live without them. If only he could break through that iron wall that separated him from the people he loved most.

Chapter Twenty-Seven

November was with them once again. Janet knew she couldn't go to Kansas for Thanksgiving and face the defeat of her divorce. Not this year. So she called her mother and asked that they come to New York.

Martha tried talking Janet into coming home. "Darling, you have nothing to be ashamed of. A divorce isn't quite the scandal it once was and no one is going to make you feel uncomfortable—"

"I know, mother, but the memories of . . . past holidays are something I don't think I could handle. It's still too raw. Please, mother, spend the holiday here with me. The Weisses will be here too."

"All right, Janet. I know how difficult this is for you. Of course we'll come."

"And you'll bring Effie?"

"Of course, darling."

She tried to appear gay and carefree. Drinking a little too much helped her carry out the deception, but she couldn't deceive herself . . .

She and Bill had wound up their lives the way they had started so long ago. Jay told her Bill was spending the holiday with Aunt Harriet and the family. Did he remember that first year, she wondered, when he'd gone to his mother's and she back to Kansas? How she'd cried during that long trip. But it was nothing to what she'd gone through since he'd walked out. God, every time she thought she'd put her anger and depression in the past, they crept up on her again. After the cruise, after that talk about Nicole and Mark, after he'd asked for the furniture of his bachelor days, and now again with the holiday season. It was like being on a seesaw in perpetual motion.

And then he made matters worse by calling. She was in the kitchen, getting more stuffing and gravy for her guests when the phone rang.

"Hi . . . it's me . . . how are you, Janet?"

How was she? Dead, just not buried. "I'm fine, Bill, and you?"

I merely hate myself, that's how I am. "I wanted to wish you a happy Thanksgiving."

"Thank you. And I wish the same for you and your family."

"I'll tell them . . . May I speak to the children?"

"Of course. It was nice of you to have called. Hold on and I'll get them."

Thanksgiving was only a dress rehearsal. Christmas was the finale. The curtain had come down. Janet was devastated as she looked at her tall Christmas tree, all white lights and silver tinsel. She remembered Maine and how it looked that first winter. The fireglow, and she and Bill making love in front of the open hearth. Pictures faded, but memories became sharper.

She heard the phone ringing. Her heart beat a little too rapidly . . . she knew it was Bill. It was difficult but . . . "Hello?"

"Merry Christmas, Janet," Allan said. "I just wanted you to know I was thinking about you." About almost nothing else, he added to himself.

Taking a deep breath . . . "Thank you, Allan . . . and merry Christmas to you."

"I suspect it's not all that merry for you, Janet, but remember, you made it this far. Take the voice of experience, if you'll forgive it . . . next year will be a lot easier, and the next . . ."

A long silence.

"Janet? Are you still there?"

"I think so. Tell me, Allan, does it ever stop hurting?"

"Yes. The first holidays are the toughest, but nothing lasts forever and this, I promise you, won't either."

"I wish I could believe that."

318

"Please try, and don't forget we have a date the first Saturday in January."

"I won't . . . You've helped so much, Allan. It's a lovely gift."

New Year's Eve she sat by the fire, trying to warm herself.

Jason had gone to a party. She'd turned down Kit's invitation. She thought back now to what Allan had said . . . it will get better . . . Well, she had a long way to go. The questioning never seemed to stop . . . why hadn't she moved to New York when Bill had asked her? . . . because the children came first . . . but you're not exactly blameless, Janet . . . everyone feels Bill was the villain and you the victim . . . not exactly, by half . . . if I'd loved him enough I *would* have given up this *house* . . . that's all it is now . . . not a *home* . . . just wood and stone . . . it has a roof, but no foundation . . .

Her parents. Kansas was what she needed at this moment. So it wasn't all over, neat and clean, no doubts, no regrets, no guilts. God, what a presumption to think otherwise. You can't just hang up new curtains and shut away the past. It has to be acknowledged before it can be buried, and a new life really begun . . .

New Year's Day Nicole and Mark came by to drive her to Kit's. No party, just family.

After dinner they sat in the spacious living room.

Nicole clapped her hands. "I want everyone's attention. You're all invited to a . . . wedding. Mark and I are the stars and we've decided on Temple Emanu-El, same as you, Aunt Kit and Uncle Nat. *And* . . . I'm converting to Judaism."

Looking at her child, a kind of chill came over Janet . . . Nicole was the fifth generation to come from the genes of Yankel . . . a Jewess born to perpetuate the faith Janet had, in a sense, been deprived of . . . a heritage she herself had longed to embrace since she'd been awakened to it. And in spite of herself the thought came . . . If Bill had been a Jew, would their lives, their marriage, have turned out differently? . . . Janet, Janet, you're so confused. Allan still was very important . . .

319

What was it he'd said? "I would never have left Joyce . . ." His former wife had finally called him a despicable Jew, or some such, and yet even now he didn't really hate her. Was there a difference in Jewish men, husbands . . . ? Dear God, why was she asking such stupid questions? People were people. Jews were people. Jews got divorced. She cut off her thoughts and walked, unnoticed, from the room. . . .

Amidst tears, cheers, hugging, toasting, Janet had to be alone to try to put her thoughts together. Right now she very much felt the need of Allan's warmth, of his wisdom . . .

Nicole's future mother-in-law was saying, "You're not going to call me Aunt Kit anymore, I hope?"

"Yes, I am. I always have and that's something very special to me. In fact, if you can stand it, you're about my favorite person in the whole world. Well, at least the part of it I've seen. The only reason I'm marrying Mark is so I can get into the family legally. But you can be my mother-in-love, okay . . . ? We're going to be married this summer."

Kit blinked back the tears. Tough Kit wasn't so tough . . . This was the little girl she'd once diapered. She and Nat had better start counting their blessings. With a daughter-in-law like Nicole, it might take a lifetime.

Nicole suddenly realized her mother was the only one who hadn't congratulated her. In all the excitement she just had not noticed Janet's absence until this moment. She looked around the room, suddenly realizing that her happy announcement might well have been bittersweet for her mother, reminding her of her own marriage—and how it had turned to ashes.

Nicole hurried up the winding stairs to the Weisses' second-floor sitting room. When she entered she found Janet in a wing chair, staring out of the window. She went to her mother, knelt beside her.

For a moment, neither spoke, then Janet quietly said, "I'm sorry, honey," and both understood what she meant, though Janet quickly added, "I mean that I didn't congratulate you and Mark. Strange . . . I just felt I had to be alone, so many things . . ."

"I understand, mother . . . I really do."

320

"Thank you, darling." And then almost abruptly, "Your father left me with a great deal, you know. I mean that. I have you and Jay. I *don't* want you to think that your marriage is in any way an unhappy reminder for me. I couldn't be more pleased, and proud. What affected me, though, was when you announced you were becoming a Jew. When you and Jay were children and I told you about your great-grandfather and your Jewish heritage, you were the one who asked the most questions, seemed to reach out to know more. Just before you came in I was thinking about the last time I saw Fayge Kowalski, the day she fastened the Star of David around my neck and said, 'Remember your *zayde* and remember to tell the story to your children.' I kept my promise, Nicole, but I didn't quite realize the effect Yankel Stevensky and Fayge Kowalski would have on our lives . . ."

Janet got up and crossed the room to the sofa, where their coats had been piled. From inside the zippered pocket of her purse she drew out a small, felt envelope containing the gold star Fayge had given her. "I pretended for a little while you were my child, Janetel . . ." Fayge now lay side by side with her Mendele and the rest of Fayge's family was also gone. When Janet and her father had arranged for two bronze memorials, one in a Wichita temple for Yankel Stevensky and one in Miami for Fayge, they'd never dreamed that this part of their heritage would be perpetuated in their family.

"I've never been without this since the day Fayge gave it to me, but I have the feeling that it was really meant for you. Here, darling, let me put it on you the way Fayge once did for me. Wear it with pride, and with the love with which it was given to me."

Chapter Twenty-Eight

Nicole sat in her small apartment trying to study, then finally gave up. When she had spoken to her father on New Year's Day she'd been reluctant to tell him she was getting married. How would her mother feel, seeing him escort her to the altar? Nicole felt pulled apart by her love for her father, no matter what he'd done, and for her mother too . . .

Her parents would finally be divorced in March . . . Wow, what a birthday present that was going to be. She could cut her birthday cake reading their bill of divorcement . . . Would her parents even be talking to each other in June? Maybe she and Mark should just get married with no frills, go to Reno . . . No, damn it, she wanted a real wedding, even if marriage had become all but obsolete among her peers. Nicole couldn't share the philosophy of her friends. She knew why she wanted to be married, and felt *good* about it. The commitment between Mark and herself was so strong they wanted to announce it . . . before God and the world. To her and Mark marriage signified being honestly willing to pledge one's life to another.

She quickly phoned her mother at the shop and arranged to meet her for lunch . . .

Two hours later Nicole and her mother were finishing their meal, and Nicole still hadn't been able to talk about what was bothering her. She sat there, stirring her coffee.

"You seem to have the world on your mind, Nicole."

"Well, something, anyway . . . Mom, I haven't told dad about our getting married yet—"

"Why?" Janet said, trying to keep her voice even.

"Because I—"

"You think it's going to be awkward?"

322

"Something like that . . . yes."

"Nicole, our problems must not become yours . . . we created them, they must not be part of your life. I'm just grateful that you're not afraid or bitter about marriage. I think it's a tribute to both you and Mark."

"And to you, mom," and dad too, she thought. After all, they *had* been in love, there had been all the good times together . . .

Janet smiled. "Thank you for that, honey . . . well, there's no need to delay telling your father . . ."

"Thank you, mother . . . I just needed to know how you felt."

"I feel it's only right that your father should give you away." She fought to keep the irony out of her voice, to push aside the thought that in a way Bill had given his daughter away a long time ago . . .

"Mom," Nicole was saying, "I do love dad, but sometimes . . . well, sometimes I don't terribly much like him."

"I know, honey . . . it's not always easy to accept people as they are . . ."

"Have you been able to do that?"

"I won't lie to you, darling. Of course it still hurts, but not the same way. I ran the gamut of all the emotions most divorced women do. But now what I feel for your father is . . . well, I guess in a way it's a sense of pity . . . and that's not so bad—"

"Not love?"

"Maybe it's part of loving someone, but everything is different now."

"Do you think you'll ever love anyone that way again?"

"No . . . I wouldn't want to."

"What about getting married again?"

"I don't think so, honey."

"Then you *are* bitter?"

"Not anymore."

"What about Allan Blum?"

". . . What about him?"

"Could you . . . well, care for him?"

"I do, as a matter of fact . . . very much. Allan's a wonderful man, and a very good friend, but I'm never going to marry again—"

323

"I'd like to see you happy, mom."

"I'll settle for what I believe is known as a little inner peace. I made a lot of mistakes in my marriage, Nicole . . ."

"Well . . . you're such a remarkable woman—"

"Hardly . . . if I'd been so remarkable you and I wouldn't be having this conversation today."

When Nicole returned to the small apartment, she found Mark waiting for her.

"Hi, honey, where you been?"

"I met my mother for lunch. God, she's really great, Mark. Remember all the misgivings I had about the two of them at the wedding? Well, my mother's just got to be the most incredible lady in the world. Mark, I want to see my father tonight and tell him."

"Okay. But let's get fortified with pizza first. I'm starved."

"I'll call and see if he'll be home."

The line was busy.

"He's on the phone. I'll call after we've eaten."

She got into her coat, put on a woolen cap and wrapped a knit muffler around her neck.

As they sat in the restaurant, munching on crusty wedges of pizza that dripped with mozzarella, Mark saw how nervous Nicole was about telling her father their plans. Mr. McNeil had come down hard on her about their trip to Europe and he'd almost hit the roof about their living together. Nicole was still embarrassed about their living arrangement whenever she saw her father, and Mr. McNeil was always a little stiff when he was around. Well, it probably *was* a little tough to accept someone who was sleeping with your daughter, Mark thought. Maybe he'd be that way himself . . .

"I wonder how many of these we've eaten, say in the last six months?" he asked, trying to distract her . . . and himself . . . from her worries.

"What?"

"I said . . . it's not important. Look, Nicole, I know you're feeling uptight about telling your father. But we haven't done anything to offend anyone, and if your father's a little off-base that's a problem he's going to have

324

to deal with. Besides, he should be happy I'm making an honest woman of you."

"You're right . . . I just wish I didn't feel so guilty when I'm with him. He always thought I was so perfect—"

"You thought he was perfect and he didn't feel too guilty about—"

"I don't want to discuss it. He did *and* he's suffered *and* besides, he's my father . . . *and* I'd like a dime so I can call."

The line was still busy.

"He's home, so let's go."

When Bill answered the door he was wearing his robe. The look of surprise on his face went unnoticed by Nicole as she gave him a hug, but as she looked past him into the living room she suddenly froze.

Sitting on the sofa was a young blonde woman dressed in a sheer peignoir.

For a moment Nicole thought her knees would give way. She looked at her father, then without a word ran down the hall, with Mark and Bill going after her.

"Nicole, please—"

The elevator opened and she nearly ran inside. When Mark caught up to her she was running along the street, her eyes blinded with tears. He tried speaking to her but she wouldn't answer.

Finally winded, she sat down on a cement stoop. Her whole body shook as Mark pulled her into his arms.

"How could he?" she whispered, repeating the words over and over again.

"Shh, Nicole," Mark said, holding her even closer. "Come on, honey, let's go home. . . ."

Back in their apartment, Nicole was sitting, wordlessly, on the bed.

Mark went to her. "I know this was a shock. But please let's talk about it. Your father's a single man. He can't live in a monastery, Nicole. He has no one—"

"He has me . . . us. Aren't we anything?"

"Sweetheart, you're not thinking right. I mean he has no wife."

"My mother doesn't have a husband and she doesn't go

325

to bed and—oh God, I hate him, Mark . . . Is that why he left my mother, so he could sleep with any little—"

"Nicole, please listen to me—"

The doorbell rang, and when Mark went to answer it he found Bill, ashen white, standing outside.

"Come on in," Mark said. "Let me take your coat. Can I get you a drink?"

"Please," Bill said.

Mark saw that Bill's hand was shaking as he took his drink.

"Sit down, Mr. McNeil. I'll tell Nicole you're here."

Bill slumped into a chair, unable to close out the hushed voices in the next room . . . "Honey, your father's come to see you . . ." "Tell him I never want to see him again . . ." "Nicole, you're really blowing this out of proportion, you were shocked, you're hurt but you know you love him . . . Take a leaf from your mother, who you think is so incredible, at least talk to him . . ."

Slowly she got off the bed, went into the living room, not acknowledging her father's presence.

The three of them just sat there in awkward silence, like characters out of a Camus novel.

Bill downed the last of his drink . . . "Nicole, what do I say . . . ? I wish this hadn't happened, I wish you'd called, I wish I were dead . . ."

She looked at him, for the first time since she'd come into the room. "Your line was busy. Do you take the phone off the hook when you're *occupied?*"

"It happens to be out of order, but—"

"Oh for God's sake, let's spare us all the nasty little explanations. Except tell me, I'm curious . . . is that what you left mother for? Is *that* your freedom?"

"Nicole, please, I'm asking, begging you not to blow this up out of proportion . . . I have to make a life of some kind . . . please understand that I can't live completely alone—"

"Wasn't that your choice? You had a family, you left it. Why? Try to make me understand, *daddy.*"

"Darling, I can't explain any more than I already have. We've already been through all the reasons why I left a million times, and I can't say it's much clearer to me than

326

it is to you. Or much easier. Just know one thing . . . I love you, Nicole, and I'm sorry about tonight—"

When he broke off, the pain in his voice was unmistakable. If it was an act, she decided, it was an awfully good one. She wished she could obliterate the memory of that woman sitting in her father's house. It was impossible to understand how he could desire someone else when he had her mother, still the loveliest woman she'd ever known. But she also couldn't stand seeing her father the way he was now, and she could no more deny her love for him than she could deny her own pain and anger.

She went to him, put her hands on his shoulders, kissed him. There was nothing to say. She had said it all.

"I love you, princess," he finally did say, reaching out and taking her to him. "You just got a rotten shake."

"No, I didn't. I guess it's just that people are so damned complicated . . . it confuses me. I guess I have a lot of growing up to do."

"You're not the only one, princess."

Nicole smiled, went to make coffee for them. After she'd come back with the tray and handed them each their cups, she sat and blew into her steaming cup for a moment before she said, "The reason I came to see you tonight . . . was to tell you we're getting married in June. Dad, I want you to give me away."

He looked from his daughter to Mark. Mark had persuaded Nicole to see him tonight, even knowing how much he had disapproved of their past relationship. Well, one thing was for sure. He wasn't going to louse things up for them by reacting the way his mother had when he and Janet had announced their marriage. And beyond that, Mark was like a son to him. He'd been there when Kit had had the twins, Mark and Deborah, he was their godfather . . .

"I'm very proud of both of you. And I envy you, Mark, more than you know . . . *you* seem to have no doubts, no hangups. I'd say that's the great legacy your parents gave you. I hope you appreciate it."

In June two momentous events took place. Mark graduated from Columbia with honors, and Nicole finished her conversion to Judaism. *Now* she was ready to become Mrs. Mark Weiss.

Mr. and Mrs. William McNeil
request the honour of your presence
at the marriage of their daughter

Nicole

to

Mr. Mark Weiss

on Sunday the twenty-second of June
nineteen hundred and seventy-five
at one o'clock in the afternoon
at Temple Emanu-El
New York City

Janet read it over and over, then took out the small enclosed card . . .

Reception
Hotel Pierre, Fifth Avenue
in the Regency Room
Luncheon will be served in the
Cotillion Room

Janet was even happier about the event than she'd imagined. Nicole was going to wear her wedding dress, the one her mother and her grandmother had worn before her. She just prayed that the dress would never bring her daughter any sad memories. She dismissed the thought immediately.

And so the day came.

Two hundred people sat in the flower-filled temple watching Nicole and Mark become husband and wife.

Bill had escorted his daughter down the aisle, then took his place beside Janet. Tears were in both their eyes . . . dear God, the memories . . . regrets . . . all that might have been . . . They sat in a kind of awe as these two young people pledged their troths to each other, in their own words.

There was something very special about this wedding. Janet *felt* the presence of Yankel Stevensky. It was as though he were looking down and nodding his approval . . . Nicole was the one to carry on the tradition of three lost generations, and now he could rest in peace . . .

They stood facing each other under the canopy. Nicole looked at Mark through her sheer face veil. Barely audibly she said, "Mark, I give myself to you with my total being. I will have no greater love than you. I ask for all your tomorrows, and even beyond. I promise to give you all my devotion and ask for yours in return. I will stand by you in happiness and adversity. I pledge to you all my trust and ask you to accept and respect me as your wife. Will you do that?"

"Yes, I will. And I ask you to love me with all my weaknesses, and to forgive them. I promise to stand by you, hold your hand in the darkest of nights and be there for you to reach out to in sorrow. I pray our lives will be built upon love and understanding, and our home be one of joy. I ask for all the days of your life . . . Will you accept me as your husband?"

"Yes, I will."

Exchanging rings, they said in unison, "I give this ring as I give you myself. It is a round circle without end. Such is my love for you." As Nicole lifted her veil, Mark was handed the traditional goblet of wine. He held it to her lips, then took a sip himself.

The rabbi blessed them and pronounced them man and wife. Then Mark stomped on the empty napkin-wrapped goblet the rabbi placed on the floor, and the ceremony was complete. As the rabbi watched them walking up the aisle, he felt far more confident than at most of his marriage ceremonies that their union would indeed last 'til death did them part. . . .

The reception was in full swing as Kit came up to Janet and said, "I guess maybe God had a plan, kid. We've been through the good and the bad times and we made it."

"We did, indeed, my dearest best friend."

No bad thoughts or recriminations tonight.

As Bill danced with Janet he said, "You look beautiful . . . more so than ever. I want to thank you for allowing me to take my daughter down the aisle."

"No need for thanks. It's where you belonged."

Chapter Twenty-Nine

Mark was an assistant professor and Nicole was in her last year at Columbia when they learned they were to become parents. After two years of trying, it was most welcome news. They moved to Westchester when Bill, the proud grandfather-to-be, gave them the down payment on a house. Bill was delighted when they *insisted* he spend weekends and vacations with them. Nicole even furnished a room that was his alone. The nameplate on the door read: "Private—McNeil's Pad."

Nicole had more than one purpose in inviting her father to come out on weekends. She still hoped that her mother and father, seeing each other so often, would eventually be brought together again.

And it began to look as if her plan might work. Bill was included in all family affairs now. In fact, Janet and he had become friends, as he had once said they should be so long ago. The bitterness seemed gone. There was no need for it any longer. Now they shared their anticipation of the things to come.

Family traditions began to evolve. Thanksgiving was at Kit's, Christmas was Janet's . . .

Bill was beginning to be more at peace with himself, and the part his children played in his life was no small part of it. Jason had gone to M.I.T. after all, and was not only tops in his class but was making basketball history. What pleased Bill most was the solid relationship that had grown between them. It was only a matter of time before Jason joined the firm. And only a matter of time before Bill became a grandfather. How proud he was at the sight of his daughter becoming large with his grandchild. . . .

Two weeks before the baby was due, Nicole and Mark moved into Bill's apartment. Janet, Kit and Nat took a suite at the Regency. On the fifteenth of June Nicole presented her husband; not to mention the world, with a nine-pound baby boy. Gerald Weiss. With this tiny new human being, life renewed itself . . . The two grandfathers—they could hardly believe *that*—peered through the glass partition. Bill looked even more closely than Nat . . . he'd received the greatest gift of his life on his birthday. . . .

The years, time, had their way, and so there was not only the joy of birth, but the tragedy of death. Time, the balance wheel . . .

Janet had just come home from the shop and was about to step into her shower before dinner when the phone rang. The moment she heard her mother's voice, somehow she knew. "Janet, your father is very ill, he wants you to come home right away."

"What happened, mother?"

"A severe coronary . . . it happened about three this afternoon, they think . . ."

"Why didn't you call me sooner—"

"I did, but Renée said you'd left and—"

"Never mind, I'll come immediately." Quickly she dialed Nicole's number and told her what had happened.

"Oh, God, mother. I'm so sorry. I'll be right over."

"No, darling. I'll just pack a few things and see what plane I can get out on."

"Are you sure you can manage alone?"

Manage alone . . . my God, if her father should . . . well, then she'd really know the meaning of being alone . . . "Yes, darling, I can handle it."

"Well . . . I know you can, but you're not going to. I'll put a few things together and Mark and I will be right over. We're going with you."

Thank God for her children.

After hanging up, Nicole called Kit. "From the sound of my mother's voice, I think she's in a state of shock."

And Kit remembered the day of her parents' plane crash. "Of course she is, but she's not alone. Make sure she knows that . . . Nat and I will make the plane arrangements . . . Oh, Nicole, unless you object, I'm going to call your father. He felt close to your grandparents . . ."

Janet sat now at her father's bedside, holding his hand and listening to his shallow breathing as he spoke. "Do you remember, Janet, what I told you so long ago? I mean, that when my time came I wanted to be buried as a Jew?"

Janet couldn't control the tears.

"You mustn't cry, darling. I've had a wonderful life . . . your mother, you . . . my work . . . But remember, I want to be buried beside my father and grandfather. And since you, darling, are my immortality, it would please me very much to know that I will be remembered with the *Kaddish* . . ."

Janet and her mother stayed with him through the long vigil. Seeing him slip away made them feel so helpless, so humble in the face of the Almighty. There *was* a power beyond them that made the real, the final decisions of life, of birth and death . . . Between the cradle and the grave people were allowed the illusion of leading their own lives, but in the end they were all His. . . .

At precisely 5:26 of a Thursday afternoon, James Stevens ceased to exist.

As though it were happening to someone else, she sat in the chapel with her mother, her children, dearest friends . . . and Bill, listening to the rabbi's eulogy. Then she watched as the casket was placed into the hearse, and it was Nat who became her solace. In her grief she had wanted her father not to have been buried so quickly. It seemed so sudden, abrupt. She wished they could have stayed just a while longer, but Nat explained that a Jew who died on Thursday had to be buried before sundown on Friday, since Saturday was the Sabbath. He also explained that in that tradition, what belonged to God must return without delay, that we came from the earth and to the earth we were obliged to return.

As Janet watched the coffin being lowered into the ground, she once again felt a deep awareness of her Jewishness, a heritage more felt than practiced, in her case. But she would create a memorial in the name of her father, his father and the father that went before them. She would never forget to say *Kaddish*. She would learn how . . . She and her mother lingered a short time after the others had walked slowly down the paths to wait. A final goodby from the two people most important to him in life . . . and now in death.

That evening friends and family came to pay their respects. Even in her bereavement Martha stood with dignity and thanked everyone for their kind words.

The next day Nat helped Janet begin the traditional week of mourning. Each evening they went to the synagogue for memorial services, and by now Janet could say, *Yis-gad-dal v'yis-kad-dash sh'meh rab'bo, b'ol'mo . . .*

Sitting in the sanctuary with Nat, she silently spoke to her great-grandfather, Yankel Stevensky . . . "I thank you for the spiritual feeling that runs so deep in me. I promise never to forget."

There came a time to accept . . . to rejoice in life and accept one's loss at the same time. . . .

But in spite of Janet's plea, Martha refused to live with her. No, she would stay where she had been most happy . . . where she could sit quietly, speak to James, not needing an answer, knowing him so well she needed no answer . . . no, she told her daughter, she had to stay, to bring fresh flowers to his resting place . . . Her memories would keep her company through the long winter nights. They were enough. They were her life.

Chapter Thirty

Jason, now a part of McNeil & Son, had taken an apartment in the city. So now that Janet's children were settled in life, she was left living alone in the house with only the echoes of the past. But they had become muted and distant. . . .

One Sunday in summer she sat on the terrace, reading the paper. A little later the house would be full. Jay was driving up with his girl friend. Nicole, now pregnant with her second child, would be coming with Mark and Gerald, Kit, Nat and Bill.

After an hour of relaxation, she was just getting up to go in for a glass of cold lemonade when the phone rang.

It was Bill. "I'm here at Nicole's. Mind if I come over ahead of the others for a little visit?"

"Sure, come on over."

A half hour later they sat together on the terrace, drinking lemonade and looking out over the garden.

"You know, Janet, I wonder how many divorced people stay as close as we have."

"Not many, I'd guess."

". . . Have you ever forgiven me?"

"Bill, I thought we agreed a long time ago . . . the past is past, let's not dwell on it . . . Did you hear the phone ringing?"

"Yes." He would have liked to have ripped out the wires.

She got up and answered it in the living room. Through the open French door Bill could hear . . . "Allan! How nice to hear from you. I always find time. When will you be here? . . . Fine . . . so am I, Allan. See you then."

Still smiling from the sound of Allan's voice, she walked back and sat down.

Bill was not only curious but abruptly . . . jealous? And angry? He couldn't push back his feelings. . . . "Is that your friend from Chicago?"

She looked at him. "Eavesdroppers never hear well of themselves."

"Are you serious about him?"

"It's really none of your business, but no . . . He's a very good friend who saw me through a lot of the rough spots."

Had she slept with him? Janet was right, though. Even if she had, what business was it of his? Still, sitting on his former terrace with his former wife made him damned . . . damned annoyed. He knew it didn't make any sense, no more than anything else he'd ever done—except marrying Janet, and he'd screwed that one up with his crazy obsession about his *freedom*. What a laugh. What freedom? The only thing he was free of was his analyst. Lately he'd been thinking more and more of getting up the courage . . . the nerve . . . to ask Janet out. Crazy? Sure. Just as crazy as he was to resent that call Janet had just gotten. But damn it, it was like someone taking his . . . his property away. They'd been divorced five years, but face it, he *was* jealous. "Janet?"

"Yes?"

"I'd like—"

Just then they heard a car in the driveway. It was Kit and Nat.

Well, he thought, during the week was best. He'd never get her alone today.

On Wednesday he called the shop, only to be told by Renée that Ms. McNeil was having her hair done. *Ms.* McNeil . . . ?

That evening he called her at home.

"What are you doing tomorrow for dinner?"

She paused, not quite believing what she'd heard. "I have a date."

"Break it."

"I can't."

"It's that friend from Chicago, right?" There was an obvious edge of anger in his voice.

Janet, in spite of herself, was rather pleased. "That's right."

336

"Oh? . . . I thought you said you weren't interested."

"It's really none of your business, Bill, but I wouldn't stand up a friend."

"I see . . . Well, have fun."

"I might do that." She laughed. He didn't.

As she hung up she wondered if maybe that shrink, as Jason called him, had finally gotten to him . . . the singles bars, the one-night stands. Being a grandfather didn't seem to bother him; in fact, just the opposite. He really seemed to adore that little boy Gerald, and he talked constantly about the next addition, which he hoped would be a girl. Times certainly had changed. She remembered his resentment—and fear—of going to his mother's, feeling so obligated and yet hating to do what was expected of him. It was what had ignited the volcano inside him. And yet lately he had been spending more than just weekends at Nicole's; he couldn't wait to get back to the old homestead. Well, mothers were different from grandchildren. He'd despised Long Island but now, finally, looked forward to Westchester. The prodigal grandfather returned . . .

On Thursday morning Janet left the shop at eleven. Renée hadn't seen her this excited in a long time. Come to think about it, not since Nicole's wedding.

"You got a little secret, Ms. McNeil?"

"Not a secret. I just feel . . . sort of great."

"I could tell. Got a hot one on the wire?"

"Renée! Allan Blum is coming for the weekend."

"So how come you're this excited? You never acted this way before when he came to town."

"Well, let's just say it feels good just being liked by a man, having a man just interested in you."

"I hear you but I don't believe you, Janet. I think, you will forgive the expression, that you're ripe for love."

Janet pretended a frown. "Don't get carried away—"

"And why not? Take it from a lady who knows. Mr. Allan Blum hasn't exactly been crazy about the idea of your platonic friendship."

"Just watch the store, Dear Abby. I'll be at Orlane's body shop. I need a treat and a treatment. I'm going for the works."

"That's the first sign."

Janet shook her head. "You've been reading Erica Jong . . . try Shakespeare."

"*He* knew all about sex."

It was five in the evening when Janet returned to the shop.

"My God! You look gorgeous. You really did go for the works. That makeup job and hair . . . he'll flip."

Janet looked at herself in the mirror. Today she really did like herself. She really did. Well, at least the way she looked.

"What time you meeting Romeo?"

Janet grimaced. "At six . . ."

"Where?"

"The Plaza."

"He travels first class, doesn't he? Here, I pressed your silk suit."

Janet went to the back of the store and slipped into the suit. When Renée saw her, she said, "Wow, that color's so delicious I could eat it. You should always wear mauve. It does something for your skin tone. Makes it glow. And your eyes are fabulous." Renée sighed. "What a figure . . . Why does my mother stuff me with matzohballs? Boy, if you can't make it tonight, call the undertaker. He's got to be far gone."

As Janet waited for Allan in the lobby of the Plaza she felt rather uncomfortable . . . Somehow she'd never gotten accustomed to having people stare at her, to the double-takes and admiring looks. Still, she couldn't help feeling a little flattered. Imagine, a grandmother . . . forty-five, and the men still looked.

"Hi, gorgeous. Doing anything tonight?"

"*Allan?*"

He kissed her as she stood up. "You recognized me?"

"Barely. You grew a beard and moustache!"

"Thought I needed a new image . . . Like it?"

"I love it, you look simply great."

"I wasn't sure how you'd take it."

"I adore beards, especially when they're trimmed the

way yours is . . ." She shook her head. "But you look so different."

"Different than what?"

"Oh, you know what I mean . . . and you've changed your hair style." The deep red hair was longer now, and together with the new beard it made him look even more distinguished.

"You noticed."

She laughed. "I noticed . . . Allan, it's so good to see you."

He squeezed her hand and smiled in reply. "Now, where would you like to go?"

"You decide, please."

"I'd like candlelight and wine, someplace quiet so we can catch up on old times."

They sat in the restaurant's shadows and spoke of unimportant things. How the shop was doing, about her grandson and the new one coming. How Bill had come back into the fold and had asked her to dinner. "It's so strange, Allan. I guess he's found his niche . . . being an unmarried husband. He'd like us to really be good friends once again—"

"And how do you feel about that?"

"I don't. Bill's become like a fixture in the family. I neither feel hurt nor anger anymore, so it's easy for me to be charitable."

"Is that really why you're being so . . . benign toward him?"

"Well, not altogether . . . I think it's important to the children that we get along together. Besides, at this point, what point would it serve to be hostile?"

Allan looked searchingly at her. "Are you sure about no longer feeling hurt or are you just being stoic? Or plain kidding yourself?"

"No . . . I really believe it's all gone. What's sort of strange . . . sad, I guess . . . is his sudden attention. Now that I'm not his wife, he wants to woo me."

"You know what's happening to him, don't you?"

"What?"

"It turns out he didn't quite make it to Camelot and now he's having a second look at what he left behind.

You've taken on a different dimension for him. I think he'd like you back, Janet."

"Would he? Well, I'm afraid I wouldn't have him. On any terms."

"I can't say that doesn't make me happy." He reached over and took her hand. "Janet, it's no secret I've been in love with you for a long time. I'd say—and don't laugh—from the moment I saw you walk into that dining room aboard ship. I know . . . love-at-first-sight, mid-forties edition, but there you are. Since then my feelings have grown much, *much* stronger . . ." He took a sip of wine, looked intently at her. "I came to New York for two reasons. The most important is to ask you to marry me . . ."

She had seen Allan whenever he came to town for some five years now, and in all that time he had never acted as much more than a devoted friend. She'd known, felt that a change was inevitable, although she had never expected anything quite like this. The answer she must give made her suddenly afraid she might lose what had become a very valuable friendship, and substitute something else that might quickly evaporate . . .

"Thank you, Allan, but I can't marry again. I mean, I've decided I never will."

"You mean, if I may say so, that you're still frightened."

"Naturally there are scars, I admit it, but it goes beyond that—"

"In what way?"

"Well . . . my children. I just feel it's wrong—"

"Why?"

"Well, the notion of bringing another man into their lives—"

"Janet, maybe you ought to be honest with yourself. It sounds very much like you're still in love with Bill—"

"No, you're wrong. Not anymore, believe me."

"Okay, I'll believe . . . especially since I so badly want to . . . but don't you think your children would actually be happy, seeing you live a more natural life?"

"I don't know, Allan . . . at my age, to start a new marriage? Yes, all right, I admit it . . . I'm terrified I might fail again."

340

"To answer the first part first—I know, spoken like a true lawyer—you're still a young woman, and even if you weren't, since when does the heart get wrinkles? People can and do fall in love at any old age. And as we grow older, well, there's the need for companionship that becomes even more important—though I repeat, you *aren't* old . . ."

Janet toyed with the crumbs on her dessert plate. "Of course, logically what you say is true, but—"

"How much do you *like* me?"

"Oh, Allan, you know the answer to that. You're the most open and unselfish person I've ever known. You never demanded anything of me—"

He held up his hand. "*Thank* you, but let me tell you, my virtue got pretty thinned out. I've spent more than a few sleepless nights wanting you, but I knew, or suspected, you weren't ready."

"And you were right, Allan. I'm not sure that I am now." Not that she hadn't thought about it. But every time she had begun to wonder what it would be like with Allan her mind had abruptly and unerringly shifted to Bill, the only man she'd ever slept with, the man she'd made her life with, and who had smashed it. She had never been able to think it through to the end, and now she felt mighty uncomfortable with the subject. Better change it . . .

"Earlier you said you wanted to see me for *two* reasons . . ."

"Right . . . Last week one of my partners died . . . heart attack. A young man, forty-six. He'd never been sick a day in his life. Left a wife and three children. It hit me right in the gut, really shook me up and forced me to step outside myself and take a good look at what I was going to do with the rest of my life. I began to come up with a few answers."

"Such as . . . ?"

"Most people wait until they retire to find Shangri-la, but sometimes it's too late. Even if they reach that age, time collects its dues and life tends to play some dirty little tricks on you . . . bad kidneys, hardening of the arteries, et cetera, et cetera. It sounds hackneyed, but I decided that life *shouldn't* be put off. I'll never be

341

forty-eight again, and I know I'm taking my retirement at the most productive time, when my earnings are probably greatest . . . But I say to hell with it. I want to do all the things I've dreamed about while I'm still relatively young, healthy and vigorous. When I get *ready* to come back I'll work my butt off, as long as I don't get arthritis of the mind . . . But I want it *now*, not later. There are no guarantees, no second chances."

He paused, took a sip of coffee and looked closely at her. "Janet, I booked passage on a freighter. I don't know how long I want to be away—two years . . . maybe longer . . . Now, that's not too much to steal out of a lifetime, is it?"

Janet merely shook her head, thinking that Allan was even more extraordinary than she'd thought. Lots of people talked about doing such things, but that's as far as it ever went, even among those who had the freedom and money to do what they wanted. It was as if they didn't take life seriously enough to find out what it was about, to do more than just go along . . .

"I don't know whether you're with me on this or not, but that's the point . . . to have you with me would really give it all some meaning . . ."

Still she couldn't answer.

"I asked you before how much you liked me, Janet. I don't think you quite answered that."

Almost in a whisper she said, "More than anyone I know—"

"Then come with me . . . there's a whole world out there, Janet. Let's share it with each other. I love you enough for the two of us, and if we have nothing more than this trip together, I think we'll be able to say at the end it was at least worthwhile. That at least we were *living* our lives, not just going along . . ."

There were tears in her eyes.

"Will you come?"

As with Bill, there was some of the old confusion about where sex and love began and ended. But Bill and Allan were so very different . . . and suddenly, as she looked across at Allan, she no longer felt like hesitating . . . there was a *good* feeling not to be ignored . . . How would the children feel about her going away with a strange man? They'd probably disapprove . . . and the role reversals here made her smile. And her mother . . . ?

As though reading her thoughts, or at least tuned to them, he said, "Janet, you don't owe anybody anything, you don't need the approval of anybody . . . except yourself. You paid your dues a long time ago. You belong to yourself. That's quite a change, I admit. Are you up to it?"

"Will you let me think about it?"

"Until Sunday . . . only until then."

She looked at him uneasily.

"Think about it, darling . . . carefully . . . Now I'll take you to your car."

She took in a very deep breath. "I've decided to stay in the city tonight."

He squeezed her hand gently. "I've waited a long time to hear you say that."

Chapter Thirty-One

She stopped at the shop and picked up her overnight case, then they took a cab back to the Plaza.

There was nothing strained or awkward when she was finally in his arms.

He undressed her unhurriedly, pausing to kiss her as each garment came off. The touch of skin on skin, each new caress, brought them the knowledge that it had been worth waiting for, and yet the wish that they'd never waited at all.

They made sweet, gentle love. Janet had never known the tenderness of such giving. Her needs had been locked away for so long she was shocked at the intensity of her desire. Imagine . . . Allan Blum, her "very good friend" . . .

The second time it was she who set the pace.

Her pleasures were his rewards. He wanted more than anything to achieve happiness for her, and in doing so his own became supreme.

In the morning she awoke in his arms, delighting in how she felt, marveling that it had been possible after so long . . . Curling herself to fit him even closer, she asked, "What's the ship like, Allan?"

"Well, it's a freighter as I said, with the best staterooms afloat. But what I like best is that they take on only twenty-five passengers. It's a Japanese line, and it's not the circus we had going to the Caribbean. This time I don't want to share my life with a hundred people I don't give a damn about. I don't want a programmed vacation, when you have to be *on* for people. I want to relax, feel I can be myself, shave off my beard and grow it back if I want and not give it a second thought."

"I love beards. My grandfather had one and my father

344

wore the loveliest mustache. You'd have loved my father, Allan . . . I realized yesterday how much like him you are." A strange and moving thought came to her . . . James Stevens and Allan Blum were the products of five thousand years, emerged out of the desert at Canaan . . . and *she* was a part of it too.

"That's quite a compliment, darling . . . Now, what's your pleasure today?"

"Let's not plan."

"You're right. We'll just do, as they say, what comes naturally. . . ."

On Saturday morning Janet said, "I'd like to go home . . . with you. Your ship doesn't sail until midnight on Sunday. Would you like that?"

"Need you ask?"

"I'm anxious for you to meet my closest friends and, of course, my daughter. Unfortunately Jason's away on a job in Arizona. I wanted so much for the two of you to meet. Well, one can't have everything, can one?"

"Not everything, but more than enough, Janet, if one really wants it. Dreams can't come true, sayeth the sage, unless you decide to make them reality. Well, this lucky one has so decided . . ."

Allan drove Janet's car into the driveway and turned off the motor. Coming around to her side, he helped her out. She stood there for a moment, lost in the past, then she looked closely at Allan. Her Westchester home seemed more beautiful today than even the first time she and Bill saw it together. She'd been so frightened he wouldn't buy it, and secretly she knew he hadn't wanted to . . . Do you like it, Bill? . . . It's really for you, Janet . . . a house is a woman's domain . . .

Quickly she took Allan by the hand, walked up to the front door and unlocked it. . . .

Allan clearly adored the house. It was everything he expected, as were Kit and Nat, who couldn't have been more gracious from the moment they walked in to meet him.

Nicole, on the other hand, couldn't have been more reserved, though Mark's warmth made up for her aloofness—which sat poorly with Nicole. The idea of Allan

Blum staying overnight in her mother's house didn't seem to faze Mark in the least . . . well, it did her.

She was even more upset when Mark drew her aside and said, "You seem to have forgotten how it was your *mother* who came to our defense when we went off to Europe that summer—"

"True, but I'd say this is *slightly* different."

"How so?"

"Mark! This happens to be my *mother*. Don't you see the difference?"

"No, except that you're acting more like a fluttery mother than a daughter. Put it another way . . . you're more than a little like your protective father. Why isn't your mother entitled to do what you and I did? Or *he* did . . . ?"

"Because she's an older woman and she's my *mother*, damn it, *and* I don't like it *and* I don't want to talk about it—"

"Well, I think maybe you should. You can't use one set of standards for yourself and another for your mother. It doesn't exactly make sense. Last I heard, she was over twenty-one and—"

"Mark . . . I don't want to talk about it—"

"Why? You still want your mother to be some tower of virtue, your eternal virginal mother? Well, darling, you just don't have the right to lay that kind of thing on her. She deserves a little—"

"I told you I don't want to talk about it . . ."

Mark suspected, though, that what Nicole really was upset about was that now her mother and father wouldn't get back together. Allan Blum was a threat to getting her parents back, and for her mother to have anything to do with him was to make her darn near some sort of scarlet woman . . . a betrayer of her father. Daughters and fathers . . . well, he certainly would stay off *that* subject with her . . .

After everyone had left, Janet took Allan by the hand and led him down the hall to her bedroom.

He looked about the room, then at the bed.

"When Bill and I divorced I sold all the old furniture.

346

It seemed too painful a reminder of . . . anyway, Allan, you sir, are the first man to sleep in *this* bed."

He smiled . . . she'd read his mind. He sure as hell wouldn't have wanted to make love in a bed that held any memory of her former husband. . . .

Next morning Janet took special pleasure in watching Allan through the kitchen window as he dove into the pool. His body was firm and slim. Not an ounce of flab. He looked as good as he had felt to her the night before . . .

She basted the chicken with the marsala wine, added fresh mushrooms, then went to the bedroom and changed into her bikini.

They splashed about the pool and raced each other the length of it and back like a couple of kids.

He got out first, then helped her up over the side.

"Did you ever try scuba diving?" he asked.

"No, never. Is it exciting?"

"Unbelievably. That's just one of the things I intend to do on this trip."

For a while they lay on the pool chaises, letting the sun warm their bodies. They held hands, content just to be near each other, but Allan couldn't help his thoughts from returning again and again to what her answer would be. So far she had said nothing about going with him. The decision, of course, had to be hers alone or it couldn't possibly work out. No prodding, no pleading. It had to be that way.

"It's noon. How's the old appetite?" she asked.

"Like a lumberjack's."

"Okay, let's go get changed and have at it."

Janet wheeled out the chicken and salad on a tea cart as Allan opened a bottle of extra dry white wine. They sat quietly, lunching and enjoying the peace of the summer afternoon.

"I love this house. I guess maybe it was always more mine than Bill's. He hated it . . . and now it's as though he never lived here. I mean, he's just no longer a part of this house, if that makes any sense."

"It makes a lot of sense. Especially to me."

Taking a sip of wine, Janet asked, "How long did you say you'd be away?"

"I don't know, darling. For as long as it takes. This is

347

the kind of thing you have to play by ear. That's sort of the whole point of it."

"Allan . . . I've thought about us."

"I hoped you had."

"Well, I've done more than think. I've watched you, watched *us* . . . I've decided . . . I want to live with you . . . I mean really live with you . . . permanently."

He closed his eyes . . . Thank God, it had been uphill, but he'd made it. *They'd* made it . . .

He got up and kissed her. "Janet, I promise you this . . . I'll spend the rest of my life trying to make sure you're never sorry."

"And I'll try to do the same for you . . ." She looked away for a moment, then . . . "Allan, what in the world do I tell the children?"

"The truth . . . it's not exactly a sin to be in love. Even if we are over forty."

Janet called Nicole and asked her to come over, said there was something important they needed to talk about. . . .

When Nicole arrived she was more than relieved that Allan Blum wasn't there. Sitting on the sofa, she watched her mother, who seemed enormously happy. Still, there was a peculiar knock in her pregnant tummy . . . she just couldn't accept that Allan Blum had slept with . . . "You said there was something important to talk about . . ."

Janet smiled uneasily. "Darling, I never thought that this would ever possibly happen to me again, but a kind of miracle has happened to your mother . . . It seems I've been given that much talked about second chance at life. Now don't laugh, but it's true . . . I'm in love, Nicole, and I'm going to take it as a rare gift . . . I'm going away with Allan Blum tonight. We're taking a—"

"You mean you're just going off with a *stranger?* Just like *that* . . . ?"

"He's *not* a stranger. Not anymore."

"He is to me, and he always will be."

"If you'll forgive me, dear, I think your attitude is a little unfair. I know this *seems* sudden, and it may be confusing to you, but—"

348

"No, I think you're the one who's a little confused, mother. I feel this is . . . do you want the truth?"

"I'm sure I can depend on you to give it to me, dear."

"Well, I don't think what you're saying is love is love at all. It's just more of the same sort of thing that happened to daddy, only delayed a little . . . Now it's *you* trying to recapture *your* youth. If this Allan Blum is so important to you, why don't you get married, for God's sake?"

Janet had always known that Nicole hoped she and Bill would remarry. Now she was just showing her disappointment, and in the process making Allan the scapegoat . . . But she couldn't help but be struck by the irony of the situation, her daughter the righteous one, the pillar of convention . . . she, the mother, the naughty rebel, for God's sake. Talk about your signs of the times, or was it really a new kind of prejudice . . . youth against the notion that older people—especially parents—could actually talk about love, especially the *act* of love . . . as though it were the exclusive domain of the young and innocent. Well, my darling daughter, much as I love you, I'm just going to have to take my chances of incurring your stern disapproval. I'm going to go on living, my way, on my terms . . . It was a speech she would have liked to have given out loud, but she thought now was a bit premature. Nicole was upset, so what she said in an even tone was, "Darling, I don't want to get married just now for some of the same reasons you didn't want to marry Mark in the beginning. And I really do have as much right to my choice as you did, dear. And Nicole, I would like to suggest that love isn't shameful or sinful, not at any age."

Unable to cope with her mother's remarks, Nicole came back with, "You can rationalize *anything*, mother. But I still say a woman your age living with a man is . . . You know, I have to say this in dad's behalf . . . at least he keeps his little romances discreetly hidden behind his closed door . . . My God, mother, what will people think?"

Janet couldn't resist the answer. "I know it's a bit corny, Nicole . . . but frankly, my dear, I really don't give a damn."

The humor of it sailed high over Nicole's outraged, dismayed sensibilities . . . Only just last week her father had asked her, "Do you think there's maybe at least a chance your mother might consider coming back to me?" And she'd said . . . "If you really went after her, I'm almost positive." And when he'd asked, "You really think she still might care for me?" she'd told him, "Oh, daddy, of *course* she does . . ."

Her poor father. It was so unfair, he'd hoped and tried but now she knew there was simply nothing else she could do to try and persuade her mother that this thing with Allan Blum would *have* to lead to disaster . . .

"I never thought I'd say this to you, mother, but I don't see what else I can do . . . What's going to happen when you come home? And you'll have to, you know, sooner or later. In more ways than one. Suppose it lasts . . . is *he* going to move in and the two of you live here . . . ?" Her anger building, she repeated, or rather amended, "*If it lasts* . . . how will you feel having to explain living openly with a man to your grandchildren, knowing they have a *real* grandfather . . . can you answer me that?"

Good Lord, Nicole, you sound like a prig . . . Once again, reversing roles, mother sounding like daughter . . . "I'll handle it, Nicole, when the times comes. Honey, be happy for me, please. I really do love this man."

"I also remember you really did love dad a whole lot—"

Janet's patience was getting a bit thin. "Nicole, be sensible. I think *you're* getting slightly confused. Of course I loved your father, but *he* left *me*. It wasn't, you know, the other way around. And thank God, Nicole, that human beings seem to have the capacity to love more than once. What a world it would be if we couldn't. I want your blessing, darling . . . Believe me, I know this is right. I'd like you to respect my feelings, the way I've tried to respect yours."

Nicole fought back the tears, then slowly put her arms around her mother. "I hope you're right, I only hope you really do know what you're doing. I just don't want you to be hurt anymore . . . I love you, mother."

"I love you too, darling . . . and thank you. Thank you . . ."

350

When Nicole went home after her emotional bout with her mother, she sat in her living room, watching her father play with his grandson, tossing the little boy into midair, delighting in his squeals of laughter. "Again, grandpa."

"That's enough, Gerald," she said.

"One more time, mommy."

"All right, but just once. You're wearing your grandfather out."

"Who says? Hey, buddy, your mother seems to think we're a couple of old men. Come on, fellow, up you go."

After Gerald had been put down for his nap, Nicole came back and found her father sitting in his favorite chair. He seemed to be born to his new role. "You know, Nicole, I'm sure glad you're raising your children in the country. It's the only way. Gerald's healthy, brown as a berry, and swims like a fish. Damn, he sure is a handsome little guy . . . in fact, I'd say he looks just like your mother, wouldn't you?"

If Nicole hadn't been so rattled at this moment, she might well have at least been tempted to remind her father that one of his biggest complaints had been Westchester . . . he seemed to have forgotten all that, when it came to his grandson . . . But the mention of her mother made the thought unimportant, frivolous. Her very pregnant stomach did somersaults as she wondered how to tell him . . . God, where did she find the right words?

Her silence was so abrupt Bill wondered if she were having premature labor pains. "You feel okay, Nicole?"

She wanted to cry. "I'm really fine . . . physically, that is."

"Which I take it means you have something momentous on your mind? You can tell me anything, you know that."

Anything but this . . . "I know, daddy . . . but some things are more difficult than others—"

"Well, come on, we've shared a lot together. If you're having a little problem with Mark, remember I've been there, that even the best marriage has its ups and—"

"It's not Mark or . . . I just don't know how to tell you this."

351

"Look, princess, whatever's on your mind, it's got to help to talk about it."

She braced herself, and said, "Daddy . . . mother's . . . involved . . . she says she's in love and . . ."

His shoulders slumped. He closed his eyes and ran his hand across his forehead. "I think I'll have a drink. Can I get you anything?"

She shook her head.

He sat down in his not-so-favorite chair at the moment and took a long swallow. "Well . . . I guess that was inevitable. Your mother's a beautiful woman . . . still young and, God knows, desirable . . . It's that Allan Blum, right?"

She nodded.

"Did she say when they were getting married?"

"They're not," Nicole said, wincing.

"They're *not?* But you said they were in love—"

"True, but she says she doesn't ever want to marry again . . ." And now Nicole had begun to cry and ramble, as though she were speaking to herself. "I literally prayed that the two of you would remarry . . . I know you still mean a lot to her . . . I just can't see her . . . well, you know what I mean . . ."

He damn well did know what Nicole meant. It was far more difficult for him to visualize her with this Blum or any other man the way she and he had once been together . . . "Except you've got to remember, Nicole, that apparently your mother's in love with this man . . . remember how it was with you and Mark." He was really talking to himself as much as to his daughter.

"I know, daddy, but that just seems so different from this. Besides, I was so sure of your relationship . . . the two of you are so close that I have to remind myself you're not married . . . Daddy, how much do you love mother, really?"

"All I can say is, I always have . . . I always will." (Even though it might have been hard to tell from his actions.)

"Then why don't you try to stop her . . . fight for her?"

Kit had asked that question a long time ago in a hospital room . . . *I love her, Kit . . . Then fight for her, Bill.*

But this was different. This was someone else's ballgame. If Janet was ready to give herself to this man . . . "I can't fight for her, Nicole . . . I don't have that right any longer."

Showing more anger than she intended, Nicole said, "Right? All's fair in love and war and if you really cared about your grandchildren you'd try to keep another man from coming into their lives, our lives . . . My God, don't you see what this will do to our *family?* Can you imagine spending the holidays with this . . . this man sitting at our table?"

"I imagine your mother must have thought about that."

"You're being damned placid about this, taking it remarkably calm for someone who just last week was wondering if she still cared for him . . ."

"Nicole, please . . . don't carry on like this in your condition . . . it's not good for you—"

"Carry on! You want me to stay calm, knowing my mother's going to live openly with a man? You know something? I think you're glad . . . it's like letting you off the hook."

Bill bit his lower lip, got up and poured himself another drink. Sitting opposite his daughter, he said, "You're wrong, Nicole. For quite a long while now I've even been trying to get up the nerve to ask your mother to remarry me, and it just *might* have worked, because for the first time in my whole damn life I'm ready to make a total commitment to someone, to belong to someone . . . I can admit that I need that. But like most of my life, I'm in the right place at the wrong time . . . When I said I didn't have the right to interfere in your mother's life, it was because I've *lost* that right. Knowing her the way I do I also know she wouldn't take this step . . . unless she loved the man. And I'm not going to be the one—not again—to louse up her life. I'll just have to live with the fact that I left the best woman I'll ever know . . . If I'd had the brains I have now things would have been different, but it took a few million hours of psychiatry to make me understand myself, and my damn fears . . . too bad it happened too late. Anyway, Nicole, be happy for your mother. She deserves it. As for me, it may be tough but I'm going to try to accept this man . . . not for him, but because it's the least I can do to make up for all the years she lived alone on account of me."

Nicole was shaking her head. "You know, I guess I have the most incredible parents in the world."

"Your mother is, anyway . . . And now, baby, if you'll excuse me, it seems I'm a little beat, after all. . . ."

Shutting the door bearing the name plate, McNeil's Pad, Bill sat on the edge of his bed, allowing himself the indulgence of reliving years past. The times of Janet and Bill . . . small things adding to . . . ? Champagne running down his suit . . . a naive young girl in a marbled lobby waiting for him to step out of an elevator . . . the virginal young woman who'd given herself so completely . . . the anxious months . . . the insecurity of waiting . . . Maine in November . . . a vision in white satin walking down the aisle to become his wife . . . the joys of the first-born, and then another . . . nineteen years of living . . . a shattering, awful parting . . . five long years of separation . . . And now, for her, a new love . . . Oh, God, Janet, how could I have been so blind to lose so much? Well, be happy, my darling . . . And then even the silent monologue was washed away in the tears he could no longer hold back.

When Nicole finally left, Janet felt almost lightheaded. She had a greater sense of herself than ever before in her life. She felt a huge relief. A weight was now truly gone. She could fly. She called Kit. To share her joy with her, who better, more appropriate for that, than Kit? She was going to grab the brass ring, you bet.

Kit closed her eyes, said to herself, *I love you, God. You really did work it all out.* To Janet she said, "Have a ball, baby . . . have a *ball.* I'll take care of your mail and the bills. What about the shop?"

"Give it to Renée."

There were still a few calls to make. She wondered if there'd be the same confrontation, explanation with Jason. Well, the Fates, never mind the facts, were on her side . . . "Darling, I have some wonderful news to tell you. I'm going away for a while, with Allan Blum. It all sort of happened very unexpectedly, but I'll write you a

354

long, long letter explaining everything. What's *important*, Jason, is that we love each other and—"

"That's enough for me, mom . . . the past is past. Be happy, mom. You deserve it."

Janet brushed away the tears. "Thank you, Jay. You know, for a very young man you're pretty damn smart. Also, it seems I've been blessed with two wonderful children."

Hanging up, she wondered how best to tell her mother. A phone call? Too abrupt. A long letter would be the right way. Unlike Nicole at first, Janet knew her mother would understand, not judge her. The most painful thing was anticipating Bill's reactions. He would be sad, regretful, look back at all they'd had and lost, the way she had done so often in the beginning. It would not be easy for him to accept another man in her life. And in a strange way she still loved him, as she knew he loved her. But life had its own way of dealing . . . the acute, malignant losses eventually became benign. And Bill did have the children and grandchildren, and she would never pretend he didn't exist, that they had not existed . . . their family, if nothing else, proved otherwise. But from now on the man in her life was Allan . . . it was the way it was. . . .

When Allan had taken out the last of the suitcases and put them in the car, Janet locked her door, and didn't once look back. . . .

Epilogue

It was two years now, two years that they had been away, two years lived as a lifetime, not just a *new* beginning, but a beginning all on its own, at once an evolution for both Janet and Allan from their pasts and a revolution in the quality of their lives.

Neither would have claimed, or even intimated, that what had come before they met was somehow merely a prelude, to be forgotten or somehow downgraded. Without the acknowledged pain—and yes, pleasure too—of their relationships with their previous spouses, and without for Janet the love and special growth through her children and their lives, none of this would have been possible for either of them. An Allan Blum whose life had not been seared by a rejecting wife, who had not learned the price of presumed happiness through outward appearances, would never have had the wisdom, the compassion, and above all the patience to make himself available for a woman as complex and surely apprehensive and confused as Janet was when they first met. And Janet, without her testing, without the *living* that had taken her from the well-meaning if remarkably naive nineteen-year-old girl who came out of Wichita, Kansas, would never have had the courage to take advantage of the new depths of feeling and involvement that a man such as Allan offered her.

And perhaps paramount among what he offered her, gave to her, reinforced in her, was his sense of origins, his Jewishness that gave room for her own to grow and merge with her hardly Jewish upbringing. The process, on a personal level, that had begun for her all those years ago on a tenement street in New York City with a woman with, to her then, the improbable name of Fayge, and that

356

was further opened up by her long-delayed talk with her father about his background, and therefore hers, was now accelerated and given fresh meaning by her association with a man who had lived as a Jew—and all that that meant, regardless of his station in life. Janet Stevens no longer felt like an outsider, looking in at her origins. Now she *felt* she belonged to her own roots, whereas before she had only occasional reminders of them. *This* was indeed the entirely new part of her life, and with Allan she was free and able to pursue it in a way never before possible. It was one thing to have a Jewish son-in-law like Mark Weiss, and to have a daughter who had converted, embracing her husband's religion, its special teachings and joys *and* deep sorrows. But now it was she, she becoming for herself, she was learning to feel and know who she was and whence she came at a level altogether new and en-riching. Not that they dropped off in every synagogue in every city they visited—although they did some of that and she was astonished, for instance, to discover that Jews and their traditions were not only known but impor-tant in such faroff places as Brisbane, Australia—but there was a new tone, a new sense of belonging in her life that was an undercurrent to the person that was now Janet Stevens.

As for Allan, it was a surprise and a matter of great satisfaction for him that he was of some help to Janet in coming into her own in terms of her Jewish origins and sensibilities, but there was much more that he received from her. Janet was a woman in a way that he had never quite understood the term. He was not inexperienced with women, and had thought that in both his personal and professional life he had had perhaps more understanding of the opposite sex than most men. But Janet was a new experience, a kind of revelation. She had a generosity of spirit, an openness to new things and ideas in a way that was exciting and enormously gratifying to him. Yes, he was in some ways her teacher, but she, on perhaps an even more profound level, was his as well. The law, as he knew it, was a profession of adversaries, of combat, of an-ticipating the worst in people more often than the best, and finding out that such expectations were not only justi-fied but often conservative. Add in the bitterness from the

357

experience of his marriage and Allan Blum was a man who had a genuine skepticism about the innate goodness of the human animal, and in particular about women. In Janet he had sensed, as he said, from the beginning a woman of a different sort, and he responded. But actually living with and sharing life with Janet had gradually allowed him to let his excessive guard down, to be more open in his fashion to the pleasures of life without doubting them so much, and in particular to the unique kind of giving, of trusting love that Janet was able to offer him.

Together they were a quite remarkable complement, in nearly every respect, including the one without which all the rest might have been nice but irrelevant—they were simply crazy about each other. They *liked* each other out of bed as well as in it, and they even learned to make each other laugh sometimes, not always to take themselves too seriously. They knew it was impossible for a person to be perfect, not to annoy and grate at times on the other's nerves—they had plenty of experience in those negative areas—and so they did not demand or expect the impossible. Perfection was possible, Allan would remind her, only in the cold ground of the grave, or the chiseled marble of a statue. They were flesh and blood, and that was a fact of life to rejoice in. . . .

Today, sitting in a deck chair aboard the *S.S. Eastern Pearl*, en route to Tokyo, Janet had some of these thoughts as she waited for Allan to come up from his swim. When he appeared, she was almost startled, unaware how deeply she had been in her thoughts about these remarkable two years together.

"You look mighty thoughtful, my lady, though, no question, as beautiful as ever. What's up?"

She took hold of his hand. "Oh . . . I was just looking back at me, at us. My God, how much I've changed. Hopefully, for the better, and surely because of you. Darling, you know you've made me happier than I ever, ever thought possible."

"After seeing me twenty-four hours a day? Maybe I'm just an addiction."

"Definitely."

He bent over and kissed her. "Darling, maybe we should go down and change, it's almost five."

"Is it that late?"

"No . . . that early, and I'm ready to pour the wine."

Hand in hand, they went off to their cabin . . .

He looked at her, dressed in her white chiffon gown, held her close and had the nerve to whisper, "Come grow old with me and be my love . . . the best is yet to come."

She smiled, kissed him soundly. "Oh, yes, my dearest. Oh, *yes.*"

Kit looked at the dateline on the cablegram. Tokyo. Quickly she tore it open, then laughed out loud. It read . . .

> RABBI ABOARD MARRIED AT SEA WILL BE HOME FOR THANKSGIVING LOVE TO ALL
>
> MR. AND MRS. ALLAN BLUM

ABOUT THE AUTHOR

CYNTHIA FREEMAN was born in New York City and moved with her family to California. She has lived most of her life in San Francisco with her husband, a prominent physician. They have a son, a daughter and three grandchildren. A believer in self-education, Cynthia Freeman has been determined since childhood to pursue knowledge for its own sake and not for the credentials. Her interest in formal education ceased in sixth grade, but, at fifteen, feeling scholastically ready, she attended classes at the University of California as an auditor only, not receiving credit. Her literary career began at the age of fifty-five, after twenty-five years as a successful interior designer. "People seem quite shocked," she remarks. "It doesn't seem strange to me. You do one thing in life and then another. I'd been writing all my life—little things for Hadassah, plays for the Sisterhood. I never thought of myself as a writer, but the simplest thing seemed to be to put a piece of paper in the roller and start typing." That typing has led to her very successful novels, *A World Full of Strangers, Fairytales, The Days of Winter, Portraits, Come Pour the Wine, No Time for Tears,* and *Catch the Gentle Dawn.*

THE LATEST IN BOOKS
AND AUDIO CASSETTES

DON'T MISS
THESE CURRENT
Bantam Bestsellers